THE BOUNDARIES WE

CROSS

Also by Brad Parks

STANDALONES

Unthinkable

Interference

The Last Act

Closer Than You Know

Say Nothing

CARTER ROSS SERIES

The Fraud

The Player

The Good Cop

The Girl Next Door

Eyes of the Innocent

Faces of the Gone

THE BOUNDARIES WE CROSS

A NOVEL

BRAD PARKS

OCEANVIEW PUBLISHING
SARASOTA, FLORIDA

This book is a work of fiction. Names, characters, businesses, organizations, places, and incidents either are the products of the author's imagination or are used fictitiously. Any resemblance to actual events, businesses, locales, or persons living or dead, is entirely coincidental.

ISBN 978-1-60809-624-4

Published in the United States of America by Oceanview Publishing
Sarasota, Florida

www.oceanviewpub.com

10 9 8 7 6 5 4 3 2 1

To Lindsy Gardner,
a great librarian and an even better friend.

PROLOGUE

As a rule, I don't like prologues.

They're either lazy or dishonest—a sign that the writer hasn't worked hard enough to decide where to start the story or that they're about to cheat you in some way.

Ordinarily, I would find a much more artful way to do this.

But I'm under a tight deadline to get this book finished, and before I let you read the rest of it, there are some things you need to know about me.

I am a teacher—sorry, was a teacher. And in that role, I always tried to maintain a delicate balance.

F. Scott Fitzgerald once wrote, "The test of a first-rate intelligence is the ability to hold two opposed ideas in the mind at the same time, and still retain the ability to function."

For me, Idea One was that in teaching, as in life, relationships are paramount.

I've long understood I couldn't just stride into a classroom, turn on the knowledge firehose, and expect children to gulp down whatever I pumped out. Before I could reach students as learners, I had to first demonstrate that I cared for and respected them as human beings.

That was especially true for adolescents, who are naturally preoccupied with their rapidly emerging identities—all those messy *who am I, what am I becoming, how do I fit into the world* questions.

Part of my job as an educator was to facilitate that process of self-discovery. The end goal was that my students grew into empathetic, compassionate humans who were capable of caring about someone *other* than themselves.

I taught English and creative writing. Particularly in the latter, I needed to foster a psychologically safe space where students could open up to me and others—through their compositions—about things they may have never been able to admit to anyone, even to themselves.

There was no way I could do that without first establishing a nurturing, supportive relationship. It was the *terra firma* upon which mountains could be built.

But this leads me to the tension between Idea One and Idea Two in the F. Scott Fitzgerald challenge: it is equally important to maintain proper boundaries.

I was friendly with my students; but I was not Charles Bliss, their friend.

I was Charles Bliss, their teacher.

Full stop.

That's why I began every class—from the first day of school to the last—in the same manner. I stood at the door, looked each student square in the eye as they entered, shook their hand, and said, "Hi, I'm Mr. Bliss."

Always Mr. Bliss.

They were expected to then introduce themselves with their chosen honorific and last name.

This may strike you as stuffy, if not cloyingly pedantic, but I adopted this ritual for at least three reasons.

The first was just a pet peeve. In this high-five, fist-bump world of ours, kids need more practice with proper handshaking.

The second was symbolic. I wanted every student to know that they were starting each day with a blank slate. Past deeds—be they feats or foibles—no longer mattered.

The third? It was a subtle but effective way of maintaining boundaries.

I never wanted kids to become excessively familiar.

That could be a challenge at a place like Carrington Academy; and not because it was rigorously competitive—average SAT score: 1420; or because it was exorbitantly expensive—annual tuition: $72,400; or because, as a Carrington alum myself, I felt additional pressure to distance myself from my students.

It was because Carrington is a boarding school. Within the zoo of secondary education, boarding school is simply a different animal. The kids don't take the bus home at three o'clock or get picked up by their parents at six. They are an overwhelming, exhausting, twenty-four-hour-a-day presence.

As a faculty member, I was expected to be what is known as a triple threat: teaching throughout the school day, coaching or leading extracurriculars in the afternoons, and supervising dorm activity at night.

It wasn't just my job. It was my life.

Given that conflation, it's perhaps not surprising that some of my colleagues were known to get a little too chummy with their charges, developing minor cults of personality, reveling in their popularity, muddying lines that should have been kept distinct.

They gossiped with—and about—their students. They subtly advantaged their darlings while carrying out vendettas against their adversaries. They became overly involved in the students' personal lives, even prying into their romantic entanglements.

You could often tell who these faculty members were because they permitted—or even encouraged—the use of informal nicknames like "Rip" or "Stew" or "Dr. T."

Not me.

I was Mr. Bliss.

By the start of my eleventh year at Carrington, my boundaries had become hardwired. I was the teacher who wore a tie, every day; even on dress-down days and spirit days and all the other occasions when the school permitted a loosening of the dress code. I was a caring professional but did not make projects out of my students or lavish excess attention on any one of them. I was a mentor who maintained appropriate distance at all times, keeping my office door open and my hands to myself.

If it sounds like I am giving a sermon, forgive me. It's only because I came to believe these things with a religious fervency.

And I hope you can keep that in mind when you read what comes next.

CHAPTER 1

SIXTEEN DAYS EARLIER

During my many years of affiliation with Carrington Academy—first as a student, now as a faculty member—I have never once been commanded to appear in the head of school's office.

The order to do just that arrives simultaneously via text and email one Monday morning in mid-January: Wellington Ambrose needs to see me. 8 a.m. sharp.

There is no accompanying explanation. I'm curious, of course; but not overly concerned. It is the first day of classes after a long and restful Christmas break. My assumption is that some calamity must have been visited upon one of my students over the holidays.

Even still, I find myself knotting my tie a little tighter than usual, then taking a little extra care to make sure the dimple is sufficiently puckered.

Like approximately three-quarters of the faculty here, I live on campus, in housing provided by the school. I share a two-bedroom dorm apartment with my wife, Emily, who is in the throes of a doctoral dissertation that feels like it will never end. She is in the next room, still dozing and therefore unaware of my unusual summons.

At five minutes to eight, I begin the short walk across campus. Carrington Academy is modeled after the elite New England colleges to which its graduates aspire, so its campus is a pleasing pastiche of gracefully curved walking paths and picturesque red-brick buildings designed in Georgian Revival style.

Ambrose's office can be found on the top floor of a stately, ivy-covered building with twelve-foot ceilings and leaded glass windows. He is just the fifteenth man—and, yes, they've all been men—to serve as head of school in the 184-year history of Carrington Academy. Portraits of his fourteen predecessors—all but one of whom are currently deceased—adorn the outer sanctum of Ambrose's suite, peering down judgmentally on me as I enter.

Pleasantly avuncular, well-liked by students and staff alike, Ambrose is a onetime Latin teacher whose tenure at the top began shortly before I arrived as a student. Our relationship has always been close.

I was a scholarship kid, a boy from the upper reaches of Maine who won an essay contest for indigent applicants. Ambrose took special interest in me—he often dotes on scholarship students—and he helped ease my transition as I learned how to eradicate my down east accent and fit in with the trust fund babies from Greenwich. We kept in touch after I graduated and went off to Yale.

Four years later, he hired me to be one of his teachers. In addition to our interactions on professional matters, we've enjoyed many long conversations about literature, politics, and other matters far afield from Carrington Academy.

A few years ago, when I published my first and only novel, he graciously allowed me a monthlong leave in the middle of a term while I went on book tour. Ambrose is as close as I've ever had to a father figure, especially because I've never met my own.

His secretary isn't in yet, so I approach his door and—at precisely eight o'clock—give it a tentative tap.

"Come in," Ambrose calls.

I nudge the door open to see the head of school, with his crisply parted white hair, sitting behind his massive cherry-topped desk.

My jaw muscles immediately clench when I recognize who's with him. Victoria Brock is a member of the Carrington board of trustees, a onetime Carrington parent and a former two-term Connecticut attorney general who cultivated a tough-on-crime reputation.

Smart, incisive, and cheerless, she's someone you never want to find yourself stuck in a conversation with during a board-staff cocktail party.

Whenever Ambrose needs to discipline or fire someone, Brock is usually part of the proceeding.

"Have a seat," Ambrose says, in a tone that gives nothing away.

Determined to stay calm, I park myself in front of Ambrose, who tents his hands in a way that perhaps only a man who had been in charge for nearly a quarter-century can do.

"Charles, I'm afraid this is not going to be a pleasant conversation," he says. "It seems Hayley Goodloe came down with a case of chlamydia over break."

"Oh, that's terrible," I reply with due concern.

Ms. Goodloe, as I call her in class, is a senior in my honors creative writing class and is also one of the co-editors of *Carrington Crossings*, the literary magazine I oversee. If you click over to the admissions section in the school's website, you will see her in the scroll of photos: the archetypal Carrington girl with straight blond hair and a crisp uniform, smiling back at you with a gleaming set of straight teeth, poised to take over the world.

But she isn't one of my advisees and I'm not the school nurse, so I'm a little mystified as to what her diagnosis has to do with me.

"Her mother was understandably concerned as to how her daughter contracted a sexually transmitted disease while under school supervision," Ambrose says. "And Hayley said she got it from you."

He announces this without any special emphasis, but his words trigger an explosion behind my eyes.

This is every teacher's nightmare: the accusation of sexual impropriety that, founded or not, immediately takes the shape of an executioner's axe.

And this is not just any student making the accusation. The Goodloes are a wealthy, well-connected Connecticut family that has sent their offspring—and their generous support—to Carrington for generations. Hayley's mother is a longtime member of the Connecticut state legislature. Hayley's grandfather served two terms as governor of Connecticut and also chaired Carrington's board of trustees. Her great-grandfather's name graces a dormitory.

I suddenly know what it is to be a tiny electron getting sucked into a rapacious black hole. I am hurtling through space at astonishing speed, with no control over my fate.

Time seems to slow. Galaxies pinwheel around me. The forces in play are almost incalculably more massive than me.

I don't know what my life is about to become. The only certainty is that, at least from the perspective of those on the outside, I will cease to exist, swallowed whole and never heard from again.

"Hayley has told her mother the relationship was consensual," Ambrose continues. "The family is not interested in pursuing legal action against you. They don't want to put Hayley through any unnecessary drama. All they're asking is for you to be terminated and immediately leave campus. Hayley hasn't yet returned to school for the new semester and they don't feel comfortable with her being on campus while you're still here."

Brock jumps in: "The age of consent in Connecticut is sixteen, so as far as the school is concerned, there is nothing that we're legally required to report to the authorities. Assuming this stays quiet"—she pauses significantly over this—"we're prepared to continue paying you, with benefits, through the end of the school year. But you are to depart immediately. You are not to say goodbye to any students or faculty members or explain your departure. If we become aware you have initiated contact with anyone affiliated with Carrington Academy, we will immediately discontinue your severance payments."

Back to Ambrose: "We'll pay to put you and your wife up in a hotel until you can make new living arrangements. In the meantime, we'll have maintenance move your things into a storage facility, which we'll pay for as well. If you choose to continue your career in independent schools, I'll give you a positive recommendation. We'll say you were looking for a change of scenery."

I gape at this man who I considered a mentor and friend. But that benevolent presence has vanished.

There is only a shrewd dealmaker. And the offer is plain.

Shut your mouth. Leave quietly. If you're lucky, you'll live to teach another day.

In the boarding school world, this is known as "pass the trash." It is how a whole subclass of well-credentialed degenerates remain employed long after they should have been discarded.

My mouth has gone suddenly dry. With difficulty, I say, "Aren't you even going to ask me if I did it?"

"Frankly, that's immaterial at the moment," Ambrose replies.

"How can it be immaterial? Carrington is . . . it's everything to me. You know that. I would never do something to jeopardize my position here. It's the only place I've ever worked. It's all my friends. It's my home. It's—"

"Mr. Bliss, Connecticut is an at-will employment state," Brock cuts in. "That means we can fire you at any time, for any reason we want, as long as it's not for a handful of protected reasons. And giving a student a venereal disease is certainly not one of them."

Hearing Brock make this proclamation—as if it is somehow incontrovertible—injects a spurt of calcium back into my spine.

Even in my diminished state, I recognize someone overplaying her hand.

"But I signed a contract," I volley back. "It says I can only be terminated for 'just cause.' Something can't be considered 'just cause' if I didn't actually do it."

I catch the quick, uneasy glance that passes between Ambrose and Brock. This is not how they planned on this playing out. I was supposed to scamper out of this office with my tail tucked firmly between my legs.

Pressing my advantage, I turn to Ambrose. "Wellie, please. You *know* me. Do you really think I'd do something like this?"

He shakes his head. "Whether I personally believe you doesn't matter. Hayley Goodloe says this occurred and her mother believes her. Diane Goodloe is not some neophyte. She's aware of the seriousness of the accusation and she's not backing off. I'm in no position to determine who is telling the truth."

"But before something can be considered 'just cause' for termination, you have to at least try," I say. "You have to perform an investigation, find the facts. Look, I'll take a chlamydia test right now. Let's go to the nurse's office. I'll pee in a cup or give blood or do whatever I have to do."

"That wouldn't solve anything," Brock says. "Fifty percent of men who carry chlamydia don't have symptoms. Or your infection could have cleared up. You still could have previously passed it on to Hayley Goodloe."

"There has to be some way I can prove my innocence," I say. "What does Hayley say about where and when this occurred? Press her on the details. I guarantee you her story will fall apart. Look, I'm not naïve. I know who the Goodloes are. But I've given this school everything I have for eleven years. Doesn't that earn me a little benefit of the doubt?"

Ambrose crosses his arms. Brock shifts uncomfortably. Everyone in the room recognizes the potential for mutually assured destruction.

A wrongful termination suit brought by an employee at an elite prep school would surely spill into public view. It would ruin any chance I had of ever again working in education, but Carrington Academy would also be stained. Top students might be less likely to apply. Wealthy donors might find another use for their checkbooks. The stench of scandal would waft around the school for years.

And one of Wellie Ambrose's primary roles as head of school—and Victoria Brock's obligations as a board member—is to safeguard the Carrington brand.

Brock speaks first: "Mr. Bliss, your service to the school is the only reason you're receiving this generous offer of severance and relocation assistance. Your options here are pretty straightforward. Your contract is up in June. I can assure you it will not be renewed. You have nothing to gain by fighting this. Even if you win, the most the courts will award you is what we're already trying to give you: payment through the end of your existing contract. If you lose, you walk away with nothing. Either way, you're gone. Take the soft landing."

"But if I don't fight this, I'm tacitly admitting my guilt. People would find out why I left, including people who I consider my closest friends. You can't stop the rumor mill from churning."

"There's nothing we can do about that," Brock says remorselessly. "All we can promise you is that those rumors wouldn't come from this office or the board."

"Yeah, that's not much solace to someone whose life is about to be destroyed for something he didn't do," I say. "Look, I'm entitled to some due process here. A hearing. A chance to face my accuser. If Hayley Goodloe is willing to look everyone in the eye and say I did this, if she can back it up with a story that holds up under a gentle degree of scrutiny, then I understand the school has no choice. You have to believe her. But I honestly don't think she'll be able to do that because nothing inappropriate happened between us. *Nothing.*"

We sit in silence for a moment, clearly at an impasse.

Ambrose breaks it. "Listen, I know this is a rotten situation, Chuck," he says, using the name I went by as a student, sounding more like himself than he has at any other point during this conversation. "If you really want to put everyone through that kind of ordeal, I guess we'll have to explore that."

Brock looks pained by this concession, which she did not seem ready to make; but she also doesn't dispute it.

Ambrose continues: "But why don't you take a day to think it through? Think about our offer. Think about what's best for you and your wife moving forward. This could be a great opportunity to start over somewhere else. Let me help you do that. You come up with a list of places you want to go and I'll make some calls. Most schools are just starting their hiring for next year. It would be perfect timing. Don't let this accusation destroy your whole life."

I am about to begin an impassioned plea about how I don't *want* to leave Carrington.

Then I stop myself.

There's truly no point.

"Fine," I say, standing, because it's pretty clear this meeting is over. "I'll think about it."

"We'll expect your answer by this time tomorrow," Brock says. "In the meantime, you are to have no contact with anyone at Carrington. Especially not Hayley Goodloe."

MIDLOGUE

Isn't it strange how there's a word for a section of explanatory text that comes before a story (prologue), and after a story (epilogue), but not during a story?

So I guess I'll call this the midlogue.

I can invent a word if I want to, can't I? Shakespeare made up words all the time.

(Let me be clear: I'm not trying to compare myself to the Bard, whoever he/she/they were. But I guess I wouldn't blame you if you scampered off to Amazon and gave me a one-star review for being a colossally arrogant prick. Though, to be honest, I have bigger things to worry about at the moment.)

Anyhow, I promise I'm not going to keep interrupting like this, but I need to break in for a second to explain the next section. It is taken from Hayley Goodloe's journal, a copy of which I obtained, under circumstances that will be explained later.

I'm not going to reprint every day of Hayley's journal. That would get tedious. I'll often skip days or even weeks of entries. What's included is just the highlights.

The journal starts at the beginning of the school year—four-and-a-half months *before* the action I'm describing in the book. But she will be writing about events that become relevant throughout my narrative, which begins in January.

Just to be explicit about it, you will know when I'm going to Hayley's journal because those sections will begin with a date—and not "chapter" or a word that ends with "logue."

Publishers get nervous when an author goes back and forth across timelines like this; but, frankly, publishers underestimate readers' intelligence.

You're smart. I have every faith you'll be able to keep up.

JOURNAL ENTRY: TUESDAY, SEPTEMBER 5

I have made at least five attempts to start this journal already, and they've all been cringey cringe bad. I guess I should just keep it simple.

Hello. This is my journal.

According to Mr. Bliss, we have to write in our journal every day—a minimum of 250 words—and he stressed the word *minimum.* He said beyond that there were no rules, that this was just for us, and that we could make it anything we wanted.

Supposedly he won't even read it. He showed us how to change the file settings so it's completely private. The only thing he can see is that the file is being accessed every day and that the file size keeps growing.

I don't know what's to prevent us from just pasting in SpongeBob memes or writing "blah" 250 times.

Someone asked him about that, and he admitted we could. He said the only person we'd be cheating if we did that was ourselves.

He suggested that if we were stuck, we could make our first journal entry about our goals for the class. That way, at the end of the year, we could look back to see how well we accomplished them.

So, okay. I'm basically taking honors creative writing because, someday, I am going to write a book about my intensely dysfunctional family, and it will become a huge bestseller, because nothing spreads more joy than the knowledge that rich people are just as miserable as everyone else.

My working title is *Searing Memoir.* Just so no one misses the point.

But before I do that, it would probably help if I actually learn how to, you know, write.

According to Mr. Bliss, journaling will help. He said that writing is nothing more than—and nothing less than—the process of transferring thoughts from your brain to the page. He said it's like a muscle, and the more you work that muscle, the stronger it gets.

He knows. He's an author. I read his book over the summer. It was really good.

Mr. Bliss said journaling is a great way to track our personal progress and growth, to reduce stress and anxiety, and to get to know ourselves better.

So, hello, self, your name is Hayley Goodloe, you are seventeen years old, and you are a senior at Carrington Academy. Your best friend is Calista Fergus. She's also your roommate. She's from Canada. The two of you are co-editors of *Carrington Crossroads*, the school literary magazine.

You play soccer in the fall and tennis in the spring, not because you're super amazing at either, but you're captain of both so that looks good for college applications.

You are also: the daughter of the Honorable Diane Goodloe (D as in Democrat-Connecticut) and the dishonorable W. Johnson Goodloe III (D as in Douchebag–New York City), who have been divorced most of your life and never should have been married in the first place; the grand-daughter of Ward J. Goodloe Jr., who no one will ever live up to; and the great granddaughter of the original W. J. Goodloe, who made the monster assload of money that his descendants now do nothing but fight over.

Wow. That got a little unseemly. And a Goodloe is never unseemly.

Let me try that again: Your name is Hayley Goodloe, of the Hartford Goodloes.

You keep your chin up . . . and your shoulders back . . . and one leg slightly in front of the other . . . and smile and . . . *Click.*

Good girl, Hayley.

Mr. Bliss said some of his past students have found it helpful to write their journals as if they're writing for their future selves, so we should put details into it that we know now—like what we were wearing or what the weather was like—but that we might forget later. He said he has had students who came back years later and thanked him for making them journal, because now they have this indelible record of their high school years.

Blah blah blah. I think I'm already well over 250 for the day.

Is Mr. Bliss *really* not going to read this thing?

Let's find out.

Hey, Mr. Bliss, guess what? I think you're kinda hot!!

CHAPTER 2

I emerge from the head of school's office concussed and dazed. There's a metallic taste in my mouth that I can only ascribe to some kind of bizarre stress reaction.

It takes massive effort just to keep putting one foot in front of the other.

Students are streaming past me on their way to their first period classes, their breath steaming the frigid morning air. A few of them offer me a cheery "Hi, Mr. Bliss," but it barely even penetrates my ears.

Don't they notice I look like I've just come from my own autopsy?

Up until twenty minutes earlier, my chief concern for the day had been whether the seniors in my literature seminar would bring sufficient depth to our discussion of Jesmyn Ward's *Sing, Unburied, Sing.* That now seems ridiculously picayune.

I feel disgusting. Dirty. Nauseous. I know what I would think if I read about someone like me. I would barely even bother with the facts, just go straight to my base assumptions.

A pretty seventeen-year-old girl.

Her worldly thirty-three-year-old creative writing teacher.

No question: That guy totally did it.

What scum.

The standard line about existence at Carrington Academy is that it's like living in bubble wrap. The sharpness of the world is out there, but as long as you're inside the fence—and there really is a white fence that rings the entire 425-acre campus—you seldom feel it.

That protection is now gone. It is nothing but broken glass and jagged rocks unless by some miracle a prevaricating teenager suddenly relocates her conscience.

That's tremorous enough. But as I approach my dorm apartment, an even more seismic thought shakes me.

I have to tell my wife about this.

Mine is not the only life that's about to be massively disrupted.

My steps slow. My guts twist again. This is at least as cruel to Emily as it is to me.

And we really, really don't need this right now.

Our marriage is just recovering from a trial separation this past fall. Our reconciliation is so recent—and so tenuous—she hasn't even fully unpacked her stuff yet.

I already hate that this is happening to us. For whatever our recent struggles have been, Emily is more than just my best friend, more than the love of my life. She is my sustaining force, a person who has been—at certain low times—the only reason I could carry on.

I simply don't function very well without her.

We met nearly seven years ago, at what now appears to be my zenith: that brief moment in time when I was trying out for the role of Charles Bliss, literary phenom.

Coming out of Yale, I could have followed the easy, well-trod path down Interstate 95 to Wall Street and/or any number of the consulting firms that came to campus to recruit.

There were two reasons I had decided to become a teacher. One was that I wanted to give back to Carrington, a place that had given me so much.

The other was that it would give me summers off to write.

Working maniacally during that time, and more sparingly when school was in session, it took me four years to produce *Washington County*, a sharply drawn multigenerational portrait of a family struggling for existence in down east Maine.

I began looking for a publisher in early 2017, at perhaps the most portentous moment ever for a book about poor white people. Trump had just won the White House. *Hillbilly Elegy* was in the midst of a dash to the top of the *New York Times* bestseller list. White grievance was still new, with its claws and fangs not yet as apparent as they would later become. It was then just a trendy curiosity for limousine liberals.

Riding that wave, I landed a prominent New York literary agent, Jane Janikowksi, who quickly sold *Washington County* to an eminent publishing company for a quarter of a million dollars.

It was a ludicrous sum for someone who grew up as poor as I did. I immediately wanted to leave teaching and live off my fat advance, but Jane convinced me to hold off. Many an author had quit their day job too soon and regretted it, she said; she counseled clients to wait until they got their *second* book deal.

As such, I spent most of 2017 balancing two jobs: teaching and polishing *Washington County* under the aegis of my editor, Portia Swan, a legendary book whisperer and one of the true tastemakers in the business. Over the course of four rounds of tough-love edits, she helped me bring the manuscript to heights I did not think it could reach, then scheduled it for publication.

With everyone certain the novel and its author were bound for literary fame, the publisher booked me for a series of long-lead lunches. These are meetings with chain store book buyers, independent bookstore owners, and reviewers. They are meant to generate buzz for a work, such that it bursts out of the chute with a full head of momentum that puts it high on the *New York Times* bestseller list.

It was a ten-city tour, which I undertook as soon as school let out in June 2018. My escort was a publicity assistant named Emily Vanderburgh, a dark-haired former professional ballerina with an effervescent personality and a collection of sleeveless summer dresses that made my heart arhythmic.

She was twenty-five, two years younger than me, single, and fearsomely competent at everything—a trait I have always found incredibly sexy. We were traveling first class on the publisher's dime, enjoying the attention of important people, shutting down hotel bars, laughing the whole way.

Some of the attraction was circumstantial and, surely, superficial. We had read the same books, binged the same shows.

But there was also something much more profound. She had this fundamental honesty to her. About who she was. About what she was feeling. There were no games, no coy deceptions, no pretend sophistications.

It was just easy, simple, straightforward: Hey, here I am. Take me or leave me.

And I was taking. All the way.

By the end of the trip, I had fallen deeply for her. Our last night together was in St. Louis. I confessed my feelings for her. She reciprocated. We made love awkwardly that night, then perfectly the next morning. We were flying so high we barely needed an airline to get us home.

Things moved quickly from there. New York City and central Connecticut felt altogether too far apart for two such lovestruck youngsters. Emily had been thinking about leaving publishing anyway, and I convinced her to take the leap.

The big leap. Carrington has a long-standing policy that forbids significant others or even fiancées from cohabitating in campus housing. Only lawfully married spouses could live together. By then I had already received a third of my book advance. I plowed it into a magnificent engagement ring, a fairy-tale wedding, and a two-week trip to Hawaii.

But even after we returned, it was like the honeymoon never stopped. I was teaching again, but we talked dreamily of where we would move—and the adventures we would embark on together—when I became a full-time author, living untethered from the demands of conventional employment.

All signs pointed to *Washington County* becoming a massive hit. The publisher had ordered a huge print run. My blurbs were almost embarrassingly purple—"virtuosic" . . . "luminous" . . . "a book like this comes along once a decade." *Publishers Weekly* gave it a coveted starred review. *Kirkus Reviews* did, too, calling me "a Steinbeck for the new millennium."

Then publication day finally came and it was like I died but no one told me.

The world had changed. The 2018 midterms had come and gone. Literate America decided it had heard quite enough from poor white people. Barnes & Noble pulled back on a promise to give *Washington County* preferred store placement. Costco decided not to make a buy after all.

All those independent bookstore owners we romanced during the long lead lunches months earlier seemingly forgot my name. The reviews continued to glow, but no one noticed.

In short order, the book tanked, selling fewer than five thousand copies.

Over the coming months, everything unraveled. Portia Swan took weeks to return my emails, if she wrote back at all. Jane Janikowski wouldn't even entertain a pitch for another book. She brusquely informed me that with my sales track record—despite the large sums that had been invested in the book and its publicity—no major publisher would come within five area codes of me ever again.

Charles Bliss was effectively radioactive.

Only one person stuck by me.

Emily.

Her devotion to me seemed to grow in equal measure with my self-disgust. When the publishing company stopped even pretending to put effort into publicity, she used her contacts to line up blog interviews and podcasts, hoping that each media hit would be *the one* that finally made the book achieve liftoff.

When *Washington County* was shortlisted for a National Book Critics Circle Award, she was sure that moment had finally arrived; that it would be overlooked no more.

Even when that proved to be a fantasy, her belief in me did not falter. She retained this unshakable certitude about my talent. Someday, she said, I would write another novel that was so terrific, publishers would line up to give me a second chance.

In the meantime, she applied for, and was accepted to, a Doctor of Psychology program at the nearby University of Hartford. We paid for her tuition—a checkbook-choking thirty grand a year—with the rest of my book money. I joked that it was an investment in my future as a kept man, which I would become someday when she went into lucrative private practice.

With her encouragement, I started writing again, though it was difficult to keep the faith. The pandemic certainly didn't help—either with my writing or my rapidly deteriorating mental health.

I finished a manuscript and threw it away. It was solid gold crap.

Then I finished another manuscript. It was even worse.

After that, I stopped writing and, in my spare time, took to sulking. I wasn't easy to be around. I know that now. She hated that I had given up on myself after all the encouragement she had poured into me. She complained I was drinking too much, and there was probably some truth to that.

Our marriage fell into a rut. Our solution to pull ourselves out of it—misguided though it may have been—was to try for a baby.

Month after heartbreaking month, we failed. Her period arrived every twenty-eight days, like it was set on some automatic calendar reminder.

Until, one month, it didn't. She waited a few days, then peed on a stick. We took turns leaping up and down when that second line appeared. During the next few weeks, we excitedly began making plans.

Until she miscarried. We were both devastated. Everything I did to try to console her was wrong. It only made her angrier and me more depressed.

A few weeks later, she announced that she was moving out, subletting an apartment for the fall semester that was closer to Hartford. She said she couldn't take care of herself *and* me anymore.

I thought for sure we were on our way to divorce.

For a few months, the only time I saw her was at weekly couples counseling. Slowly, we chipped away at our issues. I acknowledged that I had been putting too much of a burden on her, and that I needed to take responsibility for my own mental health. I even promised to start writing again, which she took as the most positive sign of all.

Two weeks before Christmas, she decided to move back in and give our marriage another chance. We were just barely getting our footing back underneath us.

Now this.

* * *

I stagger into the main room of our apartment, which is a living room that flows into a small kitchen.

There's no sound coming from the bathroom or our bedroom. Emily must still be asleep. Her typical Monday schedule is to TA an undergraduate psychology class in the late morning, then lock herself in the library for the remainder of the day to work on her dissertation.

I walk softly into the kitchen, opening the cabinet above the oven, where I keep a bottle of Glenmorangie, a single malt scotch.

All I want is a shot or two to dull the pain. I've got one hand on the bottle when I hear the click of a medicine cabinet door closing in the bathroom.

I hastily put the Glenmorangie back in its place and, wanting to get this over with, call out, "Hey, Em? You have a second?"

My voice is shaky. I'm already on the verge of tears.

"Hang on," she calls.

After a few more moments, she emerges from the bathroom with sleep-rumpled brown hair falling past her shoulders. She is wearing one of my Yale T-shirts. Her lean dancer's legs, still ropy with muscle, jut out from a pair of boxer shorts.

The moment she looks at me, she asks, "What's wrong?"

At my insistence, we settle onto the couch. I give her a full account of the scene in Ambrose's office. She sits stoically, wordlessly, absorbing the whole terrible thing.

There's a pause when I finish. Finally, she says, "Hayley Goodloe, huh?"

Emily knows a lot of the kids. She sees them in the dining hall. She cheers for them when she joins me at athletic events or performances. From time to time, she picks up extra money by chaperoning off-campus trips to a nearby mall or other such activities.

"Yes," I say.

"I didn't realize she was in any of your classes."

"Senior honors creative writing."

"You never mentioned that before."

"There's nothing to mention. I don't mention most of my students."

Emily seems to shrink. "Charles, she's not most students. She's . . . she's very pretty."

"So?" I say, sounding more defensive than I might like. "She's seventeen. She's a child."

"She doesn't look like a child."

"What's that supposed to mean?"

"If Hayley Goodloe threw herself at you, you'd be flattered. I wasn't around. You were lonely. Especially if you were drinking—"

"There is no amount of alcohol that would make me think it was okay to hook up with a student," I assert.

"I'm just saying, the rules of society aside, you're a healthy, attractive man and she's a beautiful young woman. I'd understand if you couldn't resist."

"There was nothing to resist. And even if there was, it's completely wrong and I'm married."

"You were married when you hooked up with Jessica the Bartender."

She says this without rancor. During our separation, I had a drunken one-night stand with Jessica, a bartender at Mick's, a local watering hole. For her part, Emily had a brief fling with Gary, a fellow grad student.

When we reconciled, we decided Jessica the Bartender and Gary the Grad Student canceled each other out. We called it a hall pass and moved on.

"This is very different," I say.

"Charles, honey," she says gently, though I can hear her voice fraying at the edges. "I just . . . No matter what happened, I just . . . I need the truth. Right here, right now. Please. We can get through this. We can call it another hall pass. Just tell me."

She studies me carefully. After Jessica and Gary, we had long discussions about the subject of monogamy. I know her worldview. When you study the sexuality of other human cultures, it makes the Judeo-Christian model—one man, one woman, 'til death do us part—seem downright weird.

Truly, it is not adultery that sends most couples into divorce court. It's dishonesty.

So I attempt to give her the truth.

"Em, come on," I say softly. "Nothing happened."

She holds my glance a beat longer, and in that moment, something passes between us. It is palpable, as real as the air we're breathing even if we can't see it. It's this resolve, this mutual understanding of who we are and what we've been through together.

What we are made of is stronger than this flimsy allegation.

"Okay," she says. "So what are we going to do?"

"I honestly don't know," I say, relieved at her use of the plural pronoun.

"But come tomorrow morning, you're going to ask Ambrose for a hearing?"

"I have to, don't I? If I just take their money and slink off to some other school, I might as well rent a sky plane and fly it over campus with a big banner that says, 'I did it.' Everyone would look at me like I'm some big creep. Hell, I would *feel* like a big creep."

Emily accepts this without argument. "Okay, then. What we have to figure out is: Why would Hayley invent something like this? This isn't exactly a girl who lacks for attention."

"Believe me, I wish I knew," I say. "I haven't had a lot of time to think about it, but I've been trying to put myself in her situation. Obviously, *someone* gave her chlamydia. It's probably some guy she doesn't want her parents to know about. She thinks if she blurts out my name, that will distract everyone. And, congratulations, it worked."

"You think she cares that little about ruining someone else's life? That makes her a sociopath."

"No, that makes her a teenager. You're the one who's always reminding me the frontal lobe doesn't fully develop until age twenty-five. She just didn't think things through."

"And by the time she realizes she's gone too far, it's already too late, and she feels like she can't walk back her story," Emily says.

"Something like that, yes."

"Then our only hope is that she decides to come clean."

Again, with the plural pronoun. It is giving me optimism. I am not in this oceanic trench alone. There is a hand reaching down, trying to help pluck me out of the abyss.

"Or we figure out who the guy is," I say. "We get him to talk. He admits it burns every time he pees. He goes to Ambrose, and Ambrose convinces the family to back off."

"Okay, so who's the guy?"

"I don't know," I say. "But we'd better find out fast."

JOURNAL ENTRY: FRIDAY, SEPTEMBER 8

THIS. JUST. IN.

Mr. Bliss's wife left him!

Sorry, I'm being a total bitch. I shouldn't make it sound like I'm happy about it or something. (Mr. Bliss, if you're actually reading this, I'm sorry!)

Her name is Emily. Or do I say, was Emily? I mean, she's not dead or anything, but . . . Yeah, anyhow, she's gone.

You used to see them sitting in the dining hall together or walking around campus. They seemed like they were totally in la-la-love, but my dad always says you never know what happens when the bedroom door closes.

(My dad gives me a lot of weird advice.)

Mr. Bliss's wife is really pretty, of course. Correction: she's smoking hot. Especially for an older woman. She was apparently this big dancer or something. You can definitely tell.

I had noticed Mr. Bliss was suddenly eating alone this term. And you never saw them walking together. I thought, I don't know, maybe she's just busy?

But then Calista told me she heard some sophomores gossiping about how she left him right before school started. She just packed everything in a U-Haul and took off.

That poor, poor man! I feel so bad for him.

I'm also like: What is *her* problem? Like, seriously, Mr. Bliss is practically a cliché of what women find attractive. He's tall—at least six feet two. He's broad-shouldered and solidly built, neither too thick nor too thin. He's got a jawline like a Greek god.

Plus, he's got these beautiful blue eyes. And those eyelashes! Ninety-nine percent of people could only get eyelashes like that from the cosmetics aisle at the drugstore.

On top of that, he's super smart, and charming, and nice.

Honestly, who would leave a guy like him?

She must be crazy.

CHAPTER 3

Emily lingers well past the time when she ought to have departed.

I keep trying to shoo her out the door, and she demurs, almost like she's afraid to leave me alone.

Finally, I suggest a compromise: if she agrees to go to school, I'll head out for a run.

Emily knows that, at least for me, running is the best antidepressant around. It's also when I do my best thinking. Many a glutinous bout of writer's block has loosened up after a few good miles on the road.

I kiss Emily one last time on my way out. Bundled against the cold, from my leggings to my knit cap, I soon fall into a rhythm that allows the thoughts to begin flowing.

As I begin strategizing, I am mindful that I am forbidden to have contact with anyone at Carrington, lest I jeopardize my generous severance and Ambrose's offer to help place me elsewhere. I need to go about this cautiously.

Who would know the intimacies of Hayley's dating life? I can think of at least a half-dozen girls she hangs with.

The problem is, Carrington students are required to keep their phones off during the academic day, much to their consternation. Being caught with one is an Honor Code violation, which is grounds for expulsion. If I text any of them, I wouldn't hear from them until after classes are through seven hours from now. I feel like I don't have that kind of time to waste.

But approaching them in person is also risky. Ambrose constantly roams around campus. You never know where he'll pop up.

That leaves faculty members: her advisor and her teachers. In theory, none of them will know that I've been marked for extermination. Yet. And because the phone ban doesn't apply to staff, I can reach out to them without leaving the apartment.

As soon as I return from my run, I open my laptop, pull up our online school management system, and tap into Hayley Goodloe's file.

Her contact information is at the top of the screen. She has two sets of parents. Diane Goodloe and Steve Graham live at 23 Rogers Road in West Hartford. His occupation is listed as "campaign manager." Diane's occupation is not listed; but, of course, I already know she's a state senator.

Out of curiosity, I google 23 Rogers Road. According to a real estate website, it is valued at $4.1 million.

Hayley's other parent is Ward Johnson Goodloe III. His occupation is "artist." His address is on West 20th Street in New York City. There's no apartment number, which suggests he owns the entire building. Its value is $23 million.

Sometimes, the money these families have just baffles me.

The separate addresses tell me the Goodloes are divorced. This is hardly unusual in our student body. Divorce is among the leading causes of boarding school attendance. The campus serves as a neutral ground for the parents and an oasis for the child.

Some kids just need what we call a parent-ectomy.

Her advisor's name comes next. It's Molly Millrose, whom I know well. She's a science teacher a bit older than me but still very much my contemporary. She was hired at Carrington out of

Wesleyan maybe three or four years before me. We've shared jokes about being unable to quit Connecticut.

Molly is a great human being: smart, kind, and multitalented. She makes her own dresses using fabric with fun prints on them—science teacher zombies for Halloween, photos of the Wright Brothers' plane for when she teaches Bernoulli's Principle, wedges of 3.14 pie for Pi Day, that sort of thing.

As a colleague, Molly is top drawer. There's no greater gift than when she suddenly switches onto your weekend duty team. She never lets a ball drop and is a helper by nature. There's a reason one of her jobs here is to organize the new faculty mentorship program.

She's also incredibly kind to Emily, treating her like part of the Carrington family. Emily might be even better friends with Molly than I am.

But she still wouldn't think twice about getting a text from me. So I pull up Molly's name in my phone and tap out: HEY, HAYLEY GOODLOE TEXTED ME THIS MORNING ASKING IF I COULD GIVE SOMETHING TO HER BOYFRIEND BUT I HAVE NO IDEA WHO HER BOYFRIEND IS. ANY IDEAS?

It's flimsy, but Molly will know the phone ban means I can't get an answer from a student during the day. I hit SEND before I can talk myself out of it.

Continuing my journey through Hayley's file, I get down to her current transcript. It is a mix of A-minuses and A's, including the one she currently has in Creative Writing. I scan down her list of teachers. I want to send a text to at least one more teacher, in case Molly doesn't answer or doesn't know.

My eye stops on Ken Rippinger, the aforementioned "Rip." He's her math teacher and soccer coach. Rip and I are friendly, though he's definitely one of those overly chummy teachers with what I consider to be poor boundaries—especially with his players, who he refers to as "my girls."

Will Rip help me? In truth, he's a bit of a wild card on all fronts. An Englishman who brought his passion for "football" with him from Liverpool, he's a notorious hothead who annually leads the New England Prep School Athletic Conference in yellow cards.

But his intentions are usually good. Nothing makes him lose his mind more than when the refs allow the game to get too physical. He can't stand to see any of "my girls" get hurt.

I send the same text to him that I sent Molly.

By the time I'm out of the shower, they've both replied.

Molly wrote: I DON'T THINK SHE HAS A BF THE MOMENT BUT I CAN NEVER KEEP TRACK OF THAT STUFF. GOOD LUCK. LET ME KNOW IF I CAN HELP WITH ANYTHING ELSE.

Rip's response: I THINK AIDAN BROADMOOR BUT IDK

I give both messages a thumbs-up. This is a good break. I coached Aidan Broadmoor his freshman year, when he was the star of my JV baseball team. He's now being recruited by several Ivy League schools in both baseball and football. He is, in general, a very Big Man on Campus type—handsome, outgoing, adored by peers, respected by teachers.

He's also Black. Is that why Hayley felt she couldn't say anything? Are the Goodloes *that* kind of family?

I google Johnson Goodloe, then Diane Goodloe. Neither seems like the kind of person who would be hung up on an interracial relationship. Hayley's father has used some portion of his fortune to support a variety of arts organizations, all of which are progressive by nature. Hayley's mother is a left-of-center legislator in a left-of-center state.

Then again, you never know how someone's views will change when they're suddenly dealing with their own daughter. Isn't that the essence of elite modern racism? It's largely covert, and often carefully hidden within a lot of self-righteous talk about DEI initiatives.

I shift back to the school management screen and bring up Aidan Broadmoor's schedule. His morning is packed with classes that are held in older buildings that form the center of campus. Way too close to Ambrose's eyes.

But after lunch he has AP Environmental Science. Like a lot of schools with jewel-encrusted alumni bodies, Carrington recently built a ritzy STEM building. It's named after one of its benefactors, but everyone just calls it "the STEM building." It blends into a forested part of campus up in the northwest quadrant.

That will my best chance to quietly intercept Aidan Broadmoor without being caught.

CHAPTER 4

I leave on the early side, in case—as would be typical of a Carrington student—Aidan eats a quick lunch and goes straight to class so he can cram in a small window for extra studying.

Rather than cut through the heart of campus, the most direct route, I take the southern exit and walk around through the suburban neighborhood that butts up against Carrington's northern and western sides. Then I dart through a stranger's lawn and duck under the white fence.

I pass Parsons Pond, created long ago by a wealthy alum who thought Carrington students should be able to get in touch with their inner Thoreau. "The pond," as it's so creatively called, has long been a favored hook-up spot for amorous Carrington students.

Once around it, I make a hard cut toward the STEM building.

In my attempt to not attract much notice, I am wearing my usual teaching outfit: slim fit stretch dress pants, a button-down Oxford shirt, and a tie. Since I am standing outside, a charcoal-colored pea coat tops the ensemble. Perfect faculty camouflage.

No more than ten minutes after the dining hall opens for lunch, students are back trickling by me, some of them with jaws still working on the food they quickly grabbed.

A few kids notice me, but I pretend to bury my attention in my phone. My eyes keep cutting toward the path that comes from the center of campus, where students are coming in twos and threes.

With fifteen minutes until class starts, he still hasn't materialized.

Ten minutes. Still no Aidan.

Suddenly, there's someone coming up on me fast. It's Molly Millrose, Hayley's advisor, whose classroom is on the second floor.

I can feel myself go rigid—*busted!*—but she gives me a smile that is typical of Carrington faculty when we greet each other. It's a mix of *it's nice to see you, fellow traveler* and *I could really use a two-hour nap right now, how about you?*

The fact that she's still smiling tells me she doesn't know a thing about Hayley's accusation. Maybe Ambrose really will manage to keep this quiet.

Between the homemade dresses and her side-parted, pin-curled hair, Molly has a classic look about her, like she's hoping the world will revert to a past decade. There's something about her that reminds me of a 1940s war bride.

She stops in front of me. I wish she wouldn't. I have no idea how I'll get rid of her if Aidan should happen to come this way.

"Hey, Charlie," she says.

She's the only person in the world who calls me Charlie. I have no idea why.

"What's going on?" I say, trying to keep my tone casual.

"Did you ever figure out who Hayley's boyfriend is?"

I don't want to say Aidan's name or hint that I'm here to talk to a student.

"I've got some leads," I say, keeping it vague.

"Ambrose sent an email saying she's going to be out of school for a few days but he didn't give me any details. Is she okay?"

"No clue," I say. "She just asked if I could give something to her boyfriend for the, uh, the literary magazine."

The lies are stacking up so fast I can't make eye contact anymore. It's too uncomfortable.

"Oh," Molly says. "Well, I've got to do a little more prep before class. See ya, Charlie."

She gives me a little wave.

"See ya," I say, waving back as she disappears into the building.

Only then do I fully exhale.

A few minutes later, I see Aidan, striding manfully my way. Aidan is my height but probably outweighs me by twenty pounds.

I go into bustle mode, walking away from the STEM building like I've just come from a meeting there and have somewhere else to be, as would be typical for a faculty member at this time of day. I keep my head down until Aidan is a few feet away and then look up just as he's about to pass.

"Mr. Broadmoor!" I say cheerfully. "How have you been?"

I stop, which forces him to stop. He's an earnest, polite young man who respects his teachers.

"Hey, Coach Bliss," he says.

I have already determined I can't tackle this issue straight on. The circumstances call for a sideways approach.

With this in mind, I ask, "What's the latest in the Aidan Broadmoor recruiting wars? Does Yale still stand a chance?"

He smiles. "Sorry, Coach. It's down to Harvard and Dartmouth. I like the vibe better at Dartmouth, but Harvard is Harvard, you know?"

"Yeah, that's a tough one. They're both great schools. You can't really go wrong," I say, giving the classically unhelpful advice.

Then I subtly shift subjects. "What does your girlfriend think?"

Aidan's face lifts just a little. "My girlfriend?"

"Yeah. Aren't you dating Hayley Goodloe?"

"Oh. We broke up."

Crap. Though that doesn't totally preclude him giving her a venereal disease.

"Sorry. I hadn't heard," I say. "When did that happen?"

"Before Thanksgiving break."

That was nearly two months ago. But I had already done some hard googling on chlamydia. It typically takes one to three weeks after unprotected sex with an infected person for symptoms to appear. However, there are instances when it can take a little longer. Aidan's timing still fits, especially if Hayley came down with it before Christmas.

"How long had you guys been together?" I ask.

"A few months."

"Oh, so it was pretty serious, then."

"I mean, sort of."

From the way he shifts his weight, I can tell there's something under the surface he doesn't want to tell me about. This is exactly the kind of subject I would ordinarily never press a student about. It crosses boundaries I know need to stay in place.

But I'm not going to let that stop me now.

"You guys were pretty close," I venture. "What happened?"

"Oh, I don't know. Nothing major. We just broke up."

"Yeah, but that still had to be pretty hard for you. She was your first, wasn't she?"

"Huh?"

"It's okay, Aidan," I say, lowering my voice and going into concerned-mentor mode. "Breaking up with the person you lose your virginity to—that's a big deal. You need to talk about it?"

He recoils a little. "No, sir. I mean, I didn't . . . we never—"

"You don't have to be embarrassed about it. The important thing is that you were safe. You were safe, right?"

"You don't understand. I'm in Fellowship of Christian Athletes. We sign a purity statement saying we won't have sex before marriage. I think that's one of the reasons Hayley broke it off with me. She kept wanting us to, you know, go further and stuff. And I'm . . . I'm just not about that."

Aidan Broadmoor is standing a little straighter now. He is chaste. Pure.

"Anyhow, I got to get to class," he says.

"Of course, of course. Well, good luck with the Dartmouth-Harvard thing. Let me know if you want to talk about it again sometime."

"Okay. Thanks, Coach."

He practically runs away.

JOURNAL ENTRY: SATURDAY, SEPTEMBER 23

Parents Freaking Weekend. Could someone *please* just shoot me instead?

But, hey, I guess this gives me practice for *Searing Memoir*, writing about my stupid—

Sorry. Mr. Bliss says that, whenever possible, we should avoid uninspired, vague word choices like "stupid."

As I was saying: my inconsiderate and self-absorbed parents.

So here goes.

Meet Diane and Johnson Goodloe. They are both raging narcissists. When I was a kid and I needed something—nothing crazy, just the basic attention every child requires from time to time—they would say I was "acting out."

Because heaven forbid all the focus wasn't on *them* every single second of every single day.

They don't really give a damn about me, but they are both into the *display* of being good parents, so of course they had to show up today.

Mom looked particularly plastic. I think she just got Botoxed again because when she fake-smiled at me, nothing on her face moved except for her mouth. I swear the only reason she spends time with me is in the hopes that some old creeper will mistake us for sisters so she can *laaaauuugh* and say, *Oh, no, no, no, you dear man. This is my daughter!*

My mom has been in therapy for years. She has more issues than *National Geographic.* And, honestly, I wouldn't have a problem with that . . . if she would just *admit* it. She acts like she's this perfect person—the fact that she's in therapy is this big secret I'm not allowed to tell anyone—and all the while she needs two Lexapro just to get through the day.

Her other big charade is her thing with money. She acts all poor around her constituents and makes this big deal about how she's only paid $28,000 a year as a state senator, as if this makes her a Woman of the People. But if she needs to spend money on herself and her appearance? Suddenly she's not so frugal.

The really funny thing is the only reason she's rich at all is because of the child support my dad pays her. I was three when they split up, so it's not like I understood this at the time. But a few years ago, my dad explained to me what a prenup is. (Welcome to *Growing Up Goodloe*: you learn about important legal instruments for protecting wealth around the same time as you're taught to tie your own shoes.)

He told me that his father and his lawyers made my mom sign a prenup before the wedding. It ensured she wouldn't be able to put a single finger on the Goodloe fortune if they divorced.

All she got to keep was the name. But that turned out to be worth a lot, politically anyway. She's basically State Senator for Life, because everyone has these warm memories of my grandfather, who served two terms as governor during the 90s, when the economy was booming and it was hard to screw up anything too badly. Plus, she's in a super-safe district, so she wins 80 percent of the vote without even trying.

She remarried when I was five. My stepfather's name is Steve. He's also her campaign manager. He's very . . . Steeeeve. By which I mean he's kind of doughy and balding and just kind of . . . Steeeeve.

He's got this son named Grayson who is three years older than me. Grayson lived with his mom until he turned sixteen and became "too much to handle." By which I mean: his mother caught him masturbating. Then he moved in with us.

To this day, Grayson couldn't tell you my eye color, because all he ever does is stare at my tits. He's sort of in community college but is basically this loser who does nothing but play video games and watch porn all day. It's gross. He needs to get a life.

And so does Steeeeve. Mom is underachieving with him in every way. Except, since she's a narcissist, he's *exactly* what she wants, because he worships the ground she walks on—as he should, honestly—and lets her be the star of everything.

Basically, for her second marriage, my mother picked the exact opposite of Johnson Goodloe, the Man She Could Never Tame.

I don't know how many times Dad cheated on her during their relatively brief marriage, but he still acts like he's making up for lost time. He cycles through girlfriends so fast it's hard to keep track of them. The only thing they have in common is that they're all thin and between the ages of twenty-five and thirty-four.

But I think he has an even lower limit. The way he was looking at Calista today was like, seriously, Dad, *ewwwwww*.

Someday, he's going to be with someone younger than me, at which point I get to officially throw up.

He lives in Manhattan, in this massive brownstone he inherited from my grandparents and then pumped a ton of money into. He "works" as an "artist," which I use in quotes because it's a freaking joke. He does all these nude portraits of women that he pays to model for him. Then he screws them.

Gallery owners fawn over him, because he buys way more paintings than he sells. Also, if he shows up for their gallery opening, paparazzi follow. Whenever my dad is photographed—always with some hot young babe on his arm—the caption refers to him as "Billionaire Playboy Johnson Goodloe," as if "Billionaire Playboy" is part of his name.

Whatever. I just have to put up with them both until I turn eighteen and get my hands on the trust my grandparents set up for me before they died. Last time I checked in with the lawyers, it was worth $60 million.

Then I can do whatever the hell I want.

CHAPTER 5

I take the long way back to my apartment, remaining unseen.

It's possible Aidan Broadmoor is lying, of course. But I'm starting to think that maybe Hayley didn't get her chlamydia from anyone at Carrington. It might be someone from back home; some guy her parents disapprove of, which is why she blamed me instead.

But how am I supposed to figure out who that is?

I'm still puzzling on that when I reach Wentworth, where I've lived for the past eight years. It's the last dorm at Carrington that hasn't been thoroughly renovated to modern standards, so it still has old doors, old windows, and old-world charm. It's a bit detached from the rest of campus—the only structure on the other side of the soccer and baseball fields—which means it's quieter than most.

Through the years, I've been given several opportunities to move off-dorm to one of the freestanding faculty apartment buildings on the fringes of campus, but I've always declined. I split dorm duty with two other faculty members, which means that one weeknight out of every three, I oversee study hall starting at eight thirty, followed by lights out from ten thirty to eleven. There's a comfort and convenience to doing that a few steps from where I live, especially once Connecticut winter takes hold.

My apartment is tacked to the side of the dorm along with one other. We share a common entrance, which consists of a small vestibule. I've just entered that space when two hairy hands reach out, grab me, and slam me hard against the wall.

"You piece of crap," a voice growls.

There's an elbow at my throat, pinning me against the bricks. It's Ken Rippinger. He's several inches shorter than me but startlingly strong. My eyes focus on the angry V where his eyebrows come together.

"You're a disgrace, Bliss. You know that? A total disgrace."

Spittle flies from his mouth, landing on my chin. That animates something inside me. I give him a hard shove that at least momentarily dislodges his arm from my Adam's apple and sends him to the middle of the hallway.

"What is your problem?" I yell back.

"My problem is that you shagged Hayley Goodloe."

He takes a swing at me, then another, and another. My arms are up, warding off the blows, but I still feel his fists colliding with my forearms and shoulders.

"Knock it off," I snarl, reaching toward his head, trying to grab hold of his hair, his face, anything to make him stop hitting me.

I haven't been in a fight since the fifth-grade playground. I have no idea what I'm doing.

He throws a few more ineffectual punches but, at some point, I shunt him out of range. He stops, more out of exhaustion than anything. This may just be a rest. His hands remain balled.

His tone goes high and full of mockery as he says, "'Hey, who's Hayley's boyfriend? I need to give him something.' You just want to know who the competition is, Bliss? Is that what's going on? You're disgusting."

"Would you shut up for a second? I've never touched that girl. Not once. Not a stray hand on the shoulder. Not a casual brush-by in the hallway. Not a hug when she scores a goal."

I stare at him extra hard after that one, because we both know he hugs his players all the time.

"Then why I am hearing the reason she left school is that you gave her the clam?" he demands.

"Because she's lying, okay? Someone else gave it to her. You think a seventeen-year-old kid would never lie?"

"That's not the kind of kid she is."

"But you really think that's the kind of teacher I am?"

He takes a step closer to me and jabs a finger toward my face.

"I don't know what you are. But I hope they scoop out your nuts and nail them to a wall."

"Rip, I don't know how to tell you this another way: I. Didn't. Do. It."

"You better hope you didn't," he snarls. "Because I'm going to be asking all my girls if they've seen you laying a finger on Hayley. And if any of them say yes, I'm marching them straight to Ambrose's office."

"Be my guest. It never happened."

He utters a few curses at me, then departs.

How did Rip hear about the accusation? To a certain extent, it doesn't matter. Nothing stays secret for very long at a place like Carrington. When it comes to rumors, boarding schools are witch's cauldrons. There's always something brewing.

The problem is, having Ken Rippinger stoking the fire will only create more smoke.

Will some girl *think* she saw something—something that was actually innocent—and put more insidious intentions into it?

Or, in an effort to seem supportive of Hayley, will one of her friends invent some secret rendezvous between us? Will they say they saw Hayley emerging, uniform askew, from my closed office door? Or, worse, my apartment?

As a creative writing teacher, I am familiar with the inventive powers of high school students. They are formidable fiction makers.

If my hearing with Hayley comes down to she-said-he-said, all it could take is one more she-said to completely doom me.

And if that were the case, I wouldn't even blame Ambrose for firing me. When #MeToo first started gaining traction a few years back, some of my students wanted to organize a protest in support of sexual assault survivors.

I encouraged them, and even joined them. If memory serves, the sign I wound up carrying read, simply, "I believe women."

Which, in general, I do.

Just not this one.

But how do you say that without sounding like every despicable man throughout history?

I drag myself into my apartment, my hand gently massaging my throat in the spot where Rip mashed it.

Whatever zeal I had for performing this half-ass investigation of mine is rapidly fading. Confronting students comes with risk. And if the word is out among the faculty, they're not going to be very forthcoming either.

It takes all my remaining energy just to hang my jacket on the hooks behind the door. From there, I walk shakily to the cabinet above the stove, where that Glenmorangie is now calling out to me in a high, clear voice that belongs in a chorus of angels.

Except now that I have opened the cabinet, I find myself staring at it, feeling like I might be drunk already.

The bottle is missing.

I swear it was there this morning. I was wrapping my fingers around it before the sound of Emily in the bathroom made me reconsider.

Was that a dream? A hallucination?

Or am I simply losing my mind?

JOURNAL ENTRY: MONDAY, SEPTEMBER 25

I've been thinking a lot about some things Mr. Bliss said in class today.

He got off on this tangent about how everything we write—whether it's for an assignment, for *Carrington Crossroads*, for our journals or anywhere else—needs to be *true.*

If what we write isn't true, we're not just cheating everyone who reads us, we're also cheating ourselves.

Then he warned us that writing the truth is not as easy as it sounds.

With nonfiction, some people think that if they just get the facts right, that makes what they write true. But that's not the case.

Mr. Bliss pointed out that if you only give "facts" from a certain point of view, what you write will be *factual* but not necessarily *true*, because important things may have been left out. He said especially these days, a lot of people can't tell the difference between factual and true.

He explained that human beings are prone to misinformation in all kinds of ways. He started throwing all these terms at us: confirmation bias, belief perseverance, the illusory truth effect, and other things that make me want to take a psychology class when I get to college.

Mr. Bliss said finding the truth means guarding against these natural biases, letting go of your preconceived notions, and doing the hard work necessary to discover what *actually* happened or what's *actually* real.

And that's not easy.

It's even more difficult with fiction.

In fiction, Mr. Bliss said truth begins with honesty. Intellectual honesty. Material honesty. Above all, *emotional* honesty.

Even if what we're writing is completely made up, it ought to reveal something deeper and *true* about the human condition, or the world we live in, or the nature of our subject.

He brought up the example of Harry Potter. Those are books about a boy who does magic—clearly "fictional." Yet they show us all kinds of truths about the importance of love and friendship, and about the nature of bigotry, and about the corrupting influence of power.

"Book Five could be read entirely as a polemic against fascism," he said.

I wrote that down word-for-word because I had *no idea* what it meant, but I wanted to be able to look it up later.

Then he started rattling off great works of fiction—*To Kill a Mockingbird*, *The Grapes of Wrath*, *Beloved*—and talking about how each one can teach us more about those time periods than any history book.

"In order to understand the truth of any era, you must first read its fiction," he said.

I wrote that down, too, because I thought he must have been quoting someone important, like Walt Whitman or Barack Obama or Reese Witherspoon. But then I googled it and, nope, it's a Charles Bliss original.

He was saying all of this stuff completely off the cuff, like he hadn't even planned to talk about it. But the whole class was completely rapt. You could tell everyone was thinking: *Why haven't any of our English teachers ever explained it this way?*

But even if they had, I'm not sure it would have sunk in. There's something about the way Mr. Bliss says it.

He just has so much passion when he talks. You can tell how much he cares about writing, and about teaching writing, and about us. He's not just saying these things because he read them in a textbook. It's like he's lived it, and he believes it, and he wants us to believe it, too.

It's just so inspiring. The man is simply brilliant—both in the sense that he is incredibly smart, but also in the other sense of that word.

He is this light that shines brighter than any other. In this world of ordinary people—people like Grayson, who just want to jerk off and play video games—Mr. Bliss is special.

Definitely the most brilliant person I've ever met.

He makes me want to be a better writer. A better person.

Truth begins with honesty.

I think I know exactly what he's talking about. I should probably start practicing it.

So, yeah, this is something I've known for a few weeks now. But it's time to admit it.

Deep breath. Here goes:

I honestly have a crush on Mr. Bliss.

I guess if you've already had one midlogue and you need another, you call it . . .

MIDLOGUE 2

I really am going to try to try to keep the interruptions to a minimum, but I feel I need to make it clear that throughout the fall I had no clue—*no clue*—that Hayley was developing feelings for me.

To me, she seemed like any other kid.

However—since you've just read this big lecture I've given about the importance of truth in writing—there's another reason I decided to include the above journal entry, and it's unquestionably self-aggrandizing.

I wanted you to know that, at least now and then, I wasn't a half-bad teacher.

Maybe, sometimes, I was even pretty good.

In my defense, you have to understand what it's like to stand in front of teenagers, day after day, year after year. You pour your heart into your lessons, and most of the time you get flat nothing in the way of feedback. They just stare at you—if they're even awake and paying attention—like you're some kind of lunatic.

To know one of them was really listening—absorbing the concepts, thinking critically about them, letting them inform her burgeoning worldview—is immensely gratifying.

Most of us, if we are privileged enough to occasionally live in the world of ideas, will reach that critical moment when we wonder what life is for.

Why are we here? What are we supposed to accomplish? Is there a purpose to our existence beyond mere survival?

There are those who become lotus eaters, who decide that life has no greater meaning and is primarily about the hedonistic pursuit of personal pleasure.

I legitimately feel sorry for those people. To me, the far more fulfilling path is to recognize that, ultimately, we have an obligation to our fellow humans. We are here to better each other, to make some impact on those around us, to improve the collective in some small but important way.

That's why I was so moved when I read that journal entry. Honestly, it made me want to cry.

It gave me hope that not everything I did here was a total waste.

CHAPTER 6

After a short while spent staring moronically at the gap in the cabinet, I grab the half-full bottle of tequila that's still there.

I take a long swig, savoring the burn in my mouth and throat. I'm reasonably certain that in about fifteen minutes, this will ensure I'm no longer quite so attached to reality.

But I don't want to take any chances, so I go to the fridge and grab a beer. I drink it standing up.

Between the booze and the ebbing of adrenaline from Ken Rippinger's attack, I am drained. I'm too tired to cry, too agitated to sleep; too buzzed to think straight, too sober to pass out.

I drag myself in the bedroom, where I flop face-first on the bed.

That's where I still am a short while later when, from my living room, I hear, "Hey, anyone home?"

It's the familiar voice of Leo Kastner. He was hired at the start of the school year to teach English and coach hockey. He's the same age as I am and we have similar socioeconomic backgrounds—Leo is the first former public-school teacher anyone can remember being hired at Carrington.

For lack of a better way to describe it, Leo filled the vacuum that was created in my life when Emily left. I don't mean that in the romantic sense—we're both straight—but in so many other ways, he slid into Emily's place. We quickly became brothers from another mother, confidantes, and each other's rock in the storm that is high-powered boarding school.

He has a key to my place, just as I have one for his. That's how he made it into my living room. I'm glad he decided to pop by.

"In here," I croak out, rolling over to see him standing in my bedroom doorway.

"Well, you're looking just *radiant* today, sunshine," he says, then makes a dramatic display of smelling the air. "And you smell like Jose Cuervo's bathroom."

"Don't you have class?"

"Got a sub for this period. Don't tell anyone I was here. I sort of lied and said I had a dentist appointment. Dare I ask if you want another drink?"

"You gonna join me?"

"I wish. I still have to coach. But I'll watch. You want HBT or should I fix you something stronger?"

HBT stands for hops-based therapy, aka beer. It's a code we developed so any students who overheard us wouldn't know we were talking about drinking. He's already in the kitchen, awaiting my request.

"HBT sounds great," I say.

I rise from my bed and stagger out to the couch. Leo presses a cold beer into my hands.

"All right," he says, "tell me everything."

I oblige him, running through what I know. At some point, he hands me another beer. He asks some questions but mostly just lets me vent.

Toward the end of my monologue, my phone rings. It's Emily. When she moved back in, Leo made himself scarce, not wanting to be a third wheel. He understood that Emily and I needed some space to work things out. Between his busy schedule and hers, I haven't had the chance to introduce them yet.

Now hardly seems like the time. I also don't want Emily scolding me for day-drinking. So I just let the call ring through to voicemail.

Once I'm done telling Leo about Hayley Goodloe's bombshell, he sits pensively for a moment.

"I gotta be honest, I saw her flirting with you at one point last semester. The way she was looking at you . . . haven't you seen that look before?"

He doesn't need to say the name. I've told him all about Breighlee Dumont, one of my advisees during our first year at Carrington.

Emotionally and intellectually, she was like crystal: bright, beautiful, but fragile. A single harsh word could send her spiraling into melancholia. Her inner forearms were a testament to this, an elaborate meshwork of delicate scars. I took it as my personal mission to keep the razor blade out of her hands with a steady stream of gentle encouragements.

As the year pressed on, I thought I was succeeding. The cutting stopped. She was flourishing. The more I praised her, the more her self-esteem grew. She would sometimes hug me, but I thought of it as a strictly platonic gesture.

And then one day, I was utterly blindsided when she confessed her love to me. She told me she fantasized about me ripping off her clothes and the two of us having sex on the desk in my office.

My first instinct was to report this discomfiting interaction to the English Department chair, who would have taken it to Ambrose, who would have reported it to Breighlee's parents.

But then I thought twice. I honestly feared what she might do to herself.

Instead, I let her down easy, quietly, mindful not to break the glass. She ended up going to Vassar, where I'm told there was a sociology professor who was not as successful at resisting Breighlee Dumont's attentions. He was relieved of his position as a result.

But by that point, I didn't need the cautionary tale. I had already learned my lesson. Breighlee Dumont was the reason I developed many of those aforementioned boundaries.

"It's not the same," I say. "With Breighlee, there was a . . . a relationship, or whatever you want to call it. There's nothing like that with Hayley. I swear, I learned my lesson."

"Yeah, but Hayley still *wanted* it to be more. And you never returned her affection so now she's pissed off and she's going to get back at you."

"You think that's it?" I ask.

"Oh, I don't know, I'm just spitballing. But, at risk of stating the obvious, you know you're screwed unless you can prove Hayley is lying, right?" he says. "Otherwise, the board is going to side with the Goodloes, and Ambrose will never go against the board. There's a reason guys like us don't win fights against Connecticut blue bloods."

"Believe me, I know."

"They'll tolerate us as long as we behave ourselves and mind their children for them," he says. "They'll even pretend to respect us. But at the end of the day, we're just the help. We're never *really* equals. Not when it counts."

I lift myself from the couch and walk over to the window, which affords me a view across the sports fields to Jennings Chapel, with its perfect New England church bell tower. It's where I got married.

A picture of it reliably appears in nearly all of the alumni giving appeals.

Right now, it's practically taunting me.

You know you never really *belonged here, right?*

I hate to admit it, but I sound like my mother. Roberta Bliss—everyone calls her Robbie, even me sometimes—has an, at best, ambivalent relationship toward Carrington.

She was always a big believer in the *idea* of education. She didn't want me cleaning houses and hotel rooms—her occupation—or working as a commercial fisherman—like every other man in her family. She knew that learning was the route to an easier life. It was why the apartment she rented for us—we lived above this older couple's garage—was walking distance from the town library.

Robbie was proud when I won the essay contest that guaranteed me free room and board to this prestigious boarding school that was so, so far away from down east Maine, where she still lives. But she also never stopped being resentful of Carrington for taking away her son and turning him into something she didn't fully understand.

Even now, she is loath to admit to anyone that I work at a school that primarily exists to serve the wealthy. "Chahles is a teachah," is all she'll say, with her Maine-bred aversion to the letter "r."

She is automatically suspicious of anyone with money or power. Government is stuffed with crooks. Corporations exist to screw the little guy. The stock market is rigged.

You can't trust any of them.

Ah, Robbie. Maybe you're right.

Turning back to Leo, I say it out loud: "It's like I never really belonged here, you know?"

"Wait, you're not giving up, are you?" Leo asks, sounding alarmed.

I sigh dramatically. "No, I guess not."

"That's good. Look, *someone* gave this girl chlamydia, and it wasn't you. Eventually, the truth is going to come out. You just have to keep the faith."

"Let's hope," I say.

"Attaboy. Look, I have to go. But keep your head up, okay?"

He departs. I return to my bed and lie there with my eyes closed. The unanswerable why-mes and what-nows pound out endless laps in my head.

At some point, I drift off. When I come to, it's already nighttime. Emily has texted me four more times and called twice, so I'm sure she's getting frantic not hearing from me. I fire off a text saying I'm sorry for not answering and that I'm fine.

After that, I just sit on the couch in the dark, alone with my misery, wondering how I'm going to get anyone to believe me.

It's what I'm still doing perhaps a half hour later when the front door eases open.

"Hello?" Emily calls.

She is striking, with the light from the vestibule pouring around her. Her beauty sometimes catches me off-guard like this. She has this way of holding herself that only magnifies her appeal. I still can't believe someone so exquisite decided to marry me.

"Right here," I say.

"What are you doing, silly, just sitting in the dark?" she chides. "Punishing yourself?"

"I don't know. Something like that."

She enters the apartment, closing the door.

"Well, come here and get a hug from your wife."

It's the first thing all day that actually sounds enticing to me. I rise from the couch. Just as we're about to embrace, she stops short.

"Why do you smell like a brewery?" she asks.

"I just . . . I guess I needed to fuzzy things up a little."

"And, let me guess, you were drinking on an empty stomach?"

I shrug. "I wasn't thinking about food."

"Are you still drunk?"

"A little. Not really."

"All right," she says, sighing. "Well, I guess this will help you sober up, then."

She turns on a light, then bends over to pick up a brown paper bag from the floor. I recognize the logo of our favorite local Thai place.

Her kindness is so touching I have to stifle a sob. These are familiar roles for us. I am woebegone. She is coming to my rescue, picking up pieces of me and reassembling them into human form.

I am reminded of what helped me pull through my funk after *Washington County*'s spectacular flop. Really, it became a mantra: *As long as I still have Emily, I can't have fallen too far.*

After a quiet dinner, we binge a few old episodes of *Scrubs*, then go to bed. The carbs from dinner have put me into enough of a food coma that I'm actually able to drift off.

But it doesn't last.

What feels like an eyeblink later, I am startled out of sleep by three sharp knocks on our front door.

The urgent red numbers on the clock next to my bed tell me it's 11:06.

"Hang on," I call out, hastily pulling on a pair of pants because otherwise all I'm wearing is boxers and a T-shirt.

Emily is sitting up in bed but says nothing. There's no such thing as a good interruption at this time of night.

I walk across our darkened living room and pull open the door to see Wellie Ambrose.

His hair is lightly tousled. A dark trench coat is belted at his waist. Behind him are two people who I do not recognize, both with stern faces.

Behind them are two uniformed police officers with their hands resting on their gun belts.

"What's going on?" I ask stupidly.

"The police would like to talk to you," Ambrose says. "Hayley Goodloe is missing."

JOURNAL ENTRY: MONDAY, OCTOBER 2

Future self, you're going to think you're a bit of a slut when you read this.

Thank goodness your current self is less judge-y.

So, okay, to set the scene, it was *hot* today. It hit ninety. No lie. Ninety. In October. In Connecticut. Apparently, it's an all-time record not just for the day but for the entire month.

Ms. Millrose is always reminding our advisory group that weather is *not* climate, and we shouldn't be like those idiots who say "so much for global warming" every time it snows.

But whatever. After a day like this, we're all like, *Hello! Climate change is real!*

Everyone was miserable. The administrative offices have air-conditioning, but the classrooms don't, because Carrington's teaching philosophy is that suffering builds character.

It certainly doesn't help that the uniform at Carrington was set during the last ice age. For girls, it's a pleated wool skirt that must go down to at least the knee, a long-sleeve blouse that is buttoned allll the way to the top, and a sleeveless sweater with a school crest that's basically the size of a stop sign.

Believe me, no one was wearing their sweater today. And most of the girls had their sleeves rolled up and a button or two popped. Even the biggest dickhead teachers in this place wouldn't hand out a uniform demerit on a day like this.

Possibly the most sweltering classroom at Carrington belongs to Mr. B.—Yes, I've started calling him "Mr. B" in my mind . . . though not to his face because that would probably piss him off!

Anyway, Mr. B is on the fifth floor, up in what used to be the attic of this old building. Did I mention that heat rises? I swear, it felt like 109 in there.

Anyway, we always start the class with what Mr. B calls "wind sprints," where he gives us a prompt and we have to write like crazy for five minutes, just pushing out whatever comes to mind, even if it's total trash.

Most kids type, but I like to write longhand. I sit in the front row, right near his desk, which hasn't gotten me any special attention—until today.

Suddenly, he was looking at me. A lot.

Then I realized why. An extra button on my blouse had come loose. With the way I was leaning over my paper, he could definitely see down my shirt to the cute little lace demi bra I was wearing underneath.

I could follow the trajectory of his eyes. It was like he was trying to memorize my left tit.

At one point, we made eye contact, and he looked away really fast.

I just smiled a little. I felt bad for him. His wife has left him and now he's probably just horny.

So I shifted positions to give him a better view.

CHAPTER 7

This is voluntary.

All voluntary.

Strictly, perfectly, a thousand percent voluntary.

My departure from the apartment, without Emily, after they gave me a few seconds to toss on some clothes. *Don't worry, we'll have him back to you shortly.*

My trip to the police station in the back of a patrol car. *Sorry it's not more comfortable back there.*

My parade past a coterie of gawking cops and through a door with a nameplate that reads "Interrogation Room 1." *Would you like some coffee? No? You sure?*

But it's voluntary. They remind me of this at least a dozen times. I am not in their custody; no sir, not at all. I can leave any time I choose. They're just hoping I can shed light on a few things, help them with a timeline they're assembling, assist them in finding Hayley, if I could just bear with them a little while longer.

I'm not stupid enough to believe their act, of course. If they really just wanted my help finding Hayley, they would have asked me their questions at the door to my apartment and then sped on their way.

The only reason I'm here is because I'm a suspect in whatever has happened to Hayley.

They know more than they're telling me. Yet whenever I ask a question, they fall back on two lines: They appreciate my cooperation, and they're sorry to keep me waiting.

They're sorry for the next three hours, as Monday turns into Tuesday.

There are two detectives who take turns entering Interrogation Room 1 to express this appreciation and sorrow. One is Michael Morin, a fortyish medium-sized fellow with the thick, wavy hair of a Kennedy. The other is Elizabeth Prisbell, a fiftyish woman with seemingly no body fat and a short bob.

I know I can ask for a lawyer if I want. I've watched enough cop shows, read enough crime fiction.

Furthermore, I know I probably *should* ask for a lawyer.

But there are several issues. One, I don't know any lawyers. At least not any that do criminal defense in Connecticut.

Two, it's the middle of the night. All I want to do is go home and curl up with Emily. Insisting on my right to counsel will only cause delay.

And, three, asking for a lawyer is what the guilty guy always does.

And I am not guilty.

So, being the friendly, innocent chump that I am, I remain lawyerless and polite. I don't express frustration about the wait. I don't make any demands. I certainly don't raise my voice.

I sit in that hard plastic interrogation room chair, the one that is molded to fit exactly no human butt that has ever existed, and try to remain calm.

The ultimate source of my patience, my goodwill, and my compliance is, quite simply, my belief in my own righteousness. Wherever Hayley Goodloe is, whatever has happened to her, it has nothing to do with me, as everyone will soon see.

It is nearing two thirty in the morning when Detective Prisbell enters the interrogation room and, for the first time, sits down across from me.

"Sorry to keep you waiting, Charles," she says once again. "I think we're finally ready for you. Would you mind answering a few questions now?"

"No problem."

"Okay, and you should know this is being recorded. It's standard procedure."

I nod. Of course it is.

"So, if you don't mind, tell me about your day," she says breezily, like she is making small talk.

"How is that going to help you find Hayley Goodloe?"

"Just bear with me. We're trying to get a sense of everyone's movements in relation to Hayley."

"But I didn't have any movements in relation to Hayley. My understanding is she wasn't at school."

"Ah," she says. "And why is that?"

She's obviously playing dumb. Since I'm certain the police already know about Hayley's accusation against me, I walk the detective through the scene in Wellie Ambrose's office. Prisbell asks a few terribly leading questions—*Did that make you angry? Were you worried being fired from Carrington would negatively impact your career?*—that primarily serve to establish her low estimation of my intelligence.

Like I was going to sit there in a police interrogation room and sputter, *Yeah, I just couldn't wait to get my hands on her!*

I then tell the detective about my efforts to ascertain the identity of Hayley's boyfriend and my ensuing chat with Aidan Broadmoor. I figure there's no harm. If she doesn't know about this yet, she'll probably find out soon enough.

"And after you talked with Aidan Broadmoor, what did you do?" she asks.

"I returned to my apartment."

"What time was that?"

"Probably a little after one."

"And how long were you there?"

"Uhh, the rest of the day. Until you guys came."

"You just stayed in your apartment, all afternoon and evening."

"Yes."

"By yourself."

"I had a visitor around one thirty. He stayed for maybe half an hour. And then Emily got home a little after seven."

"But from roughly two until roughly seven o'clock, there was no one with you."

"That's right," I say.

"What were you doing that whole time?"

"Nothing, really. I was . . . I was pretty depressed about the accusation"—that seems safe to admit—"so I laid down and tried to take a nap."

"A nap," she repeats.

I realize this is probably a lousy alibi for whatever it is she's looking into. But what else can I say? It's the truth.

"Did you talk to anyone on the phone during that time? Zoom with anyone?"

"No. And after that, it was just Emily and me, watching TV and going to bed. It's like I told you, there's really nothing in my timeline that relates to Hayley."

I shrug. It's all I've got. I'm thinking this will soon lead to the end of the questioning.

Then she asks, "And how did you get that contusion on the side of your neck? It looks fresh."

My hand flies to my throat. I had no idea Rip left a mark.

"I got . . ." I almost say *I got in a fight* but I don't want to implicate myself, so I change it to: "Someone jumped me."

"Who?"

I really don't want to get into this. Rip was just being his usual hotheaded, overly protective self. It doesn't need to become a police matter. So I leave it at, "A colleague."

"When?"

"When I got back from talking to Aidan Broadmoor."

"And who is this colleague?"

"Look, I don't want to make this some big deal."

"Why did he jump you?"

I sigh. "Because someone told him about Hayley's accusation and he was upset about it."

"And he, what, he punched your neck?"

"He kind of elbowed me, actually. It was just some roughhousing that got out of hand," I say, rubbing it again.

"Do you have any other bruises?"

"No," I say.

She pauses over this, then says, "Charles, you know that's not true."

"What do you mean?"

"Why don't you roll up your sleeves?"

Filling with dread, I do as she requests. As I unbutton the first cuff, it occurs to me I answered the door to my apartment in a T-shirt. She already knows full well what's there.

Sure enough, there are several red welts on my forearms from where Rip let me have it.

And, really, screw him.

"His name is Ken Rippinger," I blurt. "That's the guy who jumped me."

"He must have been pretty angry," she says.

"He was. Hayley plays soccer for him. He's very protective of his girls."

Prisbell takes this in without any change of expression.

I think this can't possibly get any worse for me—I was all alone for five hours, I am covered in defensive wounds—and then she says, "Charles, I want to show you something. Will you wait here a moment?"

* * *

By now, none of this is voluntary, and we both know it, but of course I acquiesce all the same.

I am trapped. Caged. Watched. This is being recorded and there is probably a room full of cops observing the small pieces of me that are breaking off as Detective Prisbell works me over.

And yet I just sit in that hard plastic chair, making an extreme effort not to appear nervous, upset, or—worst of all—guilty.

When Prisbell returns, she brings with her a computer tablet and a padded black bag. Detective Morin enters the room with her. He remains standing. She sits down across the table from me, sets the bag at her feet, then places the tablet between us and turns it on.

"There was no sign of forced entry at any of the doors or windows, which tells us that Hayley probably knew her attacker and let them in voluntarily," she says. "And we know the perpetrator didn't enter through the front door, because we didn't get footage of anyone coming in. We only got this as they left."

Her screen shows a still image that appears to have been shot by a doorbell camera. There's a time and date stamp on the bottom of the screen that tells me whatever I'm about to see took place at 3:47 this afternoon—or, by now, yesterday afternoon.

Prisbell presses PLAY. The screen shows the front porch of a nicely appointed home. There's a flagstone walkway that has been cleared of snow. The image is moving—there are trees swaying lightly in the background—but nothing is happening.

"What am I supposed to be watching?" I ask, perhaps a little too impatiently.

"Just wait," Prisbell says calmly. "Should be any second now."

On cue, a figure bursts out the front door onto the porch. You can only see her from the waist down, but it's obviously Hayley. She's wearing white pajama bottoms with black polka dots.

She takes a long step, almost like she's been shoved. Then she whips around, crouches, and juts her face into the camera, getting so close she fills the entire frame.

The terror in her eyes couldn't be more real.

"Mom, help me!" she shrieks. "It's—"

The feed immediately goes dark.

My hand flies to my mouth.

"Oh my God," is all I can say.

Prisbell is studying my reaction carefully.

"Is there more?" I ask.

"The perpetrator bashed the camera with something hard. Maybe the butt of a gun. They got it pretty good. The only reason we had this footage is because it had already been saved to the cloud."

"Oh, Hayley," I moan.

Prisbell does not give me any more time to process this. She pulls the tablet away for a moment, taps at it a few times, and brings up a photograph.

It's a girl's bedroom, tastefully decorated in creamy tones—Hayley's, I'm guessing. Though it looks like an angry animal charged through it.

Lamps have been tilted over. Things that belong atop a dresser are strewn on the floor. The glass framing for a poster has been shattered.

Morin takes over the narrative. "There was obviously quite a struggle. Diane Goodloe was the one who found it like this. Can you imagine how frantic she must have been, realizing her daughter was missing and that this was what had been left behind?"

I can't. I am speechless.

He continues: "And can you imagine what it will be like when we put Diane Goodloe on the witness stand to testify about it? There won't be a dry eye in the jury box—or anywhere else for that matter. And then we'll show them this."

Morin gestures to his partner. Again, Prisbell does not pause for further reflection. She reaches down at her feet into the black bag and removes an object encased in clear plastic. She sets it on the table with a thud.

"Perhaps you'd like to explain why we found this in her room, underneath her bed," he says. "And why your fingerprints are on it."

I recognize it immediately, because, as of roughly eight thirty this morning, it was still in the cabinet above my oven.

It's my bottle of Glenmorangie scotch.

JOURNAL ENTRY: TUESDAY, OCTOBER 10

This could just be my crush talking, but I definitely think Mr. B is starting to notice me.

Last week's act of minor sluttiness stirred his imagination. But I was trying not to read too much into that. When it comes to tits, men are like dogs with tennis balls. They can't help themselves.

This was different. This was him paying attention to *me*, not just my breasts.

And, of all things, I have poetry to thank.

We've been doing this poetry unit for two weeks now. What I have learned from this is that I'm *definitely* a prose person. Poetry is just stu—

Sorry. I find much of contemporary poetry to be inaccessible and self-indulgent, with little consideration given to the experience of the reader.

Basically, everyone is trying to be Sylvia Plath. It makes me want to stick *my* head in the oven.

My poetry is a joke. I just throw words together that I think other people will like. I wrote this one poem that began:

i am slipping on silent soliloquies
that are
too trite for the totality of trees.

I honestly have no idea what that even means. I showed it to Calista, and we were just laughing our asses off about it.

But Mr. B?

He was acting like he la-la-*loved* it.

There's this national poetry contest that is some kind of big deal, where each school is allowed to enter two people. Mr. B selected me and Silas Appleby. Silas is this total goth kid and I'm sure he wrote a great poem.

Mine is trash. I couldn't even begin to figure out why Mr. B would pick it.

Then he told me and Silas to make an appointment with him—separately!—to come to his office hours. He said he wants to really "work" our poem.

I can't help but think he has something else in mind that he wants to work.

But I can play along with that game. I signed up for an office hours slot during Tuesday evening study hours—after dinner.

Which means I don't have to be in uniform.

I can wear whatever I want.

CHAPTER 8

They want a confession.

I want a lawyer.

That's the standoff ensuing in Interrogation Room 1.

By this point I have had my Miranda Rights read to me. I have signed a document indicating I understand them. I am officially in police custody.

This is no longer voluntary.

But it is also five o'clock in the morning. There are no private lawyers answering their phones at this hour and my income is just barely too high to qualify for a public defender.

I am in this weird in-between place where they're not totally treating me like a criminal yet. They haven't taken my phone from me. Or my belt. Or my shoelaces. They photographed my neck and arms, but they have yet to take a mug shot. They also haven't handcuffed me or shoved me into a cell. They are still offering coffee, water, snacks, a phone charger, and other occasional kindnesses.

Because they think it will help them get a confession.

The perverse part of this little contest is that the more I insist I have nothing to confess, the surer they become they've got their guy.

My best hope is that Hayley surfaces somehow, somewhere. She gets away from whoever has taken her and tells the harrowing story of being taken captive by someone who is not her creative writing teacher.

Or maybe there will be a ransom demand. Doesn't that *have* to be why she was taken? The Goodloe fortune is vast. Someone decided they wanted a piece of it.

Once the kidnappers make contact, it will be clear that this has nothing to do with a case of chlamydia or my continued employment at Carrington Academy.

But this, I realize, is probably a fantasy. It certainly doesn't account for how my bottle of Glenmorangie could have teleported from my apartment to Hayley's bedroom.

The only explanation for that is that someone is trying to frame me.

For kidnapping.

Or, worse, for murder.

Who or why, I can't begin to speculate. But at least so far, they're doing a fine job of it.

And I have unwittingly helped them by having the worst alibi ever: five inexplicable hours that could scarcely be apportioned more damningly.

But there's nothing I can do about that now.

All I can focus on is what comes next. I'm already thinking many steps ahead, to the worst-case scenario where I'm charged with this crime and end up going to trial.

This is why I've already decided my lawyer should be a woman, preferably as young as possible. It's a matter of optics for the twelve jury members who will someday decide my fate.

If I have a young woman arguing on my behalf, maybe they'll be less likely to think I would harm a young woman.

My google search for "best up-and-coming female lawyer Connecticut" eventually leads me to a website for Anna Brodeur.

There's a professionally shot portrait of her, looking powerful and confident in jeans and a sweater.

Her firm, Brodeur Law, is located in Hartford, not far away. She is a Yale Law graduate. She has won a prestigious award given to attorneys who fight for civil rights. She has contributed a chapter to an important-sounding book about the use of DNA evidence.

She is perfect.

I am just done deciding she will be my lawyer when Detective Morin enters the room.

"Well, we tested those shot glasses we found in Hayley's room," Morin announces, not even trying to contain his glee. "Your prints are on both. How about that?"

I am studiously expressionless. My mouth does not move. I am only thinking about how Anna Brodeur will soon save me from this.

"Listen, I know you don't think I'm on your side, but you seem like a decent guy, so I just want to be one hundred percent straight with you," he says, and I know these are words he has probably said many times to people planted in the very chair where I'm sitting.

"We're not talking about some nobody drug-addicted runaway here. This is a former governor's granddaughter, a state senator's daughter. We've been told this case is an absolute top priority. We've got the FBI on standby. We've got resources pouring out our ears—cadaver dogs, helicopters, face-matching on the traffic cameras. We're gonna find her. We've just taken this to the media, too. There's gonna be a press conference in a little while, in plenty of time for all the morning news shows. Pretty girl like Hayley from a rich, well-known family? They're going to go berserk."

Morin strolls over to the tiny window to Interrogation Room 1 that looks out on the detective's bullpen.

"The longer you wait to talk, the worse it's going to get for you," he says. "You have a very narrow window of opportunity to control the narrative here. You tell us that things got out of hand. It was a crime of passion. Or it was an accident. Maybe she tripped over something. You didn't mean for her to get hurt. That's the difference between manslaughter and murder, right there. You start cooperating right now and it makes a huge difference at sentencing. You don't have a prior record. You get eight, ten years. You'll be out before you know it. You're a young guy. You'll still have plenty of life left."

He turns back toward the table, and now he's hovering just behind me, a few inches from my ear. I can smell the stale coffee on his breath.

"But I'm telling you right now, if you don't start talking fast, no one is going to care about your side of the story. We'll have gathered enough evidence that we don't need anything from you. You killed her while you were kidnapping her. We call that 'murder with special circumstances.' It's life in prison with no possibility of parole. So what's it going to be?"

Finally, something in me has heard enough. I jerk my head away from his foul breath and leap to my feet so I can face him.

"Look, can't you see this doesn't make the least bit of sense?" I burst. "I get accused of sleeping with one of my students and then I'm going to kidnap her and kill her? So I can save my *job*? That's insane. I would have to know I'd immediately become your top suspect. Honestly, how stupid do I look?"

"See, but that's just it," he counters. "You think you're smart enough to get away with it. You're Mr. Yale, Mr. Author. You're feeling smug right now because you think you've stashed her in a place where we'll never find her."

He takes a step closer. "But let me tell you something, Mr. Yale, everyone makes mistakes. Even smart guys like you. Take that bottle we found. Let me guess, you thought you'd go back for it, clean up a little. But then Hayley pulls that little stunt with the doorbell camera and you realize you don't have much time. Someone might be coming. You go back up to her room to look for it but, uh-oh! You can't find it! Where's the bottle? You didn't realize it had rolled under the bed. Or maybe you just forgot all about it. How many other mistakes did you make? Because we're going to find them. And we're going to find her. So you might as well start talking now."

I shake my head, exasperated. "You're wrong," I say.

The door to Interrogation Room 1 opens. It's Prisbell. She doesn't even look at me. Her focus is on Morin.

"We have to go," she says. "Chief wants us at the press conference."

* * *

Since I still have my phone, I'm able to tune into the press conference, which the local NBC affiliate is carrying live.

It becomes quickly clear to me that this is a form of theater for everyone involved.

There is a podium that is already laden with microphones and their too-large logo boxes. All the major networks and larger news radio outlets are represented, along with cable news and several prominent websites, including TMZ.

The stage that the podium sits on is crowded with people, all of whom want to make sure they get their face time.

This is already that kind of story.

The police are to the left of the dais. Prisbell and Morin are there, alongside several other cop-y looking people. One of them is wearing the uniform of a Connecticut State Police colonel, the organization's highest-ranking officer.

The colonel being out of bed and fully dressed at this hour of the morning tells me everything I need to know about the kind of attention this case is receiving.

On the right side of the dais is Hayley's family. The first person is unquestionably Hayley's mother. They have the same straight blond hair, the same facial structure, the same perfect teeth. Senator Goodloe looks like she's at a campaign event: hair coiffed, red skirt suit pressed, high heels shined.

Intensity radiates from her. She is the grown-up version of that girl who, the moment she's assigned to be your lab partner in science class, informs you that you better not to do anything to screw up her grade.

Just behind her, with a hand reassuringly on her back, is a man who must be Hayley's stepfather, Steve Graham. He is balding, and not much taller than Diane. An expensive-looking watch—Breitling? TAG Heuer?—winks discreetly from under the cuff of a suit that fits too well to possibly have come off the rack.

Finally, there is a solidly built young man who bears a filial resemblance to Steve Graham, which would make him Hayley's stepbrother. He appears college-aged, and is the only male onstage not wearing a tie or jacket. His attempts not to appear nervous are a failure.

The only person not there—and conspicuous for his absence—is Hayley's father, Johnson Goodloe. The artist. What's the story there? Did he have something more important to do? Could he just not be bothered?

I have no more time to think about it. The State Police colonel brings the assemblage to order, then rattles off a short cop-speak-ish monologue about the forced taking of Hayley Goodloe, whom he refers to as a "seventeen-year-old female," as if she's the subject of a lab experiment.

After a dry recitation of facts, he orders the doorbell camera footage to be played on the screen behind him.

Seeing it for a second time makes it no less chilling. The horror on her face is every bit as striking. The "Mom, help" seems even higher and more plaintive.

You don't have to be a mother to be affected by it. Just human.

The Colonel then invites Diane Goodloe to speak. This is what the reporters have been waiting for.

She is clutching a folder in her right hand. Once she arrives at the podium, the logo boxes on the microphones block the lower half of her face.

"Thank you for coming on such short notice," she begins. "On behalf of the entire Goodloe family, we appreciate everything our partners in the media are doing to help us bring Hayley home safely."

Her voice is deeper than I thought it would be. Perhaps unnaturally so. Some political media trainer must have told her long ago that would make her sound more electable.

"This is my daughter, Hayley Goodloe," she says.

She opens the folder to reveal a senior portrait photo of Hayley. The still photographers in the room—and it sounds like there are at least a dozen of them—respond by sending their camera shutters into spasm, filling the room with clicking noises.

With the ease of a game show hostess, Diane pivots from one side of the room to the other, making sure everyone gets their shot.

She continues holding up the photo as she continues, "Hayley is a bright, beautiful, vibrant girl, filled with potential, and she is very much loved by her family."

The phrase "very much loved by" hits my writer's ear at a funny angle. It's passive voice. Shouldn't a grieving mother say "I love her very much," or "we love her very much," or something more active?

But Diane Goodloe is not pausing for me to further parse her grammar.

"We are asking for the public's assistance in finding her," she continues. "We've set up toll-free tips line that should be appearing at the bottom of your screen right now. If you know anything, if you've seen anything, we ask you to contact law enforcement immediately."

She then lowers the photo and leans a little closer to the microphones. "The Goodloe family is offering a million-dollar reward to anyone who provides information that leads to Hayley's return. Thank you."

There's an audible reaction from the assembled press, this collective murmur / gasp / guttural noise that signals they are impressed, and they approve.

As if this story weren't explosive enough—a beautiful, wealthy heiress snatched from her home—here is another keg of gunpowder.

Diane yields the podium to her stepson, Steve Graham's son. His face is flushed from nerves, blotchy with pink. He is several inches taller than his father, but he has this man-child air about him.

"My name is Grayson Graham and I am Hayley's brother," he says, reading straight from a card he is holding in his shaking hand. Even though his delivery is robotic, like he's presenting a book report in class, he is battling to keep his composure.

"My sister is a really great person. Last summer she went and built houses for the poor in Guatemala. She's always offering to do things for other people and she's never"—his voice cracks a little—"she's never hurt anyone."

Summoning all of his bravery, he lowers the card and looks straight into the camera. "Look, to whoever has Hayley, we just want her back, okay? I just want my sister back."

This simple request is too much for Grayson, who succumbs to the tears he has been working so hard to hold back. The camera shutters bang out a percussive staccato while he just stands there, alone and helpless.

After a prolonged moment, Steve Graham comes to his son's rescue, draping a paternal arm around his shoulders and pulling out a handkerchief into which Grayson buries his now-even-ruddier face. He is soon shunted away from the microphones.

The colonel returns to center stage and announces he'll take questions. The first three are from television reporters who are not interested in any actual information; they are looking for more—and better—sound bites. Angry, authoritative cops. Emotional, frightened family members. Bonus if someone else weeps.

After all, this is theater.

Finally, the colonel points to his left and a woman with owlish glasses pops up.

"Addie Horne, *Hartford Courant*," she says. "Have you identified any suspects yet?"

I suck in a breath. The colonel can ruin my life with one sentence, a few syllables actually. If he utters my name, I will be forever transformed from a failed author of little note into an infamous felon.

The guy who took that girl.

"We have leads we're following," the colonel allows. "This is a very active investigation."

"But have you zeroed in on a suspect or suspects?"

"We're not prepared to get into the details of the investigation at this time."

"Can you tell us more about your theory of the crime? Is this a stranger abduction or do you think it's someone known to Hayley—a romantic interest, a friend, a family member?"

I'm on such a thin edge, I half expect her to add *a teacher*.

The colonel holds his ground. "We're not prepared to get into the details at this time," he repeats, then gestures toward another reporter.

That is the last substantive question. The press conference soon ends.

I stand and walk over to my tiny window. In a strange way, the press conference has given me hope. They didn't name me as a suspect.

Are there, in fact, other leads they're following? Are other people currently being sweated for confessions in Interrogation Rooms 2 and 3?

Or, maybe—despite their tough talk and their hard push for a confession—do they still have doubts? Enough that they're afraid to slander me?

The other takeaway from the press conference, as I take a moment to think about it, was just its weirdness.

Mostly from the family.

I know wealthy WASP culture altogether too well, having been immersed in it since I was fourteen. And I know that, especially in a crisis, few traits are more valued than the stiff upper lip. It's like they're all living out their version of a Winston Churchill biography.

Still, I am struck by Johnson Goodloe's absence.

And Diane Goodloe's steeliness.

And the fact that the only one who could summon any tears for poor Hayley was her red-faced stepbrother.

JOURNAL ENTRY: THURSDAY, OCTOBER 14

Eff Mr. B.
Eff him and his poetry.
Eff him and his office hours.
I showed up wearing—
You know what? Forget it.
Eff him and his 250 words, too.

CHAPTER 9

After the press conference, several hours slip by quietly.

I can feel the fatigue setting in, and I try to stretch out on the floor and get some rest. But sleep won't come.

It is making me dull, sluggish, uncoordinated. The cops are probably counting on this. A tired brain is more prone to mistakes.

As it nears 8 a.m., I decide it's finally an acceptable hour to text Emily. She must be awake by now—that's if she slept at all.

I have been trying not to read anything into her lack of contact. She probably just thinks the police have taken my phone. I open up our message thread and type:

> Hey, I'm still here, obviously. I'm officially in custody but haven't been charged with anything. They want me to "confess" and don't seem to understand I don't have anything to confess to. How are you holding up?

I hit SEND. The phone bloops out its delivery confirmation.

While I wait to hear from her, I doomscroll the headlines about the shocking disappearance of the former governor of Connecticut's granddaughter. There are already hundreds of them, from NPR, the *New York Times*, the *Daily Beast*—and spots much lower on the internet food chain, all the way down to the clickbait sites.

There are even some from overseas. Why, I wonder, would someone in Leeds or Hyderabad care about a missing American girl?

Many of the stories are joined by photos. Beyond the senior portrait released by the family, enterprising web content creators have already plundered the digital wilderness for photos of Hayley in her Carrington tennis skirt, Hayley dolled up with friends for last year's prom, Hayley standing by the seashore in a floral-print dress.

None of the pictures are even mildly salacious by modern standards—there's no cleavage, exposed midriffs, or racy hemlines—and yet there is still something pornographic about all of it.

This has nothing to do with helping to find a missing person. It is not about public safety, law and order, or the necessity of informing the citizenry that a serious crime may have been committed.

It is voyeurism, plain and simple; people leering slack-jawed over photos of a pretty girl with blond hair, unconcerned about her age (*She's seventeen!* I want to scream) or, ultimately, her fate; people whose motivations range from prurience, to idle distraction, to a fetish for the misery of others.

There is also an obvious inequity playing out. If Hayley were poor, or dark-skinned, or—heaven forbid—ugly, would this story be currently rocketing up the rankings of every news site and search engine algorithm?

I feel disgusted by humanity.

There's still no word from Emily by 9 a.m., which is when I place my call to Anna Brodeur's law firm.

After I explain my situation to Brodeur's assistant, I am placed on hold for five minutes. When the assistant returns, he informs me that Ms. Brodeur is at a trial and unavailable. But he can send out Ms. Brodeur's associate, Jerome Cordova, if I like.

It's not what I like. But I'm tired and desperate. I didn't think to have a backup plan. At this point, any lawyer has to be better than no lawyer. I thank the assistant, who tells me Jerome Cordova is on his way.

I immediately return to the Brodeur Law website to look for Jerome Cordova's bio.

He is not listed as a partner, nor as an associate. He is listed among "other staff" as "consulting attorney." Whatever that means.

As if it's not already clear I'm getting the second string.

There is no narrative beneath his name, no list of legal accomplishments or awards; only his credentials: Lehman College, 1979; University of Connecticut Law, 1983; admitted to the Connecticut bar, 2016.

I went looking for a young, accomplished woman and came up with an old ham-and-egg male hack instead. And what was he doing between 1983 and 2016 that he wasn't practicing law? Did it take him that long to pass the bar exam?

Cordova does not rate a professionally done portrait like Anna Brodeur. His bare-bones headshot depicts a man with dark bags under his eyes, drooping jowls, and a flat mess of a nose that appears to have been dropped onto his face from a great height.

Whatever. He'll do for now.

A short while later, the door to Interrogation Room 1 is opened by Jerome Cordova.

He is wearing a gray sport coat that matches both his thinning hair and his general aura. I see now the nose and jowls were merely toppers on a great mound of a body. It creates the impression of a man who is, above all, easily winded.

"Okay, Bliss," he says. "Let's go."

"I'm free?" I ask, unable to quite believe it.

"Would you rather stay?"

"No, I just . . . okay," I say, grabbing my jacket and getting to my feet with more pep than I've felt in hours.

"How did you get me out?" I ask. "Was there an . . . an arraignment or—"

"Shut up," he says.

"Sorry. I just—"

"What part of 'shut up' don't you understand?" he asks with an accent—and attitude—that are unmistakably Bronx. "C'mon, let's go."

* * *

I follow Cordova out of the police station and into the parking lot, where the weather and my company are equally frigid.

He walks with a limp so pronounced that I can't even decide which leg he's favoring. He stops at an older model Buick sedan—because of course he drives a Buick—and plops heavily in the driver's seat. Scooping a pile of papers off the passenger seat, he places it in the back seat atop other previously scooped piles. I take that as my invitation to sit beside him.

Without comment, he starts the car and puts it in drive. I don't want to look straight at him—it seems like that will only provoke him—so I study him out of the corner of my eye.

I'm fascinated by his nose. In addition to its impressive overall width and mass, it is covered in a fine spiderwebbing of red blood vessels.

It is the nose of a man who has seen some things.

We are a block away from the police station when he abruptly pulls alongside the road and puts the car in park.

"Okay, *now* we talk," he says. "Rule number one, *never* talk when the police can hear you. Never talk to the police, period.

Rule number two, the police are not your friends. No matter what they say, no matter how nice they seem, you cannot trust them. They are always looking to use what you say against you. Cops are nothing but assholes with badges, you understand?"

"Yes, sir."

"Call me Jerry," he says. "Now, please ruin my morning. What have you told them already?"

I walk him through my various utterances. When I get to the part about my glaring lack of alibi, the size of his grimace grows by an order of magnitude.

"Well, what was I supposed to do?" I ask. "Lie to them?"

"No, you were supposed to keep your mouth shut."

"But I thought if I just explained to them what happened they'd see I had nothing to do with this and they'd let me go. I didn't want to act like I was guilty."

"Yeah," he says heavily. "That's how they get you."

He looks through the windshield with these sad eyes, the bags under them seemingly having taken on extra weight.

"Okay, I understand," I say.

"Good. Now, the reason they let you go is not because I convinced them you're Mother Teresa. It's because they're being very, very careful with this one. If Hayley Goodloe were just another girl and you were just some mook, they'd slap you with some charges and worry about what they could make stick later. But this thing is already too high-profile for their usual slapdash approach. It's already got a billion sets of eyeballs on it, give or take.

"The problem they're having is: What do they charge you with? They can't do kidnapping, because the only evidence they have for kidnapping is a video of a girl calling for her mother. That could be interpreted at least fifty different ways. But they don't want to do murder, either. Yeah, the bottle of scotch looks bad and so do those bruises of yours. And your alibi flat out sucks. But, one, they still don't have a body. Prosecuting a murder without a body ain't easy. And, two, they're still not a thousand percent sure about you and they don't want to wind up looking like jackasses. If they get all hot and heavy and charge you too quick, it screws up their case if it turns out they got it wrong. They'd be creating automatic reasonable doubt for the real perp, because the first thing that guy's lawyer would say at trial is, 'My guy must be innocent because the police charged someone else first.'"

"Okay. Well, that's good, I guess."

"Don't get cocky. You're still in a world of hurt here. This already has that crime-of-the-century smell about it. You gotta understand how cops think. This is the big one, the one they'll all talk about at their retirement dinners. And right now, they only got one suspect. They're going to be throwing everything they have at you. Everything. You understand?"

"Yes."

"Good. Don't go giving them anything else for free. Make them earn it."

"Right."

"Okay," Jerry says. "We can go through everything else some other time. Right now, I'm sure you're wiped. Where am I taking you?"

I ask him to drive me back to Carrington, because I don't have anywhere else to go. As we get underway, I tentatively inquire about his fee structure. He tells me it's too early to say for sure, but if I do get charged with murder, I'll be looking at a mid-five-figure retainer just to start.

It makes me ill. But it's manageable. Emily and I have roughly $90,000 in savings. Most of that is an inheritance she received from her grandmother. It is tucked away in an investment account that is populated with AAA-rated bonds and solid, dividend-bearing, blue-chip stocks. It was supposed to be the down payment on a house for our family someday.

But you don't need a house if you're serving a life sentence.

Jerry eases the Buick past the brick entrance to Carrington, then follows my instructions around to Wentworth, pulling into the small parking lot behind it.

He pulls out a business card, writes a phone number on it, then hands it to me.

"That's my cell," he says. "If the cops approach you again, you keep it zipped, and you call me. The only word that comes out of your pretty face when I'm not around is 'lawyer.' *Capiche?*"

"Got it."

"Good man. Now go hit the sack."

I thank him then trudge heavily to the side of the dorm. The shared entrance is unchanged but the door to my apartment is barricaded with yellow crime scene tape.

It barely slows me down. After I unlock the door, I use my key to slash a line right down the middle of it.

I call out for Emily. There's no answer.

Nothing inside the apartment appears to have been touched. My laptop is still on the kitchen island next to the spent take-out containers.

I don't get more than about four steps inside when I hear my apartment door opening.

It's Wellie Ambrose.

He's trailed by Victoria Brock and our associate dean of students, Grant Warren, whose primary role at Carrington is to handle student discipline. He's a big guy, a former minor league baseball player who's an inch taller than me but pushing three hundred pounds.

Has he been brought here as an enforcer in the event that I act out? Or does Wellie really think of me as an unruly sophomore who needs to be served detention?

"Mr. Bliss," Brock says coolly, "I'm here to tell you in no uncertain terms that you are to leave Carrington Academy immediately. Your employment here has been terminated. You are no longer welcome anywhere on campus."

I draw breath to say something about being innocent until proven guilty, but Brock cuts me off.

"The tragedy of the Hayley Goodloe situation notwithstanding, you were explicitly told you were not to have contact with anyone at Carrington. And yet you went ahead and interrogated Aidan Broadmoor. Ignoring a direct request from the head of school qualifies as just cause for dismissal. Since you are no longer employed here and have no business here, I am telling you to leave. Now. If you attempt to return, we will have you prosecuted for trespassing. Am I making myself clear?"

She is, of course, but I just glare at her.

I know what's going on here. If a boarding school fired everyone who ignored a request from the head of school, it wouldn't have anyone left working there after about three months.

Using my interaction with Aidan Broadmoor to get rid of me is pure pretense. I am reminded of a slogan from the regime of Joseph Stalin: *Show me the man, I'll show you the crime.*

If it wasn't Aidan Broadmoor, it would have been something else.

"Fine," I say. "I just need to collect some things."

Brock responds with another bucketful of ice: "That's out of the question. You never should have entered the premises in the first place. The police have asked that your apartment be treated as a crime scene and the law requires us to honor that request."

"But I need some clothes," I protest. "How am I supposed to—"

"You'll have to take that up with the police," Brock retorts.

"Once the apartment is released, we'll have maintenance come and clean it out," Ambrose says. "Your belongings will be placed in a secure storage facility. We'll give you a key as soon as that happens. There will be no need for you to return to campus."

My gaze falls on Grant Warren. This is a man I've coached with. We've shared a weekend duty team for years. We've spent hundreds, even thousands, of hours together leading practices, overseeing activities, chaperoning student outings, dealing with the minor and/or major crises that inevitably arise when you are *in loco parentis* to 650 teenagers.

Beyond that, he's a close friend. He literally cried on my shoulder when his father died suddenly a few years back. A chemistry teacher and I once helped drag his large and thoroughly inebriated carcass back to his hotel room after his bachelor party. I was an usher at his wedding.

He is glaring at me like none of that ever happened, like I'm some malevolent stranger.

"I hope we're not going to have a problem here," Ambrose says.

"No. No problems," I reply. "Do you know where Emily is?"

"My understanding is she left campus earlier this morning."

"Where did she go?"

"It's really not my place to say. As a matter of fact, I have nothing left to say to you, period, Mr. Bliss. Right now, the only thing that matters is that you leave."

"Fine," I say.

My lone act of defiance is to scoop my laptop up off the kitchen island. It's technically a school laptop, but I have my whole life stored on that thing in one way or another. Ambrose doesn't seem to care.

The three of them escort me to my car like they're bouncers making sure I depart a club. After all the years I've spent as a trusted member of this community—service that everyone seems to have conveniently forgotten—it is both humiliating and infuriating.

I sink into the driver's seat of my car, a Subaru crossover we bought last year when we were being family minded and decided my aging Honda made for a lousy baby chariot. It is now my *de facto* home. I drive back through the brick front gate of Carrington Academy, scarcely able to believe I may never enter it again.

It's getting difficult to control my emotions. I'm so distraught I worry I'm going to cause an accident. I pull to the side of the road to compose myself and reach for my phone.

I suddenly need Emily. I need her more than air. She is now my whole world.

Then again, wasn't she always?

I place the call, but the line doesn't even ring.

A recording informs me, "The wireless customer you are calling is not available."

It must be a mistake. I call again.

The same message plays.

I know we've paid our wireless bill. Her phone was working fine as of last night. And if it was merely not charged—or she was out of service range—I'd at least get her voicemail.

All of this can only mean one thing.

Emily has blocked me.

JOURNAL ENTRY: FRIDAY, OCTOBER 15

I was really mad at Mr. B for what happened yesterday.

Which is to say: nothing.

But I have decided to forgive him.

Like, what did I expect? That he was just going to jump me in his office or something?

So, yeah, I tried to shut the door behind me when I came in, so we could have a little privacy.

He asked me to leave it open.

At another point, I was going to come around his desk to show him something on my laptop, so I could stand close to him and see if he'd feel the same kind of heat as that day he was looking down my shirt.

He told me I could just turn the laptop around.

It's not that he was mean about it or anything. He was just all business.

Very proper.

Which is good, right? That's how he's supposed to be with a student.

I just have to hang on for the day when I'm not a student anymore.

In the meantime, I will just keep flirting my ass off with him.

He doesn't seem to notice most of the time. But every now and then, I swear there's something more there. He'll give me this little glance that makes me feel . . . I don't know, *seen.*

Or he'll say something that makes me feel like he's not treating me like just another kid. Like we're equals somehow.

Ugh. I just wish I didn't have to wait. Like, how long until after graduation until I'm allowed to sleep with him? Is an hour enough?

In the meantime, Aidan Broadmoor asked me to be his date for Homecoming and I said yes. He's beautiful but boring. He's basically: sports, school, yes sir, no ma'am, more sports, more school.

I can only hope my mother doesn't find out. I swear, she'd use the picture of us as a campaign photo.

Vote for me, Woke White People! Look! My daughter is dating a Black!

CHAPTER 10

The logic statement my brain settles on—as a means to allow itself to continue functioning—goes something like this:

If it's true that Emily has given up on me, if she has stopped believing in me, if she really intends to sever all contact, my life is basically over.

Therefore, it cannot be true.

It's my post–*Washington County* mantra all over again. *As long as I still have Emily, I can't have fallen too far.*

This is nothing more than a temporary misunderstanding.

I will win her back. Just like I did last time.

With that decided, I manage to remain upright long enough to reach the hotel nearest to Carrington, which is one of those extended-stay places near the highway. It's a bit on the run-down side, but at this point I just need to get some sleep.

Naturally, the TV in the lobby is tuned to a news channel that is showing highlights of the Hayley Goodloe press conference. The graphic beneath it reads, "BREAKING: EX-GOV'S GRANDDAUGHTER MISSING."

I walk up to the desk clerk and ask him how much a room costs. He tells me it's $149 a night, plus tax. I tell him I'll take it and fork over my driver's license and credit card. He could have told me it was a thousand and I would have said the same thing.

"How long are you staying?" he asks.

"I don't know," I admit. "A few days."

Eventually, I'll have to look for an apartment—or something—but I can't even think that far ahead.

He begins dutifully typing on the computer in front of him, but the moment the screen flashes to a picture of Hayley, looking like every schoolboy's fantasy in her Carrington uniform, his eyes flit that way and stay locked.

Gross.

And annoying.

"Sorry, could you hurry up, please?" I snap. "I'm really tired."

He returns his attention to his screen long enough to produce two key cards, which he hands to me along with directions to the elevator that will take me up to room 213. The moment I get through the door, everything in me gives up. I fall face forward on the bed and pull the bedspread over my head.

At some point, sleep overwhelms me. It is not, however, good sleep. It is twitchy and filled with a running series of nightmares. Each time I wake up and clear one away, a new one takes its place.

In one particularly vivid segment, I am looking down at my body as parts of it fall off, one at a time. My hands at the wrists. My feet at the ankles. Then my shins. Followed by my forearms.

But that's not the worst part of the dream. It's that I am desperate to cry out for help. Emily is in the next room with several of my colleagues—or, sorry, ex-colleagues—from Carrington. They would surely come to my aid if they knew what was happening.

Yet I can't seem to make a sound. I have gone completely mute.

It's after four o'clock in the afternoon by the time I am able to pull myself out of bed. Darkness is coming on fast.

Still feeling a little stunned, I take in my surroundings. It's a lot shabbier than I noticed at first. The fixtures are all contractor grade and look like they could be carbon-dated to 1981. The walls are cracked and chipped. The ceiling has an ominous-looking stain on it. The bathroom would probably never get clean no matter how much it was scrubbed.

Whatever. It will have to do.

My mouth tastes like something died in it, so I make a quick trip to Walmart for a toothbrush and other toiletries, along with food, beer, and several changes of clothing, since everything I own is now off-limits.

The bill tops four hundred dollars. My biggest splurge is jogging shoes and an outfit to go with it.

When I return to the hotel, I am greeted by the sight of a police cruiser, stationed rather conspicuously on the street out front. I might convince myself it's not there because of me, but as soon as I get out of my car, the cop gets out of his. He stares at me all the way into the lobby.

The message is clear: *Just because we haven't arrested you yet doesn't mean you're actually free.*

How, I wonder, did they know I was here, of all places?

Then I remember that I handed my credit card to the hotel clerk.

I have a lot to learn if I'm ever going to attempt to become a fugitive.

Once I get back up to my room, I call Emily again, but I'm still blocked. How, I wonder, am I supposed to win her back if I can't even talk to her?

But then I relocate my empathy. This has surely been as difficult for her as it has been for me. She was probably up most of the night, too. The detectives spent time flame-broiling her, hoping she would surrender more circumstantial evidence they could use against me. They likely distorted everything to make me look like some monster that just crawled out of the sewer.

She doesn't want to believe them. But she also doesn't know what to think. Her mind is a muddle.

The last thing she needs right now is me in her face, pressing the issue. Especially when she's completely drained. After a good night's sleep, she'll realize the man she has known and loved for six years could not have done what he's being accused of.

Tomorrow. I will find her tomorrow.

I've just made this decision when my phone rings. It's Jerry Cordova.

"Bad news," he begins, without preamble. "The cops want you back at the station."

"Is that why there's one parked outside my hotel right now?" I ask, peeking through my blinds to see the cruiser still just sitting there.

"No, that's just garden-variety harassment. They want you to come back because they have some evidence they want to show us."

"What is it?"

"They won't tell me. But they're acting like it's a big deal and they seem to think it's going to make you want to confess. Are you going to confess?"

"No. Absolutely not. You have to understand, I didn't—"

"I got it, I got it. But I'm not going to tell them that, okay? If they think they're close to a confession, they'll keep showing us things. I like getting an early look at their case."

He unleashes a racking series of coughs. I can practically see his jowls shaking.

"Sorry about that," he says. "Anyhow, since they're being assholes, I told them I was unavailable this evening due to a family matter. Which is true. Because I consider the Knicks family and they have a game tonight. I said we'd be there first thing in the morning, nine sharp. Can you do that?"

"Sure."

"All right," he says before we end the call. "I'll see you at nine in the parking lot outside the station. Don't worry about that cop out front. Try to get some sleep."

There seems to be little chance of that now.

* * *

Simply to separate myself from my racing brain, I drink a beer. Then another. I've just opened my third when I hear a knock.

I warily check the peephole.

It's Leo.

I open the door.

"How did you know I was here?"

"I was running some errands earlier and I saw your car in the parking lot," he says. "I would have called but . . . "

He doesn't need to complete the thought. Leo is the only person I've met under the age of seventy who doesn't have a cell phone, which is a constant source of fascination to other people our age. Most find it anywhere from downright odd to completely unimaginable. I think of it as charmingly anachronistic.

Leo's standard explanation is that he doesn't like the feeling of being constantly tethered to the world, to say nothing of having his life tracked by apps that will sell every scrap of information they can gather about you to the highest bidder.

And, the truth is, he doesn't *really* need one. As a boarding school teacher, your world is actually pretty small.

He enters carrying a brown paper bag, from which he pulls out a six-pack of India Pale Ale we both like. "That cop I just passed won't try to arrest us if we engage in HBT, will he?" he asks with a cat-that-ate-the-canary grin.

I'm not in the mood for gallows humor, but I play along.

"He'll have to catch me first," I say.

I point him toward the kitchenette, where there's a microwave, a sink, and a fridge. He stows the rest of the beer, gives one to me even though I already have one in my hand, and pops the top on the other.

Opposite the kitchenette is a sitting area—a love seat and an easy chair surrounding a coffee table—and that's where we settle.

"For the record, you know I'm not here, right?" Leo says. "Ambrose would crap a piano if he found out I was talking to you."

"Got it."

He shakes his head as he takes a pull on his beer. "I know I'm always saying that you're too milquetoast and could use a little more controversy in your life, but I have to be honest, you've outdone yourself here. The cops were all over campus this morning. Someone must have told them we were tight because they were going at me pretty hard. What did I know, had you told me anything, was I aware of your quote-unquote 'affair' with Hayley."

"And what did you say?"

"That I knew nothing, that you hadn't told me squat because there was nothing to tell, and that you weren't the kind of teacher who would be messing around with a student."

"Thank you," I say softly.

"Of course, then they started treating *me* like I was in on the kidnapping. They asked me where I was yesterday around 4 p.m., and I told them I was surrounded by the smell of death, but only because my players' hockey gear smells like week-old roadkill."

"How'd they like that?"

"Not very much," he says, his grin returning. "Sorry, I'm just talking about myself. How are you?"

I catch him up on my evening/morning. He presses me for details, which I eagerly supply. It feels good to share.

At the midpoint of the tale, Leo refreshes my beer. I've finished it by the time I'm through with my story.

We sit in silence for a few moments, then he says, "I had a theory when I came in here, and nothing you've just said has made me change my mind."

"What's your theory?"

He takes a pull on his beer and says, "Rip."

"What about him?"

"He's the one behind all this. If any teacher was doing Hayley on the side, he'd be the one, don't you think?"

I had been so focused on my own troubles, I hadn't even paused to consider that *someone* committed this crime.

And it could certainly be Ken Rippinger.

Is that why he attacked me? Hayley must have told him she had blamed her chlamydia on me. That made Rip realize he had the perfect cover—it's the creative writing teacher! he's the bad guy! —and decide to get rid of Hayley before she changed her mind and ratted him out.

But, first, he roughed me up. He did it so he could look like Hayley's Sir Galahad. That it happened to leave me with bruises that appear defensive in nature—because they were—was just a bonus.

"Can you ask around about Rip with some of the students?" I ask. "Maybe someone has seen something."

He looks wary. "Bro, I wouldn't get my hopes up."

"I know, but let's think this through," I say, scooting out to the edge of the love seat. "He probably doesn't have an alibi."

"That's true. He doesn't coach a winter sport," Leo points out. "Classes let out at three yesterday. That would give him enough time to make it to West Hartford and drag Hayley out of her bedroom by three forty-seven."

I'm suddenly—and quite strangely—looking forward to my meeting with the police tomorrow. I will put them onto Rip. He's at least as good a fit for this as I am.

We work the Rip angle—his over-closeness to his girls, those hugs, the abundant opportunities he would have to commit such malfeasance, even his motivations. His wife, a chemistry teacher at Carrington, is no one's idea of cuddly. Might Rip have looked elsewhere for affection?

Leo puts another beer in my hand right around the time I work out another key detail: Rip was standing in the vestibule of my apartment when I returned from talking with Aidan Broadmoor.

He could have broken into my place, stolen a few choice items—my bottle of Glenmorangie, those shot glasses—and planted them in Hayley's bedroom when he snatched her.

It's entirely possible he didn't even need to break in. The key system at Carrington is an unwieldy hodgepodge. Every door has anywhere from one to ninety keys that might open it, though no one is ever quite sure which will work until they try.

There are an untold number of keys bouncing around campus—and copies of those keys, and copies of the copies—including several full sets of keys that are quietly passed down from one senior class to the next. They're known as "the senior keys."

Everyone knows the school needs to start over with an electronic system, except the old way has become one of those weirdly venerated boarding school traditions that no one has the heart to change. Whenever there's a prank at Carrington, people blame the senior keys. The coed *a cappella* group on campus even named themselves the Carrington Keys, which was widely understood as a sly double entendre.

Point is, Ken Rippinger could easily have a key that opens my dorm apartment. For that matter, Emily could have just left the door open. We do it all the time, intentionally or unintentionally. It's not like theft is an issue at Carrington.

I share this all with Leo, who promises to ask around. When I start repeating myself—I'm a little drunk—he stands up.

"All right, well, I got duty tonight," he says. "I need to get back."

"Right. Of course."

"But seriously, bro, if you need *anything*—and I mean anything at all—you reach out, okay? You know the saying: 'A good friend will help you move. A true friend will help you move a body.'"

He's just trying to get another laugh out of me, but this attempt is a little too close.

"Yeah, well, there won't be a need for *that*," I say.

"Right, right. Just kidding, okay, bro? Take care of yourself."

We hug on his way out.

Maybe two minutes later my phone rings. It's an 860 area code, so it's local. Sober, I'd be smart enough to realize I shouldn't answer it. But I'm not sober, so I accept the call and say, "Hello?"

"Hi, Charles, Addie Horne, *Hartford Courant*."

I take in a breath. I should hang up, but I'm too frozen to move the phone from my ear.

"I know you've probably had a pretty rough day, but I want to give you a chance to tell your side of the story. I'm not one of those reporters who just believes the first thing she hears from the authorities. I've had cops lie to me too many times."

I can't even find the words to reply.

"Are you still in town? Could I meet you somewhere so we could talk?"

"No comment," I say.

"I know you need to say that, but you have to understand—"

"Call my attorney," I say.

And then I hang up.

The room is spinning a little, and not just because of the beer. I have some dim understanding of what's about to happen.

Addie Horne is about to put my name out there. As soon as that happens, every other media outlet will quickly, maliciously, gleefully hop aboard.

There is no such thing as reasonable doubt in the modern-day court of public opinion. Everything is streamlined into packages made for clicking, sharing, and viral transmitting.

A horde of content creators will be googling me, ransacking my social media, pulling up every interview I ever did for *Washington County* to pull my words out of context. They'll probably use my full name—Charles Allan Bliss—so I can join the long list of three-named fiends who have killed young girls.

I always tell my students that every good story needs a villain. I'm about to be cast into that role in the disappearance and presumed death of Hayley Goodloe.

JOURNAL ENTRY: THURSDAY, NOVEMBER 2

I should have known the moment my dad texted me that something weird was going to happen.

He said he was hoping to see me because he missed me, which was clear and present nonsense: you can't miss someone if you don't even act like they're alive most of the time. He also said he wanted to share some news.

And, oh by the way, he was bringing along his girlfriend.

I wrote back: Which one?

He reminded me that I met her over the summer on the boat. Her name is Ashley. She's twenty-seven, a whole ten years older than me. She's like all the others—thin, pretty, big boobs. The only thing different about her is that instead of being blonde or redheaded she's got brown hair. Way to go on the diversity front, Dad.

I told him that I couldn't hang out with him because Calista and I were going to a Carrington Keys concert—she's crushing on this tenor at the moment—but Dad insisted.

He came to campus in this monster chauffeur-driven SUV and signed me out on a day pass.

And there was Ashley, glued giddily to his side. Back in the summer, on the boat, she didn't make any attempt to get to know me. She just pranced around in this bikini that probably didn't even take a whole spool of dental floss to make. I might as well have been a piece of furniture.

This time, she was all smiles and *It's so nice to see you again, Hayley!* Like we had spent the last two months Snapchatting every day.

The only Goodloe-appropriate establishment that serves brunch near campus is Swan's Mill Inn, so that's where we ended up. It's this very stodgy place with an army of waiters in black vests who wait around for you to go to the bathroom so they can refold your napkin.

So creepy. Like, who wants a stranger touching their napkin?

As soon as we got there, my dad, in his usual fine parenting form, tried to order me a mimosa, saying that we had something to celebrate. I reminded him there were rules against me coming back to campus plastered.

He then switched to straight champagne—like removing the orange juice made it *better*?—insisting that I could just have a sip or two. He said if I got in any trouble, he would smooth it over with Mr. Ambrose—in other words: stroke a fat check.

Once the champagne was poured, he held his glass aloft and made his grand pronouncement.

He and Ashley were getting married.

The way he said it, it was like he was making all my dreams come true, like this was some kind of fairy tale for me and my only possible response was going to be, *Squeee! I'm so happy!*

I fake-smiled for him, because that's what a Goodloe does. *Click, click, click!*

Then I drank some champagne, because why the hell not? I ended up drinking three full glasses, half-hoping I *would* get caught when I got back to campus, just so this would cost my dad something.

All the while, I was trying to memorize every detail of this brunch—the waiters, the way they used that little crumb-scraper thing, all of it—because Mr. B said details are what make a scene come alive, and this is going to be a *great* chapter for *Searing Memoir* someday.

Ashley faked her way through the whole thing, too. But even when her mouth was smiling, her eyes were saying something different entirely.

Don't mess with me, bitch, or I will destroy you.

I know, I know. I'm being an asshole. Really, I should be happier, right? My family grew today! In addition to Steeeeve, my loser stepfather, I now have Ashley.

My wicked stepmother.

CHAPTER 11

As Wednesday dawns, I don't even need to check the *Hartford Courant* to know that it printed something about me.

My phone already has eighty-three missed calls.

Most are from numbers I have never seen before.

Seven are from my mother.

I text her that I'm fine, that she shouldn't worry about whatever she's heard, and that I'll call her as soon as I can. Then I turn off my phone, shower, and head out. The police officer that has been standing watch over the hotel—it's a different one from the night before—drives approximately six inches from my rear bumper the whole way.

Jerry Cordova greets me in the parking lot outside the police station. He's dressed in gray again and has that hangdog look that I am starting to realize is just his face.

There's no need to ask if he's seen the news, because he gives me this very Bronx-like, "How *you* doin'?"

I tell him about my call from Addie Horne.

"Okay, we'll deal with that later," he says. "For now, I want you to keep in mind this Woody Allen flick I saw once. There's this bit where the whole thing is, 'Don't speak.' That's all the lady says is: 'Don't speak.' I'm that lady right now. Whatever those jerk bags in there tell you, don't speak."

"Got it," I say.

"All right. Let's do this."

We enter the station and announce ourselves to the desk officer. Before long I am back in the dreaded Interrogation Room 1.

Elizabeth Prisbell enters, followed by Michael Morin. She takes the chair in front of me. He remains standing.

He is carrying what I now recognize as evidence bags but he's keeping them shielded from view.

"Before you show us whatever you got to show us," Jerry says, "I want you both to know I'm very disappointed in you, or your captain, or the colonel, or whoever it was who leaked my client's name to the *Hartford Courant*. They just better hope they didn't write anything down that's discoverable, because it's going to make for a great libel suit when it turns out my client had nothing to do with this."

"Wasn't us," Morin says, holding his hands up. "The colonel made it very clear to everyone in our shop to keep it buttoned up and that he didn't want any leaks."

"Which probably means he's the leaker," Jerry bristles. "It's a low blow. This kid has a life. Your colonel just ruined it."

Morin inhales to return fire, but Prisbell quiets him. "I have to be honest, Mr. Cordova, your client has bigger problems than the *Hartford Courant*."

She turns to me. "Charles, just so you know, we are recording all of this once again. The Miranda acknowledgment you signed yesterday still applies, though I'm sure your attorney has reminded you of your rights."

"Get on with it," Jerry says.

"Okay. We got an anonymous tip saying someone who matched your description was seen throwing something into the dumpster behind Mick's Bar and Grill. I assume you know Mick's. That's, what, about a mile from campus?"

Maybe less. I hadn't been back there since the night with Jessica the Bartender. That was the weekend before Thanksgiving. But that hardly seems like something I want to brag about now.

"Officers investigated," Prisbell says, like she's already testifying about it. "And they found this."

She looks to Morin, who places something sheathed in clear plastic in front of me. It's a shiny, reusable grocery bag that looks a lot like one that used to be folded beneath the sink in my apartment.

"Do you recognize it?" Morin asks. "You should. It's got your fingerprints all over it. And it was full of incriminating items."

He does the honors of laying a series of evidence bags on the table.

The first contains the polka dot pajama bottoms Hayley was wearing in that doorbell camera footage. The only difference is, the white portions of the fabric have been stained a scabby reddish brown.

Next comes a light pink T-shirt. It, too, has ominous dark blotches down its front.

After that, there are thick, fluffy socks in a tie-dye pattern; and black-and-white Adidas slides, the kind preferred by soccer players the world over.

Finally, there are panties. I don't even look at them.

"We haven't been able to run a DNA test yet, but we're going to have someone bring this to the state crime lab in Meriden this morning and ask for this to be expedited," Prisbell says. "What are the chances this is Hayley Goodloe's blood?"

I am back to staring at the pajama pants. They look like something that would be shown repeatedly on a cold case crime show, next to a dated photo of a young woman with feathered Farah Fawcett hair, while a voice-over explains she hasn't been seen since that fateful night in 1977.

And then there's that damn grocery bag. Another item that Ken Rippinger stole during his shopping trip through my apartment.

"Tell us what happened, Charles," Prisbell says gently. "Where's Hayley?"

Jerry clears his throat and tries to break in with a gruff, "My client has—"

"Ask Ken Rippinger," I say with sudden ferocity.

Jerry pivots toward me with surprising speed. "I told you not to—"

"No," I say. "They need to hear this."

I turn to Prisbell. "You guys are all over me. I get it. But I'm telling you, I didn't do this. You really ought to be looking at Ken Rippinger. I bet he's the one who called in that anonymous tip—*after* he put the bag in the dumpster."

Morin can't stifle his smirk. It's like he just won a bet with Prisbell that I would try to pin this on someone else.

Prisbell at least keeps a straight face.

"We spoke with Mr. Rippinger yesterday," she says. "He acknowledged that he confronted you about Ms. Goodloe but he denied hitting you."

"Well, of course he did," I say. "You're cops. He's not going to admit to you that he assaulted me. But the fact is, before he hit me, he broke into my apartment and—"

"Okay, that's enough," Jerry says tersely. "Don't speak."

"But they need to hear this, Jerry. Everyone at Carrington knows—"

"I'm telling you, Bliss, if you want me to keep being your lawyer, *don't speak*. I can't protect you from yourself if you won't shut the hell up."

He is glaring at me in a way that would make anyone think he's the accused murderer in the room.

This, finally, makes me rein in my tongue.

Prisbell is waiting, giving me ample chance to continue pissing off my lawyer and potentially ruining my own case, but I'm done with both for the moment.

"Okay," she says, finally. "We should also tell you—since this will come out in discovery anyway—that we received an email just now from Carrington's attorney. He forwarded a report from Carrington's IT department. They were able to determine that user Charles Bliss accessed Hayley Goodloe's record in the school database at 10:23 a.m. That record contained her mother's address: 23 Rogers Road, West Hartford. A short time later, someone using your school-issued computer googled '23 Rogers Road, West Hartford.' Do you care to explain that?"

This is perhaps the first time in history that Carrington's famously incompetent IT department has ever surprised me with its efficiency.

But Jerry Cordova doesn't need to tell me how to respond.

I don't speak.

* * *

They're not just asking for a confession anymore. They fully *expect* one.

And regardless of whether they get one, they're starting to make noises like they intend to take me into custody. They don't want their best and only suspect wandering around free—or trying to make a run for it.

Prisbell and Morin retreat from the interrogation room for a few minutes. When they return, they're wearing smug, triumphant little grins.

"We're going to charge him with a thirty-eighty-six based on the prints on the bottle and shot glasses," Morin says.

Jerry immediately erupts. "Oh, you gotta be kidding me. That's a bush league move and you know it."

"No, Mr. Cordova, it's a crime," Morin says.

"One that half the frat boys at UConn probably committed this past weekend. Are you going to lock them up, too?"

Jerry turns to me and explains, "Thirty dash eighty-six is the statute that prohibits sale or delivery of alcohol to minors."

"It's a Class E felony, punishable by up to eighteen months in jail," Morin adds.

"And it's total bull. You can't prove any scotch ever touched that girl's lips. And even if it did, you can't prove he's the one who gave it to her. You have no chance of making this stick. It's harassment, and any judge who isn't completely blind is going to see it that way."

"There is an alternative," Morin dangles.

"Yeah, and what's that?"

"Your client voluntarily submits to wearing a GPS ankle bracelet. We won't charge him with anything. He won't be in custody. He won't have a record if our evidence leads us toward another suspect. Our only requirement would be that he doesn't leave the state of Connecticut."

Jerry leans back in his chair. He's actually smiling a little. It's half disgust, half admiration.

"Voluntarily, huh? In my old neighborhood, we would have just called it blackmail."

"Call it whatever you want," Morin says. "As long as he behaves himself and doesn't leave the state, he's free to go about his business."

Prisbell adds, "We think it's generous under the circumstances."

"And I think it's a flagrant violation of his rights, slapping a GPS on him without any due process. What, your captain is already tired of burning up the overtime to have my client watched, and so he figures he saves himself some money doing it this way?"

"We would just charge him and do it with the due process," Morin says. "But you'd better believe we'll be mentioning Hayley Goodloe at the bond hearing."

Jerry lets out a windy sigh. "If you don't mind, Mr. Bliss and I are going to take a little walk and discuss this."

"Suit yourself," Prisbell says.

I follow down the hallway. When he feels like he's out of earshot of everyone, he turns and gives me a grim look.

"I hate to tell you this, Ace, but they got you by the short hairs," he says. "A bond hearing wouldn't be a good thing for us right now."

"Why not?" I ask.

"There are basically two things up for discussion at a bond hearing: Are you a threat to public safety and are you a flight risk? Right now, with the Hayley Goodloe thing hanging over you, the State can argue you're both, and a judge just might go for it."

"Don't I get the presumption of innocence?"

"Oh, the State still has to prove what it says. And they'd probably have a tough time coming up with evidence you're a threat, since you don't have a record. But the flight risk thing could be a problem. You don't have a job anymore. You don't have kids. You're living in a hotel. What's to prevent you from bolting? I'm not saying you would, but the legal standard at a bond hearing is 'preponderance of the evidence.' That means that if a judge thinks the evidence is even 50.1 percent on the State's side, you get locked up until trial."

"How soon would that be?"

"If you're in detention, the State has eight months. After that we can file what's called a speedy trial motion that gives them another thirty days."

"Nine months," I moan.

"Or you take the bracelet. They're not so bad. I got clients who wear them all the time. At least it's winter. You don't have to worry about not being able to wear shorts."

I stare at the wall in front of me. I would feel like a champion fool if I tried to push my luck and wound up in jail for nine months.

My luck hasn't exactly been very good lately.

"How soon would they put it on?" I ask.

"It's a private company that does it. You have to make an appointment, but it's usually within a day or two."

"Fine," I say. "I'll do the bracelet."

We go back down the hallway and tell the detectives our decisions. Phone calls are made. My appointment is scheduled for the next morning at ten.

Which means I'm now in a hurry. Because I have one thing I need to accomplish between now and then: Get Emily back on my side.

And I'm pretty sure she's not in the state of Connecticut.

JOURNAL ENTRY: TUESDAY, NOVEMBER 7

I finally told Calista about my thing for Mr. B today.

For me it was this biiiig confession. Like, I kind of made her drag it out of me, even though I was dying to have it be dragged.

I thought it was going to feel so good to finally talk about it out loud. Sometimes, something isn't real until you tell someone else about it, you know?

Calista was . . . fine about it, I guess? She sort of just blew it off. Her response was basically, *Uhh, who* doesn't *have a thing for Mr. Bliss? He's gorgeous.*

Don't get me wrong, it's not like I'm mad at her. She's still my girl.

She just doesn't get it. And maybe I didn't totally explain the severity of the situation.

He's literally *all* I think about. I wake up and he's the first thing on my mind. Or I'll be doing something random, something that has nothing to do with him, and suddenly there he is, in my thoughts.

Or the other day, I was sitting in Spanish class and I was thinking about what it would be like to wake up with him one morning. You know, just to have him in my bed, holding me.

Sometimes I even dream about him.

I love those dreams. I never want them to end.

Because when I wake up, I know I can't have him. Not yet, anyway. The pain is practically debilitating.

I need to acknowledge something here that I've been thinking about a lot, or else this journal isn't going to be true.

This isn't just a crush.

I've had crushes before. They're not this severe, and they don't last this long. You get a few days of . . . whatever. And then you either get with the guy or not. Either way, you start to realize he's not all that.

This is different.

This is bigger. More special. More lasting.

This is love.

CHAPTER 12

Mindful of making the most of my remaining time, I return to my hotel and power up my phone.

I immediately wish I hadn't.

My number is under siege. There are 126 missed calls since I last turned it on.

How have all of these reporters gotten my number so fast? Did someone dox me on Twitter or something?

Doing my best to ignore the onslaught, I call a few of Hayley's friends and play the "I'm just worried about her" card. Several blow me off. One berates me for having the nerve to call her after "what you did." But, finally, one of her fellow PsyD candidates confirms my suspicion.

Emily is at her parents' house in Rhode Island.

They live in Jamestown, a swanky island in Narragansett Bay, just west of Newport. It's an hour-and-a-half drive, assuming Interstate 95 doesn't get in a bad mood.

I head out immediately, already formulating pleas and strategies.

Emily's choice of sanctuary, while not surprising, is nevertheless a disturbing sign. My in-laws and I have what would kindly be described as a complicated relationship.

It started off well enough. Miles and Katherine "Kiki" Vanderburgh are, respectively, a wealth manager and a homemaker. Like many people whose families have always had money, they are well-mannered, urbane, and highly polished.

Not long after Emily and I met, Miles and Kiki came down to the city to have dinner with us. We hit it off immediately. After a lavish meal—appetizers, entrées, desserts, two bottles of wine—that came to nearly $500, my future father-in-law nodded approvingly as I slapped my credit card on top of the check.

He didn't even try to offer to pay. But what did I care? I was going to be rich.

Emily said they went back home to their friends and raved about me: the soon-to-be-famous author who was going to marry their little girl.

Their infatuation with me lasted right until they met my mother.

Granted, Robbie Bliss is not always an easy person to like. She can be stubborn as mold stains. She is congenitally incapable of lying about her feelings, which is one of the things I adore about her; but it's also a massive social liability in the world of Miles and Kiki Vanderburgh.

When confronted by such people, my mother tends to be like a hermit crab, retreating into her shell the moment she feels threatened. If anything emerges after that, it's usually her big claw.

She's certainly not a huge believer in marriage or romantic relationships. You probably wouldn't be either if the man who impregnated you left on a fishing trip to Alaska and never came back, leaving you to raise a baby all by yourself and never sending a dime of child support. Not that my mother ever tried to extract any from him. She seemed to accept as her fate that she and I would have to go it alone.

You can nevah count on anyone but your mothah and yahself, Chahles, she warned me repeatedly throughout my youth.

Meeting Robbie Bliss was the first time the Vanderburghs were confronted with the fact that Emily was marrying below her station—like, a subway ride, Amtrak train, Greyhound bus, and dented pickup truck ride below her station.

They grinned their way through the wedding—without once offering to pay for anything. But once *Washington County* tanked, I swear they secretly hoped Emily would leave me. They were constantly giving her status updates about old boyfriends, particularly the ones that were doing well financially—*Did you hear? Henry Davenport started his own hedge fund!*

When we started trying for a baby, they took her aside and asked if she was *really sure* she was ready.

She said it was because they thought she should complete her doctorate first. But I could see through them.

They feared that if Emily had a baby, she'd be stuck with me forever.

Emily always dismissed my concerns as paranoia, insisting they loved me.

But Robbie Bliss didn't raise an idiot.

The Vanderburghs needed their daughter to marry rich in order for their grandchildren and future generations of Vanderburghs to continue in style and comfort. And she hadn't.

In truth, Miles Vanderburgh is a classic big-hat-no-cattle kind of guy. As a money manager, he has a special talent for jumping on trends that are about to be over—tech stocks in 2000, mortgage-backed securities in 2006, cryptocurrencies in 2021. The man's career is a series of burn marks and he's constantly losing clients.

He just lives like this isn't the case. He and Kiki are big in the Newport area sailing scene. She always has the latest handbag or shoes. She has long been forbidden from getting a job because he thinks it would make them look needy.

They have no savings. Quite the opposite. They were so deep in debt when Emily's grandmother died that they had basically spent their entire portion of the inheritance before the funeral was over.

They don't actually *own* much of anything. All of their possessions are leveraged, leased, or borrowed. Every time their house accrues even a little bit of equity, they refinance and pull out cash so they can go on another vacation or buy another trinket.

There is never any open hostility between us, of course. That's not the way the Vanderburghs operate.

But they still harbor a simmering disappointment about their daughter's choice of husband.

It's midday by the time I reach Jamestown. My intel about Emily's whereabouts proves correct: her car is parked in front of the garage.

As soon as I'm out of my car, I'm assaulted by a wind that is coming hard enough off the water that my pants are whipping around my legs. I lean into it on my way up to the Vanderburghs' porch.

Emily and I spend most of our holidays with her parents, rather than making the seven-hour slog up to Maine and my mother's apartment, where there's not really room for us anyway. Given this familiarity, I would ordinarily just walk in the front door.

This time, I knock.

My father-in-law answers wearing a button-down shirt with a whale on its pocket. He immediately crosses his arms.

All of Emily's dark-complected good looks come from Kiki. Miles Vanderburgh has washed-out coloring, thin lips, an upturned nose, and a fragile jaw. *A very punchable face*, is how Leo describes it.

I'm already itching to test out that theory as Miles coolly says, "Hello, Charles."

"Is Emily here?" I say, feeling like I'm some pathetic ex-boyfriend who's just been dumped.

"She doesn't want to speak to you," he informs me.

"*She* doesn't, or you don't want her to?"

"This has been very traumatic for her," he says, ignoring the question. "She needs some space."

"Well, I'd still like to speak with her."

He shakes his head. "I'm afraid that's not going to happen."

"And I'm afraid I don't accept your authority on this subject," I say hotly. "I'd like to talk to my wife, please. If she really doesn't want to have a conversation with me, I suppose I'll have to accept that. But after six years of marriage, I have a right to hear that directly from her."

"You don't have any rights here. You forfeited your rights the moment you decided to sleep with a seventeen-year-old girl."

"I didn't—"

I stop myself. There is no point getting into this with him.

"Would you just get Emily. I'm not leaving until I talk with her."

"Charles, you've already ruined your life. Please let Emily get on with putting hers back together."

"Yeah, see, that's what you don't seem to understand, Miles. This isn't just *her* life. It's *our* life. That's what happens when you get married. You go from being an 'I' to being a 'we.' And 'we' have things to discuss. Now if you'll please step aside."

He widens his stance so that he's blocking the doorway.

"You are *not* coming into this house," he snaps. "I'll call the police if I have to."

I am tempted to bum-rush him and knock him on his self-righteous ass, but adding assault charges in Rhode Island to whatever is about to happen in Connecticut doesn't strike me as a very solid idea.

Instead, I back away from the porch and yell up toward her bedroom.

"Emily," I bellow. "Can you please just come down and talk to me? Whatever the police have told you, it's not true. I had nothing to do with Hayley. You know that!"

I continue my entreaties toward Emily's window. The curtains are drawn. There is no apparent movement behind them. For all I know, she's not even there. But I don't let the futility and fatuousness of what I'm doing stop me.

Sometimes, marriage is all about pointless gestures.

Miles has pulled out his phone and brought it to his ear. I'm catching snippets over the sound of the howling wind and my own caterwauling. "Intruder" sticks out, as does "creating a disturbance."

My father-in-law, who has sat across the table from me at multiple Christmases, Easters, and Thanksgivings, is actually calling the cops on me.

JOURNAL ENTRY: FRIDAY, NOVEMBER 10

I will give them this much: my parents are remarkably skilled at one-upping each other.

When one of them does something messed up, the other always finds a way to top it.

Enter Mom, right on schedule. She and Steeeeve showed up unannounced at dinnertime today and asked if they could take me out for a meal.

Steve rubbed his hands like he was about to open a box of donuts and said my mother had some "exciting news" she needed to talk to me about.

I'm like, *Oh, perfect. More exciting news. I can't wait.*

We ended up going to Mick's, which is this dump right near campus. This is part of my mother's Woman of the People act, slumming it at divey places like Mick's.

She doesn't use a car service like my dad does. It would look too bougie. And, besides, she has Steeeeve to drive her, open doors for her, hold her coat for her, taste her food to make sure it's not poisoned by would-be assassins, all that.

On the way, I asked them what they thought about Dad and Ashley. Naturally, they didn't know anything about it. My stepfather kind of grumbled when I spilled the news. Mom's only question was: "How young is this one?"

I actually felt bad for her. It sucks to be a woman and get old.

But there are ways in which she only has herself to blame for what happened with her and Dad. Yeah, my dad cheated on her, like, a million times. That's his bad. But Mom was so focused on her career and what was happening in Hartford, she was pretty unavailable to him. From what he's told me, he used to *beg* her to spend more time with him, to make their relationship more of a priority. And she just wouldn't.

He said she would refuse to have sex with him because she didn't want to mess up her hair.

Sad, right?

Also: What kind of dad tells his daughter that?

Still, I know what it feels like to be ignored by someone you love desperately. It actually makes me feel sorry for my douchebag dad.

Sometimes, I think he cheated on her just to get her attention.

Mom's reaction to his engagement was pretty typical. She went into this whole thing about how she wasn't going to disparage him—Mom is big on never disparaging my father, as if she read in a book she wasn't supposed to do it—and then she proceeded to . . . of course, disparage him. She said he had serious issues that he needed to work out in therapy.

My mother, the Queen of Lexapro, thinks the whole world should be in therapy.

Just as long as they don't tell anyone about it, right, Mom?

Anyway, once we got to dinner, we ordered. No champagne with Mom. She doesn't even let me drink soda.

Then she told me her "exciting news." Robert Qualls, the senior U.S. senator from Connecticut, had started quietly putting out word that he was going to retire instead of seeking reelection.

Steve jumped in and explained to me that my mother had to start maneuvering *immediately* to line up party support—as if I didn't already know that—and avoid a heavily contested primary. Then he prattled on and on about how she had to walk a fine line, finding ways to keep the centrists happy while also signaling to the left flank that she was "one of them."

All she needed was that "D" next to her name and super-blue Connecticut would send her and the Goodloe name straight to the U.S. Senate.

Neither of them asked me what I thought. It's not like my opinion would have changed anything.

If there was a point to the dinner, it was simply for both of them to take turns warning me that running for U.S. Senate was a whole different level of scrutiny than running for State Senate, and that I should expect more of a spotlight to be on Mom—and, to a lesser but not insignificant extent, on me.

Neither of them said it out loud, but the subtext might as well have been written in 72-point font:

Don't do anything to screw this up for us.

CHAPTER 13

The cops show up promptly—because there's so little for them to do in Jamestown, Rhode Island—and I allow myself to be chased away.

Once I'm outside town limits, I pull off the side of the road and attempt to come to grips with my new reality.

Emily is gone.

She has forsaken me.

It's like all the air on the planet has vanished at once. I am now in a vacuum, a void. I expect tears to come any moment, but I suddenly can't feel anything. I'm just numb.

Maybe I'm still in denial.

Eventually, I get back underway and somehow make it back to Connecticut. When I reach the hotel, there are only a few cars in the parking lot, which is why I immediately notice this one particular vehicle.

It's a boxy, battle-scarred 1998 Jeep Cherokee that has over two hundred thousand miles on it. It is held together with bungee cords, duct tape, and prayers after too many Maine winters.

I know all this history because it's my mother's. As I pull in next to it, she climbs out of her car and walks around to the driver's side of mine.

"Hello, Chahles," she says as I open the door.

As soon as I'm on my feet, she wraps her sinewy arms around me. Embracing my mother is like hugging a walnut tree. She is hard, and rough, and maybe even a little knotty in places. Her hands are like a pair of calloused iron mitts clutching my back.

Robbie Bliss is five foot nine, or at least she used to be, before she began the long shrink. Her height isn't the only thing that's changed about her over the decades. I've seen a few scattered pictures of her as a young woman and it's almost like looking at a different person.

There's one photo of her from when she used to have a side hustle repairing the lacquer on boats that wandered into a nearby marina. In it, she's twenty-one years old, and she's sitting topside on some rich person's yacht.

Her body is slender and soft, still just a bit girlish. Her skin has a rich, brown summer tan. Her lustrous chestnut hair is sun-kissed.

She's beautiful. But that's not what really strikes me when I look at that photo.

It's her hopefulness. Her optimism. In that yellowing photo, she is a young woman gazing into a future that she can't wait to meet.

That picture was taken the summer before she had me, probably right around the time she got pregnant. It's like my arrival—and my father's departure—sucked away every aspiration Robbie Bliss might have ever had.

Time has since eroded her in other ways as well. Her life is not an easy one. She works six days a week, scrubbing and scouring and buffing and mopping her way to perpetual motion. Between that and a near total ambiguity about food, she probably tops out at about a hundred and fifteen pounds.

I am very glad to see her. I still just can't believe she's here.

"What are you doing here?" I ask in disbelief.

"You weren't answering your phone," she says. "I just felt like I had to check in on you. I can only stay for the night. I have to be back at work tomorrow."

My mother's decidedly Yankee sensibilities always require her to announce when she is leaving the moment she arrives.

"But how did you even know where I was?" I ask.

She releases me and says, "There was a charge for the hotel on your card."

When I went off to college, we decided I needed a credit card for emergencies. My mother co-signed for it. I've had the same card ever since. She must have kept the account information handy.

"And the Cherokee made the trip okay?" I ask.

It's probably an inane thing to say under the circumstances, but we're constantly talking about the Cherokee and its health. When you're poor and live in rural America, your car is your lifeline to pretty much everything, and its fragility is a source of constant anxiety.

"I changed the oil just last week," she says, like that's all there was to it.

She gives me a smile. My mother and I have the same bone structure—long and lean—but I have someone else's face. Some meandering commercial fisherman I have never met.

"Anyhow, let me get my things," she says.

"I'll help."

"Don't make a fuss," she says. "It's nothing."

Even though Robbie Bliss is practically allergic to accepting anyone's help, I manage to carry at least some of her things back to my hotel room.

When we enter, she barely breaks stride. She lifts this brown grocery bag and brings it over to the kitchenette.

"I thought you'd be hungry," she says. "I got you some peanut butter and jelly. Would you like one?"

When I was a kid, I was a certified freak for PB&J. I have since acquired a more adult palate, but to Robbie there's a part of me forever stuck in preadolescence.

As she pulls the ingredients out of the bag, I already want to cry.

Jif peanut butter. Smuckers jelly. Wonder Bread.

There was a time in middle school when I used to complain that my mother never bought brand-name products. I didn't understand that half of them were probably made in the same factory as the generics. At that age, being forced to eat the store brand was just another embarrassing mark of our inability to conform to my image of what a middle-class American family should be.

We're not fancy like that, Chahles, she would say when I griped.

So I immediately recognize what this is: Robbie, being fancy.

I don't say a word as she assembles my sandwich and places it in front of me.

"Here you are, dear."

"Thanks, Mom," I say through the lump in my throat.

She has just dropped everything in her life and driven seven hours in an SUV that could have died at any mile during the journey—all to come to my rescue with a peanut butter and jelly sandwich. It is incredibly touching and sweet. Even heroic.

Naturally, she's just looking at me through her seriously unfashionable rimless glasses—she's had the same pair since I can remember—without any hint of mawkishness.

I haven't seen her in person since my annual trip to Maine the previous summer. Her brown hair long ago lost its shine, and is now finally succumbing to gray. The lines on her forehead are etched just a bit more deeply.

"Where's Emily?" my mother asks as I chew.

I'm not sure how to say it, so I start a fumbling, "She, uhh, she—"

"She left you, didn't she."

It wasn't even a question. Just a statement. I nod.

"Well, there you have it," she says.

Perhaps unsurprisingly, Robbie Bliss never warmed to Emily Vanderburgh. Everything about Emily—her affinity for ballet, the books she read, the clothes she wore, her course of study—was foreign and strange to my mother.

And, of course, Emily's departure conforms to my mother's general expectations of humanity.

You can nevah count on anyone but your mothah and yahself, Chahles.

Never one to linger over uncomfortable feelings, she moves to the couch in the sitting area, testing its cushions with a firm press.

"This is a fold-out, am I right?" she asks.

"Mom, you can have the bed."

"Nonsense. I told you I'm only here for one night."

She immediately changes the subject: "Pastor Scott told me to say hello. He's going to have the entire congregation pray for you this Sunday. God is looking out for you, Chahles."

My mother attends church every Sunday. She found religion when I was in grade school and has been proselytizing me ever since.

It embarrasses me when her faith evinces itself as superstition, especially when she starts talking about "God's plan." I have a hard time believing an all-powerful, all-knowing, merciful God has a plan that involves school shootings, wars, pandemics, and ever-worsening natural disasters.

At the same time, I'm aware how uncomfortable Robbie is with my ill-defined, nouveau, spiritual non-religiosity.

And, make of this what you will, I'm grateful to know she prays for me every day.

"Now, let's get down to business here," she continues. "Do you have a lawyer yet? You need a lawyer."

"I have a lawyer," I assure her.

"What's he charging you?"

"I'm not sure yet. But, don't worry, I can cover it."

"Well, I want to help," she says, going toward a duffel bag that she had tossed in the corner.

She pulls a blank manilla envelope from it, which she drops unceremoniously into my lap.

It's heavy—way too heavy to be an amount of money she's ever been associated with.

"What's this?" I ask.

"Don't worry about it. It's just some can money."

My mother has an old metal coffee can she keeps hidden in a closet. When I was a little boy, and she was trying to teach me about the importance of saving, we used to have this weekly ritual where she would peel a bill out of her wallet—sometimes as little as $5, never more than $20—and let me stuff it into the can.

Now and then, she'd have to dip into the can, if there was an unexpected expense. Mostly, she tried to leave it alone. Then, on New Year's Eve, we'd empty out the can together and count up the year's bounty.

I never remember it being more than four hundred dollars. Some years it barely topped a hundred. We'd take whatever it was to the bank the next day and proudly add it to my mother's meager savings.

So how to account for this sudden weight in my lap? I pinch the brass clasp to open it and stare dumbstruck at its contents.

It is bricks of cash: hundred-dollar bills, banded together with paper, stacked a hundred thick. There are five of them in total.

The math isn't hard. It's fifty thousand dollars.

I am almost too stupefied to make my mouth work.

My mother is not a woman who can just make fifty grand in cash appear. If you assembled all the Blisses throughout history, going back to the invention of currency, and added up the sum total of everything they had ever been able to squirrel away, I doubt you'd make it to this amount.

"Mom, there's no way this is can money," I say. "How in the world did you get this?"

"It doesn't matter. I want you to have it."

"It does matter. I can't possibly—"

"You're taking it, and that's the end of this discussion. I don't want to hear another word about it."

There is this hysterical edge to her voice that I have only rarely heard from her. The provenance of this money is a serious no-fly zone.

Which only makes me more worried. Did she borrow it from a loan shark? Did she do something illicit or rash—sell an organ, rob a bank, something like that—to come up with it?

I close the flap on the envelope and place it on the table in front of me like this will allow me to distance myself from the stench of its origin.

"Now," she says more calmly, "who is this lawyer?"

We are not done discussing this money.

But I learned long ago that you don't win arguments with Robbie right away. If you're going to prevail at all, it takes time.

"His name is Jerry Cordova," I say. "He's very experienced."

I pull out my phone so I can show my mother a picture, googling Jerome Cordova. It's something I didn't do when I was at the police station. I had only clicked his bio on his firm's website.

That's why I find myself staring almost incomprehensibly at the results. The first thing to pop up is a story in *Connecticut Law Tribune*. It is from 2016, about how Jerry Cordova had been reinstated to the bar.

This, after having not practiced for the previous twenty years due to his disbarment.

CHAPTER 14

Gross misconduct in office.

According to the article, that's the official reason Jerry Cordova lost his license to practice law in 2002.

What that means, I'm not exactly sure. The article doesn't specify.

But I don't need to be represented by someone who is lugging a lot of drama into the courtroom.

I'll be bringing enough of my own already.

Since I don't want to fire him over the phone—I owe him at least some courtesy, given how much he's helped me so far—I call him and tell him we need to talk.

He agrees, saying he had been trying to leave voicemails for me, but had been thwarted by my already-full inbox.

Twenty minutes later, he knocks on my door. He is once again dressed in a gray blazer and he is carrying a leather briefcase.

He joins my mother and me around the small coffee table. He clears his throat, giving his jowls a vigorous shake, then says, "Okay, there are three things we need to go over—"

"Jerry, wait," I say. "Before you get going, there's something we need to talk about first. I saw . . . I saw that article about your disbarment."

"Yeah," he says without emotion. "And?"

"I think"—I've practiced this line in my head, but it still comes out faltering—"I think I need to go in a different direction with my representation."

Still no change in expression. "And what direction is that?"

"When I first called your firm, I asked to speak to Anna Brodeur. I think she'd be the better choice. It makes sense for a man who is accused of hurting a woman to be represented by a woman."

Now, finally, there's a small change in the set of his mouth. It adopts a wry grin. "Yeah, well, I'm sorry to tell you this, Ace, but you can't have her."

This was not the response I was expecting.

"Why not?"

"She does a lot of pro bono work helping women who've been beaten up by the men in their lives. She's seen as a real leader in the area of violence against women. And as of this morning you became the new poster child for violence against women. She told me she does not want the firm representing you."

"Then why are you still here?"

"Because Anna Brodeur is not just my boss, she's also my daughter. It's a bit of an awkward arrangement now and then. But up and until the time I'm too senile to know which way to drool and she packs me off to a home, she doesn't get to tell me what to do."

"Oh," I say.

"My daughter and I have a little difference of opinion when it comes to this sort of thing. She worries about the optics of things. She says appearance matters. I always come back to: facts matter more. What really happened? What are the shades of gray? Our legal system is based on considering the whole story, not just whatever the algorithms of our social media feeds decide to tell us. That's a hill I'm willing to die on."

He says it with such conviction I almost feel silly about the sentence that dribbles from my mouth next.

"I still don't know if . . . if you're the right person, given . . . you know, given the seriousness of the allegations against me and your, you know, your past."

This is another pre-rehearsed line that I am fumbling.

As he takes it in, the grin comes back. "You'd think a guy who claims to be wrongly accused wouldn't be quite so quick to judge."

"Fair point."

"You want to hear about it or would I be wasting my breath?"

"No. Go ahead."

"Okay. I was defending this guy who I knew was innocent," he begins. "Those are the worst ones, if you ask me. The guilty ones, you do the best you can for them, you protect their rights, you make sure the system treats them fair. But at the end of the day, what are you supposed to do? They're guilty. The innocent ones, those are the ones you lose sleep over."

He shakes his head. "Anyhow, there was a prosecutor who was withholding evidence and I knew it, and he knew I knew it, but he thought he could get away with it. I couldn't force his hand because if I revealed how I knew what he was withholding, it would have betrayed a confidence. I got so pissed off with the prosecutor, I broke into his office one night and copied his files so I could show them to the judge and get the case tossed out.

"The police caught me just as I was leaving the building. The prosecutor went berserk. He had me indicted on breaking and entering, larceny, obstruction of justice, the full monty. The only thing that kept me out of prison was that the person whose confidence I was protecting interceded and made it clear he'd drop the dime if the prosecutor didn't back off on the criminal stuff. But no one was much in the mood for me to keep my license, so I got disbarred—which I probably deserved, just for being stupid."

"And what did you do for the next fourteen years until you got reinstated?" I ask.

"Oh, let's see here," he says with a long sigh. "I started tending bar and became an amateur drunk. Then my wife died of cancer and I became a professional drunk. Then it occurred to me that I was killing myself slowly with the booze and I should stop wasting everyone's time and just get it over with."

I am so close to that moment myself, I feel his every word echoing inside my emptiness.

Jerry takes on a faraway look. "I bought a gun, I got loaded up on bourbon, and—you can believe this or not, I don't care—I was just about to pull the trigger when I heard a voice, telling me not to do it, telling me I had a higher purpose."

He stops, like something is stuck in his throat. His spider-veined nose seems to grow redder. He is, in his own Jerry Cordova way, overcome with emotion.

My mother reaches out and places a maternal hand on Jerry's knee. Her eyes have gone wide. "It was God, wasn't it?"

"Oh, I don't know about that, ma'am," Jerry says. "I always tell people it was an angel. I'm not so full of myself that I think the Big Fella would pay all that much attention to me."

"God loves you, Jerry," my mother replies simply, giving his knee a pat. "God sent you that angel."

"Anyhow," Jerry says with another sigh, "from there, I got sober. I did all twelve steps. I was wearing the orange bib at Home Depot forty hours a week, just trying to keep myself clean, when Anna came and told me she wanted to start her own law firm and she needed my help. I couldn't say no to that. But I couldn't do it without a license, so I applied for reinstatement. It had been fourteen years. The prosecutor I pissed off had died. Everyone else had retired, moved on, or forgotten. So here I am. You want me or not?"

Now my mother has her hand on my knee.

"Chahles, I think God sent Jerry to be your lawyer," she says earnestly. "This is God's plan for you."

Normally when my mother makes these kinds of pronouncements, I either ignore her or start enumerating reasons why she's being irrational.

But I just don't have it in me this time.

I need *someone* to have a plan.

It might as well be God.

"Okay, Jerry," I say. "I guess you're still my lawyer."

* * *

With this settled, Jerry moves on to his three items of business.

The first is that the detectives subpoenaed my wireless carrier. They shared a copy with Jerry in their ongoing hopes to force my confession.

During the entire window of time when Hayley Goodloe was being kidnapped, my phone was pinging off the cell phone tower that serves Carrington Academy.

"That's good, right?" I ask, hope surging. "That clears me, doesn't it?"

"Not necessarily," Jerry says. "Because you also received four text messages and two calls from your wife around the time the kidnapping occurred, but you didn't answer any of them. Can you explain that?"

"Not really. I was"—I don't want to say I was day-drinking around my mother, she wouldn't approve—"trying to take a nap and I was . . . I don't know, I was depressed. I just didn't feel like talking."

"Yeah, that's a bad answer," Jerry says, appearing legitimately dismayed. "It makes it look like you ditched the phone while you were off doing the dirty deed. If you take the stand, they'll hammer you for not answering calls from your own wife."

"Oh," I say, feeling my shoulders sag.

"But then if you don't take the stand, they'll hammer you anyway. You can't take the fifth on this one—it would make you look a hundred percent guilty. But when you give that lame answer, it makes you look like a liar and a schemer. Juries love to punish liars and schemers."

"How do we fix it?"

"We don't, I'm afraid. At best, it's a toss-up in the jury's mind."

I rub my temples for a moment.

"Okay, what's the second thing?"

"We need to talk about our public relations strategy," he says.

"I thought it was 'don't speak.'"

"It was, but then that girl talked to the *Boston Globe*."

"What girl?" I ask.

Jerry reaches down into his briefcase and pulls out two sheets of paper that have been stapled together. He slides them my way. Suddenly, I am staring at a printout of a face I haven't seen in eleven years.

Breighlee Dumont.

The girl who taught me all about the necessity of boundaries.

SECOND STUDENT ALLEGES AFFAIR WITH TEACHER, the headline fairly screams.

I grip onto the sides of my chair. The story doesn't bury the lede: Eleven years ago, when Breighlee was a senior at Carrington Academy, she had an inappropriate relationship with me.

By the time I am done with the story, my mouth has gone dry.

I know how this works. If I were to read about a man with one woman accusing him of something, I *might* withhold judgment until all the facts came out.

Two women? To hell with that guy. Let him burn

"Wow," I say. "This is . . . this is bad. You think we should respond to this but not the other stuff?"

"We don't speak about Hayley Goodloe because you're probably going to trial. I don't want anything you say in the press to come back and bite you on the stand. This new girl is a different matter. You're not going to face any charges here and they couldn't introduce this at the Goodloe trial, so I'm not worried about the legal implications. This is strictly about managing your potential jury pool. We don't want you looking like a serial predator. I gotta ask: Are there going to be more?"

"No. No chance."

He looks momentarily circumspect.

"Well, one is bad enough," he says. "This thing is out there now. You gotta know there are people who will bring this into the jury box with them, no matter what they say about not pre-judging you. I want to at least put some doubt in their minds. Can we refute it? Can we put out a statement saying it never happened?"

My mother, who has read the story over my shoulder, is looking at me expectantly.

I don't know what we're going to say to the *Boston Globe*.

But I sure can't lie to my mother.

"No," I say. "Not exactly."

MIDLOGUE 3

I don't want to belabor the Breighlee Dumont thing.

What I told you earlier is basically true. I started off with the best and purest of intentions.

She had come to Carrington with a few trunk-loads of baggage. Her divorced parents had weaponized her in their unending enmity toward each other. Her older brother was a drug addict who stole from her—and everyone else. Her aunt was born again and regularly told Breighlee she was going to hell. But that was still better than the uncle who fondled her.

So, yeah, Breighlee was a mess. The cutting was just the most outward symptom. She also battled an eating disorder, anxiety, depression, post-traumatic stress—it was like the DSM was an amusement park and she wanted to try out all the rides.

But the thing was, she was also brilliant, and funny, and kind, in spite of everything the world had dumped on her. I could see incredible potential in her. There was definitely a whole human being in there, somewhere, if only she could find a little daylight.

As the year got underway, I noticed that the further she got away from her family—and the more I became the voice in her ear—the healthier she became. This only encouraged me to get more involved.

I really thought I could fix her.

And it wasn't just about Breighlee. You have to remember, this was my first year on the faculty at Carrington. I was learning on the job, discovering what was possible, testing my powers as a teacher and mentor.

In a way, Breighlee became my test case. If I could save her, I could save every screwed-up kid who came to Carrington.

And, yes, I had a hero complex. And uncured hubris. And a heaping dose of youthful arrogance. You're never smarter than when you're in your first few years out of college, that heady time when you think you're smarter than everyone else because you don't yet know what you don't know.

Nevertheless, I came to care a great deal about Breighlee—too much, obviously.

There was nothing remotely physical between us at first. Then we started hugging. The first hug caught me completely by surprise but was a huge catharsis for her. I was the first person she had been able to trust in a long time.

Then, somehow, the hugs became regular. Whenever she and I spoke at length—and we had long talks two, three, four times a week—we ended it with a hug.

It could have been innocent—should have been innocent—but it wasn't. We held on a little too long. Our bodies got a little too close.

Truth was, I liked it. I was suffering from that jarring post-graduate jolt of going from a near-unlimited supply of friends and potential intimate partners—all of them similar in age, education, and aspiration—to an almost complete lack of them.

I was surrounded by people but lonely at the same time. Breighlee made me feel attractive, powerful, smart, wanted—all things men are notoriously powerless to resist.

And, hey, it was just a hug.

Then came that day toward the end of the year when she admitted she was in love with me and told me she fantasized about us having sex.

And then she kissed me.

Make no mistake, lest you think I'm claiming innocence: I kissed back, with great enthusiasm.

After about ten seconds, I came to my senses. I gently pushed her away and told her that while I had feelings for her, too, I couldn't let this go where we both wanted to go; that it had been wrong of me to let it progress as far as it had.

That was the end of it. I stopped hugging her. I reestablished all the boundaries I had allowed to become too squishy. Once she graduated, I vowed there would be no more Breighlee Dumonts.

I can justify what happened between us in all kinds of ways: I was twenty-two, just four years older than her. This was years before I met Emily. Had Breighlee been a freshman in college, or some eighteen-year-old I met at a coffee shop, it wouldn't have been a big deal.

Except she wasn't.

She was my student.

And when I think about it now, what I regret the most—beyond my own personal defects—is that I became another in a long line of adults who failed her.

JOURNAL ENTRY: TUESDAY, NOVEMBER 14

When my future self reads this, she will probably think she sounds a bit stalkerish.

Probably because it *is* a bit stalkerish.

But I've memorized Mr. B's schedule. It's really not that hard. Life at Carrington is regimented down to the minute, so I know where he's going to be and when.

And maybe I've taken to showing up in those places now and then.

I call out, *Hey, Mr. B*, and then I give him my cutest smile.

And he says, *Hello, Ms. Goodloe. And, please, call me Mr. Bliss.*

But by now that's become our little running joke. When no one is around, he's stopped correcting me. He just smiles back, like he's amused by it all. And sometimes, if I've been able to time my "bumping into him" correctly, we're able to start a conversation.

We mostly talk about writing, because I know that's his favorite subject. Or I'll ask him about something that came up in class or something I've read. I usually have a few topics of conversation stored up in my mind for when I see him, because that's what a good stalker does.

All the while, I'm in eye-contact and hair-flip overdrive. And whenever I can be dressed in something other than my

Carrington uniform, I take advantage of it. I wonder if anyone else has noticed how slutty my casualwear has gotten.

Mr. B definitely has. I can follow that brief little up-and-down his eyes give me whenever I walk up.

I am enough of an expert in guy psychology that I *know* he's into me. Whatever doubts I had about that are gone.

And I know he would act on it, if I could just get us into the right situation where he *knew* he wouldn't get caught.

I can't exactly text him and be like, *Hey, Mr. B, want to go to the pond tonight?*

But I've been thinking. His apartment in Wentworth has its own entrance. If I could summon the courage to sneak over there some night, I could just knock on his door.

And then we could just see what happens.

CHAPTER 15

We all reread the *Boston Globe* article twice.

Jerry and Robbie are looking to me for guidance.

There is little question in my mind about what I ought to do. I'm just not sure if I have the fortitude.

I often say to my students: Integrity means doing the right thing even when no one's watching.

Or, in this case, when everyone's watching.

There may be consequences. But, whatever they are, I will have earned them. I just feel like my only way out of this—with Breighlee, with everything—is to stick with the truth.

"If we issue a statement to the *Boston Globe*, I assume every other media outlet will pick it up?" I ask.

"That's usually the way it works, yeah," Jerry says.

"Good. Then first I want to apologize to Breighlee Dumont for any pain I caused her. Then I want to say everything she's said is true, that I'm embarrassed by what I did, and that I deeply regret my lapse in judgment."

Jerry lifts an eyebrow. "You sure about that, Ace? We could just leave it as a 'no comment.'"

"No. I'm always telling my students the world would be a better place if public figures stopped trying to win every news cycle and admitted when they were wrong. I should live up to my own words."

"You're the boss," Jerry says, closing his briefcase and standing. "I'll type something up and email it to you."

"I don't know if my Carrington email is going to work anymore. You should use my author address."

I recite it for him.

"You got it. You can still change your mind if you want."

"I won't," I say.

"Okay. The only other thing I need to talk about is the filthy lucre. I can continue to represent you against my daughter's hopes and dreams, but I do need to bring some kind of retainer back to the firm."

Before I can stop her, my mother grabs the envelope off the table in front of her. "Here's fifty thousand dollars. Will that cover it?"

If Jerry is surprised, he doesn't show it. He just says, "That'll be fine, ma'am, thank you."

"Good, then it's settled," she says.

I'm just opening my mouth to object when she gives me a quick, hard glance that says, *Don't you dare fight me on this.* I'd have a better chance holding back an avalanche.

"Okay, then that's all I got for right now," he says, scooping up the envelope along with the rest of his paperwork and laying it in his briefcase.

He reminds me one more time about the appointment to get the ankle bracelet the next morning. We bid him farewell and he departs.

As soon as the door closes, my mother stands up and gives me a kiss on the top of the head. "I'm proud of you for telling the truth about that girl, Chahles."

You shouldn't be, I think to myself. But I don't say it. I just mumble a "thanks, Mom" and leave it at that.

She immediately moves onto safe topics—mainly gossip from back home. The people, places, and things of Robbie Bliss's life really don't change much, so it's easy to keep track.

I welcome the distraction. I know we really need to return to the subject of where she got that $50,000. If it's as bad as I fear, I can always pay her back from my nest egg. I just don't have the energy to return to that issue at the moment.

After we've talked awhile, my mother suggests we watch an old rom-com on the hotel's streaming service. By the time it's done, it's dark and my stomach is rumbling.

Robbie offers more PB&J, but I need something a little more substantial. There's a hole-in-the-wall Chinese restaurant in a strip mall just down from the hotel. I place an order for us and head out.

The hotel's automatic doors have just closed behind me when I hear a woman's voice say, "Charles."

I turn to see a woman a few years younger than me with eyes covered by owlish glasses.

"Addie Horne, *Hartford Courant*," she says, walking up to me with her hand outstretched.

"No comment," I say, holding my hands away and backpedaling toward the parking lot

"Wait, please," she begins.

And then she utters the one phrase that she knows I will find irresistible: "I think you're innocent."

* * *

I know I shouldn't trust a reporter.

I know there is great wisdom in *don't speak*.

But damn if I don't need someone who is neither related to me nor in my employ to actually believe in me.

"What did you say?" I ask, turning back toward her.

"I think you're innocent," she repeats. "I think this has nothing to do with you. Why would you kill Hayley Goodloe right after she accused you of having an affair with her? It would make you the world's most obvious suspect. No one is that stupid."

Which was exactly the argument I made to the detectives. And they might have even believed it except every piece of evidence they had found pointed them to the conclusion I really *was* that stupid.

"How did you find me?" I ask.

"Do you remember when you checked in yesterday?"

I flash back to the man who couldn't stop staring at the photo of Hayley in her school uniform.

"Yeah, sure."

"The desk clerk posted something on social media saying you were staying at his hotel and you were an asshole. It got shared five thousand times, including with a colleague of mine."

I am sure this post must violate some canon of hotel ethics, but that's little help to me now.

"Great," I say. "Listen, you seem nice, but I really don't have anything to say other than 'no comment' and 'call my lawyer.'"

I start walking away. She gives chase.

"I'm not looking for an interview—at least not right away," she says. "All I want is a mutually beneficial information-sharing alliance."

"What's that supposed to mean?" I ask without breaking stride.

"I tell you what I know. You tell me what you know. It's all off the record until it's not. Just promise me when the time comes and you're ready to grant an interview, you'll give me an exclusive."

"But I don't even know anything."

"Sure you do. You know a lot, I bet. But, hey, I'll share first, okay? The other reason I think you're innocent is because of a theory we're developing about Hayley's disappearance. It involves her mother, Diane."

I finally stop. This is bait, obviously. But at the moment, I'm plenty hungry.

"And we're off the record."

She holds up her right hand. "Absolutely. Won't print a word without your permission."

"Okay," I say. "Then what about Diane Goodloe?"

"You saw how she acted at that press conference, didn't you?"

"What? That she was a bit . . . steely?"

"Steely? She was full-on android. Don't you think if your daughter was kidnapped you'd be a little more freaked out?"

It was exactly what I thought, though I immediately find myself playing devil's advocate. "Oh, I don't know. People react to stress in all kinds of different ways. Ultimately, she's a woman in politics. If she's tough, everyone accuses her of being a bitch. If she's emotional, everyone accuses her of being weak. She can't win."

"Thank you for mansplaining to me how difficult it is to be a woman," she says, deadpan. "I had no idea until just now."

She finishes with an ironic smile.

"Sorry," I say.

"Forget about it. The thing is, there could be something there. Our political reporter tells me it's an open secret that Senator Qualls is not running for reelection. He's expected to formally announce his retirement next week."

"What does that have to do with Diane Goodloe?"

"She wants to replace him. She's already working furiously behind the scenes to clear the primary field, lining up endorsements and whatnot."

"Okay, so someone kidnapped her daughter to . . . what, stop her from running?"

"Exactly," Horne says. "How is a woman with a kidnapped daughter supposed to announce herself as a candidate for U.S. Senate? It would look . . . bizarre, don't you think?"

"So, in this scenario, the person behind Hayley Goodloe's kidnapping is someone else who badly wants that Senate seat. But since they think they can't beat Diane Goodloe fair and square in a primary, they're trying to keep her on the bench instead?"

"Exactly. And Diane Goodloe is smart enough to have figured that out. That's why she wasn't more emotional at the presser. She knows that whoever has Hayley only has to keep her until just after the June filing deadline. Then Hayley is allowed to 'escape,' or is released, or whatever. Either way, she comes home scared but unharmed."

"You think anyone out there would really be that ruthless?"

"Politics are pretty vicious these days," Horne says. "And you're talking about a chance to waltz into the U.S. Senate and then stay as long as you like. That's a pretty good gig."

"Okay, let's say I buy that. Who is the perhaps-future U.S. senator behind this scheme?"

Horne adjusts her glasses. "Well, this is where we're deep off the record. And I mean *deeeeeep*. This name never escaped my lips, got it?"

"Got it."

"Have you ever heard of Victoria Brock?"

As soon as she says the name, I just about fall over.

"As in, former attorney general and current Carrington board member Victoria Brock?" I ask.

"She lost in a closely contested primary the last time a Senate seat opened up. Our political reporter says she's been sniffing around more than anyone other than perhaps Diane Goodloe, to the point where a lot of the party elders were already viewing it as a two-horse race."

I'm now thinking through the plausibility of this. Brock would have known full well Diane Goodloe was going to run. They walk in the same circles and have surely been hitting up the same donors and kissing the same rings for months.

She also would have known—before virtually anyone else—that I was ripe to be framed for Hayley Goodloe's disappearance. Once the family made the accusation, Ambrose's first phone call was probably to Brock.

It would have given her enough of a head start to concoct her scheme, then implement it. She surely has the money to hire people to help her with the heavy lifting.

By the time we had our meeting in Ambrose's office, she could have already had plans well underway.

Beyond that, I think of what I know about her personality—cold, ambitious, remorseless.

Someone like that could certainly think of her ascension to the United States Senate being worth a few months of Hayley Goodloe's inconvenience.

"Is there any . . . evidence of this?" I ask.

"It's just a theory at this point," she admits. "To be honest, we'd have a tough time proving it. A newspaper's investigatory powers pretty much stop at FOIA requests. But *you* might be able to help prove it."

"How?"

"By taking it to the police. They have powers we don't have. They can subpoena bank accounts, phone records, video evidence, you name it."

"Why don't you just take it to the police, then?"

"We can't," Horne says. "If we're wrong, it exposes us legally. Taking unfounded accusations of this nature to the police smells like malice, and malice is an essential element of libel. But if *you* were to take this to the police . . . you're just a private citizen, suspected of a crime, trying to clear your name."

"Right, of course. But I'm still confused. What do you get out of all of this?"

"Information. Scoops. From you. If the cops start finding stuff about Victoria Brock, you'll know it because they won't be all over you anymore. Maybe they'll even spill a little bit of what they know. Merely the fact that the police were investigating Victoria Brock would be a huge, huge story at this point. Once we get a hint about what the cops are up to, we can always leverage it for more information. Small leaks turn into big ones pretty fast. All of it ends up making you look like not-the-bad-guy. Like I said: mutually beneficial information sharing."

"And all I have to do is take this theory to the police and let them do all the hard work."

"Exactly."

I'm sure there's a way this could backfire.

But I can't think of it at the moment. If the police don't find anything, I'm no worse off.

If they do find something, I get my life back. Or at least some portion of it.

That possibility alone is the first thing I've felt hopeful about in days.

I store her number in my phone, and promise to call her if anything shakes loose.

JOURNAL ENTRY: FRIDAY, NOVEMBER 17

Today's episode of *The Diane Goodloe Show* began with a breathless phone call from the host herself.

She finally got her meeting with Robert Qualls!

Sorry about the above exclamation point. I know I overuse them. Mr. B says a good writer gets to use one exclamation point per month—and that might be an exclamation point too many.

But that was the way my mother talked about it! Apparently, Steeeeve is besties with one of Qualls's senior staffers, who arranged for her to get some face-time with Qualls! Before any of the other candidates could even get in the door! And I should be so, so excited about it!

Anyhow, Qualls confirmed for her in a roundabout way that he's calling it quits and will make a formal announcement in January. In the meantime, he asked her to keep it quiet—just like my mom asked *me* to keep it quiet, like there's anyone in my life who even cares.

He then told her he wants his successor to be a woman, because there's never been a female U.S. senator from Connecticut and he feels it's time.

Like, duh, it's actually past time, you old loser.

The only trick is, he won't say *which* woman. All he told my mom is that he'll make his endorsement before the primary is contested in August.

So my mom is now basically acting like her full-time job is to smooch Senator Qualls's ass—or any other part of him that needs smooching. She and Steeeeve are now formulating this detailed attack plan about how they're going to approach other people who are close to Qualls and recruit them into the lobbying effort.

Other moms talk to their daughters about the importance of maintaining a healthy body image or being careful to practice safe sex.

Mine talks to me about backroom politicking.

And I'm not going to repeat that she's a narcissist, but during the course of the entire conversation, she never once asked me how I was doing.

I am reminded of something my father told me a few weeks back. He said the only reason my mother even had me in the first place was because she didn't think anyone would vote for a woman who wasn't a mother.

So, basically, I owe my life to my ability to serve as a campaign prop.

CHAPTER 16

Over the course of the evening, while working our way through Chinese food and watching yet another cheesy rom-com, I make a few efforts to pry from my mother the source of the money in that envelope.

She won't give it up. We both know it's not can money. But Robbie Bliss is tougher than barnacles. I can't shake the truth out of her.

It's probably more accurate to say: I lack the energy to throw the massive tantrum that would be needed to elicit the truth from my mother, so I let her keep her secret for the time being.

The remainder of the night passes quietly. My first awareness that Thursday has begun is when I hear Robbie bustling around the hotel suite, getting ready to depart. This is not unusual for her. I've never known her to sleep past six.

As I toss on yesterday's clothes so I can walk her out, there is this strange ache inside me. I know she can't stay. There's nothing more she can do for me here; she's probably done too much already.

Selfishly, I just wish that the only person guaranteed to stay by my side could stick around a little longer.

Before we leave the hotel room, she insists on saying a prayer for me, asking God to protect me *and* Hayley Goodloe, and to deliver us both safely out of this terrible mess.

I give an amen to that.

Once out in the parking lot, she hugs me one last time.

"If you need any more money, just ask," she says. "I'll get it for you."

"Thanks, Mom. But for the last time, *how*?"

"Don't you worry about that," she replies. "God is watching over you, Chahles. That's all you need to know."

Then she climbs into the Cherokee, and I say my own prayer that its aging crankshaft makes it through the seven-hour trip back to Maine. I watch her drive away until she's out of sight.

It's still early, and I have time to kill until I need to leave for my appointment to get my ankle monitor attached, so I check my author email account to see if Jerry has sent a statement regarding Breighlee Dumont.

When I first set up charles@charlesblissbooks.com, it was part necessity, part vanity. I told myself a big-time author would need a separate email to accommodate the enormous rush of fan mail and speaker requests that were surely coming his way.

For the first few months after *Washington County* came out, I actually did receive a trickle of fan mail.

That soon dried up. From then on, it was just junk. Even when the rare email had a subject like "Your Book" or "Washington County" it would turn out to be a come-on from a company trying to get me to pay money in exchange for their surefire online book marketing program.

It got so depressing I stopped checking the account with any regularity. It was just another reminder of my failure.

Logging into the account now, I am confronted with several months' worth of unanswered missives. The older stuff appears to be the usual spam. But there are at least thirty emails from the previous day and a half, all from names I do not recognize.

Jerry's email is buried in the middle of the pile. The statement he's written is serviceable, but feels a little too lawyerly. I completely rework it. The last thing I want is for this to read like an "I'm sorry if she was offended" apology.

Also, it feels good to actually have something to write. Emily always points out that I'm happier when I'm writing.

When I'm done, I consider crafting an additional email to Jerry sharing the Victoria Brock theory, but some things are better explained in person. I send the new statement, then hit the shower.

Getting the ankle bracelet put on kills the rest of the morning. The technician who affixes it gives me the ground rules. I can't take it off, or the monitoring company will be notified immediately. I need to charge it once a day. I can shower, but I can't submerge it in water—so no baths, and no swimming. And if it ever buzzes, I have five minutes to press a button on the front to assure everyone I'm still there.

When I emerge from the building with it strapped to me, I feel this weight on me.

This is not strictly metaphorical. There's actually this damn contraption on my ankle. I feel conspicuously shackled.

No matter where I go from now on, the State of Connecticut will have means of knowing it. Big Brother has hopped onto my leg and is now hanging on for the ride.

On my way back to the hotel, I stop at a grocery store to pick up some supplies—a microwavable meal, chips, pretzels, beer—so I don't have to go out later. It's before noon and the place isn't crowded. But it's like everyone in there knows I'm a marked man.

It is unnerving. And wearying.

By the time I'm back to the safety of my shabby little hotel, I'm exhausted. I feel relief once the door closes behind me, though it's unclear to me whether my room is a refuge or a prison.

Maybe both.

I turn on my phone again and, ignoring all the new missed calls that have come in, dial Jerry's number.

"Hey, Ace," he answers.

"Hey, I just wanted to check in. I got my ankle bracelet."

"Good man."

"Did you get that new statement I wrote regarding Breighlee Dumont?"

"I did. It looks good, though I sent you a few tweaks. Did you not get that email?"

"I haven't checked yet," I say. "I'll do that as soon as we hang up. But first there's something I need to run by you."

"Okay. Shoot."

I walk him through my interaction with Addie Horne, ending with her plan to take "our" suspicions about Victoria Brock to the police.

"So," I conclude, "what do you think?"

"I think it's dangerous for you to be talking to a reporter about *anything*," he says. "You're trusting this woman you don't know with your life. If she decides to burn you and put something you said in the paper, and it happens to be something that incriminates you—or something that can be used against you in *any* way—you can be damn sure the prosecution is going to clip it out and wave it around under the jury's noses. You understand that, right?"

"I didn't really say anything she could have used. I mostly just listened to her unspool this theory."

"You'd be surprised how much talking most people do even when they're supposed to be listening."

"Well, at this point, if it's a mistake, it's a mistake I've already made. Now tell me: Does it make sense to take this Victoria Brock thing to the police or not?"

The line goes silent for a moment or two, long enough that I wonder if the call has dropped.

Then he allows, "It's not the worst idea I've ever heard."

I'm starting to recognize that, for Jerry Cordova, this qualifies as a glowing endorsement.

"You understand that if we tell the police we think someone else did it, they don't *have* to investigate it," he says. "They're not under any legal obligation to chase a cockamamie theory for us."

"Of course."

"Don't get me wrong, they probably will. They know if I'm mentioning it now, there's a chance I'll bring it up at trial. If they haven't looked into it—at least to rule it out—I get to hammer them for doing a shoddy investigation and having tunnel vision on you. It starts to create doubt, and doubt is your friend."

"So are you going to tell them about it?"

"Let me sleep on it," he says. "In the meantime, promise me you won't talk to that reporter anymore. If we have something to tell her, let me handle it, okay?"

"Got it. Anything else going on I need to know about?"

"Not at the moment," he says. "Just lay low. Oh, and answer that email."

"Right," I say. "Talk to you soon."

I power down my phone—I don't need the distraction—and open up my laptop.

Another half-dozen emails have come in since I last checked, but the one that first catches my eye isn't the one from Jerry Cordova.

It's from Portia Swan, my onetime editor, and it consists of just one question: "Why is Emily Vanderburgh shopping a manuscript with no name on it that is obviously something you've written?"

For a few minutes, I just stare at the email, trying to make sense of it.

Emily is shopping my manuscript? Without my name on it? And without my permission?

It's baffling—and not just because I think everything I've written since *Washington County* belongs at the bottom of a trash can.

What is she trying to pull here? Did she really think I wouldn't hear about it?

I would call her and confront her about this, but she's pretty effectively shut off all lines of communication. I can't go back out to her parents' house either. Not without putting my liberty at risk.

The only way to even start to understand more about what's happening is to reach out to my ex-editor. Her number is still stored in my phone, so I power it back on and hit the DIAL button.

"Hi Portia, it's Charles Bliss."

"Hello," she says. And then, because she's Portia—busy, important, direct—she skips the small talk and goes straight to the point. "Can you explain this submission I got from Emily Vanderburgh?"

"Not really, to be honest. She's, ahh . . . We're not exactly in touch at the moment."

"It's actually not bad, so far. I recognized immediately it was your voice. Plus, I know the way you format a manuscript, you tend to underuse commas. This is your manuscript."

"But she . . . she removed my name from it?"

"There's no title page. And you're not mentioned anywhere in the submission letter. You really know nothing about this?"

"Not a thing. Do you think she submitted it to other editors besides you?"

"I have no idea. You may want to have Jane Janikowski ask around. She's still your agent, yes?"

"Not . . . not really. The last time we talked was probably four years ago. She made it pretty clear she was done working with me."

"Well, you may want to reach out to her anyway. She's still the agent-of-record on *Washington County*. I actually have a call with her set up for later today."

"Why?"

"Because demand for your book is suddenly through the roof. Didn't you know?"

"No, I guess not."

"Well, you're trending right now," she says. "As I understand it, 'Charles Bliss' is top ten on Google and it's exploding on all the socials. It's certainly a boon to my employer that cable news is referring to you almost exclusively as 'author Charles Bliss.'"

"And that's selling books?"

"This is publishing, dear. Celebrity and notoriety might as well be interchangeable. We had a few hundred copies of *Washington County* sitting in a warehouse in Virginia. From what I'm told, they've all been snapped up and people are now scouring used bookstores for your book. We're actually considering whether we want to rush out another printing. It's pretty ironic. I can't tell you how many copies of that book we pulped."

I don't need the reminder.

She continues: "Listen, I don't know what's going on with you legally, and we probably shouldn't get into that. But if I were you, I'd be taking a lot of notes right now. Depending on how things turn out, we'd be definitely interested in publishing your story. You could write it as nonfiction, or maybe as a thinly veiled *roman à clef.* Think about it."

I promise her I will do more than just think about it. Then she hurries me off the phone. I sit there for a moment. My head might as well be a dreidel it's spinning so fast.

Writing another book—a book someone might actually want to read—is a dizzying thought.

But I can suddenly think of nothing else I would rather do. I open a new document on my computer.

"During my many years of affiliation with Carrington Academy—first as a student, now as faculty member—I have never once been commanded to appear in the head of school's office," I write.

I lean back and study the screen. Would I read a book that started like that?

Yes, I would.

I practically lunge at the keyboard and begin typing furiously.

Very, very briefly, I will interrupt for . . .

MIDLOGUE 4

Just so you're not confused: what you just read is the exact moment in history when I began writing this book.

JOURNAL ENTRY: WEDNESDAY, NOVEMBER 22

Wellllllll, the hits just keep on coming.

For the last few weeks I've been trying to figure out why my dad was marrying Ashley. Why not just date her until he got bored and dump her? That's what he's done with every other woman he's been with since Mom.

But it all makes sense now.

I should start by setting the scene. Mr. B says beginning writers often make the mistake of not giving readers enough context.

Remember, the point of writing is to impart meaning, he says. *And meaning often comes from context.*

So here's the context: My parents are supposed to have a deal where they swap holidays. If one person gets Thanksgiving, the other gets Christmas. Except most of the time they just ignore who's supposed to have what holiday and—without even asking me what I want—they do whatever is convenient for them.

My dad seldom finds me convenient. But this year he insisted I come to his place.

Honestly, it was fine with me. If I went to Mom's, I'd have to spend Thanksgiving with Grayson, listening to him jerk off in the next bedroom.

It's so gross. There was one time when he left his computer on and I saw the title of one of the videos he had been watching. No lie, it was something like, "Stepbrother gives petite teen stepsister cumload facial."

So, yeah, while I would be trying to catch up on homework, he would be next door, fantasizing about me giving him a blowjob.

Seriously, seriously disgusting.

So, anyway, I'm at my dad's place in the city for Thanksgiving. It's just him, me, and Ashley, which is a little depressing and weird. Like, isn't Thanksgiving supposed to be about being surrounded by lots of family?

But apparently my family is about to get a little bigger. When dinner was served tonight, he tapped his wineglass and made another one of his grand pronouncements: I was going to be a big sister.

At first, I was like, *What the hell are you talking about?*

And then he said it more plainly.

Ashley is pregnant.

Lucky her.

My dad said he's suuuuper excited to be a father again. He said he always wanted to have a second kid with Mom, but she would never go for it.

I'm skeptical. He didn't exactly show a ton of interest in fatherhood the first time. I'm not saying he's lying about how excited he is. Ashley has him wrapped around her little finger. He probably very much believes he wants to be a dad again.

Right now.

But check back two years from now.

The real truth about my father is that the only thing that has ever really held his long-term interest is attending to his own needs. This is a man who would spend one weekend a month with me and still hire a nanny.

So, literally, I would be like, *Daddy, will you please play Uno with me?* And he would be sitting there, just reading the paper, and suggest, *Why don't you ask Consuela?*

Whatever.

I just hope he hires the same lawyers he did last time. Because the moment Ashley walks in on him having sex with one of his nude models, that prenup is going to need to be ironclad.

CHAPTER 17

I write maniacally all through the afternoon.

Normally, I'm a painfully slow first-drafter. Even when my thoughts are adequately developed—and they never are—it takes time to find the right words and put them in the correct order.

This is like nothing I've ever done. Words, sentences, and whole paragraphs spring onto the page fully formed. I don't even need to stop and think about what I want to say, how I should say it, or where the plot should go.

All I have to do is write what happened next.

I stop only when I notice the sun sinking. I'd like to take a jog before it's fully dark.

When I return, I makes the mistake of powering on my phone to see if Jerry reached out.

He didn't. But the *Boston Globe* must have printed my statement, because there's a fresh round of missed calls and texts, in ever-more-overwhelming numbers.

I shut off the phone. It's after five. The beer in the fridge is calling me and I can think of no good reason not to answer it. I have nowhere to be, nothing to do, and plenty of pain to dull.

The first beer goes down fast and delicious. So does the second. Before long I hear a familiar voice outside my room.

"Special delivery. I've got an icy order of HBT for the occupant of room 213."

I welcome Leo into the suite. Writing has at least somewhat relieved my loneliness—to say nothing of my boredom—but it's always nice to have Leo's company.

Especially now.

"Thanks for . . . for coming," I say, my voice faltering a little. "You're a good friend."

"Don't get too flattered. It was either hang out with you or do grading for my freshman composition class. I have to put some of those essays through Google Translate just to understand them."

"You sure I'm not putting you in too much of a hole?"

"Eh, if I give them all A-minuses they won't whine too much," he says. "Besides, I could probably use a little HBT myself. I took a cab here tonight, so—*prost*."

He cracks open a beer and we get to chatting. He tells me about the scene on campus, where there's a candlelight vigil scheduled for Hayley tonight.

As the beer continues to flow, I share the news from Portia Swan.

He leans back and takes this all in.

Then he comes out with: "Have you ever thought Emily is the one who framed you?"

I practically spit out my drink.

"What?!? Why would she do that?"

"Isn't it obvious? She's trying to steal your manuscript."

I hadn't even considered this. It's so brazen. She couldn't possibly think she would ever be able to get away with this. And yet . . .

Did she think I'd be so occupied by other legal problems that I wouldn't be able to do anything about it? That I'd be locked up and unable to afford an intellectual property lawyer in addition to criminal representation? Is this just opportunistic theft?

Even still, I say, "I don't know, man."

"Come on. Think back to Monday morning. After you told her about Hayley, she *insisted* you go for that run. She wouldn't leave until you left. You don't think maybe she swiped that bottle of Glenmorangie and some shot glasses on her way out?"

I don't have a reply to this.

"Then think about the rest of her day," Leo continues. "She supposedly went to school, but did she really? Can anyone vouch for that?"

"Well, she TA'd classes in the morning, so there would be students who'd notice if she didn't show up."

"Yeah, but what about the afternoon, when the kidnapping actually took place?"

"She was just in the library, working on her dissertation."

"Well, now, that's pretty convenient, isn't it?" Leo asks. "And her school is, what, ten minutes away from Hayley's house?"

He gets up to refresh his beer. I am a few ahead of him and my brain is already buzzing hard enough that it's struggling to form coherent thoughts.

"Okay, but wait," I say. "How would Emily have pulled this off? I mean, she and Hayley are basically the same size. It's not like Emily could have overpowered her."

"She wouldn't have needed to overpower anyone if she had a gun. It's amazing how persuasive a pound and a half of steel can be if you shape it the right way."

"Come on. Where would Emily get a gun?"

"You underestimate how resourceful your wife is. You're the one who's always talking about what a hard-on you have for how competent she is."

"Yeah, but even if she *could* have done it . . . Why *would* she? Why would she want to destroy me like that?"

"You really need me to spell it out for you?" he says as he sits back down. "One, she thinks you've been screwing a seventeen-year-old girl. That's a lot different than a drunken one-night stand with the local bartender. There's the gross factor and there's also the jealousy factor. Emily is a *much* younger woman who also happens to be drop-dead gorgeous and fabulously wealthy. If Emily kidnaps and kills Hayley, it's like a two-for-one. She punishes the person who stole her man *and* she gets revenge against her cheating husband."

"You're making Emily out to be some kind of . . . of sociopath. She's not . . . She's not capable of something like that."

"You once told me you didn't think she was capable of walking out on your marriage, either," he points out. "You don't think she's smart enough to be able to hide who she really is? You have to face it that you don't really know who you're married to."

"Yeah, but . . . Let's just say she's a sociopath, purely motivated by self-interest, with no conscience whatsoever. Even with all that said, you really think she'd go through the trouble of stealing my manuscript?"

"Look, I know you may find this hard to believe, but maybe it doesn't suck as much as you think. She worked in publishing long enough to have at least some idea of what sells. Your name may be radioactive because of your crappy sales history but hers isn't."

I suck in a sharp breath.

"You're going to need to get me another beer," I say.

He obliges.

"Dude, I'm sorry to say all this, but I don't want to see you being played," he says. "Think about what you were when the two of you met. You were going to be this literary superstar. She thought she was marrying a famous *author*, not a high school English teacher.

She didn't sign up to be trapped at some boarding school for pampered rich kids for the rest of her life. Look at her parents. Look at how she was raised. She wants to *be* one of the pampered rich kids. She wants to be flitting around Manhattan, going to all the right parties, living the good life. She sees that book as her ticket back to that world."

I'm struggling against this whole idea. On some level, I simply don't want to believe it. I don't even want to contemplate it. This is a knife in the back *and* the guts. It burns too much. Even in boozy Connecticut, there's not enough alcohol to anesthetize that pain.

"But you said . . . I thought you were thinking Rip was the one who did this," I say feebly.

"Look, I don't know anything, right? I'm just saying look at the possibilities here. What do they talk about on those cop shows? Means, motive, and opportunity? You've got to face facts: Emily has all three."

JOURNAL ENTRY: FRIDAY, NOVEMBER 24

I would say the following is unbelievable, but it's actually a million percent believable.

The douchey behavior of W. Johnson Goodloe III is finally catching up to him.

One of his former nude models is trying to #MeToo his ass.

She's hired a lawyer who is threatening a lawsuit, public embarrassment, the whole thing.

I learned all of this today. Apparently, *this* was the real reason Dad wanted to spend Thanksgiving with me.

He waited until Ashley was out shopping (Ashley shops a lot) and then he pulled me aside and said he needed to talk to me about "some grown-up stuff"—which is normally his code for: money.

And I guess this ultimately does come down to money, because apparently the plaintiff's lawyer is going to try to recover damages from the Goodloe Family Trust, which I'm a part of. This lawyer can't get at *my* trust, which is separate from the family trust.

But still, if there's a lawsuit, I'm going to be served, too.

And my dad, narcissist that he is, wanted to give his side of the story first.

He said that I shouldn't worry, because, first of all, he makes all his models sign an NDA, which I know all about.

(More of *Growing Up Goodloe*: I got my first talk about NDAs—nondisclosure agreements—long before I ever got a talk about sex or drugs. My dad even asks his plumbers to sign NDAs.)

Dad said he also makes all his models sign a contract that makes it impossible for them to sue him in court. I don't know how that works, exactly, but he seemed pretty sure about himself.

He said that in the worst-case scenario, this will cost him a little money—Dad defines anything under a few million dollars as "a little money"—and that it's totally not a big deal and I shouldn't worry.

At no point did he talk about whether he actually had sex with this woman.

We both know he totally did.

I asked him whether Ashley knew about any of this. And, of course, she doesn't. It sounds like he intends to keep it that way.

He'll probably be successful.

People with money often are.

Still, I jotted down some notes after my dad was done talking—capturing details about the scene so I can make it come alive, just like Mr. B taught me—because this is *definitely* going in *Searing Memoir* someday.

Hey, *I* never signed an NDA.

CHAPTER 18

The sun is otherworldly bright Friday morning. It's like I went to bed on Earth but woke up on Mercury.

I didn't manage to get the blinds all the way closed the previous night, and now there's this beam of light slicing into the room. It lands in the exact place on the bed where my face is resting.

It's so dazzling, it feels like it was shot from a laser. It practically scalds my eyes through my closed eyelids.

For a while, I just lie there, meekly accepting my punishment. The entire back portion of my skull is throbbing.

When I finally summon the energy to at least roll in the other direction, away from the blinding glare, I hear a crunching sound.

It's an empty bag of potato chips, which I must have taken into bed with me the previous evening. There are also tiny shards of fried potato pressing into my midsection.

I'm not sure I believe in hell; but if there is one, this must be what it's like.

It had been my intention to get back to writing. Instead, I spend the morning drifting in and out of bad sleep, too hungover to do much else. At midday, I finally drag myself into the shower. I turn it as hot as I can stand it, then finish it off cold.

After that, I stumble across the main road outside my hotel to a diner, still feeling a little drunk. Only when I've had coffee, a greasy cheeseburger, and a pile of fries do I start to feel vaguely human again.

I'm still trying to piece together the previous evening, which feels a bit like a dream. I have a memory of Leo arriving, but not of him leaving. I hope he found a cab to take him home. I wonder if he's suffering as much as I am.

Probably not. I went at it a lot harder than he did.

After a quick grocery run, I return to the room and clean up from last night's disaster,

Then I call Jerry Cordova.

"What's up, Ace?" he asks.

I don't want to overburden him with this newest theory regarding Emily; especially when I still don't know what he really thinks about my last theory regarding Victoria Brock.

"I wanted to see how you were feeling now that you slept on the Victoria Brock thing."

"Yeah, I slept on it and I decided it couldn't hurt us to have the cops give it a walk around the block," he says. "I put in a call to your good friend Detective Prisbell about it."

"What did you tell her?"

"I told her I thought it would show good faith on their part if they looked into it."

"And how did she respond?"

"I believe the right word for her response would be 'dubious,'" Jerry says. "She said something vague about how she'd take it under advisement. I gotta be honest, Ace, I don't know how hard she's gonna chase it."

"Is there anything we can do about that?"

"Not really, unless you feel like throwing some of your own money at it."

"What do you mean?"

"I mean: hire a private investigator," he says.

"To investigate Victoria Brock?"

"Exactly."

"What would they be able to do?"

"A lot less than what the cops can do if they decided to get serious, but a lot more than what you can probably do at the moment. Basically, a PI could follow Victoria Brock around and take pictures if she's doing anything fishy or associating with anyone that raises alarm bells. You gotta remember, a PI can ask questions, but unlike the cops, they can't make anyone answer. They can't look at bank accounts or anything like that. They can only access the same public records that everyone else does—though they're usually pretty good at that."

I say nothing. I'm imagining some guy in a fedora with a camera slung around his neck, clicking madly away from the bushes.

"Why don't *you* sleep on it," Jerry suggests. "I've got a shop that I use. They're good. But they're not magic and they're not cheap. Are you ready to throw money at the *Hartford Courant*'s wild theory?"

"I don't know," I admit.

"Well, that's what you need to sleep on."

"Did Prisbell say anything else? Anything new in the case?"

"Nothing she feels like telling us about. We're not the good guys, in case you forgot."

It's unlikely I will anytime soon. As we wind down the conversation, he volunteers that I can call him over the weekend if I need to.

"I'm not exactly a big party guy anymore," he says. "And the Knicks only have one game so I won't be busy."

After we end the call, I'm about to turn off my phone—because that's how it has stayed for days now—when the urge strikes to keep it powered on. Being without my phone has been like being down a limb. If nothing else, I want the soothing comfort of my adult pacifier back.

I still don't intend to answer any of the calls or texts coming from numbers that aren't already in my contacts. But I need to be able to take calls from Jerry, my mother, and others who may need to get in touch with me.

I swipe at the screen and start wading through the digital carnage. The voicemail box is full and I'm simply going to leave it that way. If no one can leave a new voicemail, I won't have to bother with it.

The missed calls are also easy to dispatch. I simply swipe through all the recents until they're done.

Then I start rifling through missed text messages. Most are from members of the media. A small handful of the messages are from friends. None of them know what to say, but there's a lot of "hope you're doing okay" and "thinking about you" type sentiments.

It's thoughtful of them. Though there's this nervous hesitance to all the messages. Reading between the lines, what they really want to know is: *Did you actually do this? Am I going to spend the rest of my life shaking my head when someone mentions your name?*

The longer texts get a "thanks for the kind words" type response; for the shorter ones, I just hit the thumbs-up button.

I'm near the top of my messages when I come across yet another 860 area code that is not stored in my contacts list. At first glance, it's nothing special. I open it expecting it will be another enterprising reporter, trying to wrangle a comment from me.

Except it's not.

It's far more intriguing.

The person has sent three separate texts, each of which appears in their own little green bubble, which tells me they're not coming from another iPhone. The first reads:

Hello, Charles Bliss, I want to help you. I bet you're dying to know who kidnapped Hayley Goodloe. If you are, answer this question: What is Nutmeg Consultancy LLC??? And what to do they really do?

The next is:

Aren't you at least curious?

Finally, there's:

Why aren't you answering me? Don't you want to know where Hayley is?

I check the time these texts arrived, and in each case it's in the noon hour—the first on Wednesday, the next on Thursday, the final one today, roughly two hours ago.

Whoever the sender is, they're disciplined enough to wait a day between messages. But they want to engage me and have me play along with . . . whatever game this is.

It feels like some kind of riddle that I can't begin to solve.

What is Nutmeg Consultancy LLC? Connecticut is the Nutmeg State, so it's local. But I've never heard of it. I don't exactly have a lot of need for consulting services.

I open my laptop and google it. The top hit leads me to a simple website decorated with generic stock photos of Connecticut's capitol and a block of text:

> Nutmeg Consultancy wants to be your full-service partner in helping you achieve your electoral goals. Whether through traditional direct mail, targeted individual appeals, or the latest in digital solicitation, Nutmeg Consultancy will work with you to leverage your existing networks while also expanding your capacity. With decades of

EXPERIENCE ACROSS HUNDREDS OF CAMPAIGNS, WE PRIDE OURSELVES ON OUR TOTAL COMMITMENT TO YOUR SUCCESS. CONTACT US TODAY TO DISCOVER THE NUTMEG DIFFERENCE.

Jargon aside, this is some kind of political fundraising firm. That's what they mean by achieving "electoral goals," right?

I don't know much about politics, except that there's way too much money involved in it—and it seems to only grow more obscene with each election cycle. I can imagine that candidates like Victoria Brock hire experts like Nutmeg Consultancy to help them keep up.

Except whoever is texting me is suggesting they do something else? Something more nefarious?

Is that what this is? Did Victoria Brock hire Nutmeg Consultancy to, among other things, kidnap Hayley Goodloe? Is that how Nutmeg decided to help Victoria achieve her electoral goals?

There is a navigation bar at the bottom of the page with three options: ABOUT, CONTACT, and CLIENT LOGIN.

I click on the CONTACT link, which leads to a simple form that gives away nothing more about where Nutmeg Consultancy LLC might be.

The ABOUT takes me to a portrait of a rather ordinary-looking middle-aged white man in a suit, smiling benignly. Beneath him is another block of text:

NUTMEG CONSULTANCY WAS FOUNDED BY CHRIS SANDMAN, WHO BELIEVES THERE'S NO SUCH THING AS A ONE-SIZE-FITS-ALL APPROACH TO PROBLEM-SOLVING. EVERY CAMPAIGN AND COMMITTEE HAS DIFFERENT

NEEDS, FROM THE MACRO TO THE MICRO. WHETHER THE ELECTION IS ON THE LOCAL, STATE, OR FEDERAL LEVEL, CHRIS HAS LEARNED THAT SUCCESS BEGINS WITH ALIGNING STRATEGIES. NUTMEG HAS DEVELOPED A TEAM OF SEASONED PROFESSIONALS WHO WILL USE STATE-OF-THE-ART DATA MINING TECHNIQUES TO HELP YOU MAXIMIZE YOUR POTENTIAL AND ACHIEVE YOUR GOALS.

As someone who teaches writing for a living, I am constantly amazed that, while language was devised to convey meaning, human beings have developed a remarkable ability to pour out a great volume of words that mean nothing at all.

This bio is a prime example. Who is Chris Sandman? What are his credentials? Where did he attend college? Who has he worked for? Is there truly a "team of seasoned professionals" behind him or does his "team" consist of two cocker spaniels and whoever mows his lawn?

I turn back to my original Google search. Other than that first hit, Nutmeg Consultancy seems to have kept a low online profile—or at least one that Google can't seem to untangle from other consulting companies with "Nutmeg" in their name.

The same is true when I google "Nutmeg Consultancy Chris Sandman." The top result remains the same, but now I'm getting other Chris Sandmans in other parts of the country who happen to be consultants. Chris Sandman is too common a name; and, in any event, this particular Chris Sandman is not seeking personal fame.

This makes a certain amount of sense. His business likely comes primarily from word of mouth, not random candidates doing random Google searches. And most politicians probably wouldn't want a fundraising consultant that went around bragging about all the sly ways he helped his clients suck money out of the electorate.

Beyond that, if the truth about Nutmeg Consultancy could be found with a simple Google search, the person behind these green text bubbles wouldn't have needed to bother me.

I turn back to the texts. Whoever sent them—a troll? a scammer? a friend? a foe?—wants my attention.

They now have it.

What they intend to do with it is yet another unanswered question.

I weigh my options here. The first is, simply, to do nothing. Without even meaning to, that's what I've been doing already, having gone three days without answering the first text.

But I have to be frank with myself: there's no way I'll be able to continue that. I'm already too amped up by the possibility—however slim—that this person does, in fact, want to help me; and that this interaction will lead to some outcome that will extricate me from this nightmare.

Whoever is sending this is someone on the inside of . . . something. They already know *I* didn't do this. And they're posturing like they know a lot more about what's really going on.

If nothing else, they know more than I do.

Beyond that, it's hard to figure out a downside to at least attempting to engage this person. I've already lost my wife, most of my friends, my job, my home, my reputation, and—for all intents and purposes—my future. What more could this person take from me?

Besides, it's just a text. Even if this is just someone toying with me for some malicious fun, there's only so much damage this Green Bubble person can do to me with a text.

I just have to be smart and assume that whoever is texting me is a member of the media, who will then post this exchange on

Twitter; or a member of law enforcement, who will use it against me at trial. I vow to keep it simple and mostly ask questions. Those can hardly be considered incriminating.

So, here goes. I tap out: HI, MY PHONE HAS BEEN OFF, SO I'M JUST NOW SEEING THIS. WHO IS THIS?

Then I hit SEND and wait for a reply.

JOURNAL ENTRY: MONDAY, NOVEMBER 27

A sentence I thought I'd never type:

I'm so happy that Thanksgiving break is over.

It has been ten days since I've seen him. Ten days!

The dorms opened back up at noon today, and I was back by, like, 12:01. I just wanted to walk around campus and give myself a chance to bump into him.

And by "him," future self, I of course mean Mr. B. I've been thinking about him nonstop the whole time I was gone, having these conversations in my head with him.

Okay, that sounds weirder than it really is. It's not like I'm having hallucinations. It's more just that I imagine talking to him about things, and then I imagine how he might respond.

Writers do that.

Mr. B certainly does. He told us in class one time he has what he described as "a large internal world," where he has conversations with his characters in his head all the time.

I wonder: Does he ever talk with *me* in his head? What do I say?

Does he fantasize about me the way I do him?

Ah! I just miss him. I know it's pathetic. And the worst thing is, it's not like I'm ever really *with* him in a real way.

When we're in class, there are always other people in the room. And when I manufacture opportunities to bump into him, it's not like I'm getting quality time with him. It's always just in passing, a stolen moment here or there where I say whatever thing I've planned to say next.

But it's not a real conversation. It's not quality time.

I need to get him alone and actually tell him how I feel about him. I already let the first marking period go by. Soon it's going to be Christmas break. I know I promised myself I would wait until graduation—because we can't *really* be together until then—but I'm at the point where I just need to know whether it's even possible he'll ever feel the same way about me.

Keeping my feelings from him, carrying all of this inside, I'm not sure how much more of this I can take. This thing just keeps growing and growing and it's getting too big.

If I don't share it with him, I'm just going to burst.

CHAPTER 19

For the remainder of the afternoon, I throw myself into writing.

I'm trying not to make it an exercise in therapy. No one wants to read drivel that sounds like it ought to be coming from some shrink's couch.

But the fact remains, it's cathartic. It's like I explain to my grumbling students at the beginning of every year, when I tell them they have to journal: writing is a great way to gain critical perspective on yourself and the events that surround you.

In this case, it also makes the time pass.

Every now and then, the phone dings and I immediately grab it in the hopes Green Bubble has written back.

But, no, it's inevitably Alexis from Action News 10, hoping to book me for an "excloo" with their morning host.

Outside, a nasty night is brewing. Wind gusts rattle the skeletal branches of the leafless trees. The charcoal-smudge sky can't seem to decide whether it wants to rain, sleet, or snow, so it's doing a bit of all three.

I find myself wondering if Hayley Goodloe is out there, somewhere, watching a similar scene from captivity; or if this snow is now falling atop her hastily dug grave.

Chasing away that grim thought, I turn back to my phone and call my mother. The last I heard from her was a text the previous day, saying she had arrived safely back home.

We chat for a while about nothing of particular consequence. I decide not to tell her about the Green Bubble texts. Really, there's nothing to tell. Not yet, anyway.

She asks again if I need money. I assure her I don't, while making yet another feeble attempt to determine where she'd be getting it from. She remains tight-lipped.

"Don't even think about it," is what she says.

But, of course, I am.

I'm thinking about her money *and* mine. This $150-a-day palace of mine is fine, but I really need to find something more permanent—and cheap. An apartment or something. That's *if* I can find a landlord who will be willing to take in a disgraced former teacher with no job.

After I end the call, I take a quick look at my finances. Emily and I kept separate checking accounts, and the balance in mine currently reads $4,843.22.

But, in my head, I know it's less than that. I've put at least $1,500 on my credit card over the past few days, between the hotel and other purchases.

I stare at the line that tells me my paycheck for January was direct-deposited. I wonder if it's the last payday I'll ever see.

Just to reassure myself that I still have a cushion, I switch over to the app that connects to that investment account Emily and I share. The last time I looked a few weeks ago, it had ninety-one thousand and something in there.

I think the market has been up since then, so I'm anticipating a slightly larger number.

But that's not what I see.

Under Total Portfolio Value, it says $0.00.

As in, zero.

I stare at it confounded.

This must be a misprint. The server is down. I've been routed to the wrong account. The app is glitching. Something.

I switch over to my laptop, since the web version of my investment advisor's software gives a fuller suite of options.

Once again, my balance is $0.00.

Now in a full panic—but still convinced this is some mistake—I click on transactions.

And then I see this is not an accounting error. Yesterday morning, every single one of our safe, carefully chosen securities was sold. The proceeds of those sales—all $92,452.85 of it—were then withdrawn from the account via a wire transfer.

The report doesn't say where the money went or who authorized the transaction. But, of course, I already know.

There is only one person besides me who has privileges on that account.

Emily.

I can remember when we were setting up the account. Our financial advisor asked if we wanted single or joint authorization.

Single, we said.

Who wanted to bother with the inconvenience of joint authorization every time we wanted to make some little change?

I don't recall Emily touching the account since that day. Or even mentioning it. Money is this abstraction to her, a resource she takes for granted because it has always been there and therefore always will be.

Managing the money, checking on the investments, worrying about the markets, that was all my job.

Can she really get away with just . . . stealing this money from me?

Long-term, she probably can't. We'll divorce—she's divorcing me, right?—and we'll have an equitable distribution of assets.

But that takes at least a year. Or more. I'm going to need that money well before then. And I have no recourse for getting it back. My financial advisor can shrug and say the money was lawfully withdrawn and is now out of her reach.

I am reminded of that saying all lawyers know: possession is nine-tenths of the law.

Emily now possesses almost all of our money.

If I want to be charitable toward Emily, I can see my avaricious father-in-law, Miles Vanderburgh, behind all of this. He probably filled Emily's head with talk about how *I* was going to steal the money from *her* if she didn't act.

Get it now, before that son-of-a-bitch blows it all on expensive lawyers.

I bet he's even now managing the money himself, quietly pocketing commissions from his own daughter.

An even-less-generous voice in my head comes from Leo. A few of his words from the previous evening—those of them that I can actually remember—are coming back to me.

She thought she was marrying an author, not a high school English teacher . . . She wants to be *one of the pampered rich kids.*

Is this more evidence Emily is the one behind Hayley's disappearance? Is this another part of her exit strategy? She's going to steal my book *and* grab our savings on her way out the door?

Suddenly, I'm suffering this completely incongruous flashback. It is from our first full summer together, a year after we met. It had been such a tumultuous twelve months—the rise and fall of Charles Bliss.

Emily convinced me we should rent this one-bedroom cabin on a lake in Maine, a place remote enough that it lacked cell phone service. She had picked out that feature purposefully so I couldn't ruin the trip checking my miserable sales figures or looking for reviews that weren't coming.

It was a total getaway. She was determined to heal me.

The first day it rained. The second was pure Maine summer bliss: low humidity, bright sunshine, gentle breeze, temperature in the high seventies.

Midway through the afternoon, Emily went for a swim while I watched from a blanket under some trees by the shoreline. I admired her long, powerful strokes, in awe of her grace and athleticism. I had often wondered where her dancing career would have taken her if not for the torn Achilles that forced her retirement.

When she returned to shore, she joined me on the blanket. She kissed me with urgency, her lips and face still cool from the water. The next thing I knew, she was stripping off her bathing suit, tugging down my shorts, and climbing on top of me.

We made love right there along the shoreline, not caring who could see. In that moment of perfect pairing, we were the only people in the world, living on a planet made just for us.

I can still see her, arching her back, the light filtering through the trees and casting patterns that were almost like henna on her naked skin.

When we were through, both of us thoroughly spent, she whispered in my ear, *I'm keeping you, Charles Bliss. I'm keeping you forever and ever.*

It was my favorite vacation.

Where is that Emily now?

Really, Emily? Really? I want to scream. *Are you really keeping me? Or are you only keeping me as long as it's convenient?*

It's like being stabbed in the back and heart simultaneously. The pain is almost too dazzling to process.

I gaze out the window into a cold night. The precipitation has switched over to freezing rain.

* * *

The next morning, I awake early to return to writing.

After several hours hard at the keyboard, I permit myself a quick check of the news.

There are two stories sharing the top of the *Hartford Courant*'s website, both of which are of interest. The first is that Robert Qualls, Connecticut's senior senator, has announced his retirement after twenty-four years in office.

The piece reads like a combination of an obituary and a hagiography, with plenty of praise for the longtime lawmaker.

Qualls is quoted as saying he hopes his successor will be a woman; and he says he will likely be making an endorsement "in the coming months," before the Democratic primary. But there's no mention of Victoria Brock, Diane Goodloe, or any of the other would-be candidates.

The second lead story is, "West Hartford teen remains missing: Exhaustive search continues for daughter of prominent Connecticut political family."

Next to those headlines, Hayley Goodloe smiles out from her senior portrait photo.

Addie Horne's name is the lead byline, and it is joined by two others. The first six paragraphs focus on authorities' efforts to scour the state, looking for Hayley. I can feel myself rooting for their efforts.

It is not until the seventh paragraph that I am mentioned. Even then, the language impresses me for its neutrality. It says I have been questioned by police but am not currently in custody and have not been officially named as a suspect.

I can almost feel Addie Horne going out of her way to be fair to me. Feeling buoyed, wondering if perhaps the rest of the news media is showing similar restraint, I go to a different publication's website.

Huge mistake.

The picture that goes with the story is the official school portrait of Charles Allan Bliss placed side by side with a photo of a sun-kissed Hayley on a beach in short shorts and a bikini top.

This pairing alone could scarcely be more damning. There might as well be a caption underneath: *Sketchy teacher pervs on, kidnaps, kills hot young girl.*

I click off the page and close the lid to my laptop, promising myself I won't look at the news anymore.

In an attempt to clear my mind, I put on as many layers of clothing as I can make fit and force myself outside for a run. The morning air is crystalline but still. I pound out the miles for an hour and a half or so.

If only I didn't have that damn monitoring bracelet, resting atop my ankle bone, reminding me with every stride just how unfree I am.

I have returned to the hotel and am just out of the bathroom after my shower, with a towel wrapped around my waist, when I hear my phone ding. I walk over to the desk where I've got it plugged in and check to see who's texting me now.

Then I get an immediate jolt.

It's Green Bubble.

In response to my question—WHO IS THIS?—they have written: I'M SOMEONE WHO KNOWS WHAT'S BEST FOR YOU. AND WHAT'S BEST FOR YOU IS TO FIND OUT WHO WANTS TO HARM HAYLEY GOODLOE.

The phrase "who wants to harm Hayley" is a curious one. It makes it sound like the harm hasn't happened yet, which is not the case. Hasn't she been harmed plenty?

Or does this mean Green Bubble knows something about more harm that might be on the way?

Mindful of my vow to show restraint with Green Bubble and not give them anything to use against me, I type out a quick reply. HOW DO YOU KNOW HAYLEY? HOW DO YOU FIT INTO THIS?

I hit SEND, then sit on the edge of the bed. Green Bubble is texting at almost the exact same time as yesterday—and the day before that, and the day before that, and the day before that.

Why is that? Is there something significant about the noon hour? Is this someone who only texts on their lunch break or something? Or have they made a rule for themselves to only text once a day?

My phone dings again. The conversation is now flowing, with my texts in gray, and the replies in green.

Green: I CAN'T REVEAL MY IDENTITY SO STOP ASKING. LET'S KEEP ONE QUESTION FRONT AND CENTRE: YOU WANT TO CLEAR YOURSELF OR NOT?

Gray: WHAT KIND OF QUESTION IS THAT? OF COURSE I DO. YOU MUST KNOW THAT.

Green: VERY GOOD. HAVE YOU INVESTIGATED NUTMEG CONSULTANCY LLC?

Gray: YES. I GET THAT NUTMEG IS A POLITICAL FUND-RAISING CONSULTANT, BUT OTHERWISE . . . ?—I insert a shrugging emoji—BECAUSE THAT'S ALMOST LITERALLY WHAT I'M DOING—and hit SEND.

Green: NUTMEG CONSULTANCY LLC IS NOT WHAT IT SEEMS. BUT YOU'RE GOING TO HAVE TO BE ABLE TO PROVE IT OR ELSE NO ONE WILL BELIEVE YOU.

Gray: DID NUTMEG CONSULTANCY LLC KIDNAP HAYLEY GOODLOE?

Green: I THINK SO.

Gray: YOU THINK SO?

Green: THERE'S A LOT I DON'T KNOW.

That much is clear. It's like Green Bubble is toying with me. Are they going to help me or not? It feels like we're regressing to riddles again.

Gray: LET'S START WITH WHAT YOU DO KNOW. WHY WOULD NUTMEG CONSULTANCY WANT TO HARM HAYLEY?

Green: I DON'T KNOW. THAT'S PART OF WHAT YOU NEED TO FIGURE OUT. AND PROVE.

Gray: HOW DO I GO ABOUT DOING THAT?

Green: IF I KNEW THAT, I WOULDN'T BE TEXTING YOU. COME ON. YOU WENT TO YALE. USE THAT BIG BRAIN OF YOURS.

This is maddening. I'm not sure what Green Bubble thinks they're going to accomplish by taunting me. But getting upset about it won't help me. I take in a deep breath and push it back out.

Gray: I'm trying, believe me. But I need more information from you. What makes you suspect Nutmeg Consultancy is involved?

Green: I don't suspect. I know it. I just can't prove it.

Gray: Then what DO you know? What CAN you tell me about Nutmeg Consultancy LLC?

Green: All I have is an address. Nutmeg Consultancy LLC, P.O. Box 667, Hartford, CT 06106.

Naturally, it's a post office box; the least helpful type of address possible, other than perhaps no address at all. I'm still trying to figure out what else to ask Green Bubble next when another text pops in.

Green: Are you going to look into it or not?

Gray: Yes. Of course. Are you?

Green: I can't. Too many difficulties. It's on you. No more texts for now. Do some work. Show me you're serious. Then maybe I can tell you more.

Does Green Bubble really think I'm not serious? How much more of my life needs to be on the line here?

I sit there on the bed, wearing my towel, repressing the urge to scream at my phone.

JOURNAL ENTRY: FRIDAY, DECEMBER 1

Well, that didn't take long.

Dad's vaunted nondisclosure agreement lasted about as long as a virgin on prom night.

The plaintiff's lawyer told Dad's lawyer that the NDA is null and void because it's attempting to silence illegal activity. He said that because this woman signed her agreement with a business entity—my dad incorporates everything, because that's what rich people do—she's technically a whistleblower, and therefore she can say whatever she wants to whomever she wants.

This conversation, mind you, happened the day before the woman came out with her story in the *New York Post*, which was altogether too happy to slap her picture on its tabloid-size front page along with the big, blocky headline #MENUDE.

Get it? Because she's a nude model who is #MeToo'ing someone?

Very classy.

The paper used one of its stock photos of Billionaire Playboy W. Johnson Goodloe III, looking over his shoulder like he was trying to get away with something.

That was yesterday. Today, three more women came out and said my dad forced them to have sex with him. They are being represented by the same attorney, naturally. There are now stories going around the web calling him the Harvey Weinstein of the art world and also comparing him to Deshaun Watson, the lecherous quarterback.

Dad actually called me a little while ago to apologize that this had become public.

He also said he didn't force anyone to do anything, that everything he did with these women was a hundred percent consensual.

I actually believe him. My dad may be a total douchebag, but he's a *romantic* douchebag. It's not about the sex for him. It's about the seduction. The game. I've seen it too many times with all the grossly young women he's been with since my mom.

He wants them to want him. Force just isn't his thing.

Anyhow, it seems like Ashley is of another mind. My wicked stepmother has decided she doesn't want to be my wicked stepmother after all.

That's right: Ashley has canceled their engagement. She's moved out of his brownstone. He said she won't even talk to him anymore.

I almost feel bad for him.

But not for Ashley.

She'll be more than fine.

Just ask my mom. A Goodloe baby is a golden ticket.

CHAPTER 20

After getting dressed, I reexamine my text exchange with Green Bubble, parsing and reparsing each line, like I'm reading *Finnegans Wake* and want to make sure I don't miss anything.

It doesn't help much, though I think I can at least rule out a few possibilities.

I no longer think Green Bubble is a reporter. Or a cop. There was nothing in our exchange where I felt like Green Bubble was attempting to lure me into making a confession or typing anything quotable.

Upon further review, Green Bubble didn't ask me a single thing about me, my circumstances, or my frame of mind. It's like they weren't interested.

Their only goal seemed to be urging me to act. And it's because they can't seem to act themselves.

Maybe because they're not allowed to? Is Green Bubble someone at Carrington? One of my former colleagues, texting on a disposable burner phone?

I mull that idea for a moment or two. Other than Leo, no one from Carrington has reached out to me. They don't dare. I'm *persona non grata.*

Yet my ego would like to have me believe that I'm not universally despised at my former school. There are people there who know me, who respect me, who worked with me for eleven years and believe this accusation cannot possibly be true.

They want to help me. And Hayley. They've come across this small piece of information somehow—Maybe Hayley said something to them shortly before she was kidnapped? Maybe they've been looking into things on their own? Maybe they've heard some rumor on campus?—and they want to take it further.

They just can't risk sticking out their own neck. So they're telling me about it, knowing I'll take the ball and sprint with it.

Even the timing works. The first three were all sent during Carrington's lunchtime. The fourth came during brunch.

Is there something about the dining hall being open that makes this person feel safe to communicate with me? Is that when Green Bubble knows everyone who might catch them texting me will be busy and distracted? Or have they hidden the burner phone someplace that they only access during mealtimes?

Either way, it feels like one more piece of the puzzle that fits.

I'm still going to keep an open mind and remain cautious. Green Bubble might not be a friend. They might be someone who is only pretending to have good intentions toward me and is trying to manipulate me for reasons yet unclear.

Putting aside that issue for the time being, I turn back to the mystery that is Nutmeg Consultancy. The internet has nothing to tell me. I need to focus on the real world, where Nutmeg Consultancy has at least one tangible touchpoint: a post office box.

Maybe I can go to the 06106 post office and stake it out in the hope that someone from Nutmeg Consultancy—maybe Chris Sandman, maybe someone else on his team of seasoned professionals—comes by to grab their mail.

And then . . . Well, I guess I would have to follow them back to their office and see what's there. It's probably not far away.

I doubt anyone from Nutmeg Consultancy would check their box on Saturday or Sunday.

But Monday? Everyone checks their mail on Monday, right?

So now I know where I'll be Monday morning.

In the meantime, I return to my rapidly growing manuscript. Thousands of more words pass under my fingers as the afternoon slips away. I have never written at anything close to this feverish a pace.

When I finally shut the laptop and crack open a beer, it's after eight. I'm starting to think about maybe going out to a bar—after all, it's Saturday night—when I hear a familiar voice.

"Open up," Leo calls out. "Police!"

I invite him in, accepting the six-pack he's brought as tribute.

"Hey," I say, deeply relieved to see him. "What are you doing here? I figured you had duty or something."

"Nah, just a hockey game that went two OTs. What's new?"

We assume the same seats we had been in two nights earlier and I tell him about the texts from Green Bubble. Leo insists on reading the entire exchange, poring over it with great intensity.

Once he's done, I share my theory that it might be someone from Carrington.

He leans back and takes a pull on his drink.

"You know who it is, right?" he asks.

"Do tell."

"Bet you twenty bucks it's Molly Millrose."

"What makes you say that?"

"Oh, come on, let's not play games. You know Molly has always had a huuuge crush on 'Charrr-leeee.'"

He sings the name in a high-pitched voice.

"No she doesn't," I say, though perhaps unconvincingly.

During my first year on campus, she made what I later realized was probably a pass at me. It was subtle enough to remain somewhat ambiguous, but I definitely had the impression that if I had pursued it, my overtures would have been welcome.

"Uhh, yeah she does," Leo says definitively. "It's probably the worst-kept secret on the entire Carrington faculty. She's been crushing on you for years, my man."

"Then why is she such good friends with Emily? She's probably better friends with Emily than she is with me."

"Duh. Because that's *exactly* what women do under those circumstances. There's no better way to deflect suspicion that you're secretly in love with someone than to become BFFs with the person who's actually your biggest rival."

"I wouldn't call them rivals. They're—"

"Come on, dude, don't be an idiot. Haven't you noticed Molly *never* passes up an opportunity to start a conversation with you? You once told me she came to your book launch wearing a handmade dress with *Washington County* covers all over it."

"That's just her thing. She wears dresses with zombies on them, too. Do you think she has a crush on zombies?"

"Dude. Come on. When I came here for new faculty orientation this summer, she had been dating some guy—Bill? I think he was an engineer?"

"Bob. He was an accountant."

"Whatever. It sounded like it had been going on for a while, but she dropped him the moment she heard Emily left you."

"That was just a coincidence," I say, unconvincingly.

"Right. Like it was coincidence when she booty-called you two weeks later and came by your apartment at ten o'clock at night wearing a low-cut dress and do-me heels?"

"Those were just shoes. Nothing happened."

"Only because good ol' Charlie Bliss couldn't pull the trigger. Molly's old-fashioned. She wanted you to make the first move."

I bring the beer to my lips, take in a mouthful, and let it sit there for a moment while I ponder all this. Nothing he's said is exactly wrong.

"Come on, my man," Leo presses. "Her thighs sweat every time she thinks about you. And she's, what, thirty-seven, thirty-eight? The clock is ticking like thunder. This is her last chance to win you over. She probably knows Emily has left you *again* and she's working furiously to save your sorry ass so she can have you for herself. In a weird way, it's actually pretty romantic."

"Then why doesn't she just tell me who she is? Why all the subterfuge?"

"She's just exercising a little due caution. She desperately wants to help you but she doesn't want to get fired for it. Once you clear yourself, she'll reveal that she was Green Bubble, who came to your rescue in your time of greatest need, all in the hopes that you will finally bed her down out of sheer gratitude."

"And people say *I* write fiction."

He grins. "Look, why don't you text her and ask her? I bet she's dying to tell you who she really is. She just needs a little push."

I don't make a move for my phone. Yet.

But I'm tempted.

"No, better yet," Leo resumes. "Don't ask her. *Tell* her. Say you *know* it's her and say she needs to come clean because—oh, this is good!—because *honesty* is the most important part of any relationship. No way she'll be able to resist that."

The grin has grown wider, to canary-eating width. He's obviously very pleased with himself.

"Okay," I say, finally pulling out my phone. "I guess I'll give it a shot. Should I text the burner phone or her regular phone?"

"Well, you know I'm not exactly an expert on texting," Leo says. "But I'd say the burner. That's how she's comfortable contacting you. You want to keep playing by her rules."

With Leo's coaching, I craft what feels like a perfect text. I hit SEND before I can change my mind.

By that point, the urge to sleep has become too strong to overwhelm. I yawn and tell Leo it's past my bedtime.

"Yeah, absolutely," he says. "Why don't you go to bed? I'll tidy up out here and then be on my way."

Leo pretty much never offers to clean, but I'm not going to turn him down. I thank him for being a good guest, then retreat into my bedroom.

Within perhaps two minutes of when my head graces the pillow, I'm out cold.

JOURNAL ENTRY: WEDNESDAY, DECEMBER 6

This will *not* do.

No, no, no, this will not do *at all.*

This afternoon, during activities period, the whole school came together for that beloved Carrington tradition, the Blue and White competition.

We have Blue and White once a month, so this was December's installment. There are points kept, and the standings are posted in the dining hall, and some people get *really* into it because in May the winner is awarded the prestigious Carrington Cup.

Some of the competitions are sort of real, like tug-of-war. But most are really silly, like who can stack the most marshmallows on a paper plate and still be able to walk the length of the football field.

Or there's the ever-popular spaghetti pass, where the first years compete to see who can most quickly pass the entire contents of a huge bowl of spaghetti down the line over the backs of their heads without spilling a single noodle.

It's something alums get really nostalgic about and talk about years later. So, whatever, it's a thing.

One of the Blue and White rules is that once someone in your family is a certain color, everyone for the rest of time is that color. The Goodloe family has always been Blue.

Mr. B is one of the White team faculty advisors, which worries me, because what will our children be?

Kidding.

Sort of. They'll be Blue, obviously.

Anyway, Ms. Millrose is also a White team advisor, so she and Mr. B were working together to help some sophomores who were competing to see who could construct the longest-sailing paper airplane.

You should have seen the way she was looking at him. I know because it's probably how *I* look at him.

That's when I realized: My advisor has a thing for Mr. B!

How had I not noticed this before? I guess I had just never seen them together before.

But from then on, all I did was watch them. I even wandered close enough to the White side that I could hear her fawning over him. She was all *Charlie this* and *Charlie that*. He made a little joke about something that wasn't really that funny and she was immediately all giggly and girly about it.

Obviously, I'm not the only one who has noticed that Mr. B's wife is out of the picture.

I hauled Calista over and told her what a disaster this was and that it meant they were probably having sex.

But then Calista watched them for a while and she was like, *No, Ms. Millrose just* wishes *she was having sex with him.*

Calista pointed out that Ms. Millrose was flirting with him, but he wasn't flirting back.

That made me feel a little bit better, though I'm still not psyched about the fact that my own advisor is trying to steal my man.

I mean, what if he gets lonely some night? She's probably been throwing herself at him and he might get weak. He needs to know there's someone better available.

It's time to make my move.

CHAPTER 21

The first thing I do after rolling over in bed Sunday morning is check my phone.

Molly—and I'm now assuming it's Molly—hasn't answered. She's staying disciplined with her contact patterns. Hopefully once she knows I've figured out her identity, she'll become a little more available.

Rereading my, ahem, perfect text with sober eyes, I survey the unfortunate collision of alcohol and autocorrect: Honestly is the most imported part of Manny relationship, Ms. Millrose. I'm ready to be honest with you but are you really to be honest with me? I understand why you can't revealing yourself but you have to trust that I will always protect your identity. I know itself you Molly.

And then I tacked on: Sorry. I know ITS you Molly. Please just come clean.

It wasn't exactly a great performance for my fumbly fingers—and the grammar police will want to make an arrest even if the real ones don't—but she'll get the point.

Once I decide to give up on further sleep, I stumble back out into the sitting room. Leo's idea of cleaning up seems to be rather lacking—to the point of nonexistent—so I gather the evidence of the previous night's revelry and bury it in the recycling bin.

Throughout the remainder of the morning, I continue writing while keeping an eye on the clock. Just as it does on Saturday, the Carrington dining hall opens for brunch from 11 a.m.–1 p.m. on Sundays. I'm wondering if that is once again when I'll hear from Molly. What is it about the dining hall being open that makes her feel safe to text me?

Sure enough, at 12:48 p.m., a dinging sound fills my hotel suite. I check the newly arrived green bubble. Hi, Charlie. Yes, it's me. But you HAVE to keep this to yourself. I am taking a lot of risk here. Will you PLEASE look into Nutmeg Consultancy?

Knowing for sure it's Molly is a relief. I feel this rush of gratitude toward her, but also some guilt.

If she really does have a crush on me—and Leo made a convincing case—I'm essentially taking advantage of her feelings for me; feelings I will never return in quite the same way. I *like* Molly a lot as a person. I respect her. I enjoy her company.

But I'm never going to love her. Not in a romantic way. I just don't feel any chemistry with her.

Is it wrong of me, knowing that and still accepting her assistance? Especially when I still have feelings—for however complicated and screwed up they may be—for my wife?

I just have to be careful not to lead her on. No more letting Leo talk me into mentioning our "relationship," as if it's a thing. I have to keep this cordial but professional, for lack of a better word. I reply: I understand. Thank you for helping me. And, yes, I plan to stake out the P.O. Box tomorrow morning.

She immediately writes back: Thank you, Charlie. <3

There's another stab of guilt when I see the heart emoji. But I'm not sure what else I can do. Her help has been freely given, with no coercion on my part.

And the truth is, I need it desperately.

The rationalization I decide to settle on is that she's probably thinking as much—or more—about Hayley. Everything else is just incidental.

That has to be my focus here, too. With that in mind, I type: CAN YOU TELL ME MORE ABOUT NUTMEG CONSULTANCY? HOW DID YOU LEARN ABOUT THEM? IS IT SOMETHING HAYLEY MENTIONED, OR YOU FOUND OUT ON YOUR OWN, OR . . . ?

It takes a few minutes before Molly sends her reply. A FEW DAYS BEFORE SHE WAS KIDNAPPED, HAYLEY TOLD ME THAT IF ANYTHING BAD HAPPENED TO HER, I SHOULD LOOK INTO NUTMEG CONSULTANCY LLC. THEN SHE GAVE ME THAT P.O. BOX. I ASKED HER REPEATEDLY WHAT SHE WAS TALKING ABOUT OR WHAT SHE WAS WORRIED ABOUT, BUT SHE WOULDN'T ANSWER ME. SHE SAID SHE COULD GET IN TROUBLE IF SHE SAID TOO MUCH. I HAD NO IDEA WHAT SHE MEANT BY THAT. I GUESS I JUST THOUGHT IT WAS TEENAGE GIRL DRAMA, YOU KNOW? SORRY I CAN'T TELL YOU MORE.

I'm still absorbing this when my phone dings again.

I HAVE TO GO. POWERING DOWN PHONE NOW. WILL CHECK IN AGAIN TOMORROW AT THIS TIME.

After hitting the LIKE button, I stand up and look down at the hotel parking lot.

Hayley knew she was in some kind of trouble. It *wasn't* just teenage girl drama—though it's easy to forgive Molly for concluding it was; when I think of some of the wild things my students have said to me over the years, I probably would have thought the same.

I wish I could go back in time and talk to Hayley. Was she being threatened somehow? Or was this just guesswork on her part—speculation that turned out to be terribly true?

It also makes me wish that, whatever the case was, Hayley had taken her concerns to her parents or the police.

Does this have something to do with why she leveled this false accusation against me? Or how she got chlamydia?

It is a wretched Catch-22 that the one person who has the answers happens to be the same person who can't be found.

* * *

I write as late into the night as my straining eyes can bear.

The next morning, I'm up before the sun is, eager to start my surveillance. It's Monday. The world is getting back to work; including, I hope, the mailbox-checking employees of Nutmeg Consultancy.

I travel a few exits north on 91, to Washington Street in Hartford. By 6:45 a.m., I'm there.

The 06106 post office is a large brick building with a circular entryway and a perfect setup for a would-be box-stalker. The lobby has multiple bays of windows that afford me an unobstructed view inside. There's also plenty of parking out front, so I can sit in my car and watch people flow in and out.

I park and enter, just to scope things out. A sign tells me the lobby opened at 6 a.m. and will remain that way until 5:30 p.m.

There's an entire wall covered with steel postal boxes. Number 667 is easy to find. It looks like every other box, with its combination dial in front, but I still stare at it like it's electrified.

This is it; possibly, the linchpin to everything. Someone connected to this box has . . . something to do with Hayley's disappearance. I have to figure out what it is so I can start to get my life back.

All I need is a little patience and a little luck.

I memorize its exact position—three columns over from the corner, three rows down from the top. Then I return to my car, which I move into a slightly better position, farther away from the entrance but in a direct line with where box 667 is.

As if I haven't already imprinted the image in my mind, I pull up the Nutmeg Consultancy website and download Chris Sandman's photo onto my phone so I can study it again.

He's such an unremarkable guy: the middle of middle age, round head, receded hairline, neatly tended goatee. Dressed in his suit and smiling the way he is, he's every proud dad who ever showed up for a college graduation.

It's impossible to tell from the photo what his physical proportions are—tall? short? thick? thin?—so I'll just have to keep an eye out for all types.

And, of course, there's always the possibility that someone else from Nutmeg picks up the mail.

I settle in for my stakeout, fixing my eyes on the box. I made the strategic decision to eschew coffee, because I didn't want to be peeing all day. I'm relying on excitement and nerves to keep me alert.

Now and then, I turn on my car's engine so I can get some heat and play the radio.

Once the service windows open up at nine, activity picks up on that side of the lobby. The boxes get very little attention. One or two people pass near number 667 on their way to their own boxes, but that's it.

The morning passes slowly. No one pays any attention to the man in the car in the parking lot.

I wish I could return to my writing, but I don't want to risk taking my eyes off the box. To keep my brain active, I invent stories for people as they walk in.

There's a guy slinking toward his P.O. box, hoping he doesn't see anyone he knows. He only has the box so he can get the erectile dysfunction medicine his wife doesn't know about—because it's for when he's with his girlfriend.

There's a senior citizen who is going to get to the front of the line, and when the clerk asks him what kind of stamps he wants, he'll just gruffly say to give him whatever. The truth is, he used to collect stamps so he could pass something of value onto his son. But ever since his son died in a car crash, the old man can barely even look at a stamp.

There's a woman, sending cookies to her grandson in Sarasota. She's shared the recipe with her daughter-in-law; except whenever the daughter-in-law makes them, they never turn out quite right. The truth is, the woman left out one key ingredient. That way, everyone says no one makes those cookies quite like grandma.

It's fun. I used to play this game with Emily when we would go out for dinner. I would ask her to pick a nearby table of guests and give me one detail about what she saw, just to ground it in reality; and then I'd make up the rest, inventing elaborate backstories and intertwining plot points for all the characters—sorry, the people. I would fill the resulting stories with complications and tragedies, conflicts and twists.

Emily loved that game.

But even before Emily, I have always enjoyed having a large internal world, one where I can retreat for solace, idle distraction, or entertainment.

When I was a kid, I didn't just have imaginary friends. I had massive imaginary scenarios that lasted for days, weeks, or even years at a time. I lived deep inside them, immersing myself thoroughly in their nuances and complexities.

They seemed as real to me as anything else in my life.

Maybe some of that was just being the only child of a hardworking single mom. But there are whole portions of my youth where I couldn't honestly tell you whether something that happened was in the real world or the one I imagined.

As I entered adulthood, I channeled that energy into my writing; though, in some ways, nothing has changed. The characters in my books aren't just characters to me. They're people I know. I can see them. I know their stories. I have entire conversations with them.

Maybe that sounds nuts.

But there's nothing sane about writing a novel.

I am lost somewhere in those thoughts a little after noontime when Molly texts me from her burner phone, asking for an update. I confirm that I'm watching the box. She thanks me and tells me she's powering down the phone again.

As my watch continues, I wonder if I'm going about this wrong. Is the ownership of a post office box a public record? Can the post office solve some of this mystery for me?

During a slow moment in the middle of the afternoon, I slip back into the building and ask to speak with the postmaster. She comes out into the lobby to chat with me, which is perfect—it allows me to keep an eye on the box three over and three down.

She tells me that because the box is owned by a business, not an individual, she is able to confirm for me that it belongs to an entity called Nutmeg Consultancy LLC.

Whoever applied for the box would have had to present two forms of ID: one with a photo, like a driver's license or passport;

and a document that linked them to a physical address, like a mortgage or a lease.

But legally, she can't tell me who that person was. Or when it happened.

The only way she's allowed to release that information—all of which can be found on Nutmeg Consultancy's P.O. box application form—is if she's presented with a subpoena.

Which strikes me as something my lawyer can make happen.

I thank the postmaster for her information. As soon as I'm back out in my car, I call Jerry and tell him what I need—and why I need it.

"Sorry, Ace," he says. "I can't go ask a judge for a subpoena until you're formally charged with something."

"Do you think the cops would subpoena it for us?"

He sighs audibly. "They might. It would be a lot better if it wasn't coming from us. Will this friend of yours go to the police? Maybe provide them a sworn declaration about what Hayley Goodloe told her?"

"I don't know. It would take some convincing, for sure. The head of school at Carrington has made it pretty clear no one on staff is supposed to have anything to do with me. But if she was going directly to the police, maybe it would be permissible."

"Then I would say it's in your best interests to do that convincing," he says. "In the meantime, have you thought more about hiring a PI? You were going to sleep on it."

"Yeah, my, ahh, financial situation has changed a bit since then," I say, then fill him in on the suddenly vacant investment account.

He confirms for me that there's nothing I can do about that right now. I would have to start divorce proceedings before I had any legal tools to get at that money.

And I don't want to do that. Truth is, despite everything, I'm still desperate to reconcile with my wife.

"If you still had the money, would you hire a PI?" he asks. "Ten grand could go a long way with the guys I like to use. They know the kind of things that a defense attorney likes and they're pretty good at finding it—if it's there to be found."

Between Victoria Brock, my suspicions about Emily, and now Nutmeg Consultancy, I could certainly give a private investigator enough to do.

"I mean, I . . . I guess I . . . I'd have to think about it seriously and . . . yes. Probably yes."

"Then if you don't mind my asking: Where did you get that fifty grand from that you gave me? Because I got the feeling that wasn't yours."

"It wasn't," I confirm.

"Was it from your mom?"

"Sort of."

"Could she give you more?"

"I . . . I don't know. She's never had two nickels to rub together. I honestly don't know where she's getting it from. She tells me she can give me more but . . . I just don't know."

"Well, your family dynamics are none of my business," he says. "But as your lawyer? I'm suggesting it might be time to find out."

We end the call. As the afternoon grinds on, I'm considering Jerry's advice, all while waging a battle in between my ears.

Can I really ask my mother for more monetary help? After she's done so much already? And when I don't actually know where the money is coming from?

Now and then, when it gets too cold, I turn on the radio—which is why I hear the news of the hour:

Former Connecticut attorney general Victoria Brock has announced her candidacy for the U.S. Senate from the front steps of her childhood home in Cromwell, in front of a small but boisterous crowd.

The anchorperson notes that Brock is the first Democrat to declare her candidacy following Robert Qualls's retirement announcement on Friday, although others are expected to follow.

Left unstated is that State Senator Diane Goodloe—ensconced as she is in personal tragedy—remains on the sidelines. She is unable to enter the fray, lest she commit the one sin that not even our permissive politics of the moment would allow for: being a bad mother.

It's all playing out as Addie Horne predicted.

That thought nudges me in the direction I probably needed to go anyway with regard to a private investigator. And I'm going to need my mother's financial support to do it.

I just can't endanger her in the process. I need to know where that money is coming from.

In other words, it's time to throw that tantrum.

JOURNAL ENTRY: FRIDAY, DECEMBER 8

I finally did it! I knocked on Mr. B's door tonight!

Calista helped me work up the courage. We were hanging out at the dorm last night, and I was going on and on about Mr. B again—he praised the first sentence to this short story of mine in front of the whole class, and it wasn't *that* good a sentence—and she was basically like: *When are you going to stop talking a big game about Mr. B and actually do something about it?*

And my answer was: *You know what? Fine. I'll do it right now.*

It was, like, nine thirty at night. Lights out isn't until midnight on weekends.

I changed into tight jeans and a form-fitting tube top that always makes guys stare at me. Especially when I wear it without a bra.

Again: guys and nipples = dogs and tennis balls.

Calista told me I looked like a total tramp, but she said it as a compliment.

Honestly, if you're knocking on your teacher's door at ten o'clock on a Friday night, what's the point in subtlety?

Before I could change my mind, I put on a jacket and charged out.

There was definitely this sense of, I don't know, danger. If I bumped into a dean or a faculty member who started asking questions, I'd potentially be in trouble. The only thing on that part of campus is Wentworth, and that's a boys dorm where I'm not allowed.

The story I had at the ready was about how I needed to ask Mr. Bliss a question about revamping submission guidelines for *Carrington Crossroads*.

But no one stopped me.

As I approached the side of Wentworth, the light from inside Mr. B's apartment was shining out, which made me think he was home. But he had the shades drawn, so I couldn't see for sure.

The sickening thought hit me: What if he was in there with Ms. Millrose? What if they were getting busy?

What would I say then?

I didn't even stop to think about it. I just slipped into the little entryway and confronted Mr. B's door.

My heart was pounding like crazy. I was already starting to lose my nerve. But I knew I *had* to do this. I made myself tap on the door—lightly, so no one in the other faculty apartment could hear it.

No answer.

I knocked a little louder.

Still no answer.

I waited for a few minutes, listening intently for any sound on the other side of the door.

There was nothing. I don't know if he just wasn't there, or if he had already gone to sleep, or what.

I was disappointed, obviously.

Still, I'm proud of myself for doing it.

If nothing else, it was a good practice run.

I'll try again tomorrow night.

MIDLOGUE 5

Before I return to the narrative, I feel like I need to explain my thought process around why I decided to ask my mother for help.

It involved my long-standing battle with my ego.

When I was in my vainglorious early- and mid-twenties—fresh out of Yale and on an unswerving march to literary fame—my ego was so monumental it practically needed its own national park. I was constantly writing my own autobiography in my mind, convinced that someday the world would want to understand every detail of my journey to greatness.

Then *Washington County* flopped, which effectively dispelled that notion.

But if there was one benefit to that failure, it was that it pulverized my ego into a fine powder.

Through long trial and suffering, I have come to recognize that the ego is like a monster that promises protection—*Oh, Charles, you're so great!*—in return for continual feeding. And what it's ultimately thriving on is the junk food of human existence: praise from others; public recognition; power; the feeling of being liked, adored, and respected by everyone.

All of those things essentially boil down to one question.

What do people think of me?

That's all the ego cares about, all it ever allows you to see. It's a form of blindness that affects untold billions on this planet.

And here's the real catch, the thing that legions of truly miserable people never quite understand: *The ego can never get enough.*

It doesn't matter how many affirmations it receives. The more fuel you give it, the more it demands. The monster keeps growing larger, more threatening, and more voracious. Awards, accolades, and endorsements just keep disappearing down the gullet of a beast that will never truly be sated.

I finally came to realize there was just one way I could defeat my ego.

Stop feeding it.

Only then would it shrink down to a more manageable size and cease consuming everything in my life.

Caring so much about what people thought of me was essentially outsourcing my own happiness—leaving it to others to decide whether or not I was allowed to feel good about myself.

I had to decide on my own what I thought of myself.

It was actually this amazing freedom, taking back from others the power to dictate my moods.

I realize that's a lot of smug moralizing from a guy whose life is in shambles. I still suffer lapses—times when I allow my ego to slip back into the driver's seat and take control.

But at least in this case, I was able to recognize that the only reason I wouldn't ask my mother for help was that I was too proud, too conceited, too wrapped up in some juvenile—and, yes, egotistical—notion about rugged individualism and self-reliance.

The truth was, I needed her.

CHAPTER 22

One thing that is a certainty in the life of Robbie Bliss is that she's an earlier riser.

Which means, when it comes to work, she's an early finisher. It's now nearing four o'clock. She's pretty much always done—and completely wiped out—by this time of day.

I call her. We exchange greetings, then I explain to her the need to hire a private investigator.

"So I've been thinking about your offer from the other day—for more money," I finish. "And I think I really need some."

"Wonderful," she begins. "I'll—"

"Not so fast, Mom. I need you to hear me on this: I know that fifty grand you gave me wasn't yours. I can't take another dime from you until I know where it's coming from. I simply can't tolerate the idea that you might be putting yourself at risk in some way."

"But there's no risk, dear. Everything is fine. You'll just have to—"

"Mom, *stop*," I snap.

It is maybe the fifth time I've ever raised my voice to her. I can tell it gets her attention.

"Listen to me. Please listen," I continue. "This is not negotiable. There is no other way I am taking this money. Don't test me on this. There are too many other things I'm fighting right now. I can't fight you, too."

She's silent for a little while.

Then she asks, "How much do you need?"

"Ten thousand to start."

"Okay," she says at last. "Let me make a phone call and get back to you."

"And when you do, you're going to tell me how you've come up with the money?"

Another pause.

"Yes," she says.

Amazing: Robbie Bliss capitulates.

"Thanks, Mom."

And then I add, "Hey, Mom? You know I'm just being insistent about this because I care about you and I don't want you to get hurt."

"I'll be fine, dear," she says. "Don't you worry about me."

But, of course, I still do.

We end the call and I turn my attention back to box 667, where the same nothing-doing continues to unfold over the next hour. There's no one that looks remotely like Chris Sandman entering the building; no one who wanders particularly close to three over, three down.

As the sun sets, the service window closes, which all but empties the lobby. It's just a few people on their way home from work, hurrying in to empty their boxes.

Then, finally, I watch as the postmaster locks the front door. It's five thirty. My hope of catching someone from Nutmeg Consultancy has ended.

At least for today.

Before I depart, I send Molly a text to let her know I've come up empty.

She immediately writes back. WILL YOU CONTINUE WATCHING THE BOX TOMORROW?

I hit the LIKE button then start my journey back to the hotel. Molly is getting a little freer with the phone, though it is still a mealtime: the Carrington dining hall opens for dinner at five thirty.

Though maybe that's just a coincidence.

* * *

An hour later, I'm back in my hotel suite, just starting to get some writing done, when my mother calls.

"Can you be in your hotel room at nine o'clock tomorrow morning?" she asks.

Whatever thought I have about objecting—rooted in my desire to keep an eye on box 667—is outweighed by the strain in her voice. This is not a request being made lightly.

"Sure, Mom, what's going on?"

"I can't . . . I promised not to tell you."

"What does that even mean?"

"It means I can't tell you."

"But this is about the money?"

"Yes. Listen, Chahles, certain things that have happened that are . . . I need to recognize I'm not the only one involved. I've prayed a lot about this and . . . I think I just have to trust that this is part of God's plan."

I feel my back molars clamp down involuntarily. But I already know there's no point in objecting. Once Mom invokes God, there's no talking to her.

"Okay, Mom," I say wearily.

"Don't be angry with me. I can't handle that right now."

"I'm not angry, I'm just . . . whatever, it doesn't matter."

"Please don't *whatever* me, either. I've always tried to do the right thing by you as a mother, but you didn't come with an instruction manual. I don't know how to do this."

Since I have no idea what she's talking about, it's hard to know how to respond.

"It's okay, Mom. You've been a great—"

"I'm not fishing for compliments," she snaps, in typical barnacle-tough Robbie Bliss fashion. "Just be there."

Then she hangs up.

* * *

Per Robbie Bliss's instructions, I stay anchored to my hotel suite the next morning.

I take advantage of the opportunity to write more, placing myself in front of the keyboard while it's still dark. Several thousand new words flow across my screen.

It's only as the clock nears nine that I start having a hard time concentrating. At two minutes past the hour, there is a knock at my door.

Through the peephole, I see a man with an erect bearing and a charcoal gray suit that looks expensive.

I open the door. The man is a few inches shorter than me and probably twenty-five years older. I'm quite certain I've never laid eyes on him before.

And yet I've seen his face thousands of times.

Whenever I've looked in a mirror.

We have the same eyelashes. And the same eyes. And jaw. And cheekbones. It is uncanny. This man has my face.

Or, I guess I should say: I have his.

"Holy crap," is all I can muster.

"Hello, Charles," he says. "My name is Ellery Lawrence. I'm your father."

JOURNAL ENTRY: SATURDAY, DECEMBER 9

Oh my god.

Oh my god. Oh my god. Oh my god.

Oh my god. Oh my god.

There. That's got to be 250 words.

Nope. Just short. Once more, with feeling:

Oh my god.

CHAPTER 23

For a long moment, we stand on opposite sides of the transom, just gawking at each other.

He swallows. I am mesmerized by the bobbing of his prominent Adam's apple. Now I know where I got that from, too.

I probably ought to shake his hand, or give him a hug, or do something other than stand there like a statue. I just can't seem to overcome my shock.

There is nothing about this moment that I've prepared for. Maybe other kids who grew up without a father fantasized about what it would be like to have a dad to play catch with or to ask how to throw a curveball.

I never did. I just played catch with my mom. And I taught myself how to throw a curveball.

It never even occurred to me that I'd meet him someday. My mother almost never talked about him. He was not a presence in our lives; not even in a theoretical, maybe-someday kind of way. I can remember Emily once asking me if I missed having a father. My reply: You can't miss what you never had.

I had always assumed my mother never pursued my father for child support—or any kind of ongoing relationship—because he was inexorably flawed. An addict. A loser. A grifter.

It turns out, judging his suit and the way he carries himself, he is the one thing that Robbie Bliss disdains more than any of those things.

He's rich.

Finally, I say, "Would you like to come in?"

"Thank you," he says, entering my hotel room stiffly, like he's afraid he's going to break something.

I point him toward my little sitting area. He lowers himself onto an easy chair without really settling in. He clears his throat uncomfortably.

"Your mother, ah, said you needed some more cash."

"Wait, just wait," I say, flopping onto the love seat. "I need . . . sorry, this is just a lot to take in. I'm sure it's a lot for you, too. I just . . . I know you must be my father because, well, look at us."

"You do have the Lawrence chin," he confirms.

"Among other things, I'm sure. So it's not that I doubt that you're my father or anything. But, I'm sorry, where have you been my whole life? Who are you?"

He smiles a little at that. "Well, like I said, Ellery Lawrence. I'm a . . . a former lawyer turned . . . investor, I guess you'd say. I live in the Boston area. Ellery is a family name—my grandmother's maiden name. Supposedly, she traces her ancestry back to William Ellery, who was a signer of the Declaration of Independence. The Lawrences are . . ."

My mind finishes the sentence for him: . . . *Boston Brahmins of the first order.* You don't go to a school like Carrington without becoming familiar with the breed.

He has stopped for the moment. There's another awkward smile.

"I'm sorry," he says. "This isn't what you need to be hearing right now. What do you want to know?"

"Let's start with: How did someone like you ever cross paths with Robbie Bliss?"

"Right, sure," he says.

He gently withdraws a photograph from his suit jacket and slides it onto the coffee table. It's similar to that picture I had seen of her as a young woman. She's sitting topside on a yacht.

"That's your mother, obviously, and that was my boat," he says. "I had just finished law school and taken the bar exam. I was still waiting for the results. I wasn't much use to the firm until we knew I had a license to practice, so I basically took a month off to sail around New England. I needed a few minor repairs and I had pulled into this marina off the Gulf of Maine. I only planned to spend a day or two there. Then I met your mother.

"It was probably supposed to be a summer fling, but we fell pretty hard for each other. We spent every second we could together and it was . . . I don't know, it was like a dream. When I got notice I had passed the bar and it was time to return to Boston, I begged Robbie to come with me. She didn't seem to have anything in Maine that prevented her from leaving, at least to me. But she didn't want to go and she can be, ahh, pretty stubborn."

"I'm aware," I say.

He smiles for a fleeting moment, then turns sad again. "She told me that Boston wasn't her world, and that I would grow tired of her as soon as I realized she was nothing but a poor fisherman's daughter. And even if I didn't, she insisted my family and my friends and everyone else in my life would never accept her, and that it would ruin us in the end. There was nothing I could say to make her change her mind. She was staying in Maine, and that was that. I tried to keep in touch, but she didn't return my calls and I finally got the hint and moved on. I still thought about her from time to time, but . . ."

His voice trails off. He's made the last part of the speech to the floor in front of him. He finally lifts his head again and continues.

"She never told me she was pregnant. I knew nothing about you whatsoever until about thirteen years later. By then I had made partner at my firm but I was . . . just really unhappy. My wife and I were on the way to divorce. I had two kids who barely knew me because I spent ninety hours a week at the office. I didn't even know myself anymore. I was basically in full midlife crisis mode. Sorry, I didn't come here to talk about myself. I just—"

"You're fine," I assure him.

"Anyhow, I started thinking about my life, and I asked, 'When was the last time you were truly happy?' And the answer was: that summer I was with your mother. So I knew it was crazy, but I decided I was going to find her just to . . . I don't know, see how she was doing and if that summer still meant anything to her. I assumed she would be married and I would just be embarrassing myself, but I didn't care. I went to some of the places where we used to hang out and finally someone told me where Robbie lived. The next thing I knew, I was walking up to that little apartment of yours above the garage. Then I saw this skinny little kid playing outside."

A faraway look drifts across his face as he relives the moment.

"That was you, of course. I knocked on the door and Robbie was just . . . Honestly, she didn't know *what* to do with me. We had gone in pretty different directions while we had been apart. She had found God. The only thing I had been worshipping was the almighty dollar, which only made things worse—"

"She doesn't trust people with money," I interject.

"As I already knew. So it was pretty clear that we were not going to be anything. There was no talking about us. But you . . . she was thrilled to talk about you. She was so proud of you, of how you were turning out. It was clear even back then that you were very, very bright and an excellent student. I think she knew the local schools weren't giving you much of a challenge. She was worried hanging around that little town was going to stifle you intellectually. She wouldn't have put it quite that way, but I got the picture. I was the one who floated the possibility of boarding school.

"That led to more conversations over the course of several months, and the deal we came up with is that she would let me pay for Carrington as long as I didn't try to pursue a relationship with you. She didn't say this, but I think she felt like she had been doing a really good job with you on her own and she worried I would screw things up. I wasn't exactly feeling like Father of the Year with my own kids so I didn't fight her on it."

"So the, uh, 'essay contest' that I won?"

"That was fake, yes," he says. "I suspected the leap to a place like Carrington would be pretty intimidating for you and I wanted you to feel like you had earned your place there. Robbie said you were a really good writer. Hence the idea for an essay contest. She did send me the essay, by the way. It was impressive."

He smiles.

"And my *scholarship* to Yale?"

"That was all you," he says. "I'm not listed on your birth certificate, so my wealth didn't factor into the financial aid decision. Need-blind admissions took care of the rest."

"But that fifty grand she showed up with the other day. That, uh, obviously came from you."

He just gives a little shrug.

"Well, thank you," I say. "It might literally be a lifesaver."

"Don't worry about it. I realize this is probably not a great time to start a father-son relationship, or whatever we would be. But when you're ready, I'd really like to . . . I guess just be in your life in some fashion. I feel like I know you already, in a way. I've read *Washington County* multiple times. I actually . . . I keep it on my nightstand. There are some passages I like to read because it makes me feel closer to you. Plus, you have a half-sister and a half-brother who would probably like to meet you someday."

He stops himself as if he's already said more than he intended, then continues: "Anyhow, for right now, I just want to help. Your mother says you're hoping to hire a private investigator?"

"Yeah, my lawyer—the lawyer you paid for—has a guy he uses. He's going to need a ten-thousand-dollar retainer. I don't want to take advantage of you and your—"

"It's fine," he says. "I got it covered. I'm not made of money like I used to be. I kind of stopped worshipping at that altar a long time ago. But I . . . I can still help. I *want* to help. And you're not taking anything that I'm not freely giving."

He stands up. "Come on. Let's get you a private investigator."

JOURNAL ENTRY: SUNDAY, DECEMBER 10

I should probably elaborate on yesterday's entry. After all, this is for my future self, and I want to remember *everything* about December 9, the day Charles Bliss and I made love for the very first time!!!

Start with what I was wearing. I decided to be a little classier with my clothing choices. I wore a simple A-Line dress that I got during a Thanksgiving weekend shopping excursion with my wicked stepmother. It has buttons up the front and pockets that are just large enough for my phone. It's not the least bit low cut. Well, as long as you keep it buttoned, anyway.

It's way more cute than trampy. Very Goodloe-appropriate.

Underneath, though, I went full tramp. Black lace bra and a tiny little thong.

I made myself wait until nine thirty before I started getting ready, so it was ten o'clock by the time I went out. They were doing trivia in the student center, which is always very popular, plus it was cold and windy. There was really no one to bump into as I crossed campus.

Mr. B's light was on again, though the shades were still drawn, so I once again couldn't see what was going on inside.

But this time when I knocked, he answered the door quickly.

He looked surprised to see me, and he said, "Oh, I thought you were going to be Leo."

I had no idea what he was talking about, but I asked, "Can I come in?"

He didn't say "yes" but he sort of just stepped aside, so I walked in and closed the door behind myself. Then I hung my jacket on a hook.

The moment I turned back toward him I knew I had chosen the right dress. The way he was looking at me, it was pure lust.

I went to my thesaurus just now to see if there was a better word than "lust." But it actually turns out to be the *perfect* word. He was staring at me with total, total lust.

He said something like, "You look really nice."

Or, no, wait. It was, "You look *amazing.*"

I went back and checked. Amazing was definitely the word he used.

My reply was a simple, "Thanks." But at that point, I was definitely getting a little scared, because I had thought about the moment so much—what I would do when I was finally alone with him in his apartment, with no one else around—and I couldn't believe it was actually happening.

He didn't seem to know what to do either.

"So what's up?" he said.

"I see you all the time on campus," I said, "but we never get a chance to really talk."

He didn't really say anything to that other than, "Yeah, uh-huh."

But this wasn't about what was being said. The words didn't matter. There was an unspoken dialogue happening. It was me saying, *I want you so much*; and him saying, *I want you even more.*

I don't really know who moved toward the other first. Maybe we both sort of did. But suddenly we were standing very, very close—closer than we had ever been able to get in class or around campus.

His face was flushed with excitement. I could see every hair in those beautiful eyelashes of his. It was like the air between us was supercharged.

And then he kissed me.

And, just, wow.

I've kissed people before, but it's never felt like that.

There was no nervousness, no self-consciousness, no hesitation. He tasted a bit like whiskey, which only made it more exciting, more illicit. It was so different from Aidan Broadmoor or any of the boys I had been with.

This was a *man* kissing me.

He was so sure of himself. His hands were warm and strong, and when he grabbed ahold of me and pulled me close, I could feel his erection pressing against me.

"You are so hot," he said.

Before I knew what was happening, he was unbuttoning my dress.

Then the dress was on the floor. His hands were all over me. I knew he had been drinking, but it was like I was the one who was intoxicated. His alcohol was making *me* less inhibited. I began clawing at him like I was a wild animal or something.

I just wanted it to happen so much. I wanted *him*.

He picked me up like I was lighter than a feather and carried me into the bedroom. Before long, he was inside me, filling me. It was so perfect.

Like something out of a romance novel.

MIDLOGUE 6

I realize the above passage fairly demands some kind of comment or response on my part.

Am I, in fact, the kind of low-life scum who would sleep with a student?

Or is what you've just read nothing more than a fantasy born from Hayley Goodloe's adolescent crush?

I'm afraid I can't offer clarity on that just yet.

Sorry if that makes you want to throw the book across the room. I'd still appreciate it if you stick with me for just a little while longer.

It will all make sense soon enough.

CHAPTER 24

I am expecting Ellery Lawrence will be driving a late-model Mercedes, a Tesla, or some other testament to conspicuous consumerism.

Instead, he leads us to a Toyota Camry that looks to be at least five or six years old.

When we get in, he tosses me a brick of cash, identical to the one that had been in Robbie's envelope. Hundred-dollar bills. A hundred of them. Banded together with a strip of paper.

Ten thousand dollars.

"Here," he says. "This is just a little spending money in case things get tight."

I'm once again flabbergasted by the sight of so much cash. Where is it coming from? Does the man not believe in checks?

"I'll pay you back as soon as I can," I say.

"Don't be ridiculous," he replies.

We travel north, toward Hartford. Jerry Cordova has set us up for a preliminary consultation with Craig DeAngelis, a licensed private investigator with Mitchell Investigations.

As Ellery drives, he peppers me with questions about my life, my writing, and my teaching. Before long we're pulling up to a small professional building whose bottom floor is home to a dentist and an insurance company. Mitchell Investigations occupies an office suite on the second floor.

Ellery casually pulls another $10,000 brick out of the trunk. Once we're inside, he hands the money to an office manager, who gives him a receipt.

Before long, we are seated in front of Craig DeAngelis, who has close-cropped gray hair, a thick neck, and the no-nonsense air of a retired cop.

As he introduces himself, it turns out he *is* a retired cop, having spent twenty years with the New Britain Police Department.

After a brief rundown of this and other qualifications—along with promises of discretion—he concludes with: "And I have to tell you, I'm happy to be working with Jerry Cordova again. He's a helluva lawyer."

"That's good to hear," I say.

"Jerry has given me the thirty-thousand-foot view of what's going on, and of course I read the papers," DeAngelis says. "It sounds like the best thing that could happen for you is if someone finds this girl alive."

"God, yes," I say.

"Okay. I still don't think we need to focus a lot of attention on that right now. We have to assume the police are giving that search everything they have. There's nothing I'm going to be able to do that they haven't already thought of or aren't already doing."

"Agreed."

"Then what we're preparing for is, I hate to say, the worst-case scenario. And that is, either they don't find this girl, or they find her body, in which case you're preparing an affirmative defense—alternative theories of the crime that create reasonable doubt."

"Exactly."

"Okay, good. Then I just want to make sure we're all on the same page with where we're focusing our efforts. As I understand it, you want us to take a look at Victoria Brock, the former attorney general."

"That was a theory put forward by a reporter for the *Hartford Courant*," I say, sounding defensive without meaning to. "But, yes, I'm hoping you can see if she's up to anything. Can you, I don't know, bug her house? Her phone? Her car?"

"Not legally," he says. "But we can definitely keep an eye on her, see if she seems to be up to anything shady or has anyone around her who might do that kind of work. The idea is that Brock had Hayley Goodloe kidnapped to stop Diane Goodloe from her announcing her own candidacy for Senate, do I have that right?"

"Yes."

"Okay, next, there's your ex-wife."

"Current wife," I correct him.

"Yeah. Sorry. Jerry says she emptied your investment account and now she's maybe trying to steal your book?"

"That's right."

"And, obviously, she could have manufactured and planted a lot of the evidence the police have against you—the bottle of scotch with your prints on it, the grocery bag with your prints on it, et cetera."

"Yes."

"Then what we'd be doing there is poking holes in her alibi. I'll probably go up to the University of Hartford and ask people if they can remember seeing her in the library that afternoon. If she's not there, it at least opens up the possibility that she was off doing something else. What kind of car does she drive?"

"A red Honda Civic," I say, then recite the license plate.

"Okay. I'll see if I can find any cameras near the Goodloe residence that might show that car in the neighborhood. The police might not have gotten everything—and, besides, they were looking for your car, not hers."

"Good thought."

"Now, finally we have"—and here he pauses to look at some notes in front of him—"Nutmeg Consultancy LLC."

"Right."

"Walk me through this one," he says.

I explain what I know about Nutmeg Consultancy, finishing with my efforts to watch the post office box.

"It's probably best if we take over that surveillance," DeAngelis says. "No offense, but we're trained for that sort of thing."

"No offense taken."

"Great. Then it sounds like we've got our marching orders."

* * *

After we're done at Mitchell Investigations, Ellery and I enjoy a cordial father-son lunch.

It's clear that he has a sharp business mind. He insightfully—and incisively—drills into the bizarreness of the publishing business model with a lawyerly interrogatory.

He asks so many questions, I barely get the chance to learn more about my father. What kind of investor is Ellery? What are some of his larger deals? Does he specialize in any particular industry?

Whenever I try to turn the conversation that way, he shifts the topic back to me.

The lunch goes by quickly. Afterwards, he takes me back to my hotel, but doesn't come in. He needs to be back in Boston by nightfall for some kind of can't-miss meeting.

He gets out of the car to say goodbye. What starts as a handshake turns into a hug. I thank him again for his generosity, which he modestly shakes off. We promise to keep in touch.

As soon as I return to my hotel room, I call my mother and tell her about my day with Ellery. It's emotional for her, having all of these secrets exposed. She acknowledges the narrative that she had long let me believe—that my father fled—was always false.

The truth is, she pushed him away.

She cries through much of the conversation, but at length I am able to convince her that I forgive her for whatever she perceives her transgressions to be.

She actually has nothing to apologize for. Everything she did was about preservation: of herself, and of me. If I take a Robbie-Bliss-eye-level view of matters—thinking like a scared, twenty-year-old fisherman's daughter from down east Maine, suddenly impregnated by some guy who owned a yacht—I probably would have done the exact same thing.

After we hang up, I take advantage of what light remains to take a long run through the end of a blustery afternoon and into a calmer twilight.

As the miles pass under my feet, I am actually daring to feel optimistic.

Ellery Lawrence and his money have been a godsend. Craig DeAngelis will keep digging until he finds something that clears me and implicates someone else. I will write a book about my experience, maybe even forge a new career identity, writing stories about the wrongly accused.

This is all still swirling in my mind as I reach the end of my jog only to find two police cars and one police SUV, lights flashing, parked in front of my hotel.

I slow from a jog to a walk, trying to make sense of what I'm seeing.

"There he is," I hear someone say.

Suddenly an amplified voice comes booming from the loudspeaker on the SUV.

"Lie down on the ground!" it barks. "Face down. Now!"

"What's going on?" I ask stupidly.

Again, I hear: "Charles Bliss! Lie face down on the ground. Failure to comply will be taken as a sign of aggression."

Silhouetted by the flashing lights, I can see an officer with a pistol aimed at me.

I raise my hands—that's what you're supposed to do, right?—and sink down to my knees. Then I gingerly lower myself until my chin is inches off the sidewalk.

Footsteps approach. They belong to Detective Michael Morin.

"Charles Bliss," he says dramatically as he clamps a cold pair of handcuffs on my wrists. "You are under arrest for the murder of Hayley Goodloe."

JOURNAL ENTRY: MONDAY, DECEMBER 11

I'm trying not to freak out here, but it's really difficult when all I want to do is be *with* him and close to him and have him look at me the way he did Saturday night.

Instead, he's blowing me off. And it's making me cray.

Saturday night, we were as close as two people could be. Emotionally. Physically. It was just amazing, how in sync we were. Our bodies moved as one.

All day Sunday, I was still floating. I looked for him in the dining hall and around every corner as I drifted dreamily around campus, near his office, going to all the places he might usually be.

Except he wasn't on duty and he didn't show up in his office or the dining hall.

Even if I did see him, I didn't have any expectation he'd stop and talk or, like, pull me aside for a stolen kiss. All I wanted was a glimpse of him, just to catch his eye from a distance and get that shared acknowledgment of, *Yes, this really happened.*

And, whatever, it was the weekend. And since Sunday night is mandatory study hours, I couldn't escape my dorm and sneak over to his place. Too much risk.

But I could still imagine him hanging out in his apartment, savoring the thought of me, just like I was with him.

Then today came and I saw him in the dining hall for breakfast, and he didn't glance my way once, even though I paraded right past his table. Same with lunch.

When class finally came, it's not like I was expecting him to shake everyone's hand and say, *Hi, I'm Mr. Bliss, I slept with Ms. Goodloe on Saturday night.*

Still, it seemed like he could have given me a quick, sly smile; or held my hand just a little longer than everyone else's; or worked in a little wink or something.

Instead, it was just the normal handshake.

I felt like dying.

When I told Calista about everything, she sort of didn't believe that I had slept with him. After I proved her wrong, she had a little freak-out.

Then she told me to calm down and think rationally for a second.

She said he *had* to act like nothing happened, because now he's worried about being caught; and that I had better get used to this kind of behavior and even embrace it.

For the next six months or so, everything that happens between us needs to be kept strictly secret.

But I don't know.

I still think he owes me more than that.

CHAPTER 25

Four cops lift me off the sidewalk and then form a clump around me, herding me into the police SUV.

I am seated in back, with my arms pinned behind me, separated from the driver by a caged, snot-smeared plastic partition that seems more suitable for something they're transporting to the zoo.

As we get underway, we point in the direction of the police station. Morin is seated next to me. I ask him several times why I am now under arrest.

He instructs me to stop asking questions.

We turn into the parking lot and I am assaulted by the sight of a large gathering of people, split into two sections on either side of the entrance to the station. The only thing holding them back is a few strips of plastic yellow crime scene tape.

Occasional flashes of light burst from the assemblage. I recognize these are photographers, there to record my ignominy.

The SUV pulls to a stop a few feet from the scrum. As soon as my door is opened, shouting erupts from the other side of the police tape.

Charles, did you kill Hayley Goodloe?

Do you have any statement to make?

Charles, are you innocent?

Where did you hide the body, Charles?

Were you and Hayley Goodloe lovers?

The ruckus—and the camera flashes—only increase as my feet touch ground and I straighten up. This is the moment they have been waiting for.

Behind me, the SUV door closes. Morin and the officer escort me toward the throng.

We do not move quickly. The cops are savoring this moment, giving the photographers ample time to document the spectacle that is accused murderer Charles Bliss, manacled and submissive, being brought to justice.

Before long, these images will be rocketing from one side of the country to the other and making laps around the globe. People in India and Indiana alike will be ogling me in my sweat-stained jogging clothes, as if I were somehow trying to outrun my guilt.

Once we make it up the steps and through the door—and Morin and the other cops are done enjoying their moment of fame—they take me to the altogether-too-familiar Interrogation Room 1. There, they unhook my cuffs from behind my back and attach them to a loop in the table instead.

"Is that really necessary?" I ask.

Morin doesn't say a word. He's not performing for the cameras anymore. This is about reminding me how powerless I truly am.

He leaves me alone in the room for a few minutes before he returns with Detective Prisbell, who is carrying a manilla folder with her. From their grim countenances, I can tell there won't be any effort at good cop–bad cop.

They are both bad.

"We're recording this right now," Prisbell informs me. "The Miranda acknowledgment you signed last week is still in force, but I'm going to remind you of it anyway."

"Where's Jerry Cordova?" I ask.

"He's on his way. But this is not an interrogation. We're not going to ask you anything. We're just going to tell you a few things."

Morin gives a small, malicious smile and says, "We found the car, Charles."

I know I shouldn't say a word, but I can't seem to stop myself from asking, "What car?"

The detectives exchange knowing glances.

"It was reported stolen last week," Morin says. "The owner admitted he left his key fob inside before he went out of town. Big oops on his part. But, hey, his stupidity is your gain, right?"

"I have no idea what you're talking about," I say. "If you guys think I've stolen a car, you're just . . ."

A scoffing noise escape from me. I know I need to shut up. *Don't speak, Charles. Don't speak.*

"Your first mistake was leaving it in Old Saybrook," Morin chides. "It's too nice a town. People notice a car that's been left there. Someone phoned it in. You did a pretty good job wiping down the interior clean, I'll give you that much. No prints. No hair. But you missed a little blood smear on the window. That was your second mistake, because that's how we knew we needed to look a little harder at the rest of the car. Your third mistake was your biggest one. You left a pen behind. We found it under the driver's seat. It has your prints on it."

He withdraws a clear plastic evidence bag from the pocket of his sport coat. It contains a black, click-top, ballpoint Bic pen that I recognize because I once had a box of them in my desk at work. I always carry a pen in my right front pocket. It was a habit formed long ago, because I never knew when I was going to want to jot down a plot idea or snippet of dialogue that suddenly burst into my mind.

At Carrington, I'm known as the guy who always has a pen on him.

"A writer, done in by his own pen," Morin says, shaking his head as if this saddens him. "Kind of poetic, don't you think?"

I don't answer. I'm still a little confused about what this car and pen have to do with anything.

Morin leans across the table and speaks in confidential tones. "Listen, we're going to give you one more chance to come clean here. I'm serious. This is it. As soon as your lawyer gets here, he's going to shut this down. That's his job. But I'm telling you, that's not in your best interests. Any hope you have of getting away with this is gone. Once Jerry Cordova sees the evidence we have, he's going to tell you to plead guilty, and you're going to prison for a long time.

"The only question now is how long. You tell us everything, right now, and as long as it matches what we already know, it's going to help with the prosecutor's sentencing recommendation. We'll testify that you were cooperative, that you were remorseful. Judges love that stuff. But this opportunity is pulling out of the station real, real soon. So do yourself a favor and get on board."

He leans back, apparently done, and waits.

The silence fills the room. They're both sitting there, looking at me. I'm returning their gaze with a flat affect—which, I'm sure, only makes them think I'm more guilty.

This staring contest lasts a minute, maybe two.

Prisbell purrs, "C'mon, Charles. You're a good guy. Do the right thing."

I shake my head. "You don't get it. I don't know how many times I have to say it: I have nothing to confess."

Morin exhales loudly.

Prisbell gives a little grimace; like, more than anything, she's just sad.

Our impasse is broken a few moments later when there's a knock on the door.

It's a young cop, and he's got Jerry behind him.

It is apparent—from the shade of red that has overtaken his usual gray pallor—that my lawyer is furious. And when he sees me, with my hands shackled to the table, he fairly explodes.

"All right, first of all, what the hell are you doing interrogating my client outside of my presence?" he demands.

"We weren't interrogating him," Morin says. "We were just—"

"Knock it off. I didn't just get out of Romper Room, okay?" he says. Then he turns to me and asks, "Did you say anything?"

I begin, "No, I—"

"Good, keep it that way," he says. "Now take the damn cuffs off him. He's an innocent man who has never once acted as a threat to any officer here—or anyone else, for that matter. This is a completely unreasonable use of force."

Prisbell looks to Morin, who pulls a small key from his pocket and fits it into the top of the cuff.

As Morin frees me, Jerry sits heavily down next to me.

"Sorry about this, Ace," he says. "I told these assholes five times that if they wanted to arrest you, I would drive you in myself and you would voluntarily surrender. But they've decided to be pricks instead. All so they could get their perp walk. It's disgraceful. Just disgraceful."

As the cuffs come off, I rub my wrists gratefully.

Jerry turns back to the detectives. "Now, what's this all about?"

Morin keeps a straight face, but still seems to take a great deal of pleasure in announcing, "We found Hayley's remains."

JOURNAL ENTRY: FRIDAY, DECEMBER 15

I would say this is getting bad, but the truth is it's already far worse than that.

It has been *six days* since our magical Saturday night, and Mr. B still has not given a single indication that anything happened between us.

Every day in class, it's the same *Hi, I'm Mr. Bliss.* And I want to be like, *Yeah, hi, I'm Ms. Goodloe. Your mouth was on my nipples, remember?*

And then class gets underway and it's just the same old, same old. He treats me like any other student.

And, yeah, I know what Calista says and I totally get that. But the problem is, it's not just in class.

In the dining hall, he hasn't looked my way once. And I would know if he did, because I spend most of my meal staring at him like a lunatic.

And then during activity period earlier this afternoon, we had a meeting to look at some of the new submissions for *Carrington Crossroads*. I was intentionally the first to arrive. He was sitting in the corner with his laptop open, and he just looked up for maybe half a second, gave me this empty smile, then immediately went back to his laptop.

Was he just worried someone else was going to walk in right behind me? Couldn't there have at least been some warmth in the smile?

I keep hoping I can engineer accidentally running into him on campus, in some place where we would be out of earshot of other people. Then he could be free to say the kinds of things he did on Saturday.

You look amazing.

You are so hot.

But it's like he's avoiding me.

It's driving me utterly insane. To have waited so long to be with him, to have it come together so perfectly, and now to be jerked in the exact opposite direction?

I know some guys like to play games. But this isn't just a game.

It's cruelty.

I'm going over to his place tonight. We're basically free from after dinner until lights out. I need to see him again. I need to get reassurances that what we shared meant as much to him as it did to me.

Or at least that it meant *something.*

Honestly, sometimes I think I must have just imagined everything.

CHAPTER 26

That one sentence—*We found Hayley's remains*—crashes into me like a cannonball to the midsection.

Even sitting down, I am staggered backward from the force of it, unprepared for its impact.

For as obtusely hopeful as it may sound, I had been so focused on the best-case scenario—Hayley getting free from or being freed by her captors—that I never had seriously considered the worst.

But, objectively, this is it. Hayley is dead. Any chance of a happy ending has been extinguished. This has now veered into the realm of tragedy, with no possibility of reprieve.

And I wish I could report that my primary reaction was driven by basic human feeling; that I was thinking about her family, or about her friends, or her other teachers.

But no. Selfishly, all I can think about is how doomed I am. The delicate crust of earth I was walking on has given way, sending me into free fall. And it's looking like a long, long way down.

Morin is either unaware of—or ignoring—my devastation. He has turned to my lawyer.

"Just to get you up to speed, we got a report of a stolen car in Old Saybrook," Morin tells Jerry. "There was a small smear of blood on the driver's-side window. The rest of the interior had been wiped, but we found a pen with your client's fingerprints on it under the driver's seat. In the trunk, we found blood spatters, some strands of blond hair, and a ripped piece of fingernail. It's all Hayley's. The rapid DNA test results came back a few hours ago."

Jerry's eyes briefly dart my way.

Morin also shifts his focus to me and says, "Finding the car in Old Saybrook was a break for us in another way, too. Because that told us we needed to spend more time searching the water and less time searching the land. We talked to an oceanographer who helped us figure out what would happen if you tossed human remains into the water in Old Saybrook, at the mouth of the Connecticut River. He calculated that between the river discharge and the tidal outflow, it would get flushed out to Plum Island, clear on the other side of the Sound. And wouldn't you know it, our friends in the Coast Guard found Hayley's torso not far from where the models predicted. It had floated all the way to Gardiner's Bay."

He shakes his head, but I still have the distinct impression he's enjoying this.

"What, you thought if we didn't find her hands or her head we wouldn't be able to ID her? That's another mistake there, big fella. We don't need to find the rest of her. In case you haven't figured it out, this is now over for you. O-V-E-R, over."

I am so taken aback by the brutality I'm being accused of, I can't even make my mouth work at first. My gaze swivels to Jerry, hoping he'll offer an impassioned line of defense.

His head is tilted back in a way that accentuates his jowls. He looks like he's swallowed a bullfrog.

Just so this scenario doesn't go completely unrebutted, I say, "I haven't been anywhere near Old Saybrook. Check the ankle monitor."

"You didn't get the ankle monitor until Thursday," Morin says. "Hayley disappeared on Monday. That's plenty of time to take care of this."

"But I've never even—"

"Shut it, Ace," Jerry grumbles.

—been to Old Saybrook, I want to finish. Like that's going to matter to anyone.

Morin waits for a moment to see if I'll ignore my lawyer's advice and continue my protests, but I have managed to contain myself.

Once he realizes I'm done, Morin says, "We're canvassing the area right now to see if anyone saw Mr. Bliss last week—maybe walking toward the bus station. But even if we don't get lucky there, the pen puts him in the car, and that's all we need."

Jerry has sunk even further into his chair.

"We also have this to consider," Morin says, gesturing to Prisbell.

She withdraws two copies of a printed-out document from her folder.

"We got access to some of Hayley's online history—her social media accounts, her cloud drives, that sort of thing," she says. "And one of the things we found was this."

She slides the printouts across the table at Jerry and me.

"Hayley was keeping a journal," Prisbell says. "Ironically, it was an assignment for your class."

This is true, of course. I require my students to write 250 words a day. It's just a way to get them working the writing muscle. I never read what the students write—it's meant to be private.

But I already have the sinking feeling this is about to haunt me.

"We'll include the entire diary as part of discovery, of course," Prisbell continues. "There's a lot to wade through. A lot of it is just angsty teenage girl stuff. But there was one passage in particular that really jumped out at us."

She nods toward the printouts. I pick up mine and begin scanning, but it only takes a few seconds to make my eyes feel like they're going to fall out of their sockets.

The first paragraph ends with the clause, *Charles Bliss and I made love for the very first time!!!*

I already want to throw up, but I force myself to read the rest of it. I can feel the blood creeping into my face and my mouth going dry.

When I finish, I put the paper down, and clear my throat.

With as much authority as I can muster, I say, "This never happened."

"Don't speak, Ace," Jerry says, sounding more tired than anything else. He's shaking his head as he continues reading.

"No, they need to hear this. It's the truth—if that even matters to them," I say, then jab an index finger onto the document. "None of this is real. Not a single word. You can't possibly take this seriously as evidence. This is a *creative writing* class. I told the kids the journals could be anything they wanted, and that they could put made-up stories in them if they wanted. That's what this is. It's pure fiction."

"Doesn't read like fiction to me," Morin says.

"Look at the ending," I say. "'Like something out of a romance novel.' That's because this basically *is* a romance novel."

"You have an explanation for everything, don't you, Bliss," Morin says.

"All right, that's enough," Jerry says more forcefully to me. "I need a word alone with my client."

* * *

Once we are alone in a nearby conference room, Jerry is characteristically blunt.

"Okay, Ace, you pay me to give you legal advice, and here it is," he says. "Prosecuting a murder without a body is tricky. This just got a whole lot easier for them. We gotta be realistic about what we're facing here. I've seen defendants go down on a lot less evidence than this. You start with the stuff they found in this girl's bedroom—"

"All of which could have been planted," I interject.

He holds up a hand. "Just let me finish. You got that. You got those bruises on your arms and neck that make you look like you were in a fight. It's something we have to contend with. You got no alibi for the time this girl disappeared and they have you *admitting* you have no alibi. They've got the clothes from the dumpster in a bag with your prints on them. That's something we have to contend with. The pen being found in the car—*another* thing we have to contend with."

"Also planted," I say.

He ignores this. "Then there's the blood in the trunk. And the torso being found exactly where they expected it to be found. You gotta understand how it works when they present this sort of thing in court. They parade all of these scientists and experts up there, and they testify to this stuff. And, yeah, I can needle them here and there, poke a few holes. But they're not using a needle. They're using a hammer. And it's hard to beat a hammer with a needle."

"On top of all that," he continues, "now you got this girl, speaking from beyond the grave. Juries *love* that kind of thing. I'll try to keep the journal out of evidence, but I'm not going to win that one. Any judge would say a jury has a right to decide for itself what to make of something like that. Plus, it's not like it's completely out of the blue. What appears to be the last significant act of this girl's life was accusing you of giving her chlamydia. And now we see how she would have gotten it."

"But I swear, Jerry—"

"Sorry, Ace. No one is going to believe you. A trial is a story. Right now, they have all the pieces of the story, fitting together pretty perfectly."

I feel myself slumping in the chair.

Stories are what I do. I know he's right.

"So you think I'm guilty," I say.

"I'm not talking about what I think. What I think doesn't even matter. What matters is whether there's enough evidence to make twelve people who don't know you unanimously decide that you're guilty beyond a reasonable doubt. And, as your legal advisor, I'm telling you there is."

He says it with the finality of a cold, steel prison cell door slamming shut in my face.

"So what am I supposed to do?"

"Let me see what kind of deal I can get you," he says. "They're acting all tough right now, because that's what they do. They might even be lying to you about what they have, and the Supreme Court says they're allowed to do that. Believe me, they're less secure about their evidence than they're letting on. They always are. They also know that juries are unpredictable. It's not easy getting twelve people to pull a rope in the same direction, especially these days. Plus, you've got the resources to fight this thing to the bitter end, and I'll make sure they know that. All of that factors into how good a deal they might be willing to offer."

"It's insanity we're even talking about this," I say. "I didn't do anything to Hayley Goodloe. I didn't sleep with her. I didn't give her chlamydia. And I sure as hell didn't kidnap her, chop up her body, and toss it into the Long Island Sound."

"At risk of sounding like a broken record, I'm just trying to make you aware of your options."

"That, and you've given up on me," I say, not trying to hide the bitterness.

"No. And you can take that thought out of your head right now, Ace. If I was a quitter, they would have found me at the end of a rope a long time ago."

He says this without anger, but I still say, "Sorry. That was—"

"Don't worry about it. Look, it's my job to give you the whole picture. If you tell me you want to go to the mat on this, I'm with you all the way. But take some time to think about it. Take all the time you need. Nothing that happens next is going to happen very fast. It'll take at least a year before this thing gets to trial. We can ask for a deal at any time, literally right up until the jury hands down its verdict."

I take in a deep breath and let it out slowly.

It's clear the cops are no longer taking a wait-and-see approach. Any uncertainty they might have once had is gone. It will be replaced by intense scrutiny on me.

But I actually welcome that.

Maybe if they work hard enough, they'll finally realize they're digging up the wrong yard.

"Okay," I say. "In that case, I want you to keep fighting this. No plea deal. Don't even bother asking."

MIDLOGUE 7

Hemingway said you have to kill your darlings, so I'm going to respect your time as a reader and make the tough editorial decision to cut out the next chapter.

In it, I was booked and processed; then I spent a difficult night in jail, where I pondered suicide.

The next day, at my arraignment, the State's attorney made the recommendation not to offer me bail. A felony murder charge comes with the presumption of no bond.

It was looking grim for me until Jerry got up and, in his inimitable Jerry way, utterly destroyed the State's argument that I was a threat to society or a flight risk.

During a particularly dramatic moment, Jerry made me stand up and display my ankle monitor. How, Jerry argued, could Charles Bliss be a flight risk if he *voluntarily* subjected himself to one of those? Jerry then pointed to the huge horde of media in the gallery behind me and said there's no way I could flee even if I wanted to—my face was on every website and newspaper in America.

Anyway, the judge warned me, "You're going to have to be on your best behavior and not give this court any reason to doubt its faith in you." Then she sided with Jerry and set the bond amount at $1 million, with a 10 percent option.

I weighed just leaving the chapter in. It was well-written and dramatic in spots.

But, ultimately, I decided it didn't add that much to the plot, or to your understanding of the characters, or to the book's conclusion. So it had to go.

I'll now pick up the story with the next chapter. But, first, this word from Hayley Goodloe . . .

JOURNAL ENTRY: SATURDAY, DECEMBER 16

I feel like I owe it to myself to be totally honest about what happened last night.

Maybe that's the only way to work through the pain.

So, to start with: Yes, I went over there thinking we were going to make up, then hook up.

Maybe that was silly. But that's how you think when you believe you're in love.

I dressed strategically. Which is to say: I kept my school uniform on, so I could appear like I wasn't all eager to climb into bed with him.

Then, surprise! I wasn't wearing underwear. It felt perfectly naughty and kind of turned me on.

Can you believe that? I was actually going to have sex with him again.

I am such a fool.

I am done being a fool.

Okay, first though—total honesty time—here is what happened, in all its humiliating glory.

I went over earlier than I had in the past, because I wanted to give us more time together—for the making up *and* the hooking up. But then right at the end, I sort of had to detour because there was this big mob of idiot boys coming back to Wentworth after the basketball game and I didn't want them to see me and ask what I was doing over on their side of campus.

That's how I ended up on the parking lot side of the dorm.

And that's when I saw *her*.

Mr. B's smoking hot dancer wife. *Emily*.

She was in the parking lot. And so was this ugly U-Haul truck.

I sort of hid behind some bushes so she couldn't see me. The back of the truck was open. There was a light on inside, and it had a ramp coming out of it. I watched her walk down the ramp, carrying this box.

At first, I was trying to remain calm. Like, maybe she was just returning some of his stuff? Or maybe she was going to be bringing boxes back out, too? People who get divorced always have their stuff all mixed up.

She took the box into the apartment and then *he* came out and got something from the truck and brought it back in, too. And, still, I was thinking this could be nothing, you know?

But then no one was coming out of the apartment with any boxes. The stuff was only going one way.

Finally, at one point, they ended up in the back of the truck together. And he sort of stopped her to say something. I couldn't hear it, but just looking at her face, she totally lit up.

And I was like, *Oh my God, she's still totally in love with him.*

Then it got worse, because he rested his hand on her hip. She said something. Then he said something. And then his hand kind of moved up to her stomach. And then they kissed.

It was not a we're-just-exchanging-stuff kind of kiss.

It was a we're-getting-back-together kind of kiss.

That's when it finally hit me:

She's moving back in.

After that, I ran away in tears. I was just so embarrassed. So *humiliated.* Is *that* why he was ignoring me all week? Because he knew his wife was returning home?

I was just some hit-it-and-quit-it snack he could nibble on before he returned to his preferred main course.

Thank goodness Calista was there when I got back to my room so I had someone to cry with.

But this morning I woke up and decided I am *done* with the tears. I'm actually just furious right now. Like, I can barely stop my hands from shaking.

I have never been this mad in my life.

All I want to do is hurt him.

CHAPTER 27

Within the hour, Ellery Lawrence wires $100,000 into a special account that the State maintains for posting bail.

I have no idea whether he's sent it from a bank or just walked into a Western Union with ten more bricks of cash from his seemingly indefatigable supply. Jerry is the one who talked to him, so I'm ignorant of the details.

Once the paperwork is processed, I'm free.

Unbelievably, joyfully free.

It's a few minutes before five when they let me out. I walk with full, unrestrained strides out the back entrance to the courthouse, where Jerry is waiting in his Buick.

Before I hop in, I actually pause to fill my lungs with fresh air. A gray winter day in Connecticut has never looked or smelled so good.

As soon as I'm inside the Buick, I begin gushing.

"Jerry, you were really terrific in there. After that State's attorney went, I thought for sure I was done for. But you were magnificent, totally—"

"Knock it off, Ace," he grumbles. "We got lucky."

"That wasn't luck, that was—"

"She was pissed off at the State's attorney."

"Who, the judge?"

"Of course, the judge," he says. "The State's attorney filed a motion in another case that had some factual errors in it. She thought it was intentional bad faith from his office. She was looking to punish him in a nice, public way. You just happened to come along. She called me into chambers earlier this afternoon and told me that if I could give her something to chew on, she'd bite. That's all that happened."

He shifts the car into drive and pulls out of the parking lot.

"This is the thing they never teach you in law school," he says. "For whatever is written in the statutes, the law is ultimately interpreted and enforced by human beings. And human beings are congenitally screwed up."

I look over at his spider-veined mass of a nose. It's not difficult to understand where he would have gathered that worldview.

"Now keep your head down," he says. "I don't want any of these news vans giving chase when they realize who I got riding shotgun."

I duck as we glide past the front of the courthouse. We ride the rest of the way back to my hotel in silence. Jerry doesn't seem like much for talking.

As soon as I'm back in my room—which feels like a four-star suite compared to my holding cell—I take a long, hot shower to remove the stink of incarceration.

Then I call my father to thank him and give him the blow-by-blow of the hearing. The more effusive I am in my gratitude, the more uncomfortable it seems to make him.

Next, I talk to my mother. She's happy I'm free, but I can tell the money Ellery is throwing around makes her uneasy. Our conversation is noticeably subdued.

No one, it seems, is as ecstatic as I am at the moment. Probably because none of them spent the previous evening trying to sleep on a stainless-steel bed.

But that's fine. I am feeling buoyant enough to have my own celebration. I'm starving, so I order Chinese. I splurge getting it delivered, even though the tip will cost me extra, telling myself it's an earned extravagance.

Then I crack open a beer, a hazy IPA that was just waiting for me in my fridge. It goes fast, as does the second. As the buzz settles in, I steep in the feeling that maybe my fortunes have finally turned.

I'm still waiting for the Chinese food when Leo shows up.

"There's the man of the hour!" he says, beaming at me as he enters.

"What are you talking about?"

"You know that arraignment was live-streamed, right? There are right now clips of your lawyer shredding that prosecutor playing all over the place. The media is eating it up. You know how they love a good counter-narrative. They've spent a week building up the cops and now they're tearing them down, questioning whether they've gotten the wrong guy. The worm has turned, my friend."

He settles himself into his usual spot in my sitting area with a beer. It's nice to finally be in the presence of someone whose disposition matches my own.

"My only question is: How the heck did you post bail? I thought Emily stole all your money."

I tell him about my surprise visit from Ellery Lawrence and his financial assistance. When I'm done, Leo fixes on an unexpected aspect of the story.

"And this apparently rich guy drives a Toyota Camry," he says.

"Yeah. Weird, right?"

"Drives a Toyota Camry and throws around bricks of cash."

"What are you getting at?"

"Nothing, it's just . . . you know, a Toyota Camry is a drug dealer car, right?"

I practically spit out my beer. "You've *got* to be kidding me."

"That's what the cartels are into these days. They're smart businesspeople. They've figured out that if you drive a late model Mercedes through certain neighborhoods, you might as well be waving a flag that says, 'Please search this vehicle and arrest me.' But a Toyota Camry? No one notices a Toyota Camry. Not in the city. Not in the suburbs. Not anywhere."

"You're out of your mind. Ellery Lawrence is a pure-bred Boston Brahmin—"

"Who quit the law and changed the subject when you asked him about what kind of 'investing' he's into. Doesn't that strike you as a little shady?"

I just shake my head.

"Forget it," he says. "What matters is you're a free man, redeemed in the eyes of the media—and therefore of the public. It was all the buzz in the dining hall. And there were definitely some faculty members who may have been on the fence about you and are now convinced you're innocent. Including a certain special someone . . ."

He waggles his eyebrows at me suggestively. Maybe it's the beer fogging my thinking, but I have no idea what he's talking about.

"Who?" I ask.

"C'mon, dude. Molly Millrose! She was practically *floating*. Her prince will finally be hers!"

"Stop it with that."

"You know what you need to do, right? Strike while the iron is hot. You see how this is all coming together perfectly, right? Now that you've been formally charged with a crime, your lawyer can submit the subpoena to force the postal service to tell you who applied for that P.O. box attached to Nutmeg Consultancy. All you need is a sworn declaration from Molly. I'm telling you, man, she'll be thrilled to give it to you now."

"You think I should text her?" I ask, reaching for my phone.

But he's already shaking his head. "A text isn't going to do it. She's going to need some in-person convincing. You have to go over there, get down on one knee, bat those pretty eyes of yours, and beg."

"Are you out of your mind? If I got caught trespassing—"

"Duhh, the whole point is not to get caught," he says. "We should probably wait a little longer. But then the timing is perfect. You can order us an Uber. We'll have the car drop us right in front of Molly's door. I'll serve as lookout. You zip in, charm Molly, and zip out. No way anyone would see you."

That's true. Molly moved off dorm several years ago. She lives in one of the freestanding faculty apartments on the outskirts of campus.

"And even if they did, no one is going to turn you in," he continues. "They already suspected you were innocent and now, after today, they know it. It's obvious you're being railroaded. C'mon. The sooner we get this sworn declaration filed, the sooner we get the subpoena. And the sooner we get the subpoena, the sooner we figure out what's really going on here."

"What if she's on duty?" I ask.

"She's not. I checked. But she's on duty Thursday night, and then she has weekend duty. If you don't get her tonight, you'd have to wait until Monday. I don't want to say it's now or never. But how much longer do you want to prolong this?"

His logic is hard to argue with. Perhaps only Leo could convince me to do something this risky and still think it's a good idea. But I say, "You're right. Let's do it."

Over another beer, we plan out our strategy, working it until it's foolproof.

Study hours begin at eight. If Molly's not on duty, she'll probably be in her apartment by then. But, just to give ourselves a little extra cushion—in case she gets held up by something—we decide to get there at nine.

That means we have time to kill before we depart, so we turn on the television and Leo finds an all-news station.

And, of course, the coverage is exactly as Leo has described. The talking heads are cooing over me and the "new questions" about my innocence—because before this, the only questions they had been asking were about my guilt.

One particularly airy gasbag opines that Jerry must have revealed "explosive" evidence to the judge in chambers that made her feel like she should issue a bond. There's speculation as to what that evidence might be.

It doesn't seem to bother them for a moment that they have no idea what they're actually talking about.

At eight thirty, I order the Uber. Fifteen minutes later, the driver texts me that he's waiting out front. We head down to the lobby to see a perfectly anonymous-looking Hyundai sitting beyond the glass doors.

We are soon being whisked toward Carrington Academy. Leo keeps up a stream of banter the whole time, like he's nervous. Once we reach Carrington, I direct the driver through the back faculty entrance and up to the apartment where Molly lives.

This is truly the riskiest part of the venture: the roughly twenty-foot dash from the car to the front door.

Leo cranes his neck in every direction. I'm doing the same.

"You think the coast is clear?" he asks.

"Looks good to me."

"Okay. No time like the present. Do it."

I shove open the door, practically falling out of the car. I know it's well below freezing outside, but for some reason I don't even feel the cold. My body is numb—from the excitement, I suppose.

Somehow, I stumble, bumble, and trip the twenty feet to the door.

"Go, go, go!" Leo whisper-yells from behind me the whole time.

Once inside, I half-walk, half-crash my way up the steps. It's only a two-story building, and Molly is on the second floor—on the right side, separated from the other second-floor apartment by a small hallway.

At the top of the stairs, I turn right, bumping heavily into the wall. When I get to Molly's door, I'm out of breath. But I don't want to stop to compose myself. I need to get into Molly's apartment—and out of sight of anyone who might report me—as fast as possible.There's no hesitation. I raise my hand and knock on the door as loud as I dare.

JOURNAL ENTRY: THURSDAY, DECEMBER 21

I have been a hot mess all week, riding this roller coaster of feelings.

One moment I'm achy—like, it actually physically *hurts* when I think about him. And us.

Then I'm furious and scheming all the ways I can get revenge against him.

Then I get hit by this big wave of humiliation. How could I have let this happen?

Then I'm just sad.

Then the ride starts all over again.

I'm still thinking about him way too much. My mother, the grizzled veteran of the therapy wars, has taught me that the clinical word for this is "ruminating." I am "ruminating" over Mr. B, thinking about him all the time even though I don't *want* to be thinking about him. I keep going back to that night outside the dorm and imagining all the things I should have done differently.

Why did I just slink away? Why didn't I say something? Why didn't I walk up into the back of that truck and say to his wife, *Hey, you know he kissed me that way, too, right?*

Would she even care? Or would she be like, *Yeah, whatever, he's mine again. Now go away, child.*

And then I tell myself I need to stop focusing on her. She doesn't even know about me.

This isn't about her. It's about him.

Really, what does he have to say for himself? I've imagined all these scenarios where I confront him and angrily demand answers.

How could he ignore me after what we shared?

How could he sleep with me when he knew he was getting back together with his wife?

Did he even like having sex with me? Did I do it wrong or something?

No, strike that last question. I *know* he liked it.

Ugh. I really need to stop ruminating. He's back with his wife. It's time to get off the roller coaster.

I've been this silly little girl who thought she was in love with her teacher and then threw herself at him. And he was just this big dumb *guy* who took what was being offered to him, like any guy would.

And really, I'm through with it. Through with him. Classes are over for the semester. The dorms are closing. My mother is picking me up in a few hours.

I'm spending Christmas vacation with her and Steeeeve. It's not my dad's turn and, besides, he's out of the country. The #MeNude thing is not going well for him. The total number of women now accusing him is up to five. The City of New York has brought criminal charges against him and has issued a warrant for his arrest.

Dad told me it's just a bare-knuckle negotiating tactic by the lawyer who represents these women. The moment my father offers to stroke a large enough check, they will stop cooperating with the criminal probe and the charges will vanish. In the meantime, he'll be waiting it out in a warm place that doesn't extradite people to the United States.

Whatever. My dad is a high-net-worth cockroach. He'll find a way to survive.

In the meantime, I'm just happy to be going home. This is the clean break I've been needing. I tell myself I'm not going to think about Mr. B at all.

But then I find myself back in these daydreams where he *begs* for my forgiveness and for me to give him another chance. He tells me how much I mean to him. He admits to being deeply torn between *her*, the woman he married, and *me*, the woman he loves and wants to be with.

But that's not reality.

Reality is: he hasn't said a word to me, and I haven't said a word to him. We are not even ships passing in the night. We might as well be on a different ocean altogether.

Honestly, it's like it never happened at all.

CHAPTER 28

The next sensation I am aware of is that I'm lying on something hard.

It is not the merciless steel bunk bed of my former cell, but it's close. It's maybe slightly warmer. And a bit scratchy.

A rug. Made of wool. It covers a hardwood floor. That's what's beneath me.

This is all deduced based on feel, not sight. My eyes are closed tight. The insides of my eyelids are lined with some kind of adhesive that makes them impossible to lift.

Still, I can tell there is light around me. Natural light. Which means wherever I am, Wednesday night has ended. Thursday morning has begun.

As I attempt to relax into the rug and go back to sleep—because I'm still completely exhausted—I become aware of several disagreeable sensations simultaneously.

One, my lower half is wet.

Two, the top of my head feels like it has a spike growing out of it.

Three, my right side—which I have apparently been lying on for quite some time—aches from a lack of circulation.

Where am I? What am I doing there? And how come I couldn't find my way to a bed?

I roll onto my back and release a groan.

That's when I hear, "Jesus Christ, you're finally awake."

It's unmistakably Emily's voice, but it couldn't possibly *be* Emily. She's in Rhode Island, wanting nothing to do with me.

I open my eyes and will them to focus.

It *is* Emily. She is dressed in jeans and a faded blue V-neck sweater that is a favorite of hers. Her hair is up in a bun, the ex-ballerina's preferred coiffure when she's concentrating, busy, or mad.

But there's no question which one it is this time. Her arms are folded, and she's standing over me. The disapproval emanates from her.

"What are you doing here?" I ask.

"Molly found you passed out in the hallway when she got back from duty last night around midnight. She didn't know what the hell to do with you, so she dragged your sorry ass inside. Then she called me. She didn't realize I was in Rhode Island. You're lucky she didn't call the police."

"Oh," I say, struggling to prop myself up on my elbows.

Sure enough, I'm lying just inside the door to Molly Millrose's apartment, on the rug in her entryway.

I gaze down at myself. A lot about this isn't right. But there's one thing in particular that's trying to work its way to the top of my mind.

Then it finally arrives. My hand flies down to my lower leg. Something very important is missing.

"My ankle monitor," I say, panicked. "It's gone."

"It was lying next to you in the hall," Emily says, retrieving it from the small console table that decorates Molly's foyer.

She hands it to me. I immediately slide it back on. A few moments later, it buzzes at me, my cue to press the button on the front. But nothing else happens.

How come it didn't sound an alarm? Why am I not currently under arrest?

I already have so many questions, and then my focus moves to my pants. They're stained a dark color. They smell faintly of malt and ammonia.

"Yes, you pissed yourself," Emily says matter-of-factly.

I lie back down and stare up at the ceiling.

"My guess is you were drinking on an empty stomach again," she says. "Am I right?"

"I'm not sure," I admit.

Did the Chinese food I ordered ever come? Did I eat it? If so, I have no memory of it. But I'm starting to realize there's a lot about last night I don't remember.

"How many beers did you have?"

There were maybe two before Leo arrived. Then he handed me another. Then there was one while we waited for the food. Then—

"I don't know," I say.

Whatever number I came up with would be inaccurate anyway.

"You can't keep doing this," she says. "One of these days you're really going to hurt yourself."

"What do you care?" I ask. "What are you going to do, block me again?"

It is intended to sting. I think maybe it has.

While I feel like I have a little bit of momentum, I go up on an elbow again and add, "Portia Swan called me, by the way. She figured out that the manuscript you sent her was mine. You're not going to get away with stealing it."

Her face contorts into a fierce scowl. "*Stealing* it?"

"Oh, you just forgot to put my name on it when you submitted it to her?"

Emily's hands go to her hips. "Are you still drunk or something? I wasn't trying to steal your manuscript. I was trying to *sell* it. I only took your name off it because I wanted Portia to fall in love with it first. Then I was going to tell her you wrote it. I figured she would be willing to give you another shot once she saw how good it was. I mean, she's Portia Swan. She could approve a fifty-thousand-dollar contract for a fast-food menu and no one would question it. I knew the only way to really jolt you out of your doldrums was to get another book published, but I worried you were never going to stop hating yourself long enough to actually find another agent. So I took it upon myself to be your agent."

She is speaking so unequivocally it's hard to doubt what she's saying. It's also difficult to mount too much of an argument when I'm stewing in my own urine.

Then she adds, "And, by the way, I sent Portia that email in early January, before any of this happened. I have no idea why it took her so long to look at it other than that she's Portia and she probably has unopened email that's older than I am. Ask her to forward my original email to you if you don't believe me. If I recall correctly, I sent it January 4. Hang on, let me check."

Emily goes into her jeans and comes out with her phone. A few pokes and swipes later she reports, "Yes. January 4 at 3:27 p.m."

She holds out the phone so I can see it.

It certainly blows apart whatever timeline I was assembling. If Emily's attempted purloining of my manuscript was supposed to be opportunistic criminality on her part, it seems difficult to accuse her of it now. On January 4, she wouldn't have even known the opportunity was going to present itself.

"Oh," I say.

"Yeah, 'oh,'" she says, shaking her head.

Just then, Molly emerges from her bedroom wearing a polka dot dress, looking like her usual war bride self. Her high-heeled shoes take three steps on the hardwood floor before she sees me.

"Well, look who's awake," she says.

"Sorry, I, ah, came over uninvited last night."

"Do I even want to ask what you were doing here?"

She has stopped at Emily's side. Both women are now peering down at me, making me feel even smaller and dumber than I did already.

"I, uhh, I really need a favor and I was hoping if I showed up in person—and didn't just text you—I'd be able to convince you better."

"And what favor is that?" Molly asks.

"Could you please just put what Hayley told you in a sworn declaration? We need to use it to get a subpoena. I can have my lawyer write it up if you want. All you'd have to do is sign it."

A crease appears between her eyebrows as she says, "What do you mean 'what Hayley told me.'"

"The thing about Nutmeg Consultancy."

The crease turns into a furrow. She's looking at me like I'm speaking Farsi.

"The texts," I add. "From the burner phone."

"What texts?"

My head hurts too much to be doing this right now. She's obviously playing some kind of game for Emily's sake and I don't have the energy to deal with it.

"You can drop the act," I say.

"Charles, this isn't an act. I truly have no idea what you're talking about."

I go into my pocket, pull out my phone, and go to that green-bubbled text conversation, scrolling up to the start of the exchange.

"This," I say, holding out my phone for her.

She takes it and reads. After a few moments, she says, "You think *I* sent you these texts?"

"Well, yeah," I say, because that had been my assumption for days now. "I mean, when I called you on it, you—"

I stop mid-sentence, as the faultiness of that logic becomes plain to me. Green Bubble only copped to being Molly after I accused them of it.

Molly is still looking at the screen. Then she says, "You really think I'd spell 'center' with an 're'? I'm not British."

She is holding the phone out for me to look at, but I don't need to see it. Having read the exchange dozens of times in my attempts to parse it for hidden meaning, I know exactly what she's talking about. Green Bubble asked me to keep the question of whether I wanted to clear myself "front and centre."

I just hadn't thought about it when I reached the conclusion it had to be Molly texting me.

"So if that wasn't you, who is it?" I ask.

No one has an answer for that. I groan and lie back down. This is too much to handle in the grip of a raging hangover.

"What made you think it was me in the first place?" Molly asks.

"I don't know," I say, looking up at the ceiling again. "I figured it was probably someone connected with Carrington. And then Leo kind of helped me put it together. It was his idea for us to come over last night."

Emily jumps back into the conversation with: "Who's Leo?"

"Leo Kastner. I keep meaning to introduce you guys. I just haven't had the chance yet. He's . . . He sort of became my best friend this past fall when you were gone."

"And he's a teacher here?" Emily asks.

"Yeah, he teaches English and coaches hockey. He's new this fall. That's why you don't know him yet."

Then Molly says, "New . . . at Carrington?"

"Well, yeah. Where else would I be talking about?"

Molly tilts her head and says, "Charles, there's no one at Carrington named Leo Kastner."

JOURNAL ENTRY: SATURDAY, DECEMBER 23

Oh, you've *got* to be kidding me.

On top of everything else, I can't believe I have to deal with *this*.

I haven't been mentioning it in my journal because I thought it was just nothing. But, yeah, I had been noticing that it burned a little when I peed. I thought it would just go away. Those things usually do, right?

Then after I got home for break it started really burning, to the point where I was afraid to go to the bathroom.

It smelled gross, too. Like fish.

If I was at school I would have just gone to the health center—oh my God, how I wish I was back at school!—but I made the huge, massive mistake of telling my mother instead.

I thought I just had a urinary tract infection. No big deal.

But then my mother said urinary tract infections don't smell fishy and she took me to a doctor.

And, yeah, it turns out I have chlamydia.

This immediately led to my mother grilling me. Who was I having sex with? Why wasn't I being safe? Who was this unclean, unsafe guy?

She kept pressing me and pressing me, and I didn't want to tell her the truth and we got in this huge fight. Steeeeve came in to break it up, but then he got involved and of course he took my mother's side because that's what he does.

Finally, I burst into tears and told them "the truth."

That I got it from Grayson.

That Grayson raped me.

Which isn't true at all, of course. But it was just so delicious and so scandalous and so very *eff you both* that I relished saying it.

You should have seen Steeeeve's face. That, alone, was worth the price of admission.

I then told them that this was the result of Grayson's addiction to porn, and if they didn't believe me, they could check his computer, where they would see that he watches videos about stepbrothers getting blowjobs from their stepsisters.

Well, that turned out to be a big mistake on my part. Because, naturally, Grayson totally denied ever having sex with me. And when they searched his computer, they didn't find a trace of pornography. Like, not even one stray boob.

Apparently, my big dumb lump of a stepbrother is smart enough to clean his browser history.

What's more, Grayson tested negative for chlamydia. Of course he did. There's probably not a person in the entire state who would want to have sex with him.

So now they know I'm a liar and it's just a mess.

Merry Christmas.

CHAPTER 29

There's no one at Carrington named Leo Kastner.

The statement sort of floats in the air for a moment, like it's being held aloft by thermal winds.

"Well, of course there is," I say. "Don't be ridiculous."

"Who teaches English, coaches hockey, and does everything else a faculty member normally does around here?" Molly asks. "Dorm duty, Blue and White, the dining hall . . . the classic triple threat?"

"Well, yeah."

"Then how come I don't know him?"

"You've been busy. Everyone is busy."

"Not *that* busy," she says. "I've never even heard of him."

"You're in different departments. Plus, like I said, he's new."

"Charles, I head up the new faculty mentorship program. If there was someone who started this fall named Leo Kastner, I'd know about him."

I grope around for an explanation before I hit on: "He must have opted out of the mentorship program. It's not like he's some kid fresh out of college. He's our age. He's been teaching for years in public school."

"Leo Kastner," Molly says. "With a 'K.'"

"Exactly."

She has her phone out. "Why isn't he listed in the website with all the other faculty?"

"I'm sure it's just an oversight. You know how the IT people around here are. It takes them forever to do anything."

"Maybe. Except I'm seeing all the other new faculty. He's the only one they missed."

I'm at a loss to explain that one.

Emily, who has just been watching us go back and forth, suggests, "Why don't you show her a picture of Leo? Maybe that will help?"

I scroll through my pictures on my phone until I reach the previous summer. I'm not a big camera guy. There's no Leo.

"I don't . . . I don't have one," I say.

"He's your best friend and you don't have a picture of him?" Emily asks.

"We're guys. We don't sit around taking selfies."

"Okay, then how about Facebook, Instagram, something like that? He must have a social media profile."

"Nope," I say. "Leo doesn't even have a phone. He's a bit old-school."

"He doesn't have a cell phone?" Emily repeats. "Are you kidding me?"

Molly is back with, "The hockey team photo is posted on the website. All the coaches are there. No Leo Kastner."

"I'm sure he just missed picture day."

I can feel Emily's frustration increasing.

"This is crazy," she says. "You're not . . . This isn't a prank or something, is it?"

"No."

"So someone named Leo Kastner told you to come here last night. And then he joined you?"

"Yeah."

"Did he drive you?" she asks. "I didn't see your car."

"We took an Uber. Leo had been drinking, too."

"Then where did he go? You obviously passed out in front of Molly's door. Why didn't he come to your rescue?"

"He was acting as lookout," I explain. "He probably just assumed I was safely inside Molly's place and then he didn't want to interrupt us, so he went home."

"And you can't call him or text him right now because he doesn't have a cell phone."

"Exactly," I say. "I know it's weird. But that's Leo."

"Does he have a landline?"

"Uhh . . . I actually don't know. I've never asked. We just see each other around all the time, you know? I find him, he finds me. I've never really needed to call him."

A momentary silence envelopes the room.

Emily breaks it with, "Are you always drinking when you see him?"

"What do you mean?"

"All right, start with: last night, you were drinking."

"Obviously," I say.

"What about the time before that when you saw Leo? Were you drinking then, too?"

I think back to Saturday, the night I sent Molly that grammatical trainwreck of a text.

"Yeah," I say.

"And the time before that?"

Thursday night. I woke up Friday morning with that soul-crushing headache.

"Yeah."

"Has there *ever* been a time when Leo has shown up that you haven't been drinking?"

"Well, of course there has been," I say.

But, having been put on the spot, I'm at a complete loss to think of one.

"Honey," Emily says gently. "Are you *sure* Leo is real? You once told me when you were a kid you had a hard time knowing where your imaginary world ended. Is it possible you've made him up? Is Leo your imaginary drinking buddy?"

"No," I say. "That's not . . . No . . . That's absurd. Leo exists."

Both Emily and Molly are looking at me incredulously.

"I can prove it," I say, pulling out my phone. "He was with me in that Uber. We were yapping back and forth the whole time. The driver would have seen Leo, heard him, everything. I can clear this right up."

I pull out my phone and find the text the driver sent me to say he had arrived the previous night. I call the number, then put it on speakerphone so everyone can hear.

"Hello?" a man's voice says.

"Yes, hello, sir, I'm sorry to bother you, but I was one of your passengers last night and I was hoping you could solve a little mystery for me."

"Okay," he says.

"You picked me up around eight forty-five from an extended-stay hotel by the highway. Do you remember me?"

"Yes, sir. You were my last passenger of the night," he says.

Then he adds, "With all due respect, you were very inebriated. I had to ask you four times to buckle your seat belt. I was worried you were going to throw up in my back seat."

"I'm very sorry about that," I say. "But I was hoping you could tell me: Do you remember the other passenger with me?"

There is no hesitation on his part. "There was no other passenger. You were alone, sir."

"Are you . . . are you sure?"

"Yes, sir. You were the only one in the car."

* * *

Acceptance comes slowly, painfully.

I have once again allowed the boundary between my large internal world and the real one get too low. And Leo happily hopped right over it.

All those conversations we had were just . . . me, essentially talking with myself in my head.

Just like I do with my characters all the time.

Leo never actually existed anywhere except my own overly fertile mind.

Still, how did I not see it? I realize I constructed for Leo a protective set of assumptions—like that he didn't have a phone, so I couldn't call him or text him—but I am still grappling with how to explain this to myself.

Did the trauma of Emily leaving just make me willfully blind to the fact that my brain had summoned a phantasm for companionship?

Or was it my writerly eccentricities? It's not like I've ever been one to interrogate my reality too stringently.

Or was it something more general to the human condition? Haven't we all grappled with the illusory from time to time? Don't we all sometimes wonder whether a memory is merely a mirage?

Whatever the case, I'm now entering this strange phase of grief. Leo may have been imaginary, but the sense of loss I'm feeling is not.

It's like someone has died. Leo was an important part of my life. He has been there for me through some pretty tough times, comforting me, supporting me, cheering me on.

At the same time, I am being forced to confront one enormously troubling fact:

All of those beers that I thought we were drinking together? Yeah, Leo wasn't actually helping me with that.

Just like he never helped me clean up.

It was all me.

I need to acknowledge that I have been drinking an astonishing amount of alcohol. Double what I thought.

And that was already way too much.

This puts my drinking into a category that is beyond excessive, beyond inappropriate, and beyond my control.

It is downright scary. I have fallen somewhere far beyond the deep end.

Saying I have a problem barely begins to cover it. I have a psychosis. Whether you label it as some form of alcohol-induced schizophrenia or pick another well-known derangement of the mind, there is no question about the spell it has over me.

That magic—that curse—is finally wearing away, leaving me only with this grim new reality.

Hi, I'm Mr. Bliss, and I'm a drunk.

A serious, serious drunk.

And if I'm being totally honest with myself—in ways I don't think I was capable of being until just now—my drinking didn't just materialize out of nowhere this past fall.

Yes, it got worse. But it had been a significant issue in my marriage before that. I am now thinking back to all the times Emily tried to bring up the subject of alcohol. My line was always that she was overreacting, that I was fine, that I could quit on my own anytime I felt like it.

But why would I want to when I didn't have a problem?

Then, over the summer, I actually tried.

I lasted four days before I slipped. Then Emily left me. At the time, I put the blame for her departure squarely on the miscarriage. But—and I am just now beginning to be able to admit this to myself—that was just me hanging onto denial with both hands. My drinking was the larger point of contention between us, wasn't it?

Beyond that recognition, there are other questions now creeping into my newly awakening mind.

If I've made up Leo, what else am I making up? *Who* else am I making up?

Has my imagination created more surprises for me?

Are there other fictions I've been clinging to without realizing it?

I truly have no idea. Philosophers throughout the eons have pondered whether it's possible to definitively determine external reality. It's a puzzle they've never exactly solved.

With all apologies to Descartes, *cogito ergo sum*—"I think therefore I am"—doesn't really help if it's your own thoughts that are betraying you.

CHAPTER 30

It is Emily that snaps me out of this existential reverie, pointing out the risk I am taking by staying on campus.

If anyone loyal to Ambrose and company sees me and reports me, it will be trouble. The judge's words are now ringing between the sides of my aching skull.

You're going to have to be on your best behavior and not give this court any reason to doubt its faith in you.

I'm sure being caught trespassing near the scene of my alleged crime would be sufficient provocation to get my bond revoked.

With the thought of a year in prison hanging over my head, we decide to make our departure after the start of first period—a time when everyone on campus should either be in class or otherwise accounted for.

Molly is already gone—AP Chemistry waits for no one—leaving Emily to shepherd me out. We decide to reverse my entrance strategy from the previous night.

Emily pulls her car up to the same spot where the Uber was roughly twelve hours earlier. With considerably more grace than I did last time, I make the twenty-foot dash from the apartment to the door, then duck as low as I can into the well in front of the passenger seat.

I tense while I wait to hear someone shouting me down or sounding an alarm. But it remains quiet.

Before long, we are safely out of the back gate.

Only then do I exhale and return to a normal seated position next to Emily.

"Where am I taking you?" she asks.

"I've been staying at a hotel near the interstate," I say, pointing her in the proper direction.

She drives with her mouth clamped shut, staring straight ahead. A wisp of hair has come loose from her bun and is trailing down the side of her face. I want to tuck it behind her ear for her, even though this is hardly the time for endearing gestures.

This is always how it's been for me with Emily. Even when I'm not supposed to find her gorgeous, I still do.

No one speaks for a while. Since she left, I have had a million conversations with her in my head—more with her than I've had with Leo, for sure. Yet now that she's actually here, I can't seem to find a single thing to say.

I decide to start simple.

"You're angry," I say. "And you're scared."

She continues driving like I haven't even spoken.

Then she says, "No. I'm not scared. I'm terrified."

"Okay, I—"

"Do you have any idea what it's like to find the person you married—the person you agreed to spend the rest of your life with—passed out in a pool of their own urine?"

I pause over my answer. But there's really no good one.

"I don't," I said. "I'm sorry."

"I'm also just tired. Molly called me just as I was going to bed. I wasn't exactly in the mood to drive an hour and a half and play babysitter to a drunk."

"Sorry," I say again. Then I add: "Thank you for coming."

"I only did it for Molly. It wasn't fair to expect her to deal with you by herself."

"I know. And . . . Look, I just need to say this. I've probably been needing to say it for a long time, but I want us both to be perfectly clear about this: I have a drinking problem."

She lets out a long breath. "Believe me, I know."

"Now I feel like I need to repeat it, like, a hundred times. I have a drinking problem, and it's really, really bad. I honestly had no idea how much I was drinking. I thought Leo and I were just, you know, two guys enjoying beers together. And, yeah, maybe I'd wake up a little hungover from time to time but . . ."

My voice trails off for a moment only because I don't know how to complete the sentence. I finally come up with: "To think I was having all those beers by myself is just wild. I can't tell you how crazy I feel right now. But I also need to admit to you what I'm just now admitting to myself. I've had a problem for a while now. You tried to tell me. I just wasn't ready to see it yet. I obviously need help—professional help, personal help, the whole thing. I'm out of control."

Quite unexpectedly, she pulls off into a parking lot for a landscaping company. As soon as the car comes to a stop, she buries her face in her hands.

By the time she removes her hands a few moments later, her eyes are moist.

She steadies herself with a few deep breaths before she says, "I can't tell you what a relief it is to hear you say that. It's been just sickening to watch you just . . . drink yourself stupid. It's made me angry, and sad, and incredibly frustrated, and scared and just . . . awful."

I wait until I'm sure she's done, then say, "I know. I'm sorry I put you through that."

She tilts her head back for a moment.

"This needs to be . . . a much longer conversation," she says. "And it's probably not one we should have in a parking lot. There's a lot I need to say to you about this subject. But just . . . Well, like I said, I'm relieved. We can just start there."

"And I'm sorry. I can start there."

"Thank you," she says softly.

"I'm sorry about Leo, too. I don't even know what to say about that part."

"Yeah, that part is weird but . . . It's actually pretty on-brand for you. I just think of all the stuff that used to come out of your brain when we'd go out for dinner and you'd make up stories for people. It's not like I thought I was marrying an actuary."

She unwraps her bun.

I know my wife. This is a good sign.

Then, completely unprompted, she says, "As long as we're apologizing, I've also been feeling guilty about . . . how I've been handling a lot of things with you. I shouldn't have blocked you. That was juvenile of me. I should have just told you I needed a little more time."

"No, I completely get it," I say. "You were shaken. The police were telling you a lot of awful stories—none of which are true, by the way."

I pause to take measure of her, but can't read her. She's back to staring straight ahead out the windshield.

"You do know that, right?" I ask.

She shrugs a little. "Yeah, I guess."

It's not exactly a ringing endorsement, but I'll take what I can get.

"I've also been feeling crappy about something else," she says.

"What's that?"

"I emptied out the investment account."

"Yeah, I noticed."

"My father kind of bullied me into it. He kept saying, 'It's Grandma's money, it's Grandma's money. Charles doesn't have a right to any of that. Grandma left that for you.' I told him it was *our* money and I pointed out that you had been supporting me through graduate school and paying my tuition. But he . . . he kept saying that if I didn't act fast you were going to steal it all from me and use it on legal fees and I'd never see a dime. And I . . . honestly, I don't give a damn about the money, but he kept hassling me. I did it just to shut him up. You can have it all back if you want."

"We can figure that out later," I say. "It's not really important."

"Well, it is important. It's ninety thousand dollars."

"Other things matter to me a lot more," I say. "Like us. I want us to be together. I want us to work through all this together. Please stay with me."

Her gaze lands squarely on me for just a second, but then flicks away again; like the image of me is something hot her eyes can only briefly touch.

"I need you," I continue. "Please. I . . . I just . . ."

There's no other way to say it: "I don't know what's real without you."

She does not respond to this. A truck rumbles past us on the road.

"And I'm not just talking about Leo," I add. "I'm talking about everything. Nothing in my life is real without you. Nothing matters without you. That's just the truth."

I stop to let her absorb this.

Then, finally, she says, "Okay."

"You'll stay?"

She turns back toward me.

"Yeah, I guess," she says.

Another *Yeah, I guess.*

Again, I'll take it.

"Great. You can—"

"But I'm only doing this as a . . . as a friend. This is not us getting back together."

"I know," I assure her quickly. "The room has two beds, so we don't have to share. This will be more convenient for you, anyway. It doesn't make sense for you to be commuting back and forth to Hartford from Rhode Island. You'll be a lot closer to school here."

She ponders this for a second and says, "You can't drink. Like, not even one beer."

"I know that. Believe me, I know that."

She immediately shakes her head. "See, but already that's wrong. I want you to not drink for *you*, not for me. It doesn't work if you're only doing it for me."

"I'm not. I honestly wish you could read my mind right now. I'm not a guy sitting here, just saying what his wife wants to hear. I totally, totally understand that I need to change. Like, I can't drink another drop. I get that."

"It's not that easy," she says.

"I know. Look, let's just take it one day at a time," I say. "Isn't that the whole thing at AA? We'll be together today. I won't drink today. We'll leave it at that."

"Okay," she says. "One day at a time."

* * *

Emily gets us back underway, completing our journey back to the hotel. When we enter my suite, I am immediately confronted by the detritus from the previous evening's binge.

There are empty beer bottles everywhere—on the coffee table, the side table, the dresser. I count eleven of them altogether. It looks like someone had a party.

Except, of course, I was the only person in attendance.

There is no sign of the Chinese food anywhere. All of this alcohol went into my very empty stomach. My blood alcohol level must have been off the charts.

Emily's eyes are going from the bottles to me, then back to the bottles.

It's obvious to me what she's thinking: She's made a mistake; she shouldn't have agreed to stay; even if I'm now admitting I have a problem, this is still reawakening a variety of past traumas, all of which are still very alive inside her.

"Yeah, it's bad," I say. "I mean, does anyone need more evidence that I have a problem?"

"Why don't you get out of those clothes and take a shower," she says softly. "I'll clean up out here."

She's being so kind, I want to kiss her; but I know that will not be welcome. I just mumble my thanks instead.

Before I go into the bathroom, I make a show of going to the fridge, collecting the few beers that managed to survive the previous evening's onslaught, and pouring their contents down the sink.

Emily notices, obviously, but doesn't react.

And I don't need her to. It's not like I'm expecting her to burst into applause because her husband is finally doing the right thing.

After I'm done with the shower and redressed, I tell her I'm ready to have that longer conversation about my drinking.

She says she's not. She says she might not be for a while.

Then she asks me to change the subject. I fill her in on all she's missed over the past two weeks, including the visit from Ellery Lawrence, who is paying for a private investigator.

This eventually leads to me making a call to Craig DeAngelis. I put him on speakerphone so Emily can listen in.

"Good morning," he says. "I see you got a bond. Congratulations."

"Thanks."

"You ready for an update?"

"As ready as I'll ever be," I say.

"Okay. First of all, we've been looking into Victoria Brock and keeping an eye on her, listening in as best we legally can. There hasn't been a lot to see or hear. She's been busy, running from campaign event to campaign event. In between she hunkers down at her place in West Hartford. There's been no activity or people around her we would consider suspicious, but we'll certainly keep watching."

I'm now thinking about the decision to tail Brock. It was based on the idea that Hayley was still alive and perhaps being held captive by people Brock had hired, to be released after the primary was over and it was too late for Diane Goodloe to enter the race.

That idea needs updating now that it appears pieces of Hayley are scattered about the Long Island Sound. But maybe it makes sense to keep watching her for a few more days, just in case.

"Okay," I say.

"Nothing to report on that Nutmeg Consultancy P.O. box. We're still watching. I've got a man there as we speak."

"Great."

"There's no question there's *something* suspicious going on with Nutmeg Consultancy. I showed its website to our tech guy. He said it's a pretty basic WordPress site with a domain registered by GoDaddy, which means we're not going to be able to get any further without some help from law enforcement. But then he did a search on the one image of Chris Sandman. It turns out the image was lifted from another site. The original is a computer repair technician from Tennessee named Maurice Edwards."

"So whoever created the Nutmeg site just stole this poor guy's picture and said, 'This is Chris Sandman.' But it's not really Chris Sandman."

"Correct," DeAngelis says. "Now this is probably the most interesting thing. When we're looking into a person or business, we check every public database we can—including campaign finance reports. Nutmeg Consultancy showed up in one of them."

"How so?"

"Not as a contributor of funds, which is how we usually find people. But as a receiver of funds," he says. "We found two expenditures that are listed as going to Nutmeg Consultancy at P.O. box 667, Hartford, Connecticut. Ten thousand dollars for fundraising consulting in November, ten thousand dollars for fundraising consulting in December. The reports are quarterly, so we won't know about January, February, and March until the first quarter reports are filed in April."

"But at the very least Victoria Brock's campaign has paid Nutmeg Consultancy twenty thousand dollars," I say.

"No, no, sorry," he corrects me. "Not Victoria Brock's campaign. Diane Goodloe's campaign."

JOURNAL ENTRY: TUESDAY, DECEMBER 26

I'm freaking out right now.

I overheard something I definitely shouldn't have overheard, coming from my mother's office.

It was bad. Like, so bad I don't even want to type it, because if anyone does read this journal, they're going to think I'm crazy.

I mean, I *must* be crazy. Look at who's raising me.

This will definitely be its own chapter in *Searing Memoir*. Maybe even the first chapter.

That's if I live long enough to write it.

And the biggest reason I'm freaking out is that I don't know what to do about it.

I immediately confronted my mother with what I heard. It, uhh, didn't go well. The first thing she tried to do was gaslight me—of course—and convince me that I was mistaken, that I didn't really hear what I thought I heard.

When I insisted, she then just told me she flat-out didn't believe me. She said that after the whole Grayson thing, she wasn't in the mood for more of my lies.

Or, really, for me.

What's the matter with you? Do you just need attention? I really don't have time for that. You know I need to be focusing on my campaign right now.

Yep. She actually said that.

You can always count on Diane Goodloe to put herself first.

I would tell my dad, but he has his own problems. There's not much he's going to be able to do about it from whatever beach he's hiding on.

He probably wouldn't believe me anyway. The first thing he'd do is call my mom and she'd tell him *Hayley is just acting out.*

And that would be the end of it.

No, I'm on my own here. And I seriously don't know what to do.

CHAPTER 31

There is silence on the line as Emily and I stare at each other in bewilderment.

"Nutmeg Consultancy has been receiving payments from *Diane Goodloe's* campaign?" I say, just to make sure I've heard DeAngelis correctly.

"That's right," he says.

"But . . . Hayley told someone"—and I now know it wasn't Molly Millrose—"that if anything happened to her, they should look into Nutmeg Consultancy, and that Nutmeg Consultancy isn't what it seems."

"As you've said."

"But if Diane Goodloe's campaign has been giving Nutmeg money . . . Does that mean Diane Goodloe paid Nutmeg to kidnap and kill her own daughter? That makes no sense whatsoever."

"It sure doesn't," he confirms.

"Then what's going on here?"

"I don't know. All I can tell you right now is what's in the campaign finance reports."

"I realize that, but—"

"Listen, I know you're a writer, but think like a sculptor for a second. When a sculptor starts with a raw piece of marble, it's just this big block of stone. It doesn't look like anything. And then they start hammering and polishing. And the first thing they chisel out might eventually be an arm or a leg or, like, a snout—because maybe this is actually a sculpture of a dog. But you don't know it yet, because the rest of the piece isn't close to done. You follow?"

"Sure."

"Good. Then you have to keep in mind that's what you're looking at right now. Just one body part. It won't necessarily make sense until you see the whole. So it doesn't help to try and guess what that is just yet."

"Okay."

"What does help is if you do some chiseling yourself. This person who Hayley told about Nutmeg Consultancy in the first place. You any closer to figuring out who that is? Maybe we can help there?"

"Maybe," I say, thinking of all those still-anonymous green bubbles. "Can you tell me who owns a burner cell phone?"

"I could give you the long answer, but the short answer is no. Even the cops struggle with that one. It might not even be a burner phone. They have those apps now that mimic a burner phone. Those things are impenetrable."

"Damn."

"Don't get too discouraged. We just got started. Maybe someone will come by and check that P.O. box and that'll clear up everything. We just got to keep working."

I thank him, and we wrap up the call, leaving Emily and me to consider this latest development by ourselves.

Hayley Goodloe was worried about someone hired by her own mother?

I think back to Diane Goodloe at that press conference and her stony performance. Was she, in fact, unconcerned because *she* was the one who was behind Hayley's kidnapping?

But why? What would motivate a mother to harm her own daughter? What did Diane stand to gain from Hayley's death?

Was it just an accident? Something unforeseen that went horribly awry?

We sit in silence for a while, stewing on all the contradictions and impossibilities.

Then Emily says, "Okay. I've been thinking about this Green Bubble person. It's not Molly. That's pretty clear. Molly was concerned enough about you to call me in the middle of the night. She took a lot of risk harboring you in her apartment when she could have just as easily called the police. If she really was sending you those texts, she would have admitted it at that point—if not to you, then definitely to me."

"Agreed."

"But I still believe you're on the right track thinking it was a Carrington person. Whoever is sending you these texts definitely *knows* Molly. Let me see your phone again."

I hand it over. She starts scrolling through Green Bubble's messages.

"Yeah, see? When you sent that drunken text saying you knew it was Molly, the sender immediately shifts and starts calling you 'Charlie.' Only someone who has heard Molly call you 'Charlie' would know to do that."

"Then you're thinking it's another Carrington faculty member?" I ask.

"Maybe. But that's not really the direction I'm going in here. Imagine you're Hayley Goodloe for a moment. Something has happened that makes you feel threatened. You don't know who you can trust. You're worried about getting in trouble—with whom, we don't know. But I think we can assume she means getting in trouble with grown-ups, because that's what kids worry about.

Think like a teenage girl for a second. Who is the one and only person you're going to trust in that situation?"

And then I get where she's trying to lead me. "Your best friend," I say.

"Exactly. That's what I would have done when I was that age. Who is Hayley Goodloe's best friend?"

"Calista Fergus. They edit the literary magazine together. They're roommates. They do everything together," I say and then another light goes on in my attic. "Of course! Calista is Canadian. She would spell 'front and centre' with an 're.'"

I snap my fingers as another epiphany hits me. "That must also be why I only heard from her when the dining hall was open. She can't risk being caught with a phone during the day. She must have hidden the phone somewhere and then been sneaking off during mealtimes to text me. It's got to be Calista."

"Totally," Emily says.

"Should I just text her? And, if so, which phone? Her real phone or the burner?"

I have Calista's real number stored in my phone, just like I have most of my students' numbers in my phone. I long ago lost the battle of not having kids text me—that's pretty much the only way they communicate these days.

"No texting," Emily says. "This feels like something that needs to be done in person."

"You're probably right. But how are we going to do that? We can't risk sneaking back on campus. Either of us. I don't belong there any more than you do."

"Then we'll just have to wait until she leaves campus. She can't stay there forever."

"The weekend is coming up. Maybe she's signed up for an off-campus trip? Hang on. Let me just check something."

I open my laptop and click the link for Carrington's school management system. It is my hope that Carrington's IT department has returned to its famously incompetent form and neglected to cancel my log-in privileges.

My name and password are already auto-filled. I hit ENTER.

Milliseconds later, I'm in.

I navigate to Calista Fergus's information. Everything I need to know about her is laid out in front of me—including her weekend schedule.

Sure enough, she's signed up for the mall trip tomorrow night.

That will be our best chance to intercept her.

* * *

Emily needs to go back to Rhode Island to get some things if she's going to start cohabitating with me, but I can tell she's afraid to leave me—like maybe I'll go on a bender the moment I'm out of her sight.

I assure her I'll be fine. There's no booze in the room and I tell her I'm going to keep it that way. I can manage by myself for a night without drinking.

Eventually, she's convinced and makes her departure, with promises to be back by the next afternoon.

Once she's gone, I make a grocery run. I then return, do my best to shake off the hangover-related exhaustion, and will myself to continue writing.

I'm deep in concentration when I'm startled by three sharp raps on the door. My head turns in that direction, but I still don't move.

"Come on, Charles, we know you're in there," a man's voice says.

It's Detective Morin.

"Hang on," I say through a phlegm-clogged throat.

I get myself out from under my laptop and lift myself out of the love seat.

He knocks again—even more insistently this time.

"Be right there," I call out.

When I get to the door, I pull it open maybe two feet. I'm in no mood to invite them in.

In addition to Morin, there's a uniformed state trooper whose hands are on his belt, not terribly far from his holster.

"What's going on?" I ask as I eye the trooper's gun.

"We need to talk with you," Morin says. "Diane Goodloe was murdered last night."

JOURNAL ENTRY: THURSDAY, JANUARY 11

I haven't had access to my laptop for two weeks and therefore haven't been able to journal. So this is me summing up a whole lot of crazy stuff that has taken place during that time.

The short version: Diane Goodloe declared war on me.

And she won in a rout.

It started two days after Christmas, when I confronted her with the fact that her campaign had been sending checks to Nutmeg Consultancy at P.O. Box 667, Hartford, CT 06106.

I took it to her and I was like: *See? This is proof of what I was talking about! You have to believe me now!*

And how did she respond?

By accusing me of lying again.

Then having me sent away.

I wish I was exaggerating when I write that. But three days after Christmas, I woke up at four o'clock in the morning with these people in my room—two big guys in white uniforms and this woman with a creepy underbite.

They were like, *You have to come with us. Do you want to do this the easy way or the hard way?*

Then they said the easy way was that I had to let them put handcuffs on me. And I was like, *What are you talking about?*

It was basically legalized kidnapping, because my mother was in the room with them. She was the one who arranged for all of this. She said something like, *I love you, Hayley. But I don't know what to do with you anymore. This is for your own good.*

They tossed me in this van and they started driving. They wouldn't tell me where they were taking me. I started *screaming* at them—and basically acting like the crazy person my mother told them I was—and they just kept driving.

All the way down to Virginia. To this place named Bell Mountain School.

It's a "wilderness therapy program" for teens with "maladaptive behavioral issues"—their main behavioral issue being they pissed off their parents so bad, their parents decided to torture them.

In the name of greater "resilience," heightened "self-esteem," and improved "emotional regulation," I was made to hike up hills and down into valleys until my feet were bleeding.

It didn't matter if was cold or raining or whatever. We were hiking.

I quickly learned the students had another name for Bell Mountain School.

They called it Hell Mountain.

And it earned its nickname in every way.

The food looked like vomit. It tasted like it, too. I wasn't allowed to have my phone, a laptop, or anything that connected to the internet, because that would be a "distraction."

We slept in these lean-tos with no heat. The only time we ever really got warm was when we were allowed to huddle around a campfire that, of course, we had to gather the wood for and make ourselves.

All of this hard living was supposed to be good for us. And, honestly, it did give me a lot of time to think about some of the choices I had been making, particularly when it came to Mr. B.

But other than that, I'm not sure what the therapy part was, other than that what we were being put through on a daily basis was so miserable it made everyone forget their other problems.

After two weeks of this suffering, I was brought into the main office.

And there was my mother.

In total control. Her favorite place to be.

She admitted sending me to Hell Mountain was primarily a scare tactic. She never really intended to leave me there. She just wanted to get my attention.

Now that she had it, she laid out a deal for me. Carrington was still on winter break. Second semester didn't start until Monday. I could leave Hell Mountain and go back to Carrington like nothing had ever happened.

But only on three conditions.

One was that I had to stop "making up stories" about Grayson and about Steve.

Two was that I had to keep my mouth shut. I couldn't breathe a word about any of this—not that I had been to a therapeutic program, and certainly not why. She was going to make sure that no news about her unhinged, mentally ill daughter could leak out and be used against her campaign.

And, three, I had to tell her how I got chlamydia. As far as she was concerned, that was the "trigger" that started my "acting out." She said she wanted to rid this boy from my life.

After I heard this, I immediately burst into tears.

And then I told her it wasn't a boy who gave me chlamydia. It was a man.

I threw Mr. B straight under the bus.

After two weeks of Hell Mountain, I would have done anything to get out of there.

Then I started crying even harder and I begged her not to take it out on Mr. B. He's a great teacher, and I really don't want anything bad to happen to him. For as much as I once fantasized about getting revenge against him, Mr. B isn't really my enemy anymore.

Not after two weeks of forced marches with blisters on my feet. There's only one person who's ultimately responsible for that.

The main thing they taught at Hell Mountain—the cure for everything, as far as they were concerned—was mindfulness. We were trained to be mindful about our emotions and mindful about our interactions and mindful about each moment we're living in as we live it.

And I'm mindful, all right.

I'm mindful that I want to kill my mother.

CHAPTER 32

They are demanding that I accompany them to the station.

I initially refuse—I've seen what cooperating with these people gets me—but then they put me on the phone with Jerry, who is already there.

He tells me to come in. A prominent state senator is dead. I'm not going to avoid facing questions. We might as well get it over with.

Before long, I've been ushered into Interrogation Room 1.

This sense of utter dread follows me in. Because it's totally impossible that they would have any evidence that links me to *this* crime.

But, then again, I've thought that every other time, too.

What will it be now?

Jerry is already in the room, looking typically gray. He gives me his usual unreadable nod.

"How's it going, Ace?"

"I've been better."

"Yeah, well, so has Diane Goodloe. Now, I'm going to give you three pieces of quick legal advice before this begins."

"Don't speak, don't speak, and don't speak?"

"Very good."

Detectives Morin and Prisbell are soon seated across from me. Prisbell slides a photo across the table. I look at it for perhaps half a second.

It's Diane Goodloe in deathly repose, with a plastic bag wrapped around her head. Her mouth is agape in a forever scream. Her eyes are open. It gives her this look of abject terror.

I turn away, not that it helps.

It's already an image I'll never be able to unsee.

"It happened last night," Prisbell says. "Her husband and son were out of town, spending the night at a casino. So she wasn't found until this morning. When she didn't show up for a staff meeting, two of her aides went over to the house to check on her. She was on the couch."

Prisbell puts down another photo, this one of the entire living room.

"It was staged to look like a suicide," Prisbell says. "There was a note next to the body. It was laser-printed, not handwritten. It mentioned her long, hidden struggle with depression. And it said she was distraught over the death of her daughter and she wanted to, quote, 'join Hayley in heaven.'"

Noting my discomfort, Prisbell reaches across and retrieves the photos before continuing.

"Since it was an unattended death, we called in a death investigator, who pretty quickly determined this was not a suicide. Whoever did this made several mistakes. On their own, each one is pretty small. But when you add them together, they tell a pretty compelling story. To begin with, the knot on that plastic bag is tied in back. It's not totally impossible for the victim to have tied it that way, but in every other suicide involving suffocation this death investigator had ever seen, the knot was tied in the front. That's the first thing that got the investigator suspicious. But there was more.

"The bag was secured around the victim's head by duct tape, but the duct tape didn't have any fingerprints on it. It was smudged, like whoever put it on was wearing gloves. Except Diane wasn't wearing gloves, and there were no discarded gloves found anywhere near the body, or in the trash."

I look over to Jerry. He is totally focused on Prisbell, like he's taking mental notes or already preparing his defense.

"There are also signs that the victim struggled," she says. "There is light bruising on both of the victim's forearms, just above the wrists, which suggests someone pinned her arms down. An X-ray confirmed the victim has fractured ribs, so someone sat on her or held her down. There's a small tear in the victim's dress, and I think everyone can agree Diane Goodloe wasn't the sort of person to wear torn clothing. It also seems odd that someone would put on a dress just to kill themselves. Most people who go that route are wearing comfortable clothing.

"Lastly, there's no evidence of drugs or alcohol anywhere near the body. The tox screen will take a few weeks, but we're guessing it's going to come back clean, which would be another major red flag. People who suffocate themselves numb themselves up first. It's almost impossible to suffocate yourself otherwise. No human being has that much willpower. The urge to breathe is too strong."

She stops.

Morin takes over, jabbing the table in front of me angrily with his finger.

"You're not going to get away with this, Bliss," he says. "The autopsy hasn't even been done yet, and we've already found all these mistakes. How many more are we going to find? That's your downfall, you know. You always think you're smarter than you really are. Where were you last night? What's your bad cover story that I get to poke holes in?"

"He's not going to answer that," Jerry says. "Especially when you know exactly where he was last night. Have you checked the data on his ankle monitor?"

Prisbell shoots a look at Morin, who seems to shrink a little.

"That's actually a little bit of a gray area," she says. "The device stopped reporting around nine thirty last night and didn't resume until roughly eight this morning. The monitoring company didn't alert anyone because it didn't know who to alert. They normally contact a parole officer, but Mr. Bliss isn't actually out on parole. That was obviously a bit of an oversight on our part. And wearing the monitor was never formally established as one of his bond conditions. So the short version is, we have no idea where he was."

Morin immediately reasserts himself: "Even if we can't prove he was in West Hartford, it doesn't matter. The truth is, he could have been there. Or it might not matter. He could have paid someone to do the job for him. The prosecutor is crafting subpoenas for his bank accounts, his credit cards, all of his financial statements as we speak. Mr. Bliss, are we going to find that you recently withdraw a large sum of money from somewhere?"

This sends a little shiver through me as I think about my recently emptied investment account. Will it matter to them if Emily admits that *she* took the money? Can she show them the statements for the new investment account?

"He's not going to answer that, either," Jerry says. "What's your theory as to motive? My client is already in a world of trouble with a murder charge for killing this woman's daughter. He's out on bond by the skin of his teeth. Why would he possibly want to kill Diane Goodloe? How would that benefit him in any way, shape, or form?"

"She was going to be a star witness against him," Morin says. "Early on during our first interrogation, I laid out for your client how Diane Goodloe was the one who first came across the mess in Hayley's bedroom and how devastating it was going to be for him when a grieving mother took to the stand. He obviously wanted to silence her."

"At the risk of getting himself another murder charge?" Jerry says incredulously. "That's a little thin, don't you think?"

"Then there's the revenge factor," Morin continues, ignoring Jerry. "From what the head of school has told us, Diane Goodloe spearheaded the campaign to force him to fire Mr. Bliss."

"It's not like killing her would get him his job back," Jerry counters.

"I've seen people murdered for a lot less. You have to take into account the way the killing was carried out. He obviously wanted to punish her. He probably enjoyed her suffering."

Jerry actually rolls his eyes. "Look, you asked me to come in because you wanted to question my client. He's here. I'm here. Do you have any actual questions?"

Morin has a set to his mouth like he's been sucking on a lemon.

Prisbell speaks very evenly. "Yes. Does Mr. Bliss have anything he'd like to tell us about the murder of Diane Goodloe?"

"No," Jerry says without even consulting me. "And if that changes, I'll certainly let you know. Are we done?"

Morin mutters something unintelligible that may have been a profanity as he lifts himself from the chair and leaves the room.

Prisbell looks like she's almost embarrassed.

"Yes," she says. "I suppose we are."

* * *

I follow Jerry as he limps with characteristic fatigue out of the station and into the parking lot.

"Okay, what was *that* about?" I ask as soon as we reach the parking lot.

"Why don't you step into my office," he says, nodding toward his Buick. "You're gonna need a ride back to your hotel anyway, am I right?"

"Yeah."

"All right, come on."

We have pulled out and are rolling down the street when he begins speaking.

"That," he says, "was two detectives under a lot of stress, having a disagreement. Morin thinks you're the perp. Prisbell doesn't. But the truth is, they don't know what's going on. That's the only reason you're not in custody. They're in the same place they were early on with Hayley Goodloe. If they charge you with the murder, that's something that will come back to bite them if they ultimately decide they want to charge someone else. Morin wants to charge you anyway. Prisbell is being the voice of reason."

"Oh," I say.

"You got anything you want to tell me?"

"What? No! Jerry, you can't possibly think I had anything to do with this."

"Doesn't matter what I think. I keep trying to tell you that. My job is to figure out what the evidence is against you and advise you accordingly."

"Okay, then advise me. How does it look?"

"Not as bleak as it does with Hayley Goodloe, for sure," Jerry allows. "At least so far, they can't peg you to the scene. And murder-for-hire is tricky. Even if they do find money missing, they have to establish beyond a reasonable doubt that you gave it to the person who actually committed the crime. It's very difficult to prosecute unless one of the confederates flips on the other."

"Well, then we should be good, because I don't have any confederates."

He takes this in without comment.

We drive a little farther in silence, then he asks, "How are things coming with the private investigator? Anything shaking loose there?"

I catch him up on the latest with Nutmeg Consultancy. He has no more ideas about its apparent ties to the Goodloe campaign than I do.

Though, now that the candidate is dead, the question has only taken on that much more intrigue.

Then I tell him about Emily's theory that the person who has been texting me is Hayley's best friend, Calista Fergus.

Jerry agrees to write up a statement for Calista to sign. Then he asks a more pressing question: "Is this girl eighteen? She can't sign squat if she's not eighteen."

I don't know. But that's something that would be in her file with the Carrington school management system.

As soon as Jerry drops me off, I run up to my room and log in.

Sure enough, she celebrated her eighteenth birthday in December. I text Jerry the good news. He promises to have something ready for me in the morning.

I return to writing, determined to get some more pages out.

But that's just to distract me from the reality, which is that my future now depends on having a positive interaction with an eighteen-year-old.

CHAPTER 33

The Friday night mall trip is a kind of Carrington institution, one that goes back nearly forty years, to the opening of this particular mall.

More or less every Friday night of the school year since then—except on special weekends like Homecoming or Winter Festival—groups of Carrington students have trooped off to the food court, the movie theater, or the stores for a few hours of mindless American consumerism.

I've probably chaperoned the trip fifty times.

What makes it especially useful for my purposes now is that the Friday night mall trip behaves as predictably as spawning salmon. The bus and/or buses usually leave campus at 6:45 p.m. and arrive roughly twenty minutes later. They park in the same spot—the far reaches of the back side of the property, near the Macy's.

That's where we'll make our move.

I wake up early Friday and immediately return to the keyboard. True to his word, Jerry sends the sworn declaration toward the end of the morning.

It's written in Calista Fergus's voice, though only if she had suddenly turned into a jowly gray-headed lawyer.

But it makes the point sufficiently: Hayley Goodloe believed she was in danger because of Nutmeg Consultancy. There's no reason she shouldn't be willing to sign this document.

I print it out in the hotel lobby and carefully fold it into an envelope provided by the front desk.

Emily rejoins me midway through the afternoon, as planned. She's packed enough clothes and whatnot to stay for several weeks.

Our relations are in an odd purgatory of sorts. We are nowhere near being man and wife. We still have many, many tricky conversations to navigate before that's even a possibility again. My drinking has damaged us in so many ways.

I can't force the process of reconciliation. It needs to unfold at its own speed, on its own course.

That's if it happens at all.

In the meantime, she has erected these unspoken physical and emotional boundaries that I am slowly feeling out and trying to respect.

Yet—even fully acknowledging that—we still have all this history together. It weighs on every word; loads extra meaning into every gesture.

I can't look at her without another memory coming back.

As we leave for the mall, I try to put all that out of my mind. Truly, it won't help with the task at hand.

By 6:45, we are parked out by the Macy's. We say little as the minutes tick by.

Finally, at 7:06, I see a white activity bus chugging in through the usual entrance. It has the Carrington logo on its side.

It passes within a few yards of us. In the pale-yellow gloom that filters down from the floodlights high above, I can see the driver is Grant Warren, Carrington's man-mountain associate dean of students.

I don't know if this is a good break or a bad one. Grant wasn't exactly friendly the last time I saw him.

He parks a few spots away from us. Emily and I get out of the car. I arrive at the bus just as Grant opens the door for the kids to disembark.

His head swings slowly my way and then stops with a jolt.

"I'm not here to make trouble," I say, putting one tentative foot aboard the bus to stop him from immediately closing the door. "I just need to speak with Calista. It's about Hayley. It's really important."

Grant's first reaction is quiet confusion. This is not what he is expecting on his routine Friday night mall trip.

It probably helps that we are on neutral turf, not the hallowed grounds of Carrington Academy. I am allowed here. He doesn't have the authority to immediately kick me out.

"Please, man," I continue. "It'll only take fifteen minutes."

Think of all those baseball practices. Think of your bachelor party. Think of when your dad died. It's me. I'm the same guy.

I don't want to embarrass him by saying any of that in front of the students—or put him in a position where he thinks I'm trying to show him up—so I try to say it with my eyes.

Inside the bus, there's shocked silence. I can feel a dozen adolescents holding their collective breath.

Grant looks beyond my shoulder, like he's checking to see if anyone else is watching this scene. Then he turns around, toward where Calista is sitting.

"Is that okay with you?" he asks.

"Yeah, whatever," she says.

He pivots back to us.

"Make it fast," he says.

Grant orders the kids off the bus and loiters just outside the doors as Emily and I board.

I take a seat across from Calista, but not too close. She's so small—maybe five foot two, maybe ninety-five pounds—I don't want to intimidate her.

She has red hair and pale, washed-out features, making her face difficult to read in this low light.

"Thanks for agreeing to talk with us," I say.

"Sure," she says.

"I believe you've met my wife, Emily,"

"We've done some trips together," Emily confirms.

"Yeah, hi," Calista says.

She's not volunteering anything beyond that, so I plunge in.

"Listen, Calista, I know you're the one who has been texting me from that burner phone," I say. "Obviously, I assumed you were Ms. Millrose and you let me continue believing that. But we talked to Ms. Millrose yesterday, and she confirmed she wasn't the sender. She actually helped us figure out it was you. Like a good Canadian, you spelled 'centre' with an 're.'"

Calista doesn't have a reaction to this. At least not any I can see.

"It's fine. I'm not . . . I'm not mad or anything. I understand this has been a . . . a horrible, horrible experience for you, and that you're scared and you don't know what to do. But there comes a time when you have to ask yourself two things. One is, 'What would Hayley have wanted me to do?' The other is, 'What's the right thing to do?' And in both cases, the answer is to help bring Hayley's killer to justice. In order to do that, we need your help. What Hayley told you about Nutmeg Consultancy, the police *need* to hear that. If you could sign a sworn declaration attesting to that, we could use it to get a subpoena that would help us figure out who's behind Nutmeg Consultancy. That's—"

"I don't know what you're talking about," Calista says suddenly. "I didn't send you any texts."

Out of the corner of my eye, I see Emily doing a kind of double take. She doesn't believe this any more than I do.

"Calista," I say softly, in what I hope is a nonconfrontational tone. "We both know that you did."

I retrieve my phone from my pocket, tap on the Messages app, and produce our exchange, which I hold out for her to see.

"I didn't send you any texts," she repeats.

Her face is still difficult to make out. But I don't need to see her.

Sometimes a lie is that obvious.

I look to Emily for help. She offers none, so I turn back to Calista.

"Yes, you did," I say, shaking the phone a little for emphasis. "You're Hayley's best friend. It's natural she would have turned to you and confided in you. She trusted you. And she would have wanted you to help now. Don't you want to catch her killer?"

The question wasn't meant to be rhetorical. Calista still doesn't answer it.

"Look, I know I'm not a teacher at Carrington anymore, but I'd like to think the Honor Code still applies when we talk. All I'm asking you to do is tell the truth about what Hayley told you."

"*Honor Code,*" Calista snorts. "You're going to talk to me about the *Honor Code*? You're the one who hooked up with a student."

To calm myself, I take in a deep breath and hold it while I look down at the floor of the bus for a few seconds.

Then I release it and say, "I didn't hook up with Hayley."

"Yes, you did. Hayley told me everything."

"I don't know why Hayley is saying that. Nothing ever happened between us."

"Yes, it did. I didn't believe her at first either, then she let me listen to the whole thing."

I can almost feel everything in my world lurch to a halt.

"What are you talking about?" I ask.

"She recorded you when she was in your apartment."

"That's impossible," I say. "Hayley was never in my apartment."

Now Calista is the one yanking out her phone. In its glow, I can, for the first time, see her a little more clearly.

She's angry.

"Then why was Hayley able to share this with me?" she asks.

After a few pokes at her phone, she turns up the volume on the side.

Then I hear my own voice. It's slightly muffled, but it's definitely me.

Oh, I thought you were going to be Leo.

As soon as I hear myself say "Leo," I tense up. Emily lets out a grunt.

This is bad. If I'm mentioning Leo, I must have been drunk out of my mind. How does Calista Fergus possibly have a recording of me at a time like that? I was always careful never to drink around students. I—

Can I come in?

The second voice is unmistakably Hayley's. It's shocking, even haunting, hearing her as if she's on the bus somewhere.

You look amazing, I say.

This is agonizing to listen to. There's no question I'm the one saying this; and I'm definitely drunk. I can tell from the way I slurred the word "amazing."

Thanks, Hayley says in reply.

So what's up?

I see you all the time on campus, but we never get a chance to really talk.

My reply is unintelligible. But then I hear something that is even more telling than whatever words I just said.

It's my breathing. Loud and labored.

I'm practically panting.

For a short while, there's barely any sound at all. I have to lean in closer to hear what's coming from the phone, it's so faint. Then it gets louder: first a little slurp, then a kind of suck, then a sharp intake of breath, followed by more mouth noises.

It's unmistakably two people—Hayley Goodloe and I, apparently—kissing quite passionately.

Even if I wanted to deny it, I am almost immediately betrayed by my next utterance.

You're so hot, my voice says, but it's gone low and throaty.

The next noises are all rustling fabric—along with more kissing noises—followed by a loud *thunk*.

Then the recording ends.

"That's the phone falling to the floor when you took her dress off," Calista says. "Then you took her into the next room and had sex with her. Hayley told me everything. I mean, how do you think she got chlamydia? You were the only guy she was with. She was totally obsessed with you. And you took advantage of that."

Even though the bus is parked, it's like the entire vehicle is swaying beneath me. I actually have to reach out and grip the seat in front of me to keep from falling over.

I am reeling. But what's most incredible to me isn't just that I've heard myself saying such wildly inappropriate things to a student, or that I kissed her, or that I disrobed her, or even that I apparently had sex with her.

It's that—even if I drill down into the darkest place in my soul—I have no memory of it whatsoever.

MIDLOGUE 8

And I swear to all that is holy: I still don't.

It's the one event that shaped my life more than any other, and yet I'll go to my grave without the slightest recollection of it.

JOURNAL ENTRY: FRIDAY, JANUARY 12

This hardly comes as a surprise, but my mom is on the warpath.

First, she went to Mr. Ambrose. Much to her disgust, he didn't immediately promise to have Mr. B impaled by a stake and left for the vultures to devour.

Instead, Mr. Ambrose told my mother that while he was taking the allegation seriously, he would still have to perform an investigation. He couldn't just fire a longtime teacher—and Carrington alum—based on one accusation.

Biiiiiiig mistake, Mr. Ambrose!

As soon as my mother heard that, she escalated to the board of trustees and started calling individual members and reminding them how much money her family had given over the years.

Never mind that it wasn't actually her money. She still acted like she, alone, had authority over the Goodloe Family fortune, conveniently glossing over that she doesn't control a dime of it.

But, of course, this isn't totally about money. It's also about power. And influence.

Mom has plenty of that.

And she isn't afraid to use it here. She's been letting me listen in on all these conversations because it's like she wants me to learn: *This is how you get what you want in the world. This, my daughter, is how you destroy your rivals.*

She even called Victoria Brock, who is her chief competition for the Senate nomination, and acted all sweet and suck-up-y. She's *that* pissed.

And the thing is, I might be touched if I thought any of this was about me.

But it's not.

It's about her.

It's always about her.

Her chief grievance here is not that an older man gave me a venereal disease; or that a teacher has abused his position of authority; or that any of this has done lasting damage to my mental or physical well-being.

It's that Mr. Bliss thought he could get away with doing something like this to *her* daughter.

Because, obviously, *she's* the aggrieved party here.

And now she's going to get Mr. B fired.

Again, not because she really cares. She just wants to make the point that no one messes with Diane Goodloe and gets away with it.

I actually feel really bad for him. Though I still have bigger problems.

The thing that got me sent to Hell Mountain in the first place—that awful thing that I overheard and have promised my mother I won't say anything about—hasn't gone away.

It's only gotten worse. My days are numbered.

I don't even dare bring it up around my mom. She'll have me sent away again.

But I need to do something. And I'm running out of time.

CHAPTER 34

I have nothing more to say to Calista.

Nothing that matters, anyway.

Not after what I've just heard.

Likewise, Calista has nothing more to say to us. Emily made some half-hearted attempts at interrogation, but Calista sticks to her story. She's not the one who sent those texts. As far as she's concerned, we've gotten the wrong Canadian.

We have a smattering of other Canadians—we have ice hockey teams, after all—but I can't imagine Hayley would confide in any of them.

The only other person with an English background at the school is Ken Rippinger.

But would he be helping me now after trying to take my head off the Monday Hayley disappeared? He would have known Hayley had her suspicions about someone else.

As I walk back to my car, the ground still feels strangely uneven, like it's being shaken by an earthquake that I alone can feel.

Emily is walking beside me. Though I honestly don't know why she isn't running away after what we just heard.

Behind me, Calista is getting on the bus. Grant Warren shunts her protectively away from me, keeping his bulk between me and her.

I can't look at either of them. Or maybe it's just that I don't want to know if either of them is looking at me.

Me with my shame.

Me with my guilt.

Me, a total disgrace in every way.

When I reach my car, I fumble with the handle to the door. It takes three tries before I can even get it open. I flop into the driver seat but don't make a move to start the car. I'm in no shape to drive.

I can feel something inside of me crumbling, and I know exactly what it is.

It's my own ornately crafted self-image.

There are many animals in nature that will put great effort into deceiving other animals with clever camouflages or showy displays. Human beings are the only animals known to go to even more elaborate lengths to deceive themselves.

We live in these grand illusions of our own making. We do more than just cloak ourselves in them. We inhabit them fully. We allow them to define ourselves and our worlds.

A central part of my own personal mythology is that it simply wasn't possible I could have slept with a student.

I have *boundaries.*

I'm *Mr. Bliss*, for God's sake.

Except I am now being forced to acknowledge everything I thought I knew about myself is wrong.

My illusions are shattered.

My cloak is shredded.

I don't even know who I am anymore.

And now I'm just sitting in a car, staring out the windshield into an empty mall parking lot, wondering how I'm supposed to keep going on with the stranger who is me.

Emily sits quietly next to me. Since I don't know how to digest what's just been thrust at me, I can't begin to guess how she's processing it.

But as soon as she does, I'm certain she's going to leave me.

For good, this time.

Doesn't she have to? Why would she possibly stick with me now?

I feel like crying, but can't. It's like my tear ducts won't let me attempt to be the object of Emily's pity. They know I don't deserve it.

"I wasn't lying to you about Hayley," I finally say. "I really thought I was telling you the truth this whole time. You have to believe that. I don't remember any of . . . of what you just heard. It still feels like it never happened. I mean, obviously it did, but I . . . I . . ."

"Charles," she says softly. "You have a drinking problem."

"I know, but . . . That's not just a drinking problem. That's like a . . . a monster has taken over the controls."

"That's *exactly* what a drinking problem is," she says. "When I say it's textbook, I mean it's actually in the book. Have you ever looked at Alcohol Use Disorder in the DSM-5? I have. When we started trying to get pregnant, I decided I was going to stop drinking. It was the right thing for the baby, and I thought it would be no big deal, right? It was actually a lot harder than I thought. I realized how much time and energy I spent planning my drinking, and thinking about it, and looking forward to it. I had allowed it to become a much bigger part of my life than I realized. I needed to have a real reckoning with that. And I can't tell you what *you* need to do, but . . ."

She lets that thought dangle out there for a moment before continuing.

"Anyway, one of the diagnostic criteria for Alcohol Use Disorder is that you put yourself in dangerous or harmful situations because of alcohol—like sleeping with a student. Another one is that you frequently continue drinking even after a memory blackout. That's you, all the way."

"I know," I say.

But there's still part of me that can't accept that this was *really* me.

Is it possible that recording was counterfeit? You can deepfake anything these days, can't you? The technology with images and video is mind-blowing. Could someone—Hayley or someone else—have done the same thing with audio? Used a real recording of me to make "me" say something I really wasn't?

It's not that I'm in denial. I'm ready to accept responsibility for the terrible thing I've done.

The many terrible things.

I just need to be sure.

And it occurs to me there's one relatively straightforward thing I can do to find that certainty. It's something my previously disbelieving brain is finally permitting me to work out.

I start with what we writers like to call the inciting incident: Hayley had chlamydia.

That's how this whole thing began. I've been telling myself she couldn't have possibly gotten it from me; that if I could just figure out who gave her this venereal disease, I could solve the entire mystery.

But is it possible I'm the source?

Victoria Brock's words from that morning in Ambrose's office are coming back to me.

Fifty percent of men who carry chlamydia don't have symptoms and won't test positive.

What if I was in that 50 percent? Had I, in fact, recently contracted the disease?

If I did, I know exactly where I would have gotten it from.

With renewed clarity, I start the car, and begin driving.

"Where are you going?" Emily asks when I turn in the opposite direction of the highway. "The hotel is—"

"I just have a quick errand to run."

She seems confused be this. "What for?"

I reply with just two words.

"The truth."

CHAPTER 35

A few minutes later, I'm pulling into the parking lot at Mick's. It's three-quarters full. It's a few minutes before eight. Friday night festivities are well underway.

I walk into the restaurant and make a straight line for the bar.

Jessica the Bartender is there. She's older than I remember; but, then, I don't remember much from that night. She's pouring tequila into a line of margaritas, which she loads onto a tray for one of the waitresses.

When she's done, she looks up and sees me. I am treated to the sight of full recognition cascading across her face, followed by more than a dash of shock.

She remembers me. She knows what I've been accused of. She's probably been quietly telling all her friends she had a one-night stand with *that guy on the news*.

"Hey, sorry to bother you," I say. "Do you have a second to talk in private? It's kind of important."

She glances down the bar, which is full of patrons.

"I'm pretty busy," she says.

"I know. It won't take more than two minutes, I promise."

She takes a towel from under the bar and quickly wipes her hands on it.

"Okay, come on," she says.

I follow her through a swinging door into a busy kitchen, where she guides us to an out-of-the-way spot against a storage shelf.

"I thought maybe I'd see you again after that night," she says. "But I guess not."

"Sorry about that."

"It's fine. I'm a big girl."

A waitress walks past us and gawks at me for an overlong moment on her way through the swinging doors.

"Listen, there's something I have to ask you," I say. "Around the time we got together, did you by any chance have chlamydia?"

She flushes slightly.

It's all the answer I need.

"I was going to tell you if I saw you again. A day or two after we were with each other, I started developing symptoms. I thought maybe I got it from you, but the doctor said it would have taken longer to come on than that. So I kind of went back and figured it was this other guy I had been sort of seeing but, believe me, am *not* seeing anymore and . . . Well, anyway, sorry about that. It's really not a big deal. You just need to get some antibiotics. Clears it right up."

Her words have come out quickly. I've barely heard them. But I still manage to muster, "Thanks."

"Yeah," she says. "Sorry again."

I stumble out of the restaurant and into the parking lot. I have a mind to keep right on going toward the busy road that fronts Mick's.

All it would take is one fast-moving truck to end this pain.

The only thing that stops me is that it would be too traumatic for Emily. If that's the route I decide to go, I'll at least do it when she's not around.

I look up instead. The light pollution of suburban Connecticut is bouncing off a layer of high clouds, leaving a drab, gray wash of night sky above me.

There is just one star radiant enough to force its way through the murk. I need to squint a little to see it, but it's there—this small pinprick of white, twinkle-twinkling from on high, struggling to shine its light on me through the vast reach of space.

It feels like a metaphor. And, as a writer, I am nothing if not attuned to metaphor.

I have spent years of my life—maybe my whole life—avoiding this light. I have allowed my eyes to stay shrouded in thick, foggy blankets of delusion.

Those coverings are now coming off, one painful layer at a time.

What's left is a rather brutal reality.

That recording is a hundred percent real. I'm the one who gave Hayley chlamydia.

I crossed the line with her, just as I once did with Breighlee Dumont.

The huge difference is that, with Breighlee, I was sober. I recognized the error I was making as I made it. Back then, I was only a social drinker, tilting back a beverage or two at faculty parties, bachelor parties, or weddings.

That was pretty much it. The chances of Breighlee finding me at a time when I was under the influence would have been incredibly small.

The math was a lot different by the time Hayley came around.

And, in this case, I wasn't merely drinking. I was drunk; so drunk that I was expecting a visit from the imaginary friend that, I am now recognizing, is not merely the friendly figment I once thought him to be.

This is the first misapprehension I need to shed—that Leo and my drinking are somehow benign. I always told myself I was a friendly, harmless drunk; that drinking only brought out more of my natural affability; that no one was being hurt by what I was doing.

This is manifestly untrue.

In fact, it now seems entirely possible that Leo Kastner is actually a representation of some sociopath I hide deep inside me. His arrival triggers in me this Jekyll and Hyde transformation, turning me into something barely recognizable.

And dangerous.

Extremely dangerous.

Because that tryst with Hayley is not the only time when Leo's appearance coincided with something deeply tragic.

There are at least two others that I must now confront.

The first is the Monday afternoon when Hayley disappeared. Leo came to see me then. I have this memory of us talking, of him handing me a drink, of him counseling me—all things, I now realize, that were pure inventions of my mind.

And then things are dark for a while. There are several disturbingly unaccounted-for hours. I thought I laid down for a nap . . . but did I really?

Did I, in fact, black out and allow Leo to take over?

Is it possible I went to West Hartford and tried to seduce Hayley with Glenmorangie? Then, when I failed, did I kidnap her in a stolen car, cut her up, dump her remains into the Long Island Sound, and toss a bag with her bloody clothes in the dumpster at Mick's?

It seems wildly implausible I could pull this off—as drunk as I was—much less have no memory of it whatsoever.

But it also seems pretty implausible I could forget having sex with Hayley. And I somehow did that.

Just look at the evidence against me. My fingerprints are on a glass in her bedroom. They're also on that bag the police fished out of the dumpster. My pen was in the car with her blood in it.

I'm all over this crime. And, yes, I suppose it's still imaginable all of these items could have been planted as part of some conspiracy against me.

But since when am I tempted by conspiracy theories? I believe in Occam's Razor, which states that the simpler of two solutions is usually correct. And the far simpler explanation here is:

I did it.

Jerry has been trying to tell me that a jury of my peers would vote to convict me based on the evidence. Were I to find myself on that jury, would I join them in their unanimity?

Yes. Without question. And not just because I'm guilty in the technical legal sense that the prosecution's case had been proven beyond a reasonable doubt.

I would cast that vote believing Charles Allan Bliss is truly guilty.

Now move on to the next case, the second time when Leo's appearance concurs with homicide.

The night when Diane Goodloe was killed.

In my drunken stupor, I removed my ankle bracelet, so there's no telling where I actually was. Did I, in fact, travel to West Hartford? Did I subdue Diane Goodloe, secure a plastic bag around her head, and hold her down while she suffocated?

Just thinking about it, I am shocked by the savagery that would be required.

With Leo as my vicious wingman, I seem to be capable of so much more than I ever thought possible.

I am so lost in these thoughts—all while staring up at that wan little star—that I don't even hear Emily as she walks up.

But she is suddenly at my side.

"Hey," she says. "You okay? What's going on?"

I look down at her.

"Emily," I say in a thick voice. "I think I'm a murderer."

* * *

As Emily drives us back to the hotel, I vomit words onto her, talking her through all of the thoughts that are now racing through my mind.

She takes it in with little comment. I can feel her psychologist's training kicking in. She is actively listening but reserving judgment.

I wish she would judge a little more. I need a wife, not a shrink.

The conversation continues as we enter the hotel room, but we're losing steam. Once I am talked-out—at least for the moment—I trudge into the bedroom, lie on the bed, and stare up at the meringue of the stucco ceiling.

Going through everything with Emily has only made me more certain about my culpability for the death of two innocent human beings.

It leaves me with really only one option.

After all, I am not Mr. Hyde most of the time. The vast majority of my hours—including the ones in front of me for the conceivable future—are spent as Dr. Jekyll. For whatever schism may exist somewhere deep inside of me, the person calling the shots most of the time is mild-mannered Charles Bliss.

The teacher who always wears a tie; who shakes students' hands at the start of every class; who counsels them about making the right choices, even when they're hard; who tells them to admit when they're wrong and accept the consequences.

What needs to be done here is quite clear. It's what the detectives have been asking me to do since the very first time they picked me up.

"I think I have to confess," I say.

Emily has no immediate reaction. She allows the silence to fill the room for a while.

I'm fully aware of the implications of what I've just suggested—both for me and for us. A confession would make the end of my days as a free man and, for all functional purposes, the end of our marriage.

It's not fair to ask her to wait for someone who is never coming home.

Emily would move on with her life, probably get remarried. Having children, raising a family, growing old—all those things I dreamed of for us—she would end up doing with another guy, all while I steadily decayed, eroded by the slow-drip torture of incarceration.

At last, she suggests, "Why don't you think about it for the weekend, then call Jerry on Monday morning? Get his input before you make any decisions?"

"Yeah, I guess that's a good idea."

The mere thought of contemplating this over the weekend exhausts me.

"All right," I say with a heavy exhale. "I'm going to bed."

"That's fine," she says. "I'm still pretty keyed up. I'll probably just go out into the other room and read for a while."

"Okay," I say.

And then, because I have never felt so lonely in my life—or more in need of soothing human contact—I ask, "Could you . . . would you mind coming in and holding me for a little while? Just until I fall asleep?"

"Oh, Charles," she says. "I'm sorry. I just don't think I can."

She gives me this sad little smile, but there's an edge beneath it. She is here out of pity and obligation. Not love.

Whatever lifelong incarceration would do to our relationship now feels like a distant concern. My marriage is already over.

It makes me wish I had walked out in front of that truck.

JOURNAL ENTRY: SUNDAY, JANUARY 14

I've heard it said that when times are tough, you find out who your friends really are.

By that way of thinking, Calista is *definitely* my friend.

I couldn't have gotten through the last few days without her. It's just so amazing to have someone at your side you can really trust.

People always underestimate Calista, because she's cute and small. But that girl has a backbone. She's a lot tougher than she looks.

And she would walk through fire for me. Just like I'd do for her.

I love that girl. I've just really been wanting to share that. She's so good.

Anyway, things are not going well for Mr. B. Once the board started going to work on Mr. Ambrose, his desire to treat Mr. B fairly folded like a cheap card table.

It was actually really interesting to watch it happen, because in that first conversation with my mother, he was acting all principled. He was saying things like *we have a process here* and *sometimes adolescents change their stories* and *please give me time to look into it.*

And then after the whole board started crashing down on him it was *we'll take care of this* and *yes of course he'll be gone* and *yes, Mrs. Goodloe, of course, Mrs. Goodloe.*

People will do anything to save their own skin.

I should know. I did it to get off Hell Mountain.

Anyway, it looks like Mr. B is going to be fired first thing tomorrow morning. My mother made it very clear nothing else would be acceptable.

Ambrose is going to find a long-term sub to finish out Mr. B's class for the year. All of our grades are going to be changed to A's to make up for the "trauma" we have suffered—and because Ambrose is no fool and wants to keep a bunch of high-strung kids and parents from getting all pissy with him.

Whoever they bring in won't be nearly as good or as smart as Mr. B. It's just not possible.

They probably won't make us journal anymore. I doubt they'll make us do much of anything.

I guess that means this is my last entry.

So goodbye, Journal.

It's been real.

CHAPTER 36

Some amount of time later—it feels like I only just drifted off—I awaken with a start.

Emily is pressing on my shoulder.

"Come on," she says. "We have to go."

I prop myself up and look at the clock. It reads 9:37.

"Where?" I ask.

"Campus."

"Campus? Are you—"

"I'll explain on the way. We have to go."

My pants are on the floor. As I step into them and my shoes, Emily is already leaving our hotel room. Even with her moving awkwardly, on account of the walking boot, I have to hustle to keep up. She's holding the elevator door for me when I get there.

In one hand she's clutching her purse. In the other, she has the envelope with the sworn declaration.

Which must mean . . .

"Calista says she's going to sign it," Emily confirms—reading my mind, as usual.

"How did you manage that?"

"As soon as you fell asleep, I started texting with her. I knew she was lying through her teeth. I just had to go to work on her a little bit."

"You're magic."

"No, I'm a former teenage girl. Loyalty to friends is everything at that age. First and foremost, she has to feel like she's sticking up for her friend. But if you're denying you slept with Hayley, she can't do that, because that denial is a total afront. She feels like she can't help in any way, shape, or form without betraying Hayley's memory."

"Right," I say as the elevator opens onto the first floor.

Emily continues talking as she charges through the lobby, into the parking lot.

"The first thing I did was tell her you had admitted to being with Hayley. Then I told her you were about to go to prison for two murders you didn't commit and that she was the only one who could prevent that injustice."

"How do you know I didn't commit them? How does *she* know?"

"Because whatever Nutmeg Consultancy is, it's not you—not drunk, not sober, not ever."

"Okay, and now we're going to campus to . . . what, exactly?"

"We're actually going to the pond. This has all come together in the past fifteen minutes or so. She admitted she had been lying to us about not sending those texts. She said to meet at the pond at ten and she'd sign the paper."

Emily is already in her car and has started the engine. I hop in next to her. As she drives, I wonder whether knowing the owner of the Nutmeg Consultancy P.O. box will solve the puzzle—or just be another enigmatic piece.

We ride in silence. I don't need to tell her where to go. After six years living on campus, she's as familiar with Carrington's entrances and egresses as I am.

Soon, we're rolling slowly through the suburban neighborhood that is closest to the pond. It seems like a lifetime ago when I was last here—when I naïvely thought Aidan Broadmoor would confess to having been with Emily and exonerate me.

Emily pulls to a spot along the road, halfway between two houses.

It's as good a place as any.

The car's clock says 9:56.

I give a quick glance up and down the street. There doesn't appear to be anyone out.

"Okay," I say. "Let's do this."

"Lead the way," she replies.

I close the car door softly behind myself and dash through someone's front-, side-, and backyard. The evening has become even gloomier than it was earlier. There's no moon or stars to guide us, just light from a garage across the street.

That gets us only so far. As soon as we're under the white fence and into the forest, the underbrush swallows us. The darkness is near total. I turn on my phone's flashlight. Emily does the same.

Dry leaves crunch under our feet. Were this a balmy spring evening, I might be concerned about being heard or seen by someone else who chose to take advantage of the pond's privacy.

Not on a night like this. We'll be the only ones out there.

After a few hundred yards, the gleaming white of the pond's frozen surface emerges. It is ringed on all sides by a shallow, sloping bank. I don't see Calista.

In Carrington tradition, when you tell someone you'll meet them at the pond, it's understood that you'll rendezvous at the side closest to campus proper—and then go somewhere else nearby. We work around the edge of the pond until we reach the spot where the walking path enters.

There's still no sign of Calista.

I look at the time on my phone. 10:03.

"Okay, I guess we wait," I say.

"I'm sure she's on her way," Emily replies.

I blow warm air on my hands, then shove them into my pockets.

The air is still. One of the homes nearby must have a fire going. The scent of wood smoke drifts around us.

I glance toward Emily, but she's not looking back at me. She's just staring out at the pond, her thoughts inscrutable.

A few minutes pass. I keep peering up the path toward campus in hopeful anticipation, but see only undisturbed darkness.

"You think we're being stood up?" I ask.

"It was her idea to meet. Why would she stand us up?"

"Maybe she had a change of heart. Should we text her?"

"Not yet. Maybe the mall trip is late returning. Just be patient."

I take my turn studying the pond. I can see the scratches carved onto its surface by ice-skating students.

Then, in the distance, I hear a noise.

It's just not quite what I've been training my ears to listen for. Calista is just one person; and a fairly small, light-footed one, at that.

This sounds like more—and much larger—people. Twigs are being snapped. Leaves are being crushed. They are not approaching with stealth. They don't care who hears them coming.

"What's happening?" Emily asks, taking two steps closer to me, as if I can shelter her from whatever is coming.

I have no answer for her.

Are there three of them? No, four?

Suddenly, a bright light is shining in my eyes, blinding me. I instantly bring my hand up as a shield, for what little good that does.

Large, dark shapes are moving on both sides of me. There are four of them, all men, and they have the kind of bulk that suggests many hours in the gym. They form a kind of wall behind us. They are wearing black tactical gear. All four have pistols strapped to them.

"Okay, sir," the first man calls out.

There is now a fifth man coming up the path. He is tall and slender, even in his puffy jacket, and I recognize him from paparazzi photos I've seen. The too-smooth face being lit by the flashlights behind me is quite distinctive.

It's Johnson Goodloe.

* * *

Maybe it's the cold, or the darkness, or the shock of everything, but I am slow to work out what's happening here.

We were supposed to meet Calista here.

This is not Calista.

We have been set up.

But why?

What is Johnson Goodloe doing here? What does he want with us?

"Hello, Mr. and Mrs. Bliss," he says as if he is greeting us at his Aspen ski chalet. "I'm Johnson Goodloe. I wish we could be meeting in a more hospitable setting, but I'm afraid I'm operating under some unusual circumstances."

Emily and I exchange wary glances.

"First of all, Mr. Bliss, I want you to know I hold no ill-will against you," he continues. "I'm aware you slept with my daughter, and under the ridiculous rules of our patriarchal society, I realize I'm supposed to be mad at you."

"Yes, Mr. Goodloe," I begin. "I'm very sorry I—"

"Oh, stop. Believe me, I'm no one to judge. That whole cliché—that a man ought to protect his daughter's sexual purity, or whatever—is rooted in the time when women were treated like property. Having a daughter who wasn't a virgin made her less valuable. It's absurd. Shouldn't we have progressed by now?"

He shakes his head.

"For whatever you may have read about me in the media, I actually love women," he says. "Anyhow, that's not what we're here to discuss. I need a favor from you."

"A favor?"

"Yes. The first part of the favor is that I'd like you to sign these."

He withdraws a tri-folded sheath of paper from his jacket. He peels away two copies of a document, handing one each to Emily and me.

It's so dark, I'm having a tough time seeing the words. Emily, who is a little closer to one of the flashlights, is the first to make out what this is.

"A nondisclosure agreement?" she says, incredulously. "You're luring us out under false pretenses in the middle of the night to have us sign a nondisclosure agreement?"

"I admit, it's a little unusual," Johnson allows. "You have to understand, there's a warrant out for my arrest right now. It's really just a negotiating tactic by the lawyer who has managed to make some women believe they're in line for a big payday. If I wrote a large enough check right now, the women would drop their complaint and the criminal inquiry would vanish. But I still have to be careful. I can't go popping my head up in a big, obvious way and I can't have you running to the media or the police and telling them where I am. I also can't have you telling the whole world about what you're going to see."

"And what are we going to see?"

"Well, that's the second part of the favor," he says. "But before I let you see it, I really have to insist that you sign those. Don't worry. It's pretty standard stuff. I just . . . a man in my position has to be careful."

Emily has been reading the document while Johnson and I have been going back and forth.

"This is ridiculous," she says.

But then she signs her name to the second page. I do the same. We hand the papers back to Johnson.

"Excellent, thank you," he says. "Now would you come with me, please? I promise this will all make sense in a little while."

"Where are we going?" Emily asks.

"I have a shore house not terribly far from here. It was my parents' place. I honestly rarely ever use it. But it's become my hideout the last few days. I'd really appreciate if you could come with me. It'll probably be faster if we drive. We'll drop you back here as soon as we're done."

Emily just gives me a look and shrugs. Johnson and his men lead us up the path to the STEM building. Parked in front are two large black SUVs with heavily tinted windows. They are blocking the paved path that leads to campus—the one that would normally contain a steady trickle of students, were these regular school hours.

The way the SUVs are sitting there carries more than a whiff of arrogance. He is Johnson Goodloe. His grandfather's name is on a dorm. He and his family have given millions to this institution and there is always the next capital campaign to keep in mind. He can act with total impunity.

We are soon head south on 91, then west on 95. A little while later, the dark mass of the Long Island Sound is looming before us as we pull through the gate of a sizable waterfront compound.

The SUVs tires crunch across pea gravel until we reach the main house, which is faced in stone. We pull up to the front entrance and are discharged into a rather grand entrance area, complete with a vaulted doorway that looks like it belongs at St. Peter's.

Ever the gracious host, Johnson invites us inside and into a grand living room that looks out on the water.

"Okay, thank you for your patience," he says. "Just one more moment, please."

He disappears for a moment. Then he returns and sits near us.

"Okay, where to begin," he says. "I guess with Steve Graham. You know who he is, yes?"

"Hayley's stepfather," I say.

"Precisely. He's why you can't say anything about what you're about to see."

"Steve Graham is . . ." I say, trying to keep up.

"Right," he says. "Steve Graham has been plotting to kill Hayley. And he actually killed Diane."

He puts this out there like everything should all be obvious to us, except I'm more confused than ever.

"I don't . . . Why would Steve Graham kill Diane? And why would he be plotting to kill someone who's already dead?"

"Well, yeah, that's actually the main reason I had you sign that nondisclosure agreement."

Johnson turns toward the hallway. "Okay, honey," he calls. "We're ready for you."

A second later, I hear footsteps.

And in walks Hayley Goodloe.

MIDLOGUE 9

I need to make it perfectly clear that the character who is "dead" but comes back "alive" is an overused trope best left for soap operates and telenovelas.

I certainly would never use such a hackneyed device in a serious work of fiction.

But, in this case, there's not much I can do about it. It's what actually happened, and I experienced it much the same as you did.

I'll let Hayley explain.

JOURNAL ENTRY: FRIDAY, JANUARY 26

Yeah, so it turns out I missed journaling.

Who would have thought, right?

But the moment I knew Mr. B was coming over, I felt inspired to write. I even opened a new file. I'm storing it locally—not in the cloud—and password-protecting it so it stays private.

And what's really crazy is, this isn't for class.

It's for me.

Just like Mr. B said it should be all along.

So I guess I should try to get down everything that has happened for the last two weeks. As usual, it's been a lot.

Start with the day I decided to disappear rather than stick around and be murdered by Steeeeve—also known as the day the world thinks I was "kidnapped."

I had to make it look good, because I had to make sure it would fool my mother.

If she had any inkling the whole thing was fake—that I was doing it to get away from my homicidal stepfather—she would have found me and shipped me back to Hell Mountain.

So I decided to make it look like Mr. B did it. I knew she would a hundred percent believe that, because she hated him so much and was already blaming him for everything else wrong with me.

I felt a little guilty about using him that way.

But the truth is, he used me, too.

This was just evening the score.

As it turned out, framing him wasn't that hard. I had a secret weapon. Calista. People always underestimate her.

The morning I was "kidnapped," Calista used a set of senior keys to break into Mr. B's apartment. She was wearing gloves so she didn't leave prints on anything. She took a bottle of scotch, some shot glasses, a grocery bag, and one of his pens.

After school, she drove to my house. We put some of the incriminating items in my bedroom, then messed up the place a little bit, to make it look like I had tried to fight him off.

That's what they always point to in the cop shows. *There were signs of a struggle.*

To make extra sure, we put together that little scene for the doorbell camera. It was supposed to be me saying, *Mom, help! It's Mr. Bliss! He's kidnapping me!*

And then Calista was going to bash the camera with a crowbar.

She just got a little too excited and swung too early, so the second half got lost.

It didn't end up mattering. All the other evidence we planted was good enough.

She then took me to my dad's shore house. It used to be my grandparents' house until they died. It's this super-private compound on the Long Island Sound. You can't see the neighbors and they can't see you. My dad uses it maybe once a year—if that—and usually not until July 4 weekend. It's the perfect place to lay low.

Once we got there, I cut my arm and we spilled some blood on the pajamas I had been wearing. We put them in the shopping bag and she tossed it in the dumpster at Mick's on her way back to campus.

Then she used a burner phone app to call the police and anonymously report that she saw Mr. B doing it.

The last piece of the frame job took a few more days. Calista bought a car off this guy on Craigslist. She paid him an extra thousand bucks to wait a few days and then report it stolen, which he was happy to do, because it means he got to collect insurance on a car he actually sold.

We put this blood smear on the driver's-side window, so anyone who found it would immediately be suspicious. Then we placed some of my hair, a broken fingernail, and a few sprinkles of blood into the trunk so it would look like my body had been there. After that, she drove the car to Old Saybrook, wiped it clean, and made sure the pen was a little hidden—but not too hidden. She took the bus back to Carrington.

All the while I was holed up at my dad's unused house, eating DoorDash deliveries. I placed the orders in my mom's name and made the delivery people leave meals on the front porch. I told them I was recuperating from plastic surgery and I didn't want anyone to see me.

Like they cared. I'm just another rich, weird person living in a big house on the water.

Anyway, I thought everything was going perfectly.

Then Steve killed my mom.

I honestly never knew that was part of his plan.

Or maybe it wasn't and he just added that part later.

Having my mom die was . . . really, really hard to process. It still is. Don't get me wrong, she was a total narcissist, and she never parented me for me, and I know I wrote I wanted to kill her after she sent me to Hell Mountain.

But that was just me freaking out. I didn't really want her dead, you know? I always had this idea—even if it was just a fantasy—that someday she'd wake up and she'd really regret having been so focused on herself and her political ambitions, and she'd realize she had completely missed raising me, and she'd feel so much guilt that we could then have a semi-normal mother-daughter relationship as adults.

I guess I'm just going to have to leave that one for therapy someday.

Anyhow, when I read on the internet about my mother's "suicide," I knew right away it was Steve's doing. My mother may be the Queen of Lexapro, but she still thinks too highly of herself to commit suicide.

And the idea that she'd kill herself because she was all broken up over *my* death? Don't even get me started.

Anyway, it made this whole thing feel super, super real. I was already pretty frightened of Steve but this made me realize how deadly serious he really was.

It scared me—enough that I actually called my dad. I asked him to come back from Cuba and please help me.

And he did. He dropped everything for me.

He's still a douchebag, of course. But I guess he's a douchebag who loves his daughter.

All the while, I had been talking with Calista every day. As I asked her to, she had been using the burner phone app to text Mr. B the stuff about Nutmeg Consultancy being responsible for killing me. It seemed to be working out, because Mr. B hired a private investigator and all that stuff.

But then when Calista told me everything that happened with Emily and Mr. B—that he was going to confess to killing me—that's when I knew the game had gone on too long.

I never thought that I'd frame him so well that even *he* would believe he did it.

So we told Calista to text Mr. B's wife and say to meet her at the pond.

And now my dad and his bodyguards are going to retrieve Mr. B.

I'm a little nervous about seeing him again, but I guess I'll have to get over that.

We could really use that big brain of his to help get me out of this mess.

CHAPTER 37

Hayley glides into the room with the poise of a queen.

It's astonishing to see her essentially unchanged. She's still that perfect Carrington archetype. If the admissions department came right now to shoot new photos, all she'd have to do is jump into her uniform and she'd be ready.

Emily is every bit as stunned as I am. Her hand has flown to her mouth, which is hanging open.

Hayley walks up to me, looks me square in the eye, holds out her hand, and says, "Hi, I'm Ms. Goodloe."

I stand. A certain reflex takes over. I grasp her hand and say, "Hi, I'm Mr. Bliss."

She turns to Emily and says, "Hi, Mrs. Bliss. I don't think we've met. I'm Hayley."

"You can call me Emily," she says.

I can't even imagine how this is all playing out in my wife's mind.

Hayley turns back to me. "You once told us that one of the reasons you did that was that you wanted us to know we started each day with a blank slate. Can we do that? Can we start over with a blank slate?"

I'm still too stunned to know how to respond any other way. So I just stammer out, "Yes, of course, but . . . how are you . . .

the police said they found your torso floating in the Long Island Sound."

"No," she says, looking down at herself. "It's still here."

"Yeah, but . . ."

Then a few of Jerry's words come back to me.

They might even be lying to you about what they have, and the Supreme Court says they're allowed to do that.

The Coast Guard never found Hayley's torso. That was just another in a line of shifting efforts by the detectives to compel a confession out of me.

That, however, is just one in a series of revelations as Hayley begins talking, leading us through this extraordinary hoax that she has pulled off, wherein she has managed to convince the world she was dead.

With each piece of planted evidence and each manipulation she leads me through, I feel a little less crazy. This is exactly what I thought had happened. I knew someone had taken that bottle of scotch and planted it in Hayley's bedroom; I knew I had nothing to do with those bloody clothes; I knew I hadn't dumped a car with a trunk full of her blood in Old Saybrook.

At a certain point, I just stopped believing myself.

After she takes us through everything, I make a time-out signal with my hands and say, "Okay, but wait. There's still something I'm missing here: Why does Steve Graham want to kill you?"

"Because otherwise he was going to be broke," Hayley says.

Johnson Goodloe jumps in: "When Diane and I got married, we signed a prenup that shielded all of my assets from her in a divorce. Once we split up, all she got from me was child support. That was substantial, believe me—seven hundred thousand dollars a year. But that's basically been her primary source of income for the last fifteen years. She only made twenty-eight thousand dollars a year as a state senator. Steve Graham basically had no income as her permanent campaign manager. Child support paid for their mortgage, their clothes, their whole lifestyle. Except that gravy train was finally coming to the end of its tracks. Hayley turns eighteen in May. Once she graduates from high school, the payments stop. He was staring at the edge of a financial cliff.

"Even if Diane did get elected to the U.S. Senate, they would still have been in trouble," he continues. "She would have been paid a hundred and seventy-four thousand a year. There's no way they could have kept their heads above water. I'm sure they would have had to sell the house. Plus, the Senate wasn't a guarantee. He wouldn't have known until the primary in August whether she was even going to be making that much."

"Sure," I say. "But how does killing you help his money problems?"

"Because I have a sixty-million-dollar trust fund," Hayley says bluntly.

Johnson Goodloe actually blushes a little, like he's embarrassed his daughter would blurt out the number.

"It's an irrevocable trust, meaning the terms cannot be changed," he explains. "It states that she gets full access to the trust when she turns eighteen. At that point, she can do whatever she wants with it. However, if she dies before she turns eighteen, the trust states that all funds will be disbursed to her next of kin. If you're a minor, the law defines your next of kin as your parents."

"Steve legally adopted me when I was six," Hayley says. "Part of it was just practical. I had really bad allergies back then and my mom was busy all the time. Steve was the one who took me to the doctor and it was just easier if he was legally my father. But it was also this big romantic gesture. The whole 'we're one family now' thing. I'm not sure what he even knew about the trust back then.

"But what it means now is that I'm worth thirty million dollars to him if I die. And obviously he didn't want to share the money with my mother. He was tired of having Diane Goodloe calling all the shots. He probably worried that she'd plow all thirty million bucks into getting herself elected. That's why he had her killed."

"Okay," I say. "Thirty million dollars makes for a pretty strong motive for pretty much anything. But how do you know he was actually planning to do any of this?"

"Because the day after Christmas, I overheard Steve talking on the phone with someone," Hayley says. "He thought I was at the mall with my mother, returning Christmas presents or whatever, so he wasn't trying to keep it quiet. The whole conversation was about how and where this person might be able to kill me and make it look like an accident. They were talking about where I would be when, and going through all the possibilities—car crash, drug overdose, you name it."

"He was talking with, what, a professional hit man or something?"

"I guess, yeah," Hayley says. "I told my mother about it immediately and she . . . she just didn't believe me. I mean, part of me can't blame her. It sounds so crazy, right? Plus, I had lied about something else big recently, and she saw what I was saying as a continuation of that lie. She just told me to stop inventing stories.

"Anyway, when Steve had been talking to this hit man or whatever, I kept hearing him talk about 'Nutmeg this, Nutmeg that' as being, like, where the money was coming from. It was something about how he just had to keep cashing checks made out to Nutmeg. I went into my mom's campaign account and showed her how there were these checks made out to Nutmeg Consultancy at this P.O. box. She *still* didn't believe me. And then it got worse, because she took it to Steve, and he had his story all ready to go. He showed her this website for Nutmeg Consultancy, which made it look totally legit—"

"When actually it was completely fake," I interject. "The image they used for the proprietor is actually some podiatrist."

"You mean Chris Sandman," Hayley says.

"Allegedly, yes."

"Yeah, well, after Steve showed my mom the website, he actually put her on the phone with Chris Sandman to demonstrate that Nutmeg Consultancy was perfectly legit and was doing all this stuff for her campaign. After that, Steve was all over my mom with this constant stream of: *Hayley is out of control. You have to do something about her. She needs to learn to be accountable for her actions.* Blah, blah, blah. And that's when my mom packed me off to that wilderness program."

As Hayley has been talking, neurons have been firing off in my head. It's like they are brightening a new path, shining a spotlight on Nutmeg Consultancy.

It makes sense now. Why was Diane Goodloe's campaign—not Victoria Brock's campaign—doling out $10,000 a month to Nutmeg Consultancy? That was how Steve Graham, Diane's campaign manager, was paying his hit man.

In monthly installments. He didn't have any of his own money, so he was siphoning off campaign funds to do it.

Nutmeg Consultancy was the shell company Steve created so he could cash the checks being sent to that P.O. box. He then handed the money to the hit man—Chris Sandman, or whatever his name really is.

I share this theory with everyone. They're all nodding by the end.

"The problem is, I've run all of this past my lawyers, and they've pointed out that we can't prove any of this," says Johnson, a man who surely has more than his share of attorneys on retainer. "All we really have to go on is Hayley's word that she heard her stepfather plotting against her."

The first words out of my mouth are very nearly, *Yeah, that's actually not my problem.*

Except it still is. For as much as I would like Hayley to stroll down to the nearest police station and make the authorities realize they probably shouldn't be charging anyone with her murder, that's not going to happen.

As long as her stepfather is financially motivated to kill her, Hayley won't voluntarily come out of hiding. And even if she did, the police might *still* be trying to blame me for Diane Goodloe's murder.

I need to get this figured out before I can even begin to stitch my life back together.

"Well, Steve's name is probably on that P.O. box," I point out. "My lawyer says that with a sworn declaration from Calista, we can subpoena the post office to find out."

"Oh, great," Johnson says sarcastically. "We'd be nailing a murderer for a campaign finance violation. He'd probably have to pay a fine and everything."

He has a point. It's still a big leap from purloining campaign funds to murder-for-hire.

Everyone sits and stares at the wall for a while. We're all pondering the same difficult questions.

"He must have made *some* mistake *somewhere*," Emily says. "There's no such thing as a perfect crime. What weakness does he have that we can exploit?"

"Well, the main one is that he thinks that Hayley is dead, that I've done him this huge favor of killing her," I say. "He knows I've been charged with that murder. He also thinks he's gotten away with killing Diane, because the cops like me for that murder, too. So far, the police are buying his alibi, which is that he and his son were at a casino for the night, and there are probably a hundred cameras that back up that alibi. I'm sure Chris Sandman was the one who did the actual killing, but that doesn't even matter. Steve thinks he just has to sit tight, wait for the lawyers to do their thing, and he'll be thirty million dollars richer."

We lapse into silence again.

I turn to Emily.

"This is going to sound nuts," I say. "But I really wish I could talk to Leo right now. I swear he'd know what to do."

She places one hand atop mine.

"Charles, you do realize: You *are* Leo. Leo is you. Just like any of the other fictional characters you've ever created, he's a part of you."

"I know, but—"

"You've always told me your characters talk to you."

"They do."

"Then see if you can get Leo to start chatting," she suggests. "I'm sure he's around somewhere."

The Goodloes have no idea what's going on right now, but I'm ignoring them.

This is no time to start acting sane.

I take in a deep breath, close my eyes, and try to reach out for Leo. He's my best friend. Hired at the start of the year. A public school guy. He teaches English . . . He coaches hockey . . . I think of Leo and hockey gear, a favorite subject of his.

My players' hockey gear smells like week-old roadkill, Leo says.

And suddenly he's with me. I know it's just in my head, but it doesn't feel that way.

It's like he's in the room.

"Leo, I really need your devious mind right now," I say.

"I know. You're too milquetoast for something like this."

"Are you up to speed with everything?"

"Yeah," he says. "This Steve Graham guy sounds like a real grifter."

"Totally."

"Well, you know the best way to catch a grifter, right?"

"No. How?"

Leo immediately supplies the punch line: "By offering him an even better grift."

"Do you have any ideas?" I ask.

Leo gives me his best cat-that-ate-the-canary grin. "Do you even need to ask?"

MIDLOGUE 10

There's this one thing that I've been trying to work into this book all along, I just haven't found the right place to put it.

So I'm putting it right here, toward the end.

Which is appropriate, since it's about death.

This may get a little weird for a second or two. But bear with me. I promise I'm making an important point.

I read a study a few years back. People who had been given terminal cancer diagnoses and knew they only had a few months to live were fed a psychedelic compound—in this case, psilocybin, which is the active ingredient in magic mushrooms.

While under the influence of psilocybin, a trained guide prompted these deathly ill people to think about the existential crisis they were facing.

Afterwards, nearly 90 percent of them reported a diminishing of anxiety and depression toward dying.

But here's the really important part, at least as far as I'm concerned—me, this guy who has spent so much of his life at war with his ego.

It's the mechanism by which psilocybin and other psychedelics work. Essentially, these substances temporarily strip away the ego.

People on psychedelic journeys no longer run everything through the filter of "I" or "me." Their ego goes on vacation for a little while, enabling them to see things in a completely different way.

That's why people who are tripping can stand there staring at a leaf or a flower like they've never seen it before. Because, in a way, they haven't; or at least they haven't seen it quite like this.

You might even say they are finally seeing the real truth.

And that's why they was suddenly less anxious.

While on these consciousness-expanding psilocybin journeys, these research subjects later reported they came to recognize death was not some final act; rather, it was just another thing that would happen to them—not all that different from graduating high school, or getting married, or taking a new job.

Would things be different? Sure.

But it was nothing to be too worried about.

Death was just another transition.

Another boundary they were going to cross.

I like that way of thinking.

CHAPTER 38

Two-and-a-half days of planning, plotting, and scheming later, it's just about time for me to head out.

It is Monday morning. It seems impossible that only two weeks have passed since I was called into the head of school's office to have my existence capsized.

Now here I am, tentatively permitting the belief that perhaps this Monday will be the one where I am able to begin righting myself.

The forecast calls for an unusually balmy day for late January in Connecticut, with bright sunshine and a high in the mid-fifties. The sky is clear and cloudless.

I hope this is an omen.

The weekend has been a busy one. Various approaches have been proposed, rejected, and revamped. Timelines, contingencies, and worst-case scenarios have been imagined and reimagined. Potential points of failure have been proposed and stress-tested.

A plan has now been agreed upon and put into place. I just need to do my part.

I have been fully dressed for some time now—a button-down shirt, a blue sweater, and khakis. I have been killing time—and nervous energy—by pacing around the hotel suite.

During one of my laps, I stop in front of Emily.

She's on the love seat with several journal articles spread on the coffee table in front of her. Her computer is in her lap. This is dissertation work, and she is grinding hard on it. Her hair is in a bun.

After a few seconds, she looks up at me. She's wearing frumpy sweatpants and an old long-sleeve T-shirt.

I still think she looks dead sexy. Which is probably just another in a long series of signs that I remain madly in love with my wife.

We haven't spent one second of the past few days talking about the future or our relationship. There has seldom been time. And even when there has been, the moment has never been right.

It's not right now, either. And yet I feel compelled to say *something.*

"I really . . . I really appreciate that you've been here and that you've been . . . just . . . sticking by me."

She doesn't reply. Her face is this unreadable mask.

"I know it hasn't been easy for you," I continue. "I have to be honest; I still don't totally understand why you haven't just left me."

The mask stays in place for another moment or two.

And then it rather dramatically crumbles. Wetness pools in the corners of her eyes. Her hand flies to her mouth. Her shoulders begin to shake.

"Hey," I say, walking over to the couch and sitting next to her. "What's the matter?"

Tears are now rolling down her face but she's not dabbing at them. She's just letting them flow. It's all I can do not to reach out and wipe them away for her.

"I just . . . I just don't want you to do anything stupid today," she says.

"It'll be fine. Nothing bad is going to happen."

She shakes her head. "You don't *know* that. You guys have all these plans but it's like . . . I don't know, like you're plotting out a scene in a movie or something. You don't get to reshoot it if it goes wrong. This is *real*."

"I'll be careful."

This does not reassure her.

"I just," she begins, stops, then restarts, "I care about . . . about your safety."

My stomach does a flip. Even if she's just expressing the same concern for my welfare she'd extend to a stray dog walking along a highway, it's the first time she's voiced anything close to this since she's come back from Rhode Island.

It fills me with hope.

"I understand," I say.

"No, you *don't* understand. You really, really don't. You can't *begin* to understand."

Her tears are coming even harder. Her nose is flowing freely now, too. She wipes her face on her sleeve and repeats, "You don't understand."

"Emily, what's going on?"

She takes a little time to compose herself. Then she says, "I know you've been dealing with a lot, and I know you have a lot on your mind. But before you . . . before you do this, there's something else I think you need to know."

"Okay."

She takes a few deep breaths to steady herself.

And then she blurts, "I'm pregnant."

I actually gasp. I don't know what's driving my movement—if it's gravity or a greater power—but I half-fall, half-slide off the couch until I wind up on my knees in front of her.

Almost like I'm praying.

"I know I said I was going back on the pill," she continues. "I was just waiting until the start of my next cycle before I began taking it. And . . . I was supposed to get my period the Wednesday after Hayley disappeared. That was the day you came out to see me in Rhode Island. But it didn't happen that day, and I thought 'well, it's just stress.' But then I didn't get it the next day, or the next day, or . . . Finally, I went out and got a pregnancy test. I've actually been carrying it with me ever since."

She pulls a piece of white plastic out of the pocket of her sweatpants. Even through the blurring of the tears forming in my eyes, I can make out both lines.

For the first time, I *do* understand. Why it was that, even during the darkest moments of the past few weeks, she couldn't quite bring herself to leave me for good; why she didn't just expunge me from her life like a stain she needed to wash away.

Because the whole time, I wasn't just her estranged drunk of a husband.

I was the co-creator of the new life that would soon be stirring inside her.

Where that leaves us now, exactly, I can't begin to fathom. All I want to do is crawl toward her, bury my face close to her uterus, and tell that tiny embryo how excited I am to meet it.

I reach out for her, but stop short. I'm not allowed to touch her. She's made those boundaries abundantly clear.

Staying on my knees, I say, "I'm really, really happy right now. I don't know if that's the right thing to say or not but . . . I'm just thrilled."

She sniffles and says, "When we went through the miscarriage, I made this deal with myself. I swore that if I was ever lucky enough to get pregnant again, I'd just . . . I'd treat it like a miracle, and I would embrace whatever morning sickness or exhaustion or anything else that came with it. I'd be so happy and so grateful just to be pregnant again, and I would do whatever I had to do to bring a healthy baby into the world. I obviously didn't anticipate anything like *this*, but . . ."

Her lower lip is quivering.

"I'm just scared," she says. "I'm scared about what's going to happen today. But I'm also scared about the next day, and the day after that, and every day that follows. I want to raise this baby with you, but it has to be with *you*, Charles. When you're sober, you're the best person I've ever met. You're kind and honorable and wise and humble. You're exactly who I'd want my baby's father to be. But when you're drinking . . ."

She doesn't complete the thought. She scarcely needs to.

I'm all of five days sober. Any promises I made in that regard would feel utterly hollow.

All I say is, "We'll figure everything out. One day at a time. This baby . . . this baby is all that matters now. You have to know I'm going to do the right thing for the baby. Always."

She nods.

Then she says, "You have to go. It's time."

JOURNAL ENTRY: MONDAY, JANUARY 29

From all accounts, it sounds like all the plans for Steeeeve are in place.

They won't let me be there to watch, which I'm bummed about, because whatever happens is going to be an important scene in *Searing Memoir* and I want all the details.

But everyone pointed out that since I'm supposed to be dead, we can't risk letting my stepfather see me.

I talked with Mr. B last night while we were putting the finishing touches on everything. He promised he would take mental notes for me, and I took him up on the offer. He knows the kind of details that make a story come alive.

Then Mr. B and I dealt with our other piece of unfinished business.

Namely, us.

There were certain things I wanted to say to him while I still had the chance.

First of all, I told him I was sorry that I seduced him.

He immediately started in with the *You have nothing to apologize for. You're not the grown-up here. I'm the one who ought to—*

Blah, blah, blah. Times two hundred and fifty.

Eventually, I made him shut up so I could finish.

I told him how I had done a lot of thinking while I was in the wilderness. I hate to admit it, but some of that mindfulness stuff they made us do actually works.

When I look back on how I was with him—the way I crushed on him, the way I flirted with him, the way I threw myself at him—I'm completely embarrassed.

It was really teenager-ish. And I can't keep being a teenager forever.

When you think about it, that's sort of what my mom did. She was obsessed with looking youthful. She made everything about her. She needed to be at the center of attention and surrounded herself with people who would put her there.

She basically never stopped being a teenager.

And look at how that turned out for her.

There has to be something more to life than that.

I also told Mr. B I'm seriously examining my need for male affection—specifically, older male affection.

And, yeah, the simple answer would be to blame my dad for everything, because he was never all that available and he and my mom split up when I was little and that seriously arrested my development.

Isn't that what people do in therapy? Blame their parents for everything?

But that feels too easy. I can't help but think it might be deeper than that. Like it's some part of me that simply needs to be fixed before I can move on with a healthier life.

Anyway, I shared all this with Mr. B, and he was really cool about it. Once he was done listening, he said that being embarrassed by your past actions is a good thing.

It's a sign you're growing.

He said the only people he truly worries about are the ones who don't get embarrassed.

Actually, he said those are just people you should probably avoid altogether.

Anyway, it was a good talk. And it was probably our last. He made it pretty clear it was not appropriate for us to keep in touch, which I understood.

But he said he'll be rooting for me.

I told him I'll be rooting for him, too.

And I really mean it.

Once I was done with Mr. B, my dad and I also talked some. When I told him about my problem with older male affection, he admitted he has the opposite problem—he craves young female attention.

He said maybe we could work through our problem together.

We also talked about Mom. He said he worried I was putting off dealing with it emotionally, and I know he's right.

But, honestly, how do you go about mourning someone who was so flawed? How do you hate someone but also miss her desperately at the same time?

Like, I'm actually angry with her for getting murdered. How is that even fair of me? How do I reconcile all these contradictory thoughts and feelings?

But at least I know where to start sorting everything out.

Hello. This is my journal.

CHAPTER 39

The unofficial staging ground for step one of the operation is a grocery store parking lot.

This is the closest we can get to Steve Graham's home without worrying we'll alert him to our presence.

From there, I will be going it alone.

I have received my final briefing. Everything is a green light. The last person to talk to me is Jerry Cordova.

"Okay, Ace, you good to go?"

"Not really. But I'm going anyway."

Jerry responds to my lack of bravado with a jowl-rattling cough.

"Just think of how nice it'll be to get rid of that thing," he says, pointing down to my ankle.

"That's the truth."

"We can sort out all the details later, but I want to let you know my office is going to be returning most of that retainer to you. I gotta bill you for what I've done so far, and there might be a little bit of follow-up work, but that should wind down fairly quickly. Hopefully we'll have a check for you in the next week or two."

"Yeah, I guess you're not my lawyer anymore," I say.

I pause for a moment, then add, "But if you don't mind, I've been thinking about one other thing I wanted to ask you to do for me."

"What's that?"

"When you got sober fourteen years ago, you said you did the twelve steps. Are you still active in AA?"

"If you call two, three meetings a week active, yeah. I'm about to get my fifteen-year coin. Why do you ask?"

I stare down at my shoes for a moment. "Because I'm a . . ."

Then I bring my gaze back up. I know I need to get better at saying this. "Because I'm an alcoholic. I need to find a good meeting. And I need to find a good sponsor. Do you think you'd be up for the job?"

The smile starts in Jerry's fleshy cheeks and erupts across his face. I've never seen my dour advocate look so pleased.

"I'd be honored, Ace. The meeting is at seven every morning. I'll email you the details. See you there tomorrow?"

"Sounds like a plan."

We shake on it.

"Now, if you'll excuse me," Jerry says, "I got some things to do. And then I got a big date tonight."

"A date?"

"With my daughter. Back when she was trying to tell me I couldn't represent you, we made a bet."

"Oh?"

"Yeah. We bet a steak dinner on whether or not you were guilty."

His face returns to its more natural wry state. "Just so you don't need to ask: I bet on you. Facts matter, Ace. Always remember that."

He gives me one final nod.

Then he slowly limps back to his car.

* * *

A short while later, I am finally doing the thing I have been accused of twice—but have never actually done until now.

I am approaching the flagstone front walkway of Diane Goodloe's West Hartford mansion with menace in my heart.

It is all I can do to keep my nerves under control. If I don't do this right, there won't be a second chance.

This has to be perfect.

I go to reach for the doorbell, but it is still in the mangled form that one well-aimed jab from Calista Fergus left it in. I knock instead.

Twenty seconds later, Steve Graham pulls the front door open.

He's wearing a Hawaiian shirt, board shorts, and no shoes. He has an unlit cigar clamped between his teeth, and it dangles from his mouth like an obscenity—a man who ought to be in mourning over the death of his wife, chomping on a victory cigar.

The heat from the house pours out around him. He must have the thermostat set to seventy-five. It's like he knows he can't go on a Caribbean vacation just yet, not with his wife and stepdaughter so recently dead; so he's bringing the Caribbean to his home in suburban Connecticut.

"Hello, Steve," I say. "I think you know who I am."

"What do you want?" he asks tersely.

"I have a proposition that will really help you and Nutmeg Consultancy. Can I come in?"

I am studying him carefully, and the moment I say "Nutmeg Consultancy," I swear he has a tiny seizure. His face flushes. I am reminded of his son, Grayson, at that press conference, with that blotchy pink face.

"I have nothing to say to you," he says.

"Don't worry, I'll do all the talking," I assure him. "Can I come in? There's no need to let all this cold air into your house."

Steve scowls but steps aside so I can enter.

"Is Grayson here?" I ask.

"He's at school."

"Great. We have the place to ourselves, then?"

"What's this about?"

"Just answer me," I say, with pretend impatience. "Are we alone here or not? You don't have a housekeeper around or anything, do you?"

"Why do you want to know?"

"Because I don't want any stray ears on what I'm about to propose to you."

"Okay, hang on. The cleaning lady is upstairs. Let me just see what she's up to. Maybe I can convince her to take a little break and go to the store. I'll be right back."

Steve and his bare feet stomp heavily up the stairs. I look around a little, but it's mostly idle curiosity. It's not like Steve would keep evidence of his misdeeds out in the open.

The décor is expensive, but has a little bit of a trying-too-hard vibe. No one here wants to let on that this is all paid for by child support.

Steve and Diane have been living a life that's like gold-plated jewelry—it looks great as long as you don't dent it.

The stairs squeak as Steve begins his barefoot descent. The ridiculous cigar is gone, but now he's holding a snub-nosed pistol in his right hand.

"There's no cleaning lady, asshole," he says, pointing the gun at me. "Now keep your hands where I can see them and don't do anything that makes me nervous. Connecticut has a Castle Doctrine, you know. I could blow you away right now and the cops wouldn't blink. I'm just defending myself against a violent felon who broke into my house."

I hold my hands up and spread them wide.

This was a possibility that was discussed during planning: that Steve Graham might be armed.

I dismissed it as unlikely. Would the husband of one of the staunchest gun-control advocates in Connecticut really have a gun in the house?

Obviously, I was wrong.

"That's true," I say. "But then you'd never get to hear how I can help you. How we can help each other, actually."

"Great. Just don't make any sudden moves."

"You're the boss," I say.

"Damn straight."

"Okay, so now that we have that established, let's establish something else: I had sex with your stepdaughter and then killed her to shut her up."

He holds the gun up a little higher and makes a show of aiming it at me. "Are you *trying* to make me shoot you?"

"No, I just want it to be clear that I'm being honest with you. I did that. You know I did it. The cops know I did it. Now, the cops are also trying to blame me for killing Diane Goodloe, but we both know I didn't do that, because we both know *you* did that. Or, rather, you had Chris Sandman—or whoever he is—do it for you."

"I have no idea what you're talking about."

"Of course not," I say. "But ask yourself a question. It's a question maybe you've asked yourself already: Why am I still walking around free?"

"Because you have a slick lawyer who managed to get you out on bail," he says.

"For murdering Hayley, yes. But not for murdering Diane. If they charged me with a second murder, there's no way I'd get a bond. Not when I'm already out on bond for one murder. But they haven't charged me for murdering Diane yet. Why is that?"

He doesn't answer, so I do it for him: "Because they're still not quite sure. I believe you've probably met the same two detectives I have. Morin and Prisbell. Morin likes me for killing Diane, but Morin is an idiot. Prisbell is a lot smarter. She's not exactly sure what's going on. She likes someone else for killing Diane. And you know who that is?"

Steve is still quiet, so I continue: "She likes you, Stevey-boy. She likes you *a lot*. She's been talking to my lawyer about her suspicions. Did you know she subpoenaed Hayley's trust? She knows it's irrevocable and that you've got thirty million bucks coming to you now that Hayley is dead. That's one helluva motive. She knows you've been tapping Diane's campaign funds via Nutmeg Consultancy. She knows about the P.O. box and Chris Sandman. She knows the whole thing is a sham, and that this is how you paid your hit man—she just can't prove it yet. But she's going to keep digging and digging until she finds that proof. I mean, just look at her. She's nothing but skin and bones because all she does is work and work and work. There's no husband there, no kids there. Just the job. She'll find something eventually."

I am feeling so much like Leo right now. This is his dialogue, pouring out through me.

"Yeah, well, there's nothing there to find," Steve says. "Because I didn't kill anyone."

"Right, right. You and Grayson were at the casino all night. Prisbell sees straight through your perfect little alibi."

Steve's eyes are darting everywhere. I'm already far closer to the truth than he thought anyone would ever get.

"Whatever. You need to leave," he says, waving the gun toward me.

"Not yet, Steve. Because you still haven't heard my deal. Look, I killed Hayley. I thought I wouldn't get caught, but obviously I'm going down for the murder that I committed. Since that's the case, what would you think if I confessed to the murder that *you* committed?"

He doesn't say anything immediately. But he's interested. Perhaps subconsciously, he runs his tongue across his lips.

"Think about it," I press. "The moment I confess, Prisbell stops digging on you. She stops digging on this case altogether. She moves on to other cases. You would be guaranteed to get away with killing your wife. Even if for some reason they tried to pin it on you, any lawyer with a pulse would be able to get you off. Another man confessed to the crime. That's automatic reasonable doubt."

"And why would you do that?" he asks.

"Because you're going to give me thirty thousand dollars in cash to help me disappear."

"I am, am I?"

"You sure are. That's the whole reason I'm going to confess to your crime: because, believe me, I'm not sticking around to face the charges."

I lift up my pants leg so he can see my ankle monitor. "Tomorrow, I'm taking this bad boy off. I'm on every do-not-fly list known to man, so I've got a boat lined up that'll take me where I need to go, at which point I'm set."

"Set how?"

"That's none of your business."

"Everything is my business right now," he says. "I thought you were being honest with me."

I pause like I'm wrestling with this.

"Fine," I say. "Do you know who my birth father is?"

"No."

"His name is Ellery Lawrence. Google him, and you'll see our rather striking resemblance. He's a very wealthy man—and he also happens to be a professional criminal. He's got everything ready to go for me if I can get myself out of the country. Reconstructive facial surgery. A new identity. A numbered bank account. The whole deal. I'll be able to disappear forever. He just can't risk helping me while I'm still stateside, because the authorities are already crawling up his ass with a microscope. That's why I need thirty thousand dollars from someone who isn't Ellery Lawrence. I had some savings, but my soon-to-be ex-wife has made sure I can't get at that. I kept thinking, 'Where am I going to get thirty grand in cash from?' And then I realized you already had the perfect scam going on that front, and we could help each other out.

"So that's what I'm proposing," I continue. "You write another one of those checks out of Diane Goodloe's campaign account for thirty thousand dollars. You cash it for me just like you did all the other checks. If anyone asks, you can say Nutmeg Consultancy is advising you on how to properly close down Diane's campaign account. But no one will ask. No one will be asking anything anymore. That's the whole point of this.

"Once you give me the cash, I'll give you a letter to mail to Detective Prisbell in which I confess to murdering Diane Goodloe. I'll say I was pissed at her for getting me fired. If you want to supply any details that can help make the confession more convincing, that would be great. If not, I'm sure I can BS my way through it well enough. By the time that letter arrives in Detective Prisbell's hands, I'll be long gone."

Steve still has the gun in his hand, but it's not pointed directly at me anymore.

I have his attention. And his interest. Thirty thousand is not a lot of money to a man who is about to have thirty million. Especially when the money isn't even his.

Yet that pittance will guarantee him the perfect crime. It will give him the gift of a lifetime of restful nights, never having to worry that his misdeeds will catch up to him.

It's a hell of a good deal. A great grift, as Leo would say.

"How do I know you're not recording this?" he asks. "How do I know you haven't struck a deal with the cops where you're wearing a wire for them and trying to entrap me into saying something incriminating in exchange for a lighter sentence?"

"After I've just revealed my big escape plan?"

"You could be making that up."

"Fine, search me," I say. "I left my phone in the car. And I'm not wearing a wire, if that's what you're thinking."

I unbutton my shirt, then untuck it from my pants. I'm not wearing an undershirt, so he can already see my bare chest. I hold up the back of the shirt as well, so he can see my empty back.

"I'll strip naked if you want me to," I say. "I didn't think you were kinky like that. You just tell me when to stop."

I go for the top button of my jeans but he waves me off.

"That won't be necessary," he says.

"Okay," I say. "Then what do you think? I don't mean to put pressure on you, but this is a limited-time offer. This guy with the boat is leaving tomorrow, midday. He's given me until tomorrow morning to get him the money. So, really, I need to get this done today, while the bank is still open. After that, the deal's off the table and you're on your own with Detective Prisbell."

He licks his lips again.

"What did you say your father's name was?" he asks.

"Ellery Lawrence," I repeat.

Steve pulls out his phone with his non-gun hand and begins swiping at it. He stares hard at it for a moment, then puts it away.

"How come there hasn't been anything about him being your dad in the press?"

"The press doesn't know everything," I say.

"Thank God for that," Steve snorts.

He puts his phone back in his pocket and studies me again. I just stand there, trying to look like a man with nothing to hide.

"This letter," he says. "You have it written?"

"I have a draft of it out in the car. It's still not signed. I don't sign it until you've got an envelope full of cash for me. When you hand me the cash, I hand you the letter. You want to see the draft?"

"Not right now."

"All right, then. Any more questions?"

He says nothing, so I announce, "Good. I think you understand what the offer is. Why don't you take a little time to think about it? I'll come back today around three o'clock. If you want to do this, be ready to go to the bank by then."

Without another glance at him or his gun, I turn and see myself out. I retrace my steps down the flagstone walkway, then settle into the car.

Everything went about as well as I could have hoped. Now there's nothing to do but wait and see.

I have just turned the engine over when Steve Graham emerges from the front of his house.

He is no longer barefoot. He has taken time to put on flip-flops. He is no longer holding the gun.

I roll my window down as he approaches the car. He's a little out of breath.

"I don't need time to think about it," he says. "Let's do this."

CHAPTER 40

The bank where Nutmeg Consultancy keeps its account is just down the street from the 06106 post office.

Steve has already called ahead to make sure it has enough cash on hand to handle the size of the check he is about to write. The manager assured him it would be no problem.

He has changed out of his Hawaiian shirt and back into one of his bespoke suits. His watch—it is a Breitling, and my guess is it cost at least $20,000 of Johnson Goodloe's money—is back on his wrist.

This is his armor. He is once again Steve Graham, political operator. This is not the first shady deal he's cut in his long career. Nor is it the first time he's convinced himself what he's doing is the smartest course of action.

He's driving his own car. I am following in my Subaru. We are first going to the bank, then to the post office. This has all been agreed upon ahead of time.

It is nearing noontime. The main source of delay was that Steve did have a suggestion for my letter to Prisbell—including one detail for me to put in that would end any doubt as to the authenticity of my confession.

He instructed me to write that Diane Goodloe had been dosed with a veterinary form of ketamine. That's not something the authorities would know yet, because they're still waiting for the results of the tox screen.

Apparently, her ripped dress and those bruises on her arms were all inflicted while the killers were injecting her. During her actual suffocation, she was zonked out.

Steve has also asked that I taunt Prisbell a little bit for not being able to catch me, because why else would a deranged killer write a confession letter to a cop? I agree, putting on my best serial killer impersonation.

I also throw in some shots at Morin. Why not?

Other than these details—and the logistics of how we're doing the exchange—we haven't conversed much. It's all been business. Strictly transactional.

We're just two murderers, helping each other out.

He pulls into the bank's parking lot and takes the nearest spot to the entrance. I pull in two spaces away.

With no hesitation—he hasn't been much for hesitation since he agreed to my deal—he gets out of his car and walks into the bank.

He doesn't even glance in my direction.

I settle in and wait. Five minutes pass. Then ten.

Leo and I have attempted to run so many scenarios over the past few days. Would Steve attempt to double-cross me? If so, how? Where? And to what end? Where are my biggest vulnerabilities? What haven't we thought of?

We haven't been able to come up with any particularly trenchant answers.

In general, we agree that if he actually says yes to the initial proposal, he would have little incentive to attempt trickery.

We also agree that the quicker this all takes place, the less likely it is he'll even be able to try anything. That's why we created the artificial deadline of my boat leaving.

So far, this is happening very fast. Steve has basically been full-speed ahead.

This is the first time he's shifted into neutral. What's taking so long? The bank's parking lot is not even a quarter full. I haven't seen any other customers coming or going, so it's not like he's been in line.

Or at least I don't think so. But I can't see into the lobby, so I can't say for sure.

Another five minutes pass. I'm sweating and my heart feels like its throwing itself against my rib cage. If this is a panic attack, the timing couldn't be worse.

"Come on, come on," I mutter.

Another thirty seconds later, Steve emerges. He's carrying a hook-and-loop envelope with accordion-style sides. It's roughly the size and shape of a woman's pocketbook. It looks like it could easily contain $30,000 that has been meted out into hundred-dollar bills.

He gives me a little nod.

My heart still doesn't slow.

He backs out of his spot and I am once again following him. The post office is just a few blocks away. He's driving the speed limit, cautiously following all posted signs and signals.

As we reach the post office, I look around for anything that appears to be unusual or suspicious.

But it's just another Monday for good old 06106. The place looks exactly like it did the week before, when I was staking it out.

At the very least, I know there aren't any private investigators watching it. I called Craig DeAngelis this morning and told him he could stop surveillance.

I didn't want anything or anyone that might give Steve a spook.

We once again park near each other. Steve, still clutching the cash, comes over to my car and sits in the passenger seat.

"Let's see that confession one more time," he says.

I hold it up for him. He already knows he can't touch it, lest his fingerprints end up on it.

This is all prearranged.

Everything, at this point, is prearranged.

"All good?" I ask.

"Yep."

"Okay, now let me see the money."

He unwraps the string that has kept the envelope flap down. The money has been divided into three thin bricks. Each is wrapped in paper bands.

"I haven't touched it," he says. "If anything's missing, blame the bank. But they let me watch as the machine counted it twice. It's all there."

"Right. Then I guess it's time to sign."

I fish a pen out of my pocket, hold the letter against the driver's-side window of my car, and affix my signature.

Then I fold the letter, place it in an envelope, and seal it shut.

"Okay, let's do this," I say.

We're both now out of the car and walking up to the mailbox that's just to the right of the main entrance, bolted into the concrete there.

He's just ahead of me, his head swiveling to and fro, but there's truly nothing out of the ordinary for him to see.

We reach the mailbox. I open the slot and hold my letter there with my left hand.

"Okay, your turn," I say.

He reaches out with the cash envelope but does not let it go. I grasp it with my right hand.

"One, two, three," he says.

He releases his envelope as I drop mine into the mail slot.

Like that, I have confessed to killing Diane Goodloe. In exchange, I have received thirty thousand dollars in cash.

"A pleasure," I say.

He actually says, "Good luck."

* * *

The first shout comes from Detective Prisbell.

What I said earlier about Prisbell suspecting Steve was true. Even before Jerry, Emily, Johnson, Hayley, and I approached Prisbell with this plan, she really did like Steve for the murder of Diane Goodloe.

Once she realized Hayley was still alive, the detective liked Steve even more.

As she told us: *It's always the husband.*

She hadn't put the pieces together yet. But she was a receptive audience from the start. And once she heard our plan, she agreed that if Steve Graham was willing to pay me $30,000 for a fake confession, it was a significant indicator of guilt.

Then Steve went and added those details about the ketamine to the confession letter. That ended any lingering doubt the police might have had.

But, in truth, Prisbell wasn't difficult to sell on the plan that is now being perfectly executed.

"Steve Graham," she says, authoritatively. "Put your hands up. You are under arrest."

I watch as Steve swivels toward her voice, which is coming from his right.

She approaches slowly, still about twenty yards off. She is walking with a wide, well-balanced stance and holding her service weapon in both hands, pointing it toward the ground.

But she is not the only one. There are suddenly cops emerging from everywhere, all making cautious approaches.

One comes out of a van that is parked along the street to Steve's left.

One springs from an unmarked car in the post office parking lot.

Two more are emerging from the gas station behind him, across the street.

Morin is inside the post office, cutting off any thought of trying to escape into the building.

They've got all the angles covered.

I wait for a show of defeat from Steve; to see his palms spread wide, followed by a recognition that he has been outmaneuvered and that a masterful trap has been sprung.

This is the moment of the plan where no one could ever quite decide how Steve would react. Would he resist? Try to run?

"Let's see those hands," Prisbell orders again.

But Steve's hands are not going upward.

One of them—the right one—darts quickly inside his suit jacket.

When it reappears, it is grasping that snub-nosed pistol.

The weapon looms large in my field of vision, filling it with matte black steel and molded plastic. It is very close, yet also just beyond reach.

Steve's face is lit by rage and hatred. He begins swinging the barrel in the direction of my midsection. My legs tense, preparing themselves to spring me away from danger.

"Gun!" Prisbell shouts.

From all sides, officers raise their weapons.

But Steve will not be deterred. This is not a man with meek surrender in mind.

In just a few tenths of a second—before I can dive out of the way—he steadies the gun and pulls the trigger.

I hear it first: this percussive clap, coming from the weapon.

The noise alone is terrifying.

Then I feel the impact. It sends me staggering backwards—one step, two steps, then a fall.

I do not feel the hard jolt to my backside when I land, nor the bite of the concrete on my elbows, nor the collision when my head meets the sidewalk.

The agony emanating from my stomach is already so dazzling it overwhelms any other signal my brain might be able to receive.

Gunfire seems to be erupting from everywhere now—more shots than I can possibly count. Some collide with the wall of the post office, spraying pieces of brick and mortar into the air. Others shatter the glass behind me.

Most strike their target. Steve Graham seems to almost be lifted by the energy being transferred into his body by the hurtling projectiles. Small spurts of blood pop from his head, face, and neck as the bullets slam into him.

He does this odd scarecrow dance, twisting with his arms at strange angles.

Then he drops, crumpling into a lifeless heap.

The police keep firing at him even when he's down. The gun is still clenched in his hand. They are taking no chances. Even as he lies there, quite apparently lifeless, they empty their clips into him. The barrage seems like it will never end.

Finally, prompted by nothing I can discern, it does.

My ears are ringing, but they are able to register this incredible silence that has broken out.

The shock is already spreading fast in my system, practically freezing me in place.

My first thought is that I've been paralyzed. The bullet must have hit my spinal cord.

Then I realize I *can* move. I can wiggle my fingers and kick my legs. It's just that my body hurts so much, the only thought I'm truly capable of having is about the pain. It's like my stomach has been replaced by a molten ball of fire.

I look down, expecting there to be a tangle of intestines emerging from a gaping wound.

All I see is a neat, dime-sized hole in my blue sweater. Like a volcano, most of the lava is underneath somewhere.

I look up at the incredibly blue sky, in all its infiniteness.

"Emily," I say.

And then the world goes black.

EPILOGUE

When I came to the first time, I was in a hospital bed.

I can remember being astonished—simply astonished—that I could open my eyes at all. It felt like this monumental achievement.

My mother was asleep in a chair by the window. It was dark outside.

I looked down to see tubes and wires coming out of me. My torso was wrapped tightly in gauze.

Then I passed out again.

When I came to the second time, Emily was standing by my bedside, but her head was turned away. She was talking to someone, though I couldn't make out what anyone was saying. It was like their words were buried under a gooey pile of mud.

It was daylight. I desperately wanted to say something to her, to let her know I was there, but even the thought of it was too exhausting.

As was the effort it took to remain awake. Once again, I felt myself being dragged down into a sleepy abyss.

It went this way for an amount of time whose length I could not determine. Possibly it was more than a day, though I was never aware of it being nighttime again; so, probably, this all transpired over the course of one day.

Maybe the fifth or sixth time I managed to open my eyes, Robbie happened to be hovering over me. She excitedly told Emily I was awake. They gathered on either side of my bed and gave me encouraging smiles. My mom squeezed my hand and told me she loved me.

Man, that was nice.

I really wanted to tell them I loved them, too. But my throat was too dry and my eyelids were too heavy and I was just too tired to speak. Maybe I nodded just a little bit. That was the best I could do.

Later on, I managed to stay conscious long enough to learn that I had been placed in a medically induced coma that I was now coming out of. I had nearly died from internal bleeding—my blood pressure had dropped perilously low during surgery—but I had been taken to a hospital in Hartford that had plenty of experience with gunshot trauma, and a skilled team of surgeons had managed to staunch the bleeding.

From there, I stabilized. It helped that I was young and strong. They were bombarding me with antibiotics, so there was no sign of infection. They predicted I would be able to make a full recovery.

From the bullet wound, anyway.

It wasn't until the next morning that I learned about the rest of my prognosis.

Robbie was gripping my hand the entire time. Emily was standing near the head of the bed, trying to be a reassuring presence. I could tell from the thinness of their smiles the news wasn't good.

A very compassionate internal medicine specialist named Dr. Jacquelyn Lineberry explained to me that I had been struck by a .22 caliber round. Once inside me, the bullet tumbled—.22 rounds tend to do this—and really tore up a lot of flesh.

In particular, it shredded a hefty portion of my liver.

Some other healthy, young person might have been able to withstand this. But Dr. Lineberry told me I had an underlying liver condition, one that was almost certainly brought on by repeated episodes of binge drinking. The bullet served as a kind of tipping point, sending an already compromised organ into failure.

It was no longer adequately doing its job, which was to keep my blood clean enough for the rest of my body to use.

According to Dr. Lineberry, my ammonia levels were rising steadily.

The whites of my eyes had already turned yellow. My skin was jaundiced.

And would only get worse. There were measures they could take to buy me a little more time and slow the buildup of ammonia. They could not stop it altogether.

The only thing that could save me is a new liver. But even if we found a matching donor in the next few days, a team of doctors had already determined I was not a candidate for a transplant. The bullet had decimated too much of the flesh surrounding my liver. There was zero chance the surgery would be a success.

Before long—Dr. Lineberry thought it would be a few days, but she admitted I could take a turn for the worse at any time—I will pass into what is known as a hepatic coma.

It will be painless. I won't even realize it has happened.

And then I will die.

It is the paradox of life that we are all dying from the moment we're born. As someone who spends way too much time in his head, I have frequently wrestled with my mortality.

I have just never been forced to confront it with such urgency.

It didn't take me long to consider my priorities and decide how to spend what little time I have left.

First, I made sure my mother and Emily understood just how thoroughly I love them both; and that I consider that love to be eternal and everlasting, something that will stay with them long after I'm gone.

Since I don't know exactly when I'm going to slip into my final bout of unconsciousness, I wanted to make sure I was on the record with that.

Then I got to work. As a writer, I believe that the only form of immortality humans can achieve is through our stories.

Before too much longer, this one will be all that is left of me.

At my insistence, I had my laptop brought into the intensive care unit. I raised my bed to enough of an upright position that I could sit up. It hurt like hell—because of the bullet wound, not the liver failure—but I refused to let them give me morphine.

I wanted my mind to be as clear as possible so I could work on this manuscript.

The word "deadline" never had such stark meaning.

I briefed Emily about my wishes for the manuscript after I go. She will be the one who has to get the book through edits, copy edits, first-pass pages, and all the milestones that proceed publication. I have every confidence she'll do great. With everything. Probably better than me. She doesn't get tripped up by sentimentality like I sometimes do.

Hopefully, if I've become too maudlin at any point, she'll exercise some discretion and rein me back in. One of my dying wishes is to be remembered as a writer who is considerate of his readers and doesn't subject them to a lot of self-absorbed rambling.

For three full days, I worked to my utmost capacity, my fingers flying across the keyboard. Once I wrote the final scene, the one where Steve shot me, I started editing from the beginning—and adding the prologue, midlogues, and this epilogue.

Robbie and Emily were buzzing around me the whole time, but they kept their interruptions to a minimum. They knew how important it was to me to work.

I also got a visit from Ellery Lawrence. It was strange to say goodbye when we had only just said hello. We both had to achieve our peace with that.

By the way, he's not a drug dealer. He had just taken a bunch of cash out of the bank. That part was just Leo's active imagination.

I kept expecting I might get a visit from Leo, but he stayed away. He respected my need to get this story out.

On the fourth day, the work started to become a lot more difficult. I was having trouble keeping myself upright. I had to give up typing for the most part and just began dictating to Emily, who recorded me on her phone.

I was fading hard.

I'm told I've always had a tendency to wrap up my books a little too quickly.

But I hope you'll let it slide this time. I really didn't have a choice.

* * *

So here I am. At a very different kind of The End.

Life is filled with boundaries—some we create for ourselves, some that are imposed on us. I thought my boundaries were high, impregnable walls. I have learned over the past few weeks just how low and vulnerable they truly were.

But maybe, if those ego-free psychedelic travelers are correct, the line between life and death really is just another low boundary that I am now about to cross.

I'm ready. It is nighttime on the fourth day. I am going through waves of what the doctors call "hepatic encephalopathy" as rising ammonia levels begin to cloud my brain.

Ironically, it's a bit like being drunk. So, at the very least, I have plenty of practice with the feeling.

My mother, who has seldom left my bedside—even when all I've been doing is typing madly—has been persuaded to go down to the cafeteria for a late dinner. She's barely eaten anything. Even walnut-hard Robbie Bliss needs some food eventually.

That leaves Emily and me alone in the hospital room.

She is still recording me on her phone, though it's getting difficult for me to talk. My words are slurring.

"I can't keep my eyes focused," I say.

"It's time, isn't it?" she asks.

I'm so weak, I'm not even sure I manage to nod.

"Okay. There's something I've been wanting to do," she says.

She stands and puts away her phone. Then she walks over to the door and closes it. I have no idea what she's up to, and my confusion only increases when she walks up to my bed, pops open the top two buttons on her jeans, and raises the hem of her sweater.

Emily has not touched me in weeks. Not since the allegations about the kidnapping first surfaced.

But now she is grabbing my hand and pulling it toward her.

She guides my fingers until they are below her navel and just above her pubic bone, and then presses them into her flesh.

And that's when I understand.

She is still not letting me touch her.

But she is letting me touch our baby.

This will be as close to my child as I'm ever going to get. It is the best she can do; and it is the best I will get in what little time I have left.

"This baby will know who their father was," she whispers. "I will tell them what a decent, wonderful man you were. And how much love you have for us."

I cannot summon a response.

She just holds my hand there.

A powerful feeling passes through me. It's this sense of profound gratitude. I am thankful for my life, even though it has been too short. I am thankful for the people—students and colleagues, family and friends—who have joined me for various parts of my journey.

I am thankful for the baby that will soon be stirring inside of Emily.

She has tears in her eyes. I think I do, too.

I don't know exactly where I'm going next or what it will be like when I get there. But I am suddenly filled with the knowledge that everything will be okay.

All I have to do now is let go.

ACNOWLEDGMENTS

Throughout the years, I have been fortunate to be affiliated—as a faculty spouse, parent, and booster—with three terrific boarding schools: Christchurch School in Virginia, Cardigan Mountain School in New Hampshire, and San Domenico School in California.

To be perfectly clear, none of them are the inspiration for what happened at Carrington Academy.

Thank goodness.

Nevertheless, I'd like to thank my friends at those learning institutions for a lot of lovely conversations through the years—in dining halls, faculty apartments, bleachers, auditoriums, libraries, and everywhere else in between. I couldn't have written this novel without their many insights into the teaching profession and the boarding school life.

Dr. Randy Ferrance and Connecticut death investigator Michelle Clark were both kind enough to take my calls and field my bizarre questions. I appreciate their good humor and expertise.

I'd also like to thank my agent, Alice Martell, an unwavering partner and cherished advocate—who is, thank goodness, the polar opposite of the coldhearted agent described in these pages.

To the crew at Oceanview—Bob and Pat Gussin, Lee Randall, and Faith Matson—it has been wonderful working with you and I deeply appreciate your efforts to launch this book into the world.

And, finally, to my cherished wife and amazing children, who have now nurtured me through the crucible of publishing a dozen novels: Thank you for being all that matters.

BOOK CLUB DISCUSSION QUESTIONS

THE BOUNDARIES WE CROSS

1. Have you ever been accused of something you didn't do? How did you resolve it?
2. How do you think Emily handled the accusations against Charles? Would you have acted differently if it were your spouse or significant other?
3. One of the themes of the novel is about class differences—and how Charles never feels like he's truly a part of the world he's been given access to. How do you think that influenced Charles's path throughout the novel?
4. Robbie Bliss had a very different life from her son. In what ways did she shape Charles's worldview?
5. How did your feelings toward Hayley change throughout the narrative? Did you believe her version of the story? In the end, did you feel she was justified in her actions?
6. How would you describe the tone of this novel? What emotions did it evoke in you?
7. There were two points of view in this book—Charles and Hayley. Was there a character you wanted to hear more from?

8. Which character intrigued you most? Why?
9. Which twist did you find most surprising?
10. Many thrillers feature a strong antagonist. Was there a true villain in this book? If so, who was it?
11. Did Charles deserve his fate in the end? Or was it too cruel an ending?

For more information about
THE BOUNDARIES WE CROSS
and the author, Brad Parks, visit his website at:
https://bradparksbooks.com